DAVE JACKSON

FORTY
TO LIFE

BETHANYHOUSE
PUBLISHERS

Forty to Life
Copyright © 2007
Dave Jackson

Cover design by Lookout Design, Inc.

Unless otherwise noted, Scripture quotations are taken from the *Holy Bible*, New International Version®. NIV®. Copyright © 1973, 1978, 1984 by International Bible Society. Used by permission of Zondervan Publishing House. All rights reserved.

This novel is a work of fiction. Any resemblance to actual events or persons, living or dead, is entirely coincidental. However, some scenes were inspired by a shooting on the Chicago/Evanston border in the summer of 1996 and the subsequent encounter between the shooter and the victim's mother. An earlier adaptation of those events appeared as the short story "Perdonado" by Dave Jackson in *The Storytellers' Collection*, Multnomah Publishers, 2000.

Published by Bethany House Publishers
11400 Hampshire Avenue South
Bloomington, Minnesota 55438

Bethany House Publishers is a division of
Baker Publishing Group, Grand Rapids, Michigan.

Printed in the United States of America

ISBN-13: 978-0-7642-0323-7
ISBN-10: 0-7642-0323-1

Library of Congress Cataloging-in-Publication Data

Jackson, Dave.
    Forty to life / Dave Jackson.
        p.   cm.
    ISBN 978-0-7642-0323-7 (pbk.)
    1. Murderers—Fiction. 2. Revenge—Fiction. 3. Forgiveness—Fiction. 4. Chicago (Ill.)—Fiction. I. Title.
    PS3560.A2128F67 2007
    813'.54—dc22   2007011985

To Gordon McLean,
the real Mr. Gee, who has
given over fifty years of his life
to youth on the streets and in jails.

Prologue

R aymond Slewinski!" The guard yelled from his booth into the dayroom. "Admin called, says you got a visitor—a woman."

Ray's cellmate threw his cards in the air. "Yo mama!" He leaned back in his chair and swore through clenched teeth. "We ain't never gonna finish this crunked-up game! What is this, Slew? You got a bird in the bush? How you rate a hookup, anyway?" His voice trailed off in a further string of curses.

Ray sneered at the pimply African-American albino across the table. The guy swore like a throbbing tremie pipe. "Why don't you just shut up, Zitty. This ain't no conjugal visit!" He put down his cards and rose slowly, pulling down on the short sleeve of his denim prison shirt to cover the blurred tattoo on his shoulder. He wasn't for flashing his Latin Kings crown today, not to this visitor. On the other hand, why was he even seeing her?

"Come on, come on," snapped the guard. "I ain't got all day."

But he did. He'd be working here all day. Then he would go home to family, friends, whatever—while Ray wouldn't go home till the year 2037. By then he'd be twice the age of that hick guard. He threw the man a lead-eyed glance and shuffled toward the door, arriving just as the solenoid buzzed the lock open. Nothing could make him or his time move faster. His shoulders rolled with contempt as he strolled ahead of the guard, out of his brick and steel "dorm" and across the frozen yard of the Illinois Youth Center at Joliet. He moved even slower, putting off as long as possible the strip search he'd have to go through before entering the visitation room.

Why had he agreed to see this woman?

"Let's go, Slewinski!" It was the voice of the guard ushering him into the small room. "Come on! Come on! You know the routine." Ray yanked his arm away when the guard touched his elbow. If it had to be a strip search, he sure didn't want the guy touching him. He'd heard how some guards tried to make inmates their pancakes. But not him!

As slowly as he could possibly move without getting yelled at, Ray peeled off his clothes.

"Hurry up, Slewinski. Bend and spread 'em!"

Ray complied. What did the guard think? That he was going to find some boof?

Ray got dressed, but by then he didn't feel like seeing anyone, especially not a woman.

In the visitation room Ray waited and watched other guys sitting around the bolted-down tables, playing checkers with their moms, leaning forward to whisper sweet nothin's to their girls, or yelling at their misbehaving four-year-olds to show they were still the man of the house, whatever that meant. Ray continued to wait. If the woman were here, why didn't they let her in so he could get this over with? He sighed deeply and tried to calm down. He'd be cool. He saw no sense to this meeting. But then, in prison, any diversion was worth the hassle. He waited.

The door on the opposite side of the room finally opened, and Ray spotted her. Tall with short brown hair, tanned skin, and blue eyes. Maybe a little too thin, but nice looking. Somehow she seemed younger than he remembered. She threaded her way to his table and reached out. He scanned away as he gave up a brief, limp handshake. He did not rise.

"Hi. I'm Connie Mason."

"Yeah, I know. Seen you in court."

She stood there until he glanced back and let out a sigh. "Wanna sit down?"

"Thank you." She made the words sound very prim and proper as she eased into the blue plastic chair on the opposite side of the table. "I hope you don't mind." She folded her arms and hunched her shoulders as though hiding her femininity.

Ray snorted. If she was as uncomfortable as he was, why was she here? "So. Uh . . . whatchu want?" he finally asked.

"I want to talk, and—" Her eyes dropped as she searched the glossy floor tiles.

"And . . . and what?" His jaw stiffened. "Look, lady, I'm sorry 'bout your kid. It was just one of those things, you know?"

Her head jerked up, eyes flashing. "No. No, I *don't* know. And don't call it 'just one of those things'!" For several moments she just sat. Ray watched the muscles in her jaw twitch as though she didn't trust what she'd say next. Finally she took a deep breath. "I've thought about you often since . . . since then . . . and I just want to talk."

Ray shrugged and slouched back in his chair. This might be something to pass the time on a dull Tuesday morning, but it wasn't much better than playin' poker with Zitty. If not for his curiosity, he'd have gotten up and walked out right then. Ray couldn't figure out why she'd come to see him, why she'd *want* to see him, and why he'd said yes.

CHAPTER 1

A wisp of smoke snaked into Ray's eye, causing him to squint as he studied his homies hanging outside Popeyes on the corner of Clark and Jordan, just south of the Evanston/Chicago border. He took a deep drag from the Marlboro and flipped its butt into the gutter as he stepped off the curb. "Hey, Rico, what's happenin', man? Who's workin'?" The cloud of smoke floated with him as he crossed the street.

"My shorties takin' care of business. They already moved four eight balls this mornin'. They learnin', they learnin'." Rico Quiñones, the enforcer for the local Latin Kings, was leaning against the brick apartment building, smoking weed while a couple of wannabes buzzed around like flies over dropped chicken, doing tricks on their old BMX bikes. In spite of the warm June weather, seventeen-year-old Rico wore an oversized L.A. Kings starter jacket.

Rico looked Ray up and down. Then he pointed with his chin in a way that drew attention to the first few hairs of a hopeful goatee. "Hey, Slew, check out them GDs in that green Taurus."

Running his fingers through his straight black hair, combed back but falling to both sides, Ray studied the ride as it crept by. "They ain't no GDs. What would Gangster Disciples be doing cruisin' with two *blancos*?"

"Hey, white boy, who you, anyway? You just a wanksta, tryin' to pass for Latino and make everyone think you a true King. I'm tellin' you, man, they all GDs. Watch this!" With one hand Rico stabbed the air with Latin King signs, his fingers making the points of a crown. With the other hand he threw down the GD sign of the devil's fork. The two wannabes joined in the taunting.

The green sedan eased into the small Popeyes parking lot, and one of the white teenagers jumped out and ran in. The driver and the two black teens stayed in the car. One of them sneered at the Kings and then gestured with his middle finger.

"There, there! See what I told you?" harped Rico.

"See what? You crazy, man. That wasn't no gang sign. He just flipped you the bird, man. That's all."

"Nobody flips *this* Almighty Latin King the bird. That was for you, *lady*! You droppin' the flag." He turned away and mumbled under his breath. *"Cobarde!"*

Ray straight-armed the older gangbanger in the back, right between his shoulders. "What'd you say, man? What'd you call me?"

Rico lurched forward and almost went down, then turned around slowly. *"I'll call you anything I want.* You gonna do somethin' about it? Besides, anybody who can't recognize GD scum ain't no true King."

"Hey, I'm down for the Kings just as much as you, man, and I ain't no coward neither. I know that guy, the one who went inside. He's Greg Mason. Swam for ETHS. They ain't no gangstas."

"Ha, ETHS!" Rico rolled his eyes. "You should've stayed up there in Evanston! Wake up, man. This is 1997, and I tell ya, those guys are from the Juneway Jungle. Why else they be cruisin' 'round here? They're all GDs! You just won't admit it, 'cause you don't wanna do nuttin' about it. You *asustado!*" He spat the word out and turned away.

"*Cobarde! Cobarde!*" the wannabes chanted as they wheeled past.

Ray grabbed the sleeve of Rico's jacket, turning him back. "I ain't scared. Gimme the piece, man. I'll show you."

"Oh yeah? You'll show us? You can't show us squat!" Rico pulled the 9 mm semiautomatic from the depths of his huge jacket and slapped it into Ray's open hand. His lip pulled back in a sneer. "Your name may be a Slewinski, but so far, you ain't *slew* no one. So let's see if you can live up to your handle."

Ray stared hard at him, then turned around just as the door on the green sedan slammed and the car pulled out of the parking lot. Without realizing it, Ray let out a sigh of relief.

"Now ain't that convenient," mocked Rico. "They're gone, so you don't have to do nothin'. 'Course, if you had any brass, you'd go after 'em." Rico nodded at the shorties' bikes. "They won't be gettin' far in this traffic."

Ray wrapped a yellow and black handkerchief around the 9 mm and dropped it into the cargo pocket on his baggy pants. He glanced up the street, jerked a bike from one of the shorties, and jumped on.

"Five high, six die," sang the wannabes as he took off.

He rode north on the clattering contraption, weaving between the parked cars on his right and the slow moving traffic on his left. Maybe before he overtook the green sedan, he could duck into an alley, and no one would know what happened. But then he heard the *squeak, squeak, squeak* of Rico pedaling hard after him on the other bike.

"Hey, Slew, you gotta hurry, man, if you gonna catch 'em. Let's go!"

The red light at Howard Street stopped the Taurus long enough for Ray to pull up alongside it. Maybe he would just yell at them or show the gun and scare the green tea right out of 'em.

But Rico skidded to a stop on the other side of the street and started yelling. "Yo, Slew! Don't forget what our Supreme Inca says: 'Cowards die many times before their death, but Latin Kings never taste death but once.' " Then he flashed the crown. "¡Amor de rey!"

Ray's eye started twitching. If cowards died many times, then he was dying at that very moment. Greg Mason's pale face through the Taurus window was replaced by his own pained reflection. Was he *Slew* or *Cobarde*? Ray gritted his teeth, reached down, and jerked the pistol from his pants pocket. It was still wrapped in its gang rag, so Greg probably didn't even know what it was.

"Do it, man! Do it! Don't be no *cobarde*!"

The blast was deafening. Through the spider-webbed window, Ray saw blood pumping, spurting, gushing red and frothy from the hole in Greg's chest. Ray had never seen so much blood.

"*Awriiiight! You did it! You did it!*"

Rico's faint words broke through the ringing in Ray's ears.

"Come on, man. Let's get outta here. Five-Os be comin'!"

The ringing merged into sirens as Ray wheeled the bike away from the Taurus and sped back down Clark Street. He turned west on Jordan and pedaled as fast as he could.

The piece, where can I dump the piece? Ray could feel the Bryco 9 mm in his deep pocket, slapping against his leg as he pedaled at a furious pace. Rico might be mad at losing his piece, but Ray couldn't be caught with a hot gun! Sirens screamed a couple blocks away, but they weren't coming his way, at least not yet. He looked right and left for an unlocked car or one with a window down. No, that wasn't a good idea. He couldn't ditch it this close to his crib only two blocks ahead. He had to get it out of the neighborhood, away from him, far away.

And then he saw it, creeping down the alley: a big Waste Management garbage truck. Ray wheeled around and screeched to a stop as he watched the green dragon move fifty feet, then stop while the lone driver lumbered back like he had been working twenty-four hours straight to roll the next Dumpster up to its rear. Hooks on, the hydraulics whined, and then baby diapers, a week's rotting garbage, baggies of dog waste, cans and bottles and newspapers all tumbled together into the yawning back of the truck. The empty Dumpster crashed back onto the alley and the man rolled it against the building. Then he went forward to move the truck another fifty feet.

Ray shot down the alley after him and wheeled into an empty stairwell just as the truck made its next stop. Ray could hear more sirens—one sounded like it was coming his direction—as the driver got down from the cab, moving as slowly as an aging arthritic.

"Come on, man!" Ray whispered to himself. "Hurry it up, hurry it up!" But this time there were two Dumpsters, and the man stepped between them, then looked both ways up and down the alley before relieving himself against the building.

He took a deep breath—"Ahhh!"—and backed out. Then he dragged one of the bins to the truck, which slowly enveloped its contents, and then did the same with the second Dumpster. They filled the receiving tray—just what Ray had been waiting for—and the operator pulled the lever that would scoop its contents forward into the compactor. As the mechanism groaned, the man walked to the front of the truck to advance it another fifty feet, and Ray rode up and tossed his weapon deep into the trash pile.

Having a second thought, he hopped off the bike as the truck began to move and threw it in as well. It was small and old, not much more than a kid's toy. Once its wheels were crushed by the compactor, no one would look twice when the load was discharged into the landfill.

Ray emerged from the alley and turned toward home as a siren picked up again. It was an ambulance. Ray knew the difference and felt a profound dread. He hoped the kid would be okay, but how could he with all that blood pumping from his chest? Ray couldn't let himself think about those things. He was a long way from safe. Why had he done it? Why had he let Rico talk him into it? He didn't need this kind of grief right now.

When Ray got to his apartment, he went around to the back and climbed the stairs as quietly as a guy trying to sneak his lady out at night. He entered through the kitchen and smelled scorched coffee. His mother had failed to shut off the pot last night—again. But she wasn't up yet this morning. *Good.* Alice Cooper screamed "Go to Hell" from his thirteen-year-old sister, Lena's, room. *Good.* With her music turned up that loud, she wouldn't hear Ray coming in. He sneaked down the hall to the darkened living room, where he crashed on the couch, covering his head with the ratty blanket. The living room couch had been his regular bed ever since he had turned twelve and his mother said he could no longer share his sister's room.

He messed his hair and tried to fall asleep. He wanted his mother to have to wake him up so she could validate his claim that he'd come in late the night before and had been sleeping all morning: "I even had to wake him up," she'd say. But sleep wouldn't come. Every time he closed his eyes, all he could see was the red geyser erupting from that kid's chest. Was he dead yet? Was he still alive? What if the cops came right now? He needed more alibi.

"Lena!" he yelled louder than Alice Cooper, "turn that thing off. You woke me up. Lena? Lena! Mom! Make her turn that thing off, I need some more sleep!"

He heard his mother shuffling out of her bedroom. "Well, if you got in at a decent hour, you wouldn't need to sleep till noon! Lena! Lena!" *Bam, bam, bam.* She pounded on the door. "Lena, turn it down. I can't sleep either, and I had to work last night."

There, he'd done it. They both thought Ray had come in late and had been sleeping all morning. But would that hold? Who had seen him on the streets that morning? Rico—but he wouldn't dare say anything because it would implicate him—and the two wannabes. Would they talk? Not if they knew what was good for them. How much had they seen, anyway? Too much, really. Maybe he'd have to get someone to put the fear of God in them.

Of course, there were the guys in that green Taurus. A good lawyer ought to be able to discredit anything they recalled by pointing out that they were too traumatized to get it straight—or maybe just out to pin anything on a rival. He had heard of guys getting off for less.

Ray's mother was up now, fussing around in the kitchen. Maybe he should go in and make nice to her, reinforce the idea that he had been home all morning. There was no possibility of sleep. He was too wound up. But it would be nice, give his mind some relief from all this trauma . . . unless he ended up having nightmares about the blast and all that blood. Now that he listened, his ears were still ringing.

And what about that gunshot residue, or whatever they called it, the powder that gets all over your hands when you fire a gun? He'd seen a guy get put away on *NYPD Blue* for no more than that.

Ray's mind was buzzing. He got up, went into the bathroom, and took a shower, scrubbing his right hand and arm, his face, his hair. He came out and dressed in clean clothes. Then he found an old Kmart bag and stuffed his dirty clothes in it. He wished he'd been able to chuck them into the garbage truck too, but that chance had passed. Where could he dump them so they wouldn't attract attention? He considered the Salvation Army donation box up on Howard. No, no, he didn't want to go back up there, and besides, people sorted through those donations. He didn't want anybody to look at his clothes.

Somebody else's storage locker. That might work. There were gaps at the tops of each locker in the building's basement, enough to stuff his bag through, and the cops would have to have a good reason—maybe even a search warrant—to go through someone else's private stuff.

"Hey, Mom, what's to eat?" He asked as she went through the kitchen. "How about some pancakes? I'll be right back."

When he came back up, his mom was talking to someone down the hall at the front door. *Cops.* As soon as they saw Ray, they pushed their way past his mom and came toward him. He forced himself not to run.

CHAPTER 2

R aymond Slewinski? Where've you been?"

"Me? Just stepped out to grab a cigarette." He patted his shirt and pants pockets. "But wouldn't you know it, forgot my smokes."

"Where've you been this morning?" There were two cops, both in uniform, and the woman was doing all the talking.

"Me?" Ray stretched and yawned. "Just got up."

"You just got up, huh? Got up from what?"

The hall door opened and Lena came out in her "Born Naked" T-shirt, holding her hands up, fingers spread to dry fresh black fingernail polish. "What's goin' on? Am I under arrest?"

"Just stay right there in the doorway where we can see you," said the female cop. Then to Ray, "Where've you been this morning? You happen to talk to a couple kids on bikes over by Popeyes on Clark?"

"No," Ray's mom put in. "He's been here sleeping all morning. We were just gonna have some breakfast. I had to work late last night. And he got in so late, he slept till noon. What time is it now?"

Both cops glanced at their watches—Ray knew it was nearly 1 p.m.—but no one answered his mother.

"Raymond, I wonder if you would mind postponing your breakfast for a while to come down to the station with us and help us clear up a couple things with these kids. They seem to think someone stole their bikes, and they thought it was you. But if you were here all morning, then of course it couldn't have been you. So all you gotta do is show your face, and they'll realize they were mistaken. Musta been somebody else." She smiled like Mother Teresa at Ray's mom. "You know how kids are these days. Those guys probably left their bikes at the beach, and they're claiming someone boosted 'em so they won't get in trouble with their parents. But . . ." She shrugged. "We still gotta check these things out."

Ray was afraid he knew what *"these things"* were, and they weren't lost bikes. His head floated, like just before he blacked out that time he drank too much beer. He needed a reason not to go with the cops, a reason that would not raise more suspicion. Certainly they weren't sure he was the shooter, or they would have arrested him on the spot. But he didn't dare make it easy for them either.

"Oh, go ahead, Ray. Help 'em out. I'll get you a banana and fix you something nice when you get back." She turned to the cops. "You *will* give him a ride back, won't you?"

"Once we get this all cleared up, we'll be the taxi, ma'am."

Ray knew the cops suspected something. There was no way those wannabes would have gone to the police on their own over their missing junker bikes. The cops must have been questioning them about the shooting and come up with a clue that led to Ray. He'd just have to play it cool and hope he could deflect them. Lucky he'd disposed of the weapon and set up some kind of alibi.

"Okay. Let's do it, officers. Whatever the *niñitos* said doesn't involve me. So let's go show 'em."

Ray steeled himself as he rode in the back of the cruiser over to Clark Street and the few blocks south to the 24th District Police

Station. The image of Greg Mason through the car window rose in Ray's mind, and he wished he could ask them about him, but that was out of the question. He had to keep his mind off the shooting so the cops couldn't get to him. He would not admit anything. If they couldn't prove it, he might get off. He would act respectful—not tee 'em off—but without kissing up either.

Could he do it?

Ray's insides were so tight his stomach quivered. He cleared his throat. "Can I smoke?"

"You smell smoke in our car?"

"Uh . . . what about when we get to the station?"

"We'll see how things go."

When they got to the station, the cops led him in the front door—that was a good sign. The female officer spoke to the officer at the front desk: "This is Raymond Slewinski. He's here about those bicycles. Could you send him on back when you're done with him?" They went on through the door as though they didn't care one way or the other whether he followed them.

Either I'm still in the clear or they're playing a pretty cold game with me, Ray thought.

He started answering the questions as the desk man filled out some forms. But the questions went beyond name and address and when he was born to where he went to school, his mother's name, his father's name, and whether he was in a gang—he said no.

"Why all the questions? Since you know my name, you know all this other stuff. Am I under arrest, or something?"

"Does it look like it? Are we takin' your prints or mug shots or putting on the cuffs? Take it easy, son. Just a couple more questions: You had any priors?"

"No!" No need to mention the times the cops shook him down for dope or loitering.

"What's your street name?"

"Whaddaya mean?"

The cop glared at him.

"Uh, I don't got no street name . . . but sometimes they call me Slew 'cause my name's Slewinski, Raymond Slewinski, but that's all. Hey, are we done here or what?"

"Yeah, we're done. You can go through that door there. Third room on the right. An officer will be with you shortly."

When Ray stepped toward the door, the buzzer announced he was entering a secure area. Ray knew what that meant.

When it closed, he'd be locked in!

Ray stuck his head in the third room on the right and looked around. It was a bare room painted two colors of gray, a table in the middle with chairs on either side, and a fluorescent light overhead. Just like the interrogation rooms on TV except for no two-way mirror on the wall. No one was in the room. He stepped back into the hall, looking both ways. Maybe he ought to just walk out of there . . . but the door with the electronic latch had a keypad on this side. He'd have to get the desk man's attention and tell him they were through with him. But of course he'd have to wait a few minutes for that to be a convincing story.

He stepped back into the room so no one would notice him. Maybe they would forget.

"Well, there you are. Ray Slewinski?" The plainclothes detective looked too much like Andy Sipowicz on *NYPD Blue* for Ray's comfort, though this guy had more hair and no mustache. "I'm Detective Barker. Why don't you just have a seat over there, and we'll see if we can get this cleared up quickly."

The detective flipped through some pages of a notepad. "Slewinski . . . your family from the old country?"

"Isn't everybody's?" *Oops.* He didn't mean to be a smart aleck. "Actually, I think it was my grandparents." Maybe that would smooth it over.

"Yeah, mine too. On my mother's side. Otherwise, I wouldn't be a Barker, know what I mean?—Oh, before we get started, there's one little thing you can help me with about these bikes. You watch TV, don't you?" When Ray nodded, he continued. "Then you've seen 'em do the Miranda thing." He thrust a clipboard out to Ray and handed him a pen. "I'm going to go over your rights—"

"Wait a minute. I thought the guy at the front desk said I wasn't under arrest."

"Oh, you're not. You're not. Don't worry. This is just a technicality. I can't use anything you tell me unless I Mirandize you first, so just put a check in the boxes after I read each one. Okay?" He didn't wait for Ray's response.

"One. You have the right to remain silent and refuse to answer questions. Do you understand?"

Ray hesitated. This was going too far. Next thing, they'd be putting the cuffs on him.

"What's the matter? Just check the box. It's not that big a deal."

Almost automatically, Ray made a check mark.

"Okay. Two. Anything you do say may be used against you in a court of law. Do you understand?

"Three. You have the right to consult an attorney before speaking to the police and to have an attorney present during questioning now or in the future. Do you understand?

"Four. If you cannot afford an attorney, one will be appointed for you before any questioning if you wish. Do you understand? Go ahead, go ahead. Check the box.

"Five. If you decide to answer questions now without an attorney present, you will still have the right to stop answering at any time until you talk to an attorney. Do you understand?

"Six. Knowing and understanding your rights as I have explained them to you, are you willing to answer my questions without an attorney present?"

Ray swallowed. "This isn't going to get me in any trouble or anything, is it?"

"No, no, no. Of course not. Just sign down there at the bottom and we'll be good."

Ray signed. What else could he do?

Barker took the clipboard and sat down in the chair. "Now, about these bikes. Do you know these boys?" He looked at his pad. "A Juan Hernandez and an Angelo Hernandez. Hey, are they brothers?"

Ray shrugged. "Wouldn't know." This detective wasn't going to catch him that easily.

"But do you know them?"

"I might-a run into 'em around the neighborhood, but I'd have to see 'em to be sure."

"Maybe we can arrange that. So what were you doing this morning, say about ten o'clock?"

Here it comes, thought Ray. "I was home in bed. Got in pretty late last night."

"How late?"

"I don't know. Maybe two or three this morning. What's this have to do with any bikes?"

"So you weren't over near the Popeyes Chicken this morning?"

"No. You can ask my mom. The beat cops already did. What's this about?"

The detective leaned forward across the table. "It's about a shooting this morning, Ray. Certainly you heard all the sirens?"

"There are sirens all the time." *But those sirens today were for Greg Mason.* The thought almost knocked Ray off his game. He took a breath. "Besides, I was asleep till almost noon."

"Right. Home . . . in . . . bed." The detective made a little note in his pad, then looked up and narrowed his eyes. "Only these boys say you jumped on one of their bikes and headed up Clark. And witnesses say the shooter was a kid who resembled you, riding a bike. Now, you want to tell me how there could be so many coincidences?"

"I don't see any coincidences since I was home in bed. But if you really want to be talkin' about some kind of a shooting, and you're lookin' to me, then I think I better ask for that lawyer." He was thinking about the rights he had just gone over. But what good would a lawyer do?

"Oh, we're not charging you or anything. It's just these kids lost their bikes and we're trying to straighten it out. But if you did know anything about that shooting, say who was the real instigator or how it went down, this would be a good time to step up. 'Cause you know, if you help us, we can certainly help you." He leaned back in his chair. "Excuse me a minute. You need anything? A glass of water or something?"

"How 'bout a smoke?"

"Oh, sure. Be right back. By the way, I need to call your mom and tell her we'll be a little longer. Wouldn't want her to get worried." And then he left . . . and shut the door behind him.

When Ray got up and checked, the door was locked.

CHAPTER
3

Ray paced around the small locked room in the 24th District Police Station while Detective Barker went to get him a cigarette. Had he said anything that could get him in trouble? He didn't think so, but then he'd never been through this before. Cops on the street hassled you, yelled at you, pushed you around, and threatened to lock you away until you were old and gray. Ray knew how to deal with cops on the street, but he'd never been brought to a station and interrogated before.

There was no good cop/bad cop thing going on here, but Barker was more than a curious detective trying to solve a stolen bike complaint, he could tell that. He seemed as benign as Colombo but was probably just as dangerous. Barker couldn't have a solid case yet, or he would have arrested Ray by now. Still, he knew too much. Ray's only hope was to keep his mouth shut no matter what the cops said or did.

Ray kept walking around in the small room, nervously trying the door from time to time even though he knew it would still be locked. What was taking Barker so long? Where were his smokes? When was he going to get out of there? Finally Ray sat down with his elbows on the table and rested his chin on his hands.

It seemed like forever before the door opened, but probably only forty-five minutes had passed when Barker returned, extending a single cigarette toward Ray like he was passing him a blunt. He even glanced back over his shoulder. "You know, supplying cigarettes to minors is a criminal offense under Illinois State law. So don't tell anyone who gave that to you." He turned back to close the door.

"Wait a minute!" Ray jumped up. "Don't close it. Wait, I want to—"

The door clicked shut. "Sorry. What's the problem?"

"Well, I didn't steal those bikes, and I don't know nothin' about no shooting. So can I go?"

"Oh, you're free to go anytime, but sit down." He reached out with a lighter and flicked the flame in front of Ray's face until Ray sat and lit his cigarette. "Help me out just a little bit more here, will ya? Do you know a Rico Quiñones?"

Though Ray had tried to maintain eye contact with Barker—to show he had nothing to fear—he couldn't hold it and looked away. He took a long drag from his cigarette and blew a big cloud of smoke up into the air. Rico Quiñones . . . the cops had one more piece to the puzzle. They were closing in on him. He took a deep breath and forced himself to look back at Barker. "Yeah, I know him, but I don't have nothin' to do with him 'cause he ain't nothin' but a gangbanger."

"You know, that's exactly what those Hernandez kids said too. And we're thinking he might have had something to do with this shooting I mentioned to you. In fact, while I was out getting you a cigarette, I got a call. They got Quiñones down there at Area 3 Violent Crimes Headquarters right now and asked if I could come down and give them a hand. But I need some help. I need you to come with me."

Violent Crimes Headquarters? Ray didn't want to get anywhere near that place. He could feel sweat forming on his forehead. Would

Barker notice if he wiped it off? The detective was already standing to leave by the time Ray answered. "Uh, I got some stuff I gotta do for my mom at home. I don't think I can come with you." Ray stayed seated.

For the first time, Barker's voice had an edge. "Oh no. You're coming with me because I don't have time to clear you on this bike theft thing. If I left you here, I'd have to have one of the blue shirts book you, and you wouldn't want that. So you're better off coming with me down to Area 3."

Ray remained seated as Barker started to walk out. "Don't I need a lawyer before you question me anymore?"

"A lawyer? What for? You're just helping me out here with extra work those guys at Area 3 keep throwing at me. But hey, I'll make you a promise. You help me, and I'll help you. I'll make sure this bicycle thing disappears. What do you say?"

When Ray hesitated, Barker started again to leave. "'Course, if you want a lawyer, that's your right, and I won't stand in the way, not even for a moment. But I think you're smart enough to see that if you call for one now, it just makes you look like you're guilty of something." Barker turned back as if alarmed. "You're *not* guilty, are you? . . . Do you really want a lawyer?"

Ray's shoulders sagged and he shook his head like it was too heavy to hold up. Then he stood and followed Barker out the door.

The "interview" room at Area 3 Violent Crimes Headquarters that Detective Barker ushered Ray into was smaller and darker than the room at the new 24th District station. It was nothing more than a stark eight-by-ten-foot cell containing two rings embedded in the concrete floor in front of a steel bench mounted to the wall. The door also was steel, with nothing but a peephole to enable someone to look in from the outside.

"We'll be back in a minute," said Barker.

"*We*"? Who was "we"? Ray felt control slipping away. The door clicked behind Barker, and Ray didn't even try it. He knew he was locked in. The creeping feeling that they owned him inched up his back and tingled his scalp.

He waited . . . and waited . . . for over an hour. With every minute the tension wound tighter, like a guitar string about to snap. The image of the shattered window and the blood gushing out of the guy's chest flooded Ray's mind every time he tried to close his eyes. He worried about Greg Mason. Had he survived? Or had Ray committed . . . *murder?* He could hardly think of the word, let alone say it aloud. If only he could go back and begin this day over!

It wouldn't be that big a thing, would it? To set the universe back a few hours? Ray would certainly live it differently. He'd learned his lesson. Maybe this was all a dream, and he would wake up with the chance to . . . to tell Rico to bug off. He didn't care whether those guys were GDs or not. He didn't care if Rico ragged on him for not having "slew" anyone. He didn't want to be "Slew" anyway! He didn't care anymore whether he was an Almighty King. He just wanted the events of the morning to go away!

Finally, the door clicked open and Barker returned carrying a plastic folding chair. He was accompanied by a stout African-American woman with short, cropped hair tinged red at the tips— not red like red hair, red as in blood red! Blood! Ray couldn't stop looking at it. She wore half-moon glasses low on her nose and carried a folding chair for herself along with a notebook and pen and . . . a Burger King bag.

Ray could smell hot fries. His stomach growled as if on cue. It had been a long time since he'd had anything to eat.

"Oh yeah. This is for you." The woman held the bag out to Ray. "Thought that by this late in the day, you might be needin' something to eat."

It took Ray only a moment to dig into the Whopper, large fries, and Coke.

They unfolded their chairs and sat down like they were preparing for a three-way conference. "Ray, this is Officer Percell. She's a juvenile officer assigned to protect your rights. And as you can see, she's already looking out for you. The burger okay?"

Ray swallowed and looked back and forth. "Am I under arrest here?"

Barker shook his head. "Not unless you think you should be." He laughed nervously. "Look, like I told you before, we're going to make the bicycle thing go away. You just help us out like a good citizen with some of this other stuff. Okay?"

Ray shrugged. "Yeah, guess so. . . . But I didn't think this was going to take so long. Maybe I ought to go call my mom and let her know where I am."

Officer Percell looked over the top of her glasses. "We already notified your mother that we are questioning you. I think she's coming down pretty soon. Also, Detective Barker here says he asked you whether or not you wanted a lawyer, and you said no. Is that correct?"

"Well, at first I said no, but then I thought maybe I should have one. You know, with you asking so many questions, and all, so . . ." Ray looked at Barker. For an instant, hardness dropped over the detective's eyes like a plastic shield, and Ray thought about his warning that insisting on a lawyer would make him look guilty.

"So . . . so what? Do you still want one or not?"

Ray shrugged. "Guess not. But . . ." He pulled his eyes away from Barker and looked to Officer Percell. "But my mom, how will she get all the way down here?"

"Don't worry about her, Ray. You've got more serious concerns." Barker's voice turned rough as asphalt. Ray cringed. Had he just made a mistake? He had said he guessed he didn't need a lawyer, what he thought Barker wanted—the old *You help me and I'll help you* that he had promised. But now Barker sounded angry, like the gloves were off, punching a finger toward his chest. "We've been doing our homework, and we're tired of fooling around here. We think you were the triggerman on that shooting this morning. Rico Quiñones says so. . . . Oh, don't look so surprised. I told you we had him down here. He's in the other room and singing like a rapper, facts just spewing out of his mouth. The Hernandez boys too. They say you took one of their bikes and headed north on Clark just before the shooting. All the witnesses say the shooter rode up on a bike. And you fit their descriptions. That's a lot of detective work to accomplish in one day, wouldn't you say? But there's one thing—"

"I want to call my mom."

"*Your mom!*" Barker sneered as if Ray were something he'd stepped in. "What do you want your mom for? She'll just tell you to tell the truth. And that's what you should do, because there's one thing I can tell you about cops and the DAs. You make their job easier, and they will work with you." Then he switched on a smile. If this was good cop/bad cop, Barker was playing both parts. "You're young, and you don't have any priors. Right? So we're gonna give you every consideration if you make life easy for us."

The detective stopped and turned to the juvenile officer, raising his eyebrows as though seeking her approval for how he was conducting the interview. She said nothing but continued to take notes.

Ray needed to go to the bathroom. He needed to get out of there. It was too hot, too close, too small, not enough air. "Uh, could I—"

"Hold on a minute. Let me finish." Barker looked down at his little notebook as though he'd been following a script. "Oh yeah. You don't have any priors. Quiñones, on the other hand, is hardcore. He's got a rap sheet an inch thick. His kind cause trouble in the 'hood, so we'd be just as glad if he found a new address, someplace like Marion or even Pontiac Correctional Center. Know what I mean? So my guess is he was behind this whole thing, the instigator, so to speak. Can you confirm that much for me?"

Ray squirmed on the hard bench and stared down at his Nikes. Blood was oozing out of them and spreading in a puddle across the floor. He blinked and it was gone. "What'd you say?"

Barker sighed loudly and gave a knowing glance at Officer Percell. "Look at me, Ray. Focus! I'm trying to make things easier for you here. I said we'd be glad if you could verify that Quiñones was the mastermind behind this morning's shooting. Can you do that much for us?"

"*Mastermind?* He's no mastermind of anything. He's a . . . he's an idiot." Yeah, and Ray knew he'd been an idiot to listen to him too. If he could just turn back the clock.

"Yeah, but he was the one who suggested the shooting, right?"

"How should I know? I didn't even know there was any shooting."

"Oh, come on, Raymond." The detective looked at his watch. "It's almost seven o'clock, and I'll bet you're as tired as I am. Let's get this thing over with. No more games. Okay?"

"I gotta use the rest room. Can't really wait."

Barker rolled his eyes and looked at Percell. "All right, but when we come back, you're gonna work with me, right?"

Ray nodded. What else could he do?

CHAPTER 4

Ray tried to stay in the smelly rest room—only one toilet and a tiny corner washbasin—for as long as he could, but in a minute or two Barker was pounding on the door saying they had to get back to work.

In the "interview" room again—Ray considered it an interrogation room—he finished his fries and sucked on the Coke until the straw gurgled as Percell and Barker arranged their chairs in front of him.

"Look, Ray"—Barker's nice-guy face was hardening—"this is my last offer. You just tell me whether or not Quiñones had anything to do with that shooting this morning and you can go on home. How 'bout it? Was Quiñones involved?"

The shooting this morning . . . a vision of the kid's bloody chest and the shock on his face filled Ray's mind. He couldn't prevent the tears brimming in his eyes, and when a sob erupted from his gut, he disguised it as a cough. They were gonna get him. Sooner or later they'd make their case. Maybe if they were looking at Quiñones, that was his best move. Confirm that, shift the blame, and squeak out of this mess. What did he care about Quiñones, anyway? He was the guy who had set him up in the first place. He really was the guilty one. Let him sweat it.

"Yeah." Two more sobs burst forth, and he sniffed deeply. "Yeah . . . Quiñones was the one. He said those guys were GDs."

Detective Barker leaned back, his folding chair creaking with the shift in weight. Then he laced his fingers together and put his hands behind his head for a headrest. "Thanks, Ray. You've just made my day. Now Officer Percell and I are going to step out for a few minutes, and when we come back, I think we can get this thing all wrapped up." He stood, and Percell followed his lead. "You wait here."

Like he had a choice once the door clicked shut.

Barker and Percell weren't gone long this time. When they returned, Barker brought in a new writing pad—large, not his little pocket one—and a pen. He had a broad, pleasant smile on his face, no longer the intense, dead-eyed Detective Sipowicz. Now he was the jovial Andy again.

"Okay, Ray. You helped us out, and like I promised, I've helped you out. I made that bicycle thing disappear. The Hernandez boys aren't filing a complaint. So now all we gotta do is wind this thing up so we can all get some rest. The way I see it, if you heard Quiñones say those guys were GDs, then you weren't home in bed all morning like you said. In fact, you must have been right there at the Popeyes when all this started. And the Hernandez boys said both of you got on their bikes and headed north. What we're left with is one last question: Who fired the gun? Of course, Quiñones says you were the triggerman. Normally, I wouldn't be inclined to believe him—him being a lowlife gangbanger and all—except he's been telling us the truth all along while you've been lying to us from the start. So who am I to believe?"

Barker stopped and stared at Ray, the fun-loving Andy face morphing back into his determined Sipowicz glare. "You see where I'm going with this, don't you, Ray? The fact is, we got you. Now, you probably tossed that gun in some Dumpster and think you've scrubbed the gunshot residue off your hand."

What? How could Barker possibly know all that? Was he psychic? Was he guessing? Or had he come across more evidence?

"But"—Barker raised both hands, palms up—"do you know how many guys get convicted for murder without a weapon ever being recovered? The idea of 'no weapon, no crime' is a TV myth. And do you really think our CSI team can't find traces of lead, nitrocellulose, or a little barium on your hands if you shot a gun recently? That stuff goes into your pores, man, right into the pores of your skin. It doesn't just wash off, and they use electron microscopes these days. And how about your shoes? Bet you didn't even think about the stuff drifting down onto them, now, did you?"

Barker had to be bluffing. Surely that stuff would wash off—or most of it, at least. Still, at the mention of his shoes, Ray couldn't help himself from glancing down at his Nikes. At least they weren't "bleeding" this time, but—he looked twice—what was that? Gray dust? Was there gray dust on his sneakers? He couldn't keep from staring.

"And that's just the lab work," Barker continued. "There are more witnesses for us to interview, like the other guys in the victim's car, like the people in the car behind them. You think they wouldn't pick you out in a lineup? No, Ray, we may have more work to do, but it's all doable. We know it was you. The only question is: How hard are you going to make us work?" He stopped, tilted his head to the side, and stared at Ray. "Like I told you. Make it easy on us, and we'll encourage the DA to go easy on you. Now, I kept my word on the bike charge. It's gone. So you know I'll help you on this. You see, we don't think you are a bad kid, just someone who got caught up in some foolishness, foolishness that this rotten Quiñones instigated. We think he's the real troublemaker, and you can be sure, he'll get what's comin' to him. Because as far as I'm concerned, he, being the older one and all, is more responsible. So . . ."

He paused as if measuring his victim. Was he about to spring a trap? He rubbed his chin as though stroking a beard. "Do you want to tell us what happened now, or do you want us to come back and see you in the morning? Though, of course, that bench . . ." He shrugged. "That bench makes a mighty uncomfortable bed. Sorry 'bout that, but we just don't have anything else to offer. Know what I mean?"

Ray knew. Actually, what Ray really knew was that he was beat. There was no way out. He was going down for the shooting. Did the kid die? Would it be murder? Ray hadn't dared ask before this because he'd been claiming ignorance. Hadn't been there. Didn't know anything about the shooting.

He looked at the detective. "Is he going to make it?"

Barker shook his head slowly, a genuine look of sadness on his face. "He's dead."

Then it was . . . murder!

"Ray, when the cops came to your house this afternoon, they were asking about some missing bicycles. Then we discovered those bikes may have been involved in this case, and so I questioned you as a potential witness—someone who *might* have known something about the shooting. But now . . . well, the speculation has ended. I'm arresting you for the murder of Greg Mason on or about noon today."

He pulled out a little card and began to read as though he didn't know the words by heart. "You have the right to remain silent. If you give up that right, anything you say can and will be used against you in a court of law. You have the right to . . ."

They had him. It was too late to protest. What good would an attorney do now? Ray was scared. He was scared to death! He was so scared that his mouth tasted like metal filings, each breath like ammonia, scalding his lungs. He'd do anything for relief, anything to get out of this little room, anything Barker asked, just so this would be over.

"Ray . . . Ray, look at me. Son, you gotta focus so we can get this done. Do you understand your rights?"

"You already read my rights to me."

"Of course we did, but I just wanted to make sure you understood. Both Officer Percell and I want to make sure of that . . . for the record."

Yeah, for the record, thought Ray. *I'll definitely have a record now.*

"So since you understand what we're dealing with here, tell us in your own words what happened this morning."

So Ray told him while the detective took notes like a secretary doing shorthand.

When he finished, Barker said in a soft voice, "Thank you, Ray. I'm gonna go type up what you told me. Then you're going to sign it, and we'll be done."

And they were done too. As soon as Ray signed his confession, Barker and Percell left. Ten minutes later a blue shirt came in and took him to be processed: mug shots, fingerprints, and more paper work, empty his pockets, take off his belt, remove his shoelaces, sign this, sign that, confirming that all the information on their endless forms was accurate. Ray didn't read it. He just initialed what they circled and signed on the lines they told him. What difference did it make?

"Hey, Slewinski. When were you born?" said the blue shirt, frowning at the papers in his hands.

"Already told you."

"Yeah, but what you told me and what's on this intake form from the 24th District are different. It says July 10, 1981. You told me '82. What's the matter? Don't you even know when you were born?"

"'Course I know. It was '82."

"Then how come the difference? Look, we're gonna check, so don't mess with me, man. What's your school records say?"

"They say '81, but it's a long story. When I—"

"I don't want to hear it. We'll go with the school records, and believe you me, the DA will check!"

"Whatever." The cops wouldn't care why his mother had enrolled him in school saying he was a year older than he really was.

Shortly after all the forms were filled out, the cops cuffed Ray—not just handcuffs, but ankle shackles too, and a chain that ran between the two that didn't allow him to raise his hands much higher than his waist.

And then his mother and sister walked in.

"Raymond! Raymond!" his mother screeched. "What's happening? What are you doing here? And what's this . . . why do you have handcuffs on? And chains! Oh, Raymond!" His mother broke down, wailing and hanging on him as if she were losing him forever.

Maybe she was. That possibility and his mother's grief broke something in Ray, and he began sobbing. Even his sister began bawling until her black eye makeup streaked down her face as if she were Alice Cooper himself.

"All right, all right! That's enough." The blue shirt tried to pry them apart. "This boy's in custody right now. You can't be doing that."

When the officer finally split them up, putting at least a couple feet between everyone, Ray wiped his eyes on his shoulders since he couldn't raise his arms high enough to do the job. "Where were you, Mom? They said they called you."

"I tried, baby. I got so worried when they called and said they were questioning you. We borrowed Tina's car, but you weren't at the station. What's this about a shooting? No one was shooting at you, were they?" She turned to the cop. "How come you got my boy all tied up like some galley slave?"

"Ma'am, please calm down. He's just goin' to juvie where everything will be sorted out. Now stand back, like I told you." She looked back at Raymond and her face collapsed. "I'm sorry, Ray. I'm so sorry. When you weren't at the 24th, they sent me to some other station. But they hadn't even heard of you at that station until their computer finally said you were down here." She appealed again to the police officer. "Sir, you gotta let him go. He's a good boy, and I didn't mean to take so long getting here. Honest."

"It isn't your fault, lady. He's under arrest for murder. There was a shooting today, and we think your son may have been responsible. There's nothing you can do. We're taking him down to the Cook County Juvenile Detention Center." He started to put his hand on her shoulder and then hesitated. "Perhaps you can see him in court tomorrow. But don't expect to talk to him. They don't allow that." Then he explained that if she couldn't afford an attorney, a public defender would represent Raymond before the judge who would determine what would happen next.

The police officer tried to get his mother and sister to leave, but they wouldn't budge. Soon a van arrived, and Ray was taken out to it, shuffling as far as the ankle shackles would permit. When he got to the step, he had to rely on the aid of a cop and the deputy sheriff to help him up into the van. His shackles were so short, he couldn't lift his leg high enough on his own. Yeah, and if he tried to get out on his own—if he tried to escape—he'd fall on his face too. He rode alone in the back, steel grillwork separating him from the uncommunicative deputy sheriff, who drove down Western Avenue as the city lights shimmered off wet streets in the gently falling rain. His tears were gone, wrung out of him by the hopelessness of his situation, dried up by the shock of what he had done, numbed by a clock whose hands he could not turn back to a.m.

Tomorrow would begin his new life as an inmate, a convict . . . a murderer.

CHAPTER 5

Ray saw the sign—Cook County Juvenile Temporary Detention Center—as the deputy helped him out of the van and hustled him into the five-story concrete building that filled an entire city block at the corner of Hamilton and Roosevelt on Chicago's near south side. Guys on the street often scoffed at the "Audy Home," as it was commonly called. "Ain't no big deal, man, if you can stand the food. Been there three times. Little brother's in there right now."

Ray was unshackled and escorted to a small, windowless reception room, where the guard set before him a tray of cold food—a hunk of meatloaf resembling a miniature concrete block, mashed potatoes as hard as wall spackle, covered with greasy gravy, once-green beans, a cup of red Jell-O, and a carton of warm milk. Ray picked at it, his stomach protesting every bite.

The guard sat in a chair by the door, scanning through the transfer papers the deputy had handed over when he delivered Ray. "You done?" the guard said when Ray pushed back his tray. Ray nodded, and the guard said, "Let's go."

Ray walked ahead of him down a sterile corridor, not unlike the hallways in his own school, except that the guard had to unlock the frequent doors. Their destination was an office room with several desks, but only one was occupied.

"New houseguest for you," the guard announced as they came through the door.

The middle-aged white woman looked up from typing on her computer. "Why you keep bringin' me more kids, Joe? You know we ain't got room for 'em."

"Hey, I get the roster like everyone else. Three guys got shipped out of here this morning. We're down to only 678, so I know you got room for at least one more."

"Oh sure! In a place built for four-fifty? You tell me how to squeeze him in!"

He shrugged, holding his hunched shoulders high. "That's not my job, but I doubt he'll be here very long. This is the kid from that shooting this morning. Heard it on the news. I'm bettin' they'll be sendin' him along to a more permanent home out west before his bed gets warm."

The clerk rolled her eyes and motioned Ray to sit in the chair beside her desk. Then she began going over his papers, typing stuff in her computer. Finally she looked at him and smiled. "You got you a number now, son: K17868. Best remember it."

Awakened at 6:25 a.m. after his first night in intake at the Juvenile Detention Center, Ray dressed—wishing he had some clean clothes—ate breakfast, and waited. He was beginning to conclude that waiting was one of the primary forms of punishment for anyone who was incarcerated. He was taken to a small room with a narrow window looking south over Ogden Avenue, and he watched the cars go by: people hurrying to work and school, an ambulance rushing to Cook County Hospital, a woman walking three dogs that seemed to enjoy entangling her feet with their leashes. But Ray was just as entangled, sitting, waiting, and waiting some more.

Finally the door opened and an overweight woman came bustling in carrying an overloaded black leather briefcase in one hand and a mountain of manila file folders clutched to her chest with her other arm. "Whew!" She plopped down in the aqua-colored plastic chair, dumping her briefs on the table. "You must be Raymond Slewinski, right?"

"Yeah."

"Well, I'm Patty Higgins. I've been assigned as your PD, your public defender." She looked straight at him with pale gray eyes and held his stare as though she expected him to respond.

"Oh."

She raised her dark eyebrows, drawing attention to the quarter inch of white roots that outlined her heavy, grayish face, separating it from black hair. When she sat down, Ray had noticed it was held back at the nape of her neck by a large silver barrette with turquoise stones before cascading in loose tangles down her back. Her oversized brown dress with embroidered Indian symbols and her beaded leather sandals affected a Native American motif that Ray guessed said more style than ethnicity. She turned to the top file on her stack and opened it, her jowls quivering with each jerky movement.

"So you're charged with murder but . . . never been arrested before, and you confessed." She looked up at him. "Why'd you confess?"

"I don't know."

"Look, we don't have much time, and we're not going to get anywhere with 'I don't knows.' In a few minutes, we've got to go in there and face Judge Gregory Romano. I've known him for many years, and he's a fair man, especially when it comes to juveniles, but he doesn't work with 'I don't know.' You understand?"

Ray nodded.

She again studied the papers in Ray's folder. "You're fifteen, huh?" She paused for a moment, then muttered almost to herself,

"That'll put you in adult court." After flipping to the next page, she snapped her head up as though she had discovered something, drilling Ray again with her gray eyes. "Look, Ray, this is important! You gotta tell me why you confessed. Did this . . ." She glanced down. "Did this Detective John Barker hit you? Did he threaten you in any way?"

"No, ma'am."

"Did he read you your rights?"

"Yes."

"Then why didn't you ask for an attorney?"

"I don't know."

"Now, come on—"

"Okay. I didn't know they had me until all of a sudden . . ." What had happened, anyway? "Until everything just caved in, and he was offering me a deal, and I didn't know what to do."

"What deal?"

"He said he'd make the bicycle complaint go away, and then he said if I helped him, he'd help me."

Patty Higgins shook her head, making the fat under her chin jiggle. "There never was any bicycle complaint against you. What did you think you were helping Barker do?"

"He said he wanted to get Quiñones off the streets, and so I thought he might be going down for the shooting instead of me."

"What? Were you hoping Quiñones would take the fall for something you actually did?"

Ray looked down at the floor and nodded. He knew he shouldn't have tried that, but . . . "But Detective Barker said Quiñones instigated it." It was more an appeal than a defense.

"Maybe, but Quiñones was smart. He never said a word. So they don't have a thing on him."

What? Quiñones hadn't said anything? But Detective Barker had said he was—how had he put it?—*singing like a rapper.* Ray could hardly believe it.

"Did you ask for a lawyer?"

"They said I didn't need one. That it would only make me look guilty."

"How 'bout your mother? This report doesn't show that she was present. Where was she?"

"She couldn't find me. She went to the 24th, but they sent her somewhere else, and I didn't know where she was."

"Yeah, right. The musical chairs routine until you confess. Then she showed up, right? She did finally come, didn't she?"

"Yes."

"All right. It looks to me like your only chance is to get the judge to see that your Miranda rights were violated and get this confession thrown out."

The Honorable Gregory Romano wore a black robe and sat behind a raised bench in the oak-paneled, windowless juvenile courtroom, housed on the first floor of the Juvenile Detention Center. Why move alleged offenders to another location if everything could be done at "home"? It didn't *feel* like court TV to Ray. There was no jury, no reporters sketching pictures, no pomp other than the judge's black robe, which was open down the front to reveal a rumpled blue suit. A guard escorted Ray to stand before the judge and then remained within arm's reach behind him.

"Keep your hands behind your back, and don't be looking around," said the African-American deputy sheriff who looked like he had only recently retired from linebacker for the Chicago Bears. Ray spotted his PD when he came in, digging in her briefcase at a table that was now behind him and to his right. A similar table to Ray's left had to be for the assistant state's attorney. Three people bustled around it. Ray stole a quick glance. Why were three people against him and only one for him? One was searching for something on a computer monitor; the other two were talking in hushed tones.

There was no "Hear ye, hear ye!" The clerk simply said, "Court's still in session." Then she handed some papers up to the judge and said, "This arraignment petition is on that murder case, Your Honor."

The judge took the papers and began reading through them while everyone else in the court continued doing what they had been doing—talking, looking for papers, walking over to have a quiet conference with another person.

Suddenly Patty Higgins, Ray's PD, was standing at his side. He took the opportunity of her arrival to look back, and there was his mother sitting on what looked like a church pew along with a half dozen other people—probably parents and relatives of other alleged offenders. His mom had a wide-eyed expression on her face and held her hand over her mouth as if she were about to lose her breakfast.

"Face the judge," reminded the deputy in a low tone.

"Are we ready, counselors?" asked the judge. After looking from the prosecution to the defense as though they were batting a Ping-Pong ball back and forth, the judge stopped his head wagging and zeroed in on Ray. "Mr. Slewinski, you are charged with the murder of one"—he glanced down—"Gregory C. Mason, on or about June 10 of this year, 1997." He continued reading the grisly details as Ray's stomach cringed. When the judge finished reading, he looked up and said, "Does the state have anything to add?"

A finely groomed Asian man stood behind the state's attorney's table. "No, Your Honor."

"And Ms. Higgins?" the judge asked.

Ray's PD answered quickly. "Your Honor, this confession is utterly bogus. It never—"

"*Bogus?* What kind of a word is that? We're not on the street here, counselor."

"I beg your pardon, Your Honor. What I mean is that it never should have happened. My client—"

"Objection, this is an arraignment, not the trial, Your Honor."

The judge held up his hand toward the state's attorney but said to Ray's attorney, "Don't push it too far, Ms. Higgins."

"I'll try not to, Your Honor, but we must object to the confession. His Miranda rights were grossly abused."

The judge kept scanning through the documents. "Looks to me like he initialed every one of them, but as the state pointed out, you can challenge that at the trial if you want to. This is just an arraignment. Petition sustained." The judge looked at Ray. "I'm going to explain so you will understand what just happened, young man. I am sustaining the petition against you. That means I think there is enough evidence for the case to go forward. You can plead guilty or not guilty, but since you are fifteen years old and this is a murder charge, you'll be automatically transferred to adult court. You make your plea there." He stopped and looked around on his desk. "Where's the documentation on this boy's age?"

"School records, Your Honor," said the state's attorney. "They're right there in the file, and they confirm what he said at processing."

"Okay." The judge flipped through some more papers. "Yes, yes. I see he's fifteen." He looked up. "I think we're done here." He grabbed his gavel and smacked it on a wooden disk near the front of his desk, then looked over to his clerk. "What's next?"

Ray felt the deputy grip his arm just above his elbow and give him a nudge. Ray turned to his PD. "Is that all?"

Patty Higgins shrugged. "Yeah. I'll talk to you tomorrow."

CHAPTER 6

On the second floor of the Juvenile Detention Center, which included administrative offices, classrooms for the alternative school, the infirmary, and counseling rooms, Ray faced more processing. There were three other new guys. He was issued a uniform, which looked like a maroon version of hospital scrubs, and more rules than he had ever heard in his life. "If you are sick, you can report to the infirmary on this floor in the morning. No talking when walking in the halls, and you are to remain in line at all times. No conversation under any circumstances with residents from other units. You are not to go near the female units and no interaction with the female residents!"—*Female residents?* Were there girls here?—"No gambling. No smoking. No swearing or foul language. Phone calls are a privilege and allowed only at the discretion of your supervisor. When not already in your room, you have to ask permission to go to the bathroom, and you will be told when you can take a shower. There will be no groups of young men in the showers. . . ."

Ray didn't hear the rest. The orientation went on and on, but his mind went elsewhere, trying to grasp what had happened in the last twenty-four hours. What would happen in Adult Criminal Court? Would there be a jury? Were there other Latin Kings here at the JDC? What about rivals? Would he get picked on? Beat up? Raped?

Finally a guard came and collected Ray and the other three new guys to take them to their units. They rode the elevator up to the third floor. To Ray's surprise, the building was not a solid block as it had appeared from the outside. Instead, from the third floor on up, it was more like a walled city, where the outside walls were wide enough to house the units where the residents lived. In the center, the building was open to the sky because the roof of the second floor was an open courtyard divided by concrete barriers into three recreation fields where groups of guys, dressed in different colored uniforms, played football or baseball on the concrete roof.

Huh, Ray thought. *You'd soon learn not to slide into third base on those diamonds.* Ray and the other guys followed the guard down a hallway that had glass on both sides. The inside glass looked out onto the courtyard, and Ray could see that the hall went all the way around its perimeter. In addition, when he looked up, he could see identical glass and steel hallways wrapping around the inside of the fourth and fifth floors. The glass on the outside of the hallway separated it from the living units for the residents. Looking in as he walked by, he could see that each unit housed about thirty teenagers. Some units were empty—perhaps the guys were on the field or in school—but in some the guys were busy mopping the floor of their dayroom, cleaning the glass, or sitting around.

"Quit rubberneckin'," barked the guard. "Yours will be just like the rest, and you'll get a good long look once you're there."

Ray was the first one delivered to his unit. In the center of the dayroom sat a desk and a large console with buttons and lights. A supervisor sat behind it, giving orders and overseeing everything. He buzzed the door open to allow them to enter.

"Here's your new kid," said the guard.

The supervisor nodded and buzzed the guard back out the locked glass door while he continued yelling at the two guys at the other end of the dayroom to straighten up the TV area.

One TV for thirty guys?

Finally the supervisor turned to Ray. "Slewinski?"

Ray nodded.

"You got a voice? Say 'Yes, sir' when I speak to you, son. Understand?"

"Yes, sir."

"Here's a roll of toilet paper." He tossed it to Ray. "It'll need to last you a week. Room seven, down at the end of the dayroom. Go make yourself at home." His laugh sounded like he was juggling marbles in his mouth.

Ray walked past several doors with full-length shatter-proof windows in them, and he could see without staring that everything a guy might do within them—from using the toilet to sleeping—was fully visible to the supervisor and anyone else who might glance in. Ray tried the handle on door seven. It was locked. He looked back over his shoulder toward the supervisor, who was watching him, perhaps demonstrating that he was in total control of everything Ray would do.

The hint of a smirk turned down the corners of the supervisor's mouth just before he reached out his hand with exaggerated deliberateness and slowly turned the key that buzzed open the door to Ray's cell. It was a small, concrete-walled room with a high ceiling. The door locked when it swung closed.

Ray surveyed his world: a small stainless-steel toilet and sink unit, a cot with a thin, plastic-covered mattress folded into an S with two blankets on top, a pedestal stool of metal mounted to the floor in front of a built-in writing shelf, and on the far wall—not very far, not more than eight feet—a narrow window positioned too high to see anything but a streak of sky. There was no switch for the lights. Lights were controlled from the console by the supervisor, as would be every minute of the days to come.

Ray laid out his mattress and sat down. And looked around. And got up. And checked the water in his washbasin—a tiny trickle. And went to the door. It was still locked, and the supervisor didn't respond when he wiggled the handle. He returned to his bunk and lay down, studying the featureless ceiling. He got up and went back to the door to watch the guys in the dayroom. He could not quite see the TV screen.

Four guys playing cards around a small table were African American and bigger than Ray. In fact, most of the guys he could see in this unit were black. But some were Latinos—maybe Kings or Insane Popes or maybe 2-6ers—and a few were white. Would the LKs protect Ray?

He swallowed hard. His throat felt as if a cotton ball were stuck there. He returned to his bunk, where he wiped his eyes with the back of his hand. What had he done to his life? What had he done to that kid in the Taurus, blood pumping from his chest, shock on his face? Maybe Ray did belong in here where a supervisor could control everything with the buttons on his console so Ray couldn't do anything bad again.

All too soon, Ray found out what it meant to be transferred to adult criminal court. The next day his legs were shackled again and his hands cuffed and fastened to a belt around his waist. What, did they think he was a maniac about to go off and attack everyone around him, even though half of them were armed with three-foot nightsticks and some packed guns? Ray found himself hanging his head, shuffling along with baby steps like criminals he had seen in the movies. *"Yeah, boss! Right away, boss!"*

But the driver of the van flipped roles on him once the door was closed and locked. "Where to?" he asked, as if he were a taxi driver and Ray his first fare of the day—though a heavy expanded steel screen separated Ray from the driver.

Ray was tempted to say, "*Home, James*," but thought better of it and said, "To court, I guess."

"You guess? Is that because you don't really know where you're going? You ever been in criminal court, son?"

"No, sir."

"Well, let me tell you where you're goin', 'cause I got it right here on the order. You are headed to the Circuit Court for Cook County, the Criminal Division that convenes at Twenty-sixth and California. You know what that is?"

"Not sure."

The guard pulled out into traffic, then glanced in his mirror. "That's Cook County Jail, boy, one of the largest and most violent prisons in the country. Today it houses approximately eleven thousand *alleged* criminals, all awaiting trial or serving a short sentence. But don't let that *alleged* part give you any comfort. Over the years it's been home to the mobster Al Capone, gang leaders like Larry Hoover and Jeff Fort, and serial killers Richard Speck and John Wayne Gacy. You hear of any of them?" He looked at Ray in his mirror again.

"Yes, sir, most of 'em."

"Well, they were some bad dudes, and like I tell every kid I drive over there, you don't want to be among 'em. You get my drift?"

Ray nodded.

"I didn't hear you!"

"Yes, sir."

Apparently the man was done being a tour guide, because he said no more during the remaining few minutes it took to get to the court building connected to Cook County Jail. But the man's words had their effect. In the ten minutes it took to ride in the sheriff's van between the JDC and the Cook County Jail, Ray felt a resistance rising within him like the north poles of two magnets. He wanted to get away from that place as soon as possible.

An hour later Patty Higgins joined him in the holding pens where the accused waited for their cases to be called. Ray asked her, "So what am I supposed to do?"

His PD continued scribbling notes on a yellow pad. "You don't have to do anything." She looked up. "And don't say *anything* unless the judge speaks to you directly and I give you the nod to answer. Today the state will read the charges against you. Even though a boy was killed and you confessed to the shooting, I advise you to plead *not guilty*—"

"But I—"

"Don't want to hear it." She held up a hand like a traffic cop and turned her head to the side. "At this point our whole case depends on getting that confession thrown out. The only way that can be considered is with a not-guilty plea so your judge can hear the details. Later, if it proves to be in your best interest to plea-bargain, we can consider switching to a guilty plea at that time. But today all you're going to do is plead not guilty—agreed?" She paused and stared at Ray until he nodded his head. "Then you'll receive a court date for your trial, and we'll be out of there in less than ten minutes. You'll see."

And Ray did see. Just as his PD had predicted, ten minutes after his case was called, he had a court date: Monday, March 9, 1998, nearly nine months away.

"How come so long before it begins?" Ray asked when Patty Higgins accompanied him back to the holding room.

"Court schedule is full. Besides, this gives everyone time to prepare. Though, to be honest with you, no one will do anything until a couple days before. And even after it starts, there'll probably be several continuances before we actually get down to business. But I hope one of those will get your confession thrown out."

"I gotta stay at the JDC during the whole thing?"

"'Fraid so." She studied him for a few moments. "You really don't know how the system works, do you? Never had it explained to you when you were on the streets?"

"Well, I heard . . ." Ray stopped. What could he really say?

"Listen." She leaned forward like a concerned school teacher. "The JDC is supposed to be a *temporary* detention center. But many kids stay two, even two and a half years while their cases wind their way through the courts. They're relieved every time 'judgment day' is postponed by another continuance. And sometimes that gives the defense time to keep them out of prison. But frequently, it isn't until *after* a kid is finally acquitted that it dawns on him that he has just served a two-and-a-half-year sentence anyway."

Ray couldn't believe what he was hearing: two or two and a half years even for someone judged not guilty! "But why?"

Patty Higgins shrugged. "That's just how the system works. It's a sly mechanism to get troublemakers off the streets even when the state can't prove guilt, and that makes voters think they're safer. But hopefully during that time we can keep you from getting sent up to the Big House."

Ray shivered. He'd entered a not-guilty plea, but there was no way he could find hope in the *truth* even if his case got dragged out for a couple years.

CHAPTER 7

Ray's birthday came and went on July 10 without anyone noticing that he had turned fifteen. Even his mother had to work that evening and couldn't come to visit. "I'm sorry, Raymond," she said the next Sunday. "I really tried, but my boss has no heart. Maybe you will be out soon, and then we can have a late celebration."

"Yeah, maybe, Mom." Ray's face barely cracked a smile. Already he was growing cynical about his future. Any hope he had for good things to happen had been swallowed by the numbness of the routine at the JDC, and that numbness only grew in the months that followed.

Ray's days began to blur into one another: up at six, morning chores, breakfast, school, lunch, more school, back to the unit, chores, rec time or waiting for rec time, chow, back to the unit, TV or studies, lights-out.

The only things that broke up the monotony were tests, tests, and more tests: physical, emotional, mental, academic. They were not the kind of tests one passed or failed. In fact, Ray didn't know whether he had done well or not. "Don't worry about it," said the female psychologist who kept asking how he was *feeling*. "We just want to know where you are." Nevertheless, when she asked Ray if he cried at night, he said no. What business was it of hers? He was going to have to look out for himself even more than he had on the streets, because "in the system" there was no one else to look out for him.

One guy, however, had tattoos all over his arms, and Ray recognized them as Latin King insignia. "Where'd you get those?"

"Did 'em myself. Pretty good, huh?"

"Yeah, man. Think you could do one for me?"

The other guy looked around as if concerned that someone might be listening. "Probably. What do you want?"

"How 'bout a crown with L and K under it, just like that?" Ray pointed to the guy's other arm.

"You a King, man?"

"Yeah. Name's Ray, Raymond Slewinski."

"Gerardo Gomez." They bumped fists. "Hey, I don't mind doin' a crown for you, but you know the staff don't like seeing displays of gang affiliation."

Ray shrugged. "What can they do after it's done? They didn't do nothin' to you, did they?"

"No, but this ain't like goin' to no tattoo parlor for twenty minutes. I'll have to do it with just a needle and some ink. Could take a while, two or three days. Know what I mean? They might see it half done and know what's happening."

Ray grinned what he thought was a tough-guy grin. "Better get started, then."

Gomez was good, for a prison tattoo artist. The edges were a little blurred, but the proportions were good, and he was able to do it without the supervisor noticing, working a little bit at a time when the guys were watching TV or in other places.

Other than his time with Gomez, Ray kept pretty much to himself. He took care to stay out of fights because there was always the threat of Room 18, the "Gladiator Room," as some called it, where supervisors sent guys who got into it with each other to settle their disputes on their own. Ray had seen some guys come out of there pretty bloodied up, so he made peace when he could and hoped he'd never be seriously braced.

But there was this one guy, a big white guy, almost six feet tall and two hundred pounds. Word was, he'd played football for New Trier High School in Winnetka, one of the wealthiest suburbs north of Chicago. He looked like a skinhead with his blue eyes and shaved head, but he wasn't mobbed up. Claimed he didn't need any gang affiliation, that being a good customer was protection enough. Ray had pretty much ignored him until one day he was missing some of his underwear and saw this big white kid using it for rags to clean the shower, a duty he was regularly assigned for being the last guy in line for anything.

"Hey, them's my shorts. What you doin' with 'em?"

The guy held them up. "You wear girl's underwear? Is it softer or something?"

"Come on, man. Just give 'em back."

"Take 'em back." The guy squared off toward Ray.

Ray knew the guy was big enough to grind him up like hamburger, but should he lay into him anyway and take the beating just so no one would think him a coward? Or should he walk away? It was one of those miserable no-win decisions. Ray's mom used to say, *"You know, sometimes discretion is the better part of valor."* But she wasn't a guy on the bricks. On the other hand, Ray wasn't out on the bricks anymore either, and he did need to survive. What would mean survival? Finally he walked away.

Later, Ray learned the bully's name was Doug Davenport. He bragged about driving down into the city in his yellow Beemer and going home with enough yeyo to float the whole school. His dad's high-priced lawyers had gotten his first three busts for riding dirty—possession with the intent to distribute—reduced to misdemeanors with fines and probation. "Yeah, and they'll do it again too. Just wait and see." But this time the judge hadn't released him into the custody of his parents, so he was stuck in the JDC.

Ray attended classes daily but could seldom concentrate. Anytime he wasn't watching TV or involved in some other distraction, his own case flooded his mind. He thought that as time passed it would be less sharp in his consciousness. But it never went away because his case was now what defined every aspect of his life.

And that's what everybody called it. "My case *this*." "My case *that*." Never any reference to what anyone had actually done—though word got around just the same. Just like on the streets, everybody wanted respect. But the awe, the veiled fear, even the disdain with which guys looked at him was a cheap substitute for respect, and Ray knew it. They didn't really respect him for shooting an unarmed kid who wasn't even a rival.

When Patty Higgins sat down with him just before Christmas to discuss his case—she at least wasn't waiting until just before the trial to work on it—Ray noticed that she didn't seem shaken by the fact that he was accused of murder. It was as though she didn't care what he had done. She said she either had hard cases or easy cases, and it was all based on how much work they required from her. At this point, Ray's case was rather simple: "As far as I can see, Ray, your only hope is to get that confession thrown out. According to the disclosures, the police haven't collected much physical evidence and no formal statements from witnesses . . . other than from the guys in the car. But of course, that could change." She was thumbing through the papers in his file, refreshing herself on his case as they talked.

"Even the statements from the guys in the car are a little soft," she continued. "Two of them ID'd your picture, but the third one picked out a kid from Maywood who was in school that day. Trauma can mess with your memory. So . . ." She closed the folder and looked at him. Today her hair roots were black. "Like I said, my recommendation is that we work on getting that confession thrown out, and then we go from there. You have a choice between a bench trial—that's where the judge alone hears your case—and a jury trial. But there's been a lot about this case in the papers. No matter how careful we are during jury selection, jurors are bound to be influenced by the media."

"So what am I supposed to do?"

"I think a bench trial is probably safest. A judge is less likely to rely on a confession from a minor, whereas to a jury, a confession is a confession, so they could be swayed by hearing that you said you did it . . . if we can't get it thrown out."

"But . . . doesn't it matter who the judge is?"

"Perhaps. But we don't have any say over that. I still think a bench trial is best. There's just too much public emotion. People are tired of kids killing kids. So what do you say? Bench trial?"

He shrugged. What could he say? What did he know? "Okay."

In mid-February, when Ray's PD told him Judge Rolf S. Wolfson had drawn his case, his first question was, "So what's he like?"

Patty Higgins squirmed in the plastic chair, the only kind to be found in the small counseling rooms in the JDC. "I've only been before him one other time, but he has a no-nonsense reputation. However . . ." She paused and grimaced as though she had a toothpick wedged sideways in her mouth. "He's up for reelection next fall, and he's gotten himself in a bit of trouble."

"Trouble? A judge in trouble? What do you mean?"

"On the wall in his chambers, he has a plaque—I've seen it myself—with a Congressional Medal of Honor mounted on it and a framed certificate saying he was a war hero, awarded the medal for exceptional bravery during the Korean War. That's the highest honor in the land, and they don't give it out very often. They say there are only 150 or so recipients still alive. Anyway, some veterans group discovered Judge Wolfson's *not* one of them. He's an imposter, and the medal's a fake, even though I guess he was in the Marines at one time. It's been written up in the *Tribune*, the *Sun-Times*, and people are calling for his resignation. Big scandal."

"So what's that to me? He got caught. Maybe he'll know how it feels."

"Yeah, well, it may not go down that way. If he rolls over and agrees to resign, it may not mean much for your case. But if he decides to fight, he may turn very political on us, and your case has gotten a lot of press—get tough on the gangbangers and all that. If he wants votes come November, he may try to please the public."

"Whaddaya mean, please the public?"

"Kids killin' kids, Ray . . ." She paused as though waiting for a response. "You 'member the Hardaway trials, don't you?"

Ray shook his head.

Patty Higgins took a deep breath and leaned back in her chair. "Three, four years ago, Yummy Sandifer, you remember him? . . . Well, he was only eleven when he made his bid for a big rep with the Black Disciples. Walked up and shot three kids on a playground. Little girl died.

"Apparently the Black Disciples put out a contract on Yummy because of all the heat the cops brought down on 'em to turn over the shooter. Not long after that, Yummy was executed, and the police arrested the two Hardaway brothers for his shooting: Derrick was fourteen, and Cragg was sixteen. All kids!

"People were scared, Ray. And that wasn't so long ago." She shook her head. "Your case sounds like more of the same—kids killing kids! That makes the public angry. See what I'm getting at? It's in all the papers.

"Derrick got forty-five years, Cragg was given sixty. With all the trouble Judge Wolfson already has, how can he do less if he wants to be reelected? Besides, you're white. If he didn't come down on you, it'd look like he was playin' racial favorites. He can't afford any more controversy."

Ray looked down. He was having trouble taking a deep breath. Had he been a fool to agree to a bench trial? Guess that's what you get when all you can afford is an overworked PD. He sighed. "Maybe we ought to ask for another judge. Can you do that?"

"Don't think so, but I do have some more news. I got a continuance for a couple more months, until—" she rummaged through her papers "—until May 18, so—"

"Wait a minute, why would you keep stretching this out? I mean, I already been in here over eight months, ya know!"

"Ah, my young friend." Her long silver-and-turquoise earrings swung as she shook her head. "What you don't realize is that this place is like summer camp compared to where you're going if I can't get that confession thrown out. You don't want to get there any sooner than necessary. But the reason I asked for a continuance is that the police haven't yet found those telephone records showing their attempts to inform your mother. And that's crucial to proving they took your confession illegally."

"But, Ms. Higgins, you don't understand. I'm dryin' up like yesterday's pizza in here. I'm not one of these chumps who's glad for every continuance like you explained. I want out! There ain't nothin' to do. The school they got's a waste. I hate it! I want to make somethin' of my life. So how 'bout hurryin' things up?"

"Ha!" She made a wry smile and shook her head. "Nothin' like coolin' your heels in the joint to inspire higher goals. But I'm telling you, son, you don't want what's comin' down the track to arrive any sooner if we can't get you off the track. We need every opportunity, so don't rush it."

More "opportunities" did come—though Ray still thought of them as delays—and before the May date arrived, the prosecution petitioned for another continuance. It seemed the phone company's computer had crashed, and they were having trouble retrieving the backup file from some archives in Colorado. The judge granted a delay of two more months. Ray felt as if his whole life were constipated.

CHAPTER 8

Friday, July 10, was Ray's second birthday at the JDC. He could hardly remember the first one. It had all been a swirl—the shooting, his getting arrested and incarcerated. This time his mom got off work early and came down to the JDC for a visit. She brought a package with new underwear and socks. Of course, security had opened and checked everything, so there wasn't any pretty wrapping paper or anything for Ray to open, but he still got a funny lump in his throat when his mother handed it to him.

"Here's a card, and I brought you some Ho Hos for a cake. They wouldn't let me bring in anything bigger or anything homemade 'cause they said it might include drugs. So . . ." She shrugged. "Happy birthday!" She looked tired, a little shorter and heavier than he had remembered. Wisps of wiry gray hair around her face sprang out from her otherwise loose, dark curls as though they were ratting her out, giving away how wound up she was on the inside. Ray felt bad he was putting her through all this.

"That's okay, Mom. You never baked cakes anyway." He held up the underwear. "I needed these. Stuff gets stolen around here all the time."

They sat in silence looking around the visitation room. There were families at a couple of the other tables.

"Where's Lena? How come she didn't come for my birthday? I haven't seen her since I came here."

His mom held her head in her hand, elbow on the table. "They won't let kids in here, not unless you're being locked up. But I'm really worried, Raymond. She's gonna get locked up too if she doesn't make some changes. I wish you could write her a letter or something . . . talk some sense into her. You're finding out how bad it can get when you screw up, but she acts like she hasn't a clue."

"Yeah . . ." He didn't know what else to say. What could he tell his sister? At least she hadn't shot anyone.

Hands on the wall clock inched forward. Sitting across the table from his mom, Ray felt like he ought to say something, but he didn't know what to say. He couldn't just ask her to hold him like when he was a little boy, but he knew he would regret wasting the time with her once she was gone. Why couldn't he think of something to talk about, something that would matter?

Finally Mrs. Slewinski stood up, acting just as awkward as he felt. "Gotta go. Don't want to be riding the El after dark. I'll try to get back down here again before your next court date. But if I don't make it, baby, I'll see you then." She gave him a peck on the cheek and headed toward the door.

He watched her leave. Yeah, she'd see him in court, but they wouldn't be able to talk there. Maybe she'd come to the JDC again before the court date, but she wasn't coming as often as she had at first. He touched his cheek where she had kissed him. What else could she do? She had to keep her job. Ray understood.

Ray woke up sweating. By the dim light that came through his door, he focused on the calendar taped to his wall. August 11, the day when his trial was to begin. He calculated: It was one year, two months, and one day since the shooting. If only he could turn back the time. But time continued moving forward, and two hours later he was sitting in one of the holding cells for the criminal division of Cook County Court at Twenty-sixth and California. Ray's foot bounced uncontrollably as he looked around the maze of cages where defendants waited until their case was called. Ray shuddered when he looked at their hardened faces. Would he end up looking like those monsters? Had he become one of them?

For his trial Ray was wearing civilian clothes and would be allowed to sit at the table with Patty Higgins. It gave him some small sense of support that she'd be beside him when the bailiff finally escorted him into the courtroom. She had an assistant with her this time, a young man with curly red hair, wide eyes, and an open-collar shirt—perhaps a law student. Ray's mother and sister were also in court. A half-smile washed over Lena's face when Ray made eye contact with her. But otherwise she sat there like a little girl in the principal's office, shoulders hunched, eyes downcast, waiting to get whacked. Had Mom *made* her come? Mrs. Slewinski waved and smiled hopefully. She had visited him as often as she could at the JDC and brought him new underwear and various "approved" toiletries for his birthday. But he was feeling more and more removed from family, like their world was moving on while his remained stuck.

"Hey," Ray nudged Patty Higgins. "Who're they?" He pointed to some strangers over to the side of the courtroom. A man and a woman were busily writing in notebooks, and beside them a woman worked on a large sketch pad with colored markers.

"Press."

"Am I going to be on the news?"

"Perhaps . . . if there's nothing more exciting. But don't count on it."

Ray concluded that the table corresponding to the one where he sat with Patty Higgins and her assistant was for the state's attorney and his staff. Then he noticed the people sitting in the first row behind them, behind a knee-high divider that separated the court from the spectators. A woman was dabbing her eyes with a handkerchief, and a man had his arm around her, patting her shoulder. Others around them stared at Ray like frightened refugees. They had to be family and friends of Greg Mason. A feeling as cold as an iron rod pulled through his body. They no longer had a son. What had he done? Ray wished he could tell them he was sorry . . . but what difference would that make? Greg Mason was dead.

Dead!

And then Ray saw Detective John Barker and Officer Percell sitting a couple rows behind the Masons. The cops had squeezed him until his confession had come out. It had been unfair, an unstoppable nightmare. He had felt helpless. Would the trial be any different? And yet what could he say? It had yielded the truth.

The bailiff's loud voice broke into his thoughts. "All rise!" A door behind the bench opened, and a black-robed judge entered. "The Circuit Court of Cook County is now in session, the Honorable Rolf S. Wolfson presiding. You may be seated."

The judge breezed in, surveying the room before taking his seat in his high-backed leather chair behind the bench. Ray guessed he was about seventy, and he looked like he actually might have been a Marine at one time: buzz-cut white hair, thin bristly mustache, slightly bulbous nose, and ruddy complexion with a roadmap of tiny purple veins in his cheeks suggesting a little too much liquor, maybe? He busied himself shuffling papers on his desk, grabbing additional brief glances at who was in his courtroom. Ray had the sense he didn't miss a thing.

For several minutes the other members of the court continued consulting quietly with one another, shuffling papers and whispering behind raised hands until the judge said, "I'll hear the petition from the defense to suppress the confession."

Patty Higgins stood. "Thank you, Your Honor. We contend that the confession was invalid and involuntary because of three things: One, this juvenile was not granted counsel even though he asked for it on more than one occasion. Two, he was interrogated apart from a parent. And three, his statement was made as the result of a false promise from the investigating detective."

"Your Honor." The assistant state's attorney stood. He was not the Asian man Ray had seen in juvenile court, but a tall, thin white man with a short-cropped dark beard that outlined his jawline like Abraham Lincoln. "If you'll read the transcript—"

"Objection. It's not a transcript. It's a report—"

"It's a *sworn* report, Your Honor. And so far, the defense has not challenged any of the content."

The judge held up both hands. "Can we dial it down a little here? We're just getting started, and you should have dealt with this in pretrial. I'm merely hearing a petition. You're not examining witnesses."

The prosecutor and the defense looked at each other until Patty Higgins sat down and the assistant state's attorney continued.

"As I was saying, Your Honor, the *record* shows that the boy's mother was notified before any interrogation concerning the shooting began. The police can't wait forever just because someone's parent is otherwise detained—"

"Wait a minute." Patty Higgins was on her feet again. She was surprisingly quick in spite of her bulk. "Your Honor, this was a typical runaround. The parent was called from one station, but by the time she got there, they'd moved the boy. She goes to the second place, but they had never heard of him. And the phone records, which we all waited so long to receive—" She turned and glared at the prosecution—"indicate that no further attempts were made to contact Mrs. Slewinski. They can keep that up all day until they get their confession. Which they did! And then, 'Oh, of course, Mrs. Slewinski. He's down at Area 3.' "

Ray noticed that she carefully avoided using the whole name of the Area 3 station, which would have reminded the judge that it was the Area 3 *Violent Crimes* Headquarters. She was good. She was good! He took a deep breath.

"The court will take note of that, Ms. Higgins. Please continue, Mr. Musselman."

Patty sat down, and the prosecutor continued. "In addition to informing the boy's mother, a juvenile officer was brought in to protect the defendant's rights and ensure that he was not unduly pressured." He looked down at some notes in his hand. "And yes, the issue of a lawyer did come up . . . *we* brought it up in his Miranda warning, but it came up on a couple of other occasions as well. However, not once did the defendant specifically ask for a lawyer. And we have no idea what this other claim of a 'false promise' involves."

Patty Higgins stood and sighed. "The inducement was twofold. Detective Barker promised that the complaint about a stolen bike would 'disappear' if Mr. Slewinski, that is, if the boy cooperated. Then to get him to confess, he said they had him but that they would 'help' him if he helped them."

"Your Honor." The assistant state's attorney was on his feet again. "Those comments hardly constitute 'inducements.' First of all, there never was a charge made against the defendant concerning a stolen bicycle, just some questions based on what some kids said. Second, it is not an inducement to suggest that cooperation with the police and our office will result in the state not seeking the most severe penalties. Such an unprovoked murder could result in a life sentence, but we're not going to ask for—"

The judge cleared his throat and pulled the small microphone toward him as he glared at the assistant state's attorney. "That sounds like an inducement to me, Mr. Musselman, especially when dealing with a juvenile."

The courtroom sparring over Ray's confession continued for more than an hour. Ray did not follow all the details, but he felt encouraged. Patty Higgins was a fighter, a fighter in his corner. Finally the judge called for a lunch recess and said he would return with his ruling when court reconvened at 2:30 p.m.

"How are we doing?" Ray whispered to his PD before the bailiff came to escort him from the courtroom.

"Hard to say. But at least he's listening."

When court reconvened, Judge Wolfson looked around and said, "Is Detective Barker in court?"

Barker raised his hand.

"How about Officer Percell?"

"Right here, Your Honor."

"All right. First of all, I'd like to say to the two of you that I am not happy at the way this interrogation was conducted. When you are dealing with a fifteen-year-old—"

Ray slid toward his PD. "I wasn't fifteen. My birthday wasn't until July 10, a month after the . . . the—" Ray tried to sound legal "—until after the *alleged* incident."

She covered her mouth with her hand and whispered, "Shh. He's leaning our way." Then she gestured toward the judge. "Maybe he's going to give you a late birthday present!"

" . . . especially one who has not been hardened by previous arrests. It's too easy to pressure a youth into confessing just to please you." Then he paused and looked back and forth between the defense and prosecution. "However, I do not see any evidence that the accused was too physically, mentally, or emotionally immature to understand what he was doing by making a confession. There is no claim of any coercion or force or the threat of it. I do not see any signs of psychological breakdown as a result of the questioning. Every test he has been given since then shows him to be intelligent and up to grade level in terms of his education . . . something we don't often see in this courtroom.

"As for the questioning being conducted in the absence of his mother, I agree with you, Ms. Higgins, that the police may have used—" the judge cleared his throat theatrically— "some smoke and mirrors, so to speak. However, while the law requires that a parent be *notified*, the police don't have to stop questioning until the parent shows up. That could tie their hands indefinitely with some disinterested parents. And finally, the record and the signed Miranda waiver demonstrate that Mr. Slewinski had ample opportunity to ask for a lawyer, which he did not do.

"Therefore, my ruling is that the confession is admissible."

Patty Higgins sat back slowly, silently blowing out a long, slow breath. Ray looked at her, eyes widening. *Admissable? Wait . . . wait! Didn't she say my only hope was to get it thrown out?*

CHAPTER 9

Patty Higgins did not stay seated for long after Judge Wolfson denied Ray's petition to suppress his confession. Back on her feet: "Your Honor, the defense asks for a continuance."

"I should imagine," said the judge. He turned toward his clerk. "Give us something about a month out." Then he looked back and forth between the state's attorney and the PD and waved his hand as though he were shooing a fly. "You work it out. I'll be back in a few minutes." He stood and headed toward the door.

"All rise," said the bailiff.

Patty Higgins didn't have to tell Ray why she had asked for a continuance: Her plan had crumbled, and she needed time to restructure Ray's defense.

Once court was dismissed, Patty Higgins arranged for a secure room in which she could consult with Ray without their having to sit in the holding cages. Her assistant accompanied her, and the three of them sat around an old oak table.

They'd lost! To Ray it felt like the only time he had been on a Little League team and had gone all the way to the playoffs with a good record only to get skunked seven to nothing. Patty Higgins reached out and touched his arm. "Don't worry about it. It was a long shot anyway. We'll just change our strategy."

Long shot? From what she had said before, it was his *only* shot.

"So now what?" he muttered.

She took a deep breath, raising her eyebrows, and blew out in a silent whistle. "Now we focus on getting you as little time as possible."

"You mean I'm gonna do time for sure?"

"Raymond, you're charged with murder. You confessed to it, and so far I don't see any way to prove otherwise. If you have any suggestions or anything you haven't told me, now's the time to come forth. Know what I mean?"

"I told the cops I was home asleep, and Mom agreed."

She just gazed at him until he looked down at his hands in his lap. Finally she said gently, "That was before you confessed, and as far as I know, there's no one else to corroborate that story. Right?"

Ray looked up at her and then at her assistant. It was the first time Ray had actually taken note of the man, but there was no hope in his sallow face either. He was like a stranger.

Patty nodded with a wan smile on her wide face. "I'm going to work on character references, people who believe in you, believe that you can change. Teachers, coaches. You go to church? A pastor or priest would be good. Anybody like that?"

Ray shrugged. "We used to go to mass before my father left, but . . ."

"Don't worry. We'll come up with some recommendations."

Ray couldn't stop the tears rising in his eyes. He wiped at them with the back of his arm. "What's gonna happen to me? Tell me straight. I need to know."

Patty Higgins looked at her assistant public defender and then back at Ray as though she didn't want to tell him what he actually faced, how bad a charge of first-degree murder was.

"Maybe we can talk to the state's attorney about a plea bargain." She reached around to her back collar, pulling her hair free so it fell down her back. "Get your time down in exchange for making their job easier or helping them out in some way. But with murder, and this being an election year . . . like I told you, everybody's upset about gangs and super predators. You could be facing sixty years. And with the truth-in-sentencing law, there's no time off for good behavior. So we got to get it down up front."

"Sixty years!" Ray almost choked on the words. "Can't we appeal?"

Patty Higgins snorted. "Oh, we can try—and we will—but as I see it, the only thing we can appeal is your confession. And frankly, the judge's ruling is not without precedent. Confessions by juveniles have been allowed even where there was doubt about the guilt of the accused. But in your case . . . I'm afraid people see your confession as the truth. So even though you should have had counsel present, it might be upheld. It's hard to say, but I don't want to give you false hope."

Sixty years! Ray sat staring at the table. Sixty years was a lifetime. He might never come out, or if he did, he'd be an old man—seventy-five years old! He didn't even have any relatives that old. What would he do in prison for all that time? Would he turn into one of those monsters he saw in the holding cages? Would he get beat up? Owned? Or . . . offed?

He needed a miracle. He needed a God who could do miracles. But, ha! He wasn't even sure such a God existed. The constitution for the Almighty Latin King Nation spoke of "Yahve," a variation on the Hebrew *Yahweh*, but he wasn't the God Ray had heard about when he had gone to church. "Yahve" was said to be the "Almighty King of Kings," as though God himself was a Latin King. Even though Ray enjoyed celebrating January 6 as the Kings' Holy Day, he had never believed any of that superstition. It was just to pump up the organization. The Kings were of the streets, by the streets, and for the streets, nothing more. Ray needed a *real* God. But why would the real God help him? Wasn't murder one of the big ten no-nos? Why . . . how could a real God help him after he had killed someone?

"Look, Ms. Higgins. I can't do sixty years." Ray stared at the table. "They might as well give me the needle."

"Don't say that, Ray. Besides, they don't execute juveniles in Illinois." She glanced at her assistant. "They may be trying you as an adult, but that's one break you still get, no capital punishment when it comes to sentencing."

"Yeah, big break! They take away my whole life, but they keep me around to make me watch it drip away day after day. I been inside long enough to know what that feels like. That's totally wasting my life." He no sooner said the words than he realized their irony: He had "wasted" Greg Mason's life when he shot him in that car, and now he was going to watch his own life waste away.

"Look, Ray. I know it's tough. But you'll adjust. There are a lot of constructive things you can do on the inside."

"Yeah, like what?"

"Education, for one. You can always keep learning. And you can devote yourself to helping others. There'll be other guys you can help so they can have a better life on the inside and when they get out. Think of it as a way to pay society back for what you did."

Ray stared at her. So she *did* believe he had committed the murder! In fact, maybe she had considered him guilty all along, just hadn't said so. His eyes fell again to the table. Well, what difference did it make? He was guilty, and now he was going to prison for the rest of his life. He'd better focus on how he was going to survive on the inside.

"Hey, Tyrone," Ray said as he sat down at the lunch table across from the tall black Conservative Vice Lord from Chicago's westside. "Your brother's in Pontiac, ain't he?"

"*Was* in Pontiac. He out now. What's it to ya?"

"Just wondering." Ray moved the beans around on his tray. "His case very bad?"

"Nah. He shot a kid when he was thirteen, then torched an abandoned building to burn the body and hide the evidence. But that ain't what sent him to Pontiac. He'd already been in trouble a lot of times, so the judge sent him up to adult court. He got twenty years. But that was before truth-in-sentencing. He got out last year when he was only twenty-three."

"So how'd he do his time, man?"

Tyrone shrugged. "He said it wasn't too bad when he was in Joliet, but when he turned eighteen they sent him to Pontiac 'cause he nearly killed a guard at Joliet. Anyway, he said the only way to make it was to get tight with your set. They're your only protection in a high-security institution. Otherwise, you end up a prison punk or get shanked. There's just no other way."

Get tight with your set! Well, Ray would do that. It was the Kings that got him into this mess; they'd have to be the ones to see him through. The more he talked to other guys, the more he learned. There was a whole society inside the prisons. The gangs ran everything, and those who were senior in their organization got the most privileges. Yeah, he'd have to do that. He'd have to prove himself, work his way up, get some serious juice.

The next time Patty Higgins came to discuss his case, the smile on her heavy face was so big the wrinkles at the corners of her eyes looked like the cracks in caked mud.

"So what's up?" He eyed her warily as they got in the elevator to go down to a JDC conference room.

"Just wait. I got some good news for you." She inserted the key and waited until the security system allowed the elevator to descend.

When they were seated across the table from each other, she opened her folder and raised her eyebrows. "We got a plea bargain, and I think it's a good one!"

"Yeah?"

"Fifteen years if you'll testify against Quiñones. Pretty good, huh?" She nodded like it was a done deal.

Ray narrowed his eyes. "Testify against him about what?"

"Well, the state doesn't have anything on him, but Barker's convinced that he was behind the shooting and says you can put him away. They want him off the streets. If you testify, they can get him on the accountability law, maybe even conspiracy. He could end up doing more time than you, 'cause he didn't cooperate with them and you did. He didn't say a word, so they couldn't even arrest him."

"You mean he hasn't been on ice in Cook County all this time?" Something was wrong here.

"No. They held him forty-eight hours, then had to cut him loose. Detective Barker says all they could do was lean on his probation officer to make sure he didn't leave town. He's out on the streets right now."

Ray digested this news. Quiñones was out because he kept his mouth shut?! What if *Ray* had kept his mouth shut? But he hadn't, had he . . . ?

Fifteen years! The news swirled in Ray's head so that he felt dizzy. Fifteen years—he'd be thirty when he got out. *Thirty.* That would be pretty old, but he'd still have a life. Fifteen was sure better than sixty . . . or even life. With fifteen, he could still get married, have a family, maybe get a job. He could help his mom when she got old. Thirty years old, that wouldn't be too bad.

On the other hand, how would he do that time? It wouldn't be too long before he'd be moved into an adult prison, where he'd have to do most of his time. Years in an adult prison, marked as a stool pigeon who testified against a fellow King. He wouldn't make it. He'd eat a shank for sure! That might even happen at an IYC—whatever youth prison he got sent to. "*Once a King, always a King!*" He couldn't break the code. If the Kings didn't take him out for ratting on one of their own, someone else would get him because he wouldn't have the protection of his organization.

He swallowed. "What kind of a prison? How 'bout Vandalia or East Moline, something minimum security?" Maybe he would be safer there.

"Oh, I doubt it, not at first." Patty Higgins shook her head. "You're still going up on a murder rap. For a while you'll be in maximum—Stateville or Dwight. Hopefully not Menard or Pontiac. But you'll have to earn your way into a lower-security facility."

"But I haven't caused anybody any trouble. I haven't even been in any fights."

"And you just keep it that way! You can't afford to be written up for *anything*. Nevertheless, like I said, you're facing first-degree murder. The state's attorney won't talk anything less. I was lucky to get a deal on the time. And I think it's a good one too."

Ray slumped in his chair. Sure, it looked like a good deal when you were just talking numbers, but Patty Higgins didn't know anything about the Kings. They were ruthless . . . to their rivals *and* to their own members if someone defied the leadership or the code. More than once Ray had heard the story of Carlos Robles as guys hung out on the corner, passing on gang lore.

For years the Illinois Department of Corrections had wondered why that crazy Latin King Carlos Robles had escaped just one week before his parole. How dumb was that? And then someone found his skull buried in the yard at Stateville. But the Kings knew all along what had happened to him. He had disrespected Raul Gonzalez, a Latin King leader. As a result, he was grabbed and taken to the large industrial kitchen at Stateville, where he was butchered and run through the prison's meat grinder and served to the inmates in the meatloaf for dinner that night. "Robles Meatloaf," they called it, and of course, all the Kings chose to be one-day vegetarians. Ray remembered the Kings on the streets laughing about it when the story came out in the *Chicago Tribune* a couple years ago.

Apparently, Robles' head was too big to fit into the meat grinder chute, so the Kings buried it out in the yard. Yeah, at the time all the dudes thought that was a hoot. It proved they were invincible. Nobody crossed the Almighty Latin King Nation, and if they did, at least they didn't live to tell about it!

Ray shook his head slowly.

"Look." Patty Higgins must have sensed Ray's hesitation. "You don't owe Quiñones a thing. He didn't do anything for you. Oh yeah, he kept his mouth shut, but that was only to protect himself. If he had said one word, he would have incriminated himself. He wasn't protecting you."

Ray kept his eyes averted. He knew that if he testified against Quiñones, he'd be crossing the Kings . . . and facing the consequences. Should he give such a foolish thing a try? No way! Testifying against Rico Quiñones, a Latin King enforcer? How stupid would that be? It would never be overlooked, and if Ray ended up in a maximum-security adult prison—as he undoubtedly would—his life wouldn't be worth a pack of cigarettes. He knew what his answer would be, even if his PD could never understand.

He took a deep breath and blew it out. "Thanks for trying, Ms. Higgins, but I can't take the deal. Tell him no."

CHAPTER 10

Ray knew it was a dream, yet he couldn't seem to wake up. He was riding a bike north through traffic on Clark Street, Rico following close behind, laughing so hard he almost lost control of his bike. "You a foo', man! You a foo'! You know where you gonna end up, but you headin' there anyway. You a foo', man!"

No, that wasn't right. That wasn't what he had said. He'd been saying, "Do it, man! Do it! Don't be no *cobarde!*" Ray tried to correct his dream, but it wouldn't cooperate.

The Bryco 9 mm was so heavy in Ray's pocket he could barely pedal his bike, and yet there sat the green Taurus, just two cars ahead. Ray moved forward slower and slower as though swimming through sewer sludge until he came up to the window and pointed the automatic at the kid in the passenger seat. But the face looking up at him was wrong! It was his own face, frozen with horror. His hands were up, trying to ward off what was coming, and his mouth was silently screaming, *"No, no! Please no!"*

And then, just as the pistol exploded, Ray awoke with a start and snapped upright in his bunk. His heart pounded with heavy sledgehammer beats as though each contraction had to pump all the blood in his body gulp by gulp. But this was wrong! He hadn't shot himself. It was only a dream. He was safe in the JDC.

Still breathing hard, Ray looked through the window of his door into the dayroom, where a dim glow of light showed the supervisor snoozing at the console, his chest and head rising rhythmically with each breath.

Safe . . . but not really safe. The threat of Ray's future—sixty years in prison—avalanched down on him in slow motion. It was as though he *had* shot himself that afternoon back in the hood. His life was just as wasted. He would spend the rest of it in prison, no girlfriends, no wife, no kids. He'd never take a trip to Disneyworld. He'd never fly in an airplane. He'd never go fishing on Lake Michigan like his dad used to do.

Ray's heartbeat slowed, and he sank back down on his cot, turning on his side and curling into the fetal position. He'd had tough times as a kid: their family not having enough money for rent, his mom sick and unable to work for a whole month. But this beat all. All those other troubles had a tomorrow when he could hope for something better. But there was no hope in his future now, no promising possibilities, no hope of brighter days around the corner. He tried to think of his time in pieces: ten-year increments. He could remember ten years ago. He was just a little guy, and his dad was still around. That seemed so long ago, near the beginning of time as he knew it. But ten years in the future, that was just as far off. He would only be starting on his time.

Ray squeezed his eyes tightly, battling the hot tears lurking just inside. He'd just have to suck it up!

The nightmare returned almost every night, though not always the same. Sometimes Greg Mason was sitting in the car when Ray pointed the gun. But in spite of how vivid his memory was of the spurting blood during the day, he always awoke from his dream at the instant of the blast, just before the blood came gushing out. Ray told himself it was his mind's way of protecting him from the full horror of the event, yet the dream left him feeling haunted all day, as though something wasn't right, something just on the edge of his consciousness, something he couldn't get away from.

Of course, that was true. Things weren't right! He'd killed someone in cold blood, and he hadn't yet figured a way to turn back the clock. It left him constantly regretting the past and always fearing the future. Ray was only able to live in the present for brief moments before either his past or his future came crashing in on him, stealing what fleeting peace he managed to find in a TV show, a card game, a game of baseball up on the roof, even his school studies. It was like a monkey on his back that he couldn't shake off, and it was wearing him down, making him nervous, on edge, short-tempered.

How did the other guys do it? They didn't seem to care. Maybe that was it. Ray had to get to that place where he didn't care. If he was going to survive prison for the rest of his life, he had to toughen up, not let all this crap get to him. He'd killed a guy. Nothing he could do about it. Couldn't let it get to him. Build a wall around himself. Maybe he needed to embrace his status as a dangerous, unpredictable, hardcore killer. That was it. He needed a rep. And there was only one way to do it.

Earlier, Ray had discovered in a very personal way that Doug Davenport was the biggest bully in his section. Davenport thought his size and his money bought him the right to disrespect anyone he chose. And somewhere between his money and his size it seemed to work. Ray had walked away from him the first time, but it had only invited additional disrespect: "What's with you, man? You some ghetto cockroach with that LK tattoo on your shoulder? Why don't you just be a white boy? You got no pride in your race?"

Finally Ray decided this was the guy he had to brace. Also, attacking him wouldn't incur the wrath of some other set since Davenport was a *neutron*, someone unaffiliated with a gang.

To prevent guys ganging up on one another, the supervisors never allowed more than two guys to shower at a time, and there was no door on the shower room, merely a secondary wall that blocked the general view from the whole dayroom. When guys went to the shower, they couldn't take anything in with them but a washcloth and soap and the towel they wrapped around themselves as they walked to and from the shower. That was to keep anything that might be used as a weapon out of the shower.

On Friday evening Ray timed his shower for when Davenport would be in there alone. Instead of a washcloth, he took a white tube sock and a new, large bar of soap. Once inside the shower room, he slipped the soap down into the toe of the sock, wet it so the sock stretched out, and grasped it firmly by the top.

As usual, Davenport started trash talking. "Whassa matter witch you, man? You on scag? All you chump-head Latin Kings on scag? I bet even yo mama's on scag!"

Ray didn't say a thing, just waited until Davenport turned toward the shower head and closed his eyes as the full force of the water hit his face. Then Ray swung the soap in the sock with all his might and cracked Davenport right above the ear. Davenport let out a muffled moan as he went down, first onto one knee and then toppling over to sit on the floor of the shower. The water pelted down on him as he held his head and swayed like a drunken man close to passing out.

Ray pulled the sock off his bar of soap and tossed it up on top of the steam pipe near the ceiling. He stood over Davenport with his fists clenched as though he were ready to hit him again. "Got a man down in the shower," he called to the supervisor. "I think he hit his head."

In an instant the supervisor was at the door. "What's goin' on in here?"

"That LK jerk hit me! That's what happened."

By then Ray had stepped back, dropped his guard, and stood there casually. He spread his hands. "What, *me* hit *him*? How could I possibly sit him down like that? That guy's big as a mountain."

Davenport was big, and the supervisor bought the ruse. Ray couldn't have taken down Davenport with one punch. "So what'd you do? Smash him into the wall?"

"No. I never pushed him."

"He hit me, man. That's what he did. He sucker punched me."

"You boys need a little time in the gladiator room?"

Ray looked at Davenport. This would be the test. If Davenport believed Ray hit him with his fist, then it didn't much matter whether it was a sucker punch or not. Davenport was a bully and unlikely to go up against anyone who could hit that hard.

He stood up, rubbing his head and giving Ray an ugly sneer. "No. We cool, man."

Word spread. But Ray knew the problem with a rep—there was always someone looking to knock it down.

Ray's case proceeded at what seemed like a snail's pace. Nearly every day he went to court, where either Peter Musselman, the assistant state's attorney, or Patty Higgins, Ray's PD, would argue various details before Judge Rolf S. Wolfson. Sometimes a reporter sat in the courtroom. Once a class of high-school students filed in to sit on the back two rows. They left when nothing seemed to be happening. Ray's mother showed up only occasionally because she couldn't miss work. But always, members of the victim's family were present. Ray couldn't help stealing a glance at them, wondering how much they hated him, whether anyone in their family had ever been in trouble with the law like he was.

Court was a tedious routine.

"When's this thing going to be over, anyway?" Ray hunched his shoulders inside the white shirt and tie Patty Higgins said he had to wear to court to "portray a civilized image."

Patty Higgins looked at him with narrowed eyes. "You sure you want it to be over? It's not going to be any better for you when it is."

Ray shrugged. "I just don't like people talkin' 'bout it all the time, goin' over every little detail. Makes me emo, man. Know what I mean? Brings me down." Seemed like his whole world had been reduced to victims and perps, enforcers and security, prosecutors and defenders—people and locks telling him what he could and couldn't do every minute of every day.

"Actually," Patty Higgins said, "now that it's under way, your case is moving pretty fast, faster than most I've been on. The judge asked whether we'd be ready for closing arguments next time; after that, it's the verdict. If you're found guilty, it may be no more than a few weeks before sentencing. That's not very long. I wouldn't be so eager for it to move faster if I were you. You don't want what waits you." She stared at him with sad eyes. "Think about it, Ray. You sure you don't want to go for that plea bargain? It's not officially on the table any longer, but I might get Musselman to give us something if you'd be willing to testify."

Ray shook his head slowly. "You don't understand, Ms. Higgins. Once a King, *always* a King. We stick together. He didn't go up against me, and I don't dare go up against him. Might as well be dead if I did."

"Ray, I tried to tell you! The only reason he didn't testify against you was to save his own neck. Quiñones hasn't done one thing for you but get you into this mess. Have the Latin Kings put up any money for your defense? Have any of them volunteered to testify on your behalf? And in a year and a half, have any of them come to visit you even once? Have they done *anything* for your mother or sister? No. Face it. You're forgotten by the gang. Why try to maintain any loyalty to them?"

Ray studied his shoe. He'd never thought of all the things the Kings *hadn't* done for him. He just missed being out on the streets partying and gangbanging with his boys. That's the image of the outside he tried to keep alive in his mind, not that they had abandoned him in the joint. Huh. Maybe his PD had a point.

But . . . it didn't really matter. Maybe they'd forgotten Ray for now, but if he turned against them, they would remember him soon enough.

Ray lifted his eyes and met his attorney's. "Sorry, Ms. Higgins. Know you mean well an' all that, but I can't testify against Quiñones."

Just as Patty Higgins had predicted, the next time they were in court, the judge called for closing arguments. The prosecutor emphasized the cold-blooded nature of the shooting and the fact that there was no disputing what happened. He reminded the judge of the two witnesses—passengers in the victim's car—who had testified in court that Ray was the shooter. And then he concluded with Ray's confession. All very simple and short.

Patty Higgins stood and sighed. Even though the judge had admitted Ray's confession, she challenged its validity again. Then she turned to some of the prosecution's claims. "It's true that two passengers in the victim's car identified Mr. Slewinski as the assailant. A lot of images get skewed in a moment of trauma. People think they see things that aren't there. They superimpose memories. They might have confused Mr. Slewinski for Rico Quiñones. There is certainly reasonable doubt as to whether they are remembering correctly. The fourth rider failed to identify Ray. In fact, he picked out someone else when shown mug shots that included Ray's. We don't convict people on majority vote in this country. If there is reasonable doubt—such as contrary testimony by one of the witnesses—we have to take that into account.

"And don't forget, Your Honor, no weapon has been found linking Ray to the shooting, and the police didn't find any gunshot residue on him or his clothes."

Stupid pigs. Ray smiled to himself. *They were so sure they had an airtight case, they never even checked.*

"And Ray's mother told police he was home in bed that morning." It was a fact that appeared in the police report, so she could mention it in her summation, but Patty Higgins had never called Ray's mom to the stand to reinforce it. When Ray had asked why not, she had explained, *"Because she can't swear to knowing where you were all morning. I'd be a fool to put her on the stand."*

But Ms. Higgins was only getting warmed up. "The weakest part of the prosecution's case," she said, pacing back and forth and shaking her finger at the state's attorney's table, "is that the police didn't pursue the most likely suspect in the shooting, Rico Quiñones, a young gangbanger who was picked up in the vicinity but who refused to cooperate with the police. My client, on the other hand, cooperated from the beginning—he had nothing to hide. And the two young men easily could have been mistaken for the other. Ray is only an inch shorter than Quiñones, and with the baggy clothes kids wear these days, they all looked alike, especially in a tense and terrifying moment.

"Furthermore, Quiñones's fingerprints were found on the only bicycle recovered for the Hernandez boys. So why didn't the police arrest Quiñones?" Patty Higgins wheeled toward the judge and planted both hands on her hips like some aging, overweight Xena. "Why? Because they had a confession from Raymond Slewinski! And that's all they thought they needed."

She then referenced the research that showed confessions from juveniles under pressure and without counsel or a parent present were notoriously unreliable. She stopped short of declaring that it never should have been admitted, because that would have challenged the judge head-on since he was the one who had admitted it, but she did suggest it was certainly grounds for reasonable doubt.

"In conclusion, Raymond Slewinski should be found not guilty."

When she sat down, Ray felt like throwing his arms around her. Finally someone had really come to his defense! He could almost believe himself innocent . . . if he had not been there and had not been the one who pulled the trigger. Surely she had raised reasonable doubt. Hadn't she?

The judge took a fifteen-minute recess, during which Ray felt so excited he thought he was going to lose his lunch. His stomach wouldn't stop clutching and flopping. Maybe there was a God. Maybe there were miracles. Maybe he was being given a second chance.

Twenty minutes later the bailiff said, "All rise." The door behind the bench opened, and Judge Rolf S. Wolfson swooped in and court resumed. The bailiff instructed Ray, as the defendant, to rise. His defense team rose with him. Then the judge began talking, saying he had carefully considered all the evidence. Ray was preparing himself for a long lecture when the judge said, " . . . and therefore on the count of murder in the first degree, after due consideration, I find Raymond Slewinski guilty."

CHAPTER 11

"The judge says he wants to wrap up your case as soon as possible," Patty Higgins said a half hour later when she bustled into the client conference room she had arranged instead of the holding cages where Ray usually had to wait.

Ray stared at his PD. Wrap it up or drag it out, what difference did it make? His eagerness to get things over with had melted with the guilty verdict. "What about an appeal? Can't we get another judge to change this?"

Patty Higgins rolled her eyes. "I've filed your appeal—as a matter of course—but you don't get a new judge. Wolfson will look at it first, and he'll deny it when he sentences you. Later, the appellate court will review it, but I'm sorry to say, it isn't likely that they will reverse it. We just don't have enough to go on. And actually, if they granted the appeal, it wouldn't be a reverse. They'd just send it back to Wolfson and tell him he shouldn't have admitted the confession—that's what our appeal is based on. But he might still convict you on the rest of the evidence anyway."

Ms. Higgins sat in silence for a moment, staring at the paper before her. "This is not good. I've seldom seen a case get moved along so fast."

"What's wrong with fast? It don't seem fast to me." Ray's impatience returned. "I been rottin' in here for a year and a half. I'd just as soon get it over with."

"Ha!" The loose flesh under her chin bobbled as she shook her head. "I already told you, Ray. This is the JDC. You don't rot here. You may not get to hang on the corner with your homeboys, but this is not rotting. Rotting is what happens after you leave here . . . the years you're likely to spend in adult prison. That's when the rotting happens." She stared at him as though she knew telling him what lay ahead was futile.

"Look, I'm not talking about the overall time your case has taken; I'm talking about rushing from conviction through sentencing. The reason this isn't good is that November 3 is Election Day. If Judge Wolfson sentences you before then, I'm afraid it will be just to make himself look good in the eyes of the voters, take the heat off his Medal of Honor scandal. And if that's his motive, he's liable to add a few years to your sentence just to show the voters he's not soft on crime. No, this isn't good . . . unless . . . ." She got a faraway look in her eyes as she stared at the bulletin board on the wall.

"Unless what?"

"Well, we might be able to use it as grounds for another appeal, but that'd be a real long shot, and so far we haven't scored too well with our long shots. I don't know."

Patty Higgins tried everything she could to delay the sentencing, but Judge Wolfson set it for Tuesday, October 27, just a month after the verdict.

During that month Ray walked around the JDC as if he were suspended in a thick fog while the whole world continued to function without him. He went to class but had no idea what the lessons were about. He went down to the rooftop field when it was time for recreation but sat out the games, saying he wasn't feeling well. "No, I don't need to go to the infirmary. Just go ahead without me." He picked at his food, and at night he couldn't sleep.

All he thought about was the judge's one line: "*On the count of murder in the first degree . . . I find Raymond Slewinski guilty.*"

What had Ray expected? He *had* been the one to pull the trigger, and as the street proverb said, *You do the crime, you do the time!* He knew that was the way society worked, but somehow, even a year and a half after pulling the trigger, he still hadn't been able to accept that he had actually murdered someone. *A murderer? Me? How could that be?*

The day for sentencing arrived. Court had become familiar, almost comfortable: Ray sitting there beside Patty Higgins; everyone conducting their business before Judge Wolfson entered; the prosecutor conversing quietly behind his hand with his assistant, a new relaxed, satisfied look on his face. Greg Mason's family and friends were huddled on one side of the gallery, and Ray knew that his mother sat a couple rows back on his side. This morning he couldn't look at her.

Once the proceedings got underway, Ray listened impassively as Judge Wolfson denied his appeal. He wasn't surprised. Patty Higgins had warned him. But the judge had no sooner invited the prosecution and defense to offer their statements that might influence his sentencing than Ray's PD jumped to her feet.

"Your Honor, the defense requests a two-week continuance before sentencing."

"On what grounds, Ms. Higgins?"

"Well, Your Honor, we have not been able to contact the boy's father, but understanding why his father left the family could mitigate the boy's actions . . . a significant element for you to consider in determining punishment. But we think we have finally found him in . . . California—"

Ray's stomach tightened. What was she talking about? His father wasn't in California. Why'd she say that? Did she have a plan, or was she bluffing, stumbling around?

"Your Honor," the PD continued, "we'd like time to get a statement from him for you to consider before rendering the sentence."

"Ms. Higgins, after—" he counted on his fingers—"after almost seventeen months you are only now finding this man? I don't think so. And I don't subscribe to the psychological hocus pocus that we can blame all our woes in this life on our parents. This young man made his own decisions, and he must face the consequences. I don't need to know why his father left the family or even *that* he left the family. It's irrelevant."

"Thank you anyway, Your Honor." Patty Higgins sat down. Ray leaned over to whisper to her.

"My dad's not in California, is he? I thought he was in New Jersey."

"I was just trying to gain a few more days before sentencing, get past this election."

The assistant state's attorney was on his feet, making his statements that might influence the judge's sentence. He emphasized the cold-blooded nature of the crime, how the victim, Greg Mason, was by all accounts a fine student and top athlete with no association to any gang. Ray Slewinski, on the other hand, was a ruthless killer, and the public deserved to be permanently protected from his kind. Several reporters were present for this final stage of the proceedings, and it was obvious Mr. Musselman was using the media to tell the public that the state's attorney's office wasn't soft on crime either.

When Patty Higgins stood up again, Ray noted she moved like an overweight marathon runner losing the race. There was no snap in her gestures, no spark in her voice when she pointed to Ray's good grades in school, his disadvantage of being from a poor home where his father had abandoned the family. She said his test scores and psychological profile supported his good record in the JDC. She railed against a legal system that threw juveniles into the adult criminal system when there was every hope for rehabilitation if they would only be given a second chance. "You can give him that chance, Judge, if you just remember that Ray is a juvenile and sentence him to the minimum of fifteen years for his crime."

She sat down. The judge abruptly announced a fifteen-minute recess. Ray fidgeted and watched the clock. When the judge did not come back in the predicted time, Ray asked his PD, "Is that a good sign? Is he reconsidering?"

"Doesn't mean a thing one way or the other. He's often late."

Finally the door opened and the judge swept in. He read a speech that sounded like it had been written by the state's attorney, about how our communities had to be protected against the "super predators" and how the courts were society's last lines of defense. The judge put down his script and looked up; staring over the heads of everyone in court, he seemed to focus on a point a thousand yards beyond the back wall. He coughed and then swallowed. "Therefore, I sentence Raymond Slewinski to forty years in prison, to be served . . ."

Ray heard no more until the gavel came down: *Bam!*

"Oh-h-h, no!" The wail erupted from two rows behind Ray like the scream of the El train on a tight corner. It was his mother, no longer able to hold it all in. "My baby! My baby! Oh, Mother of God! Oh no! Oh-h-h . . ." Her cries trailed off as she finally got a hold of herself.

Forty years? Forty years . . . the fact that Ray had already served almost a year and a half of that sentence only demonstrated to him how long forty years really was. He tried to imagine himself in his mid-fifties—receding hairline, maybe starting to gray, the beginnings of a paunch, shoulders sagging. No . . . no, that wouldn't be him . . . would it? He would practically be a senior citizen. Did they call ex-cons "citizens"? Who knew? Forty years! How would he ever survive that long?

Ray slumped. Forty years, most of it in adult prison as number K17868. What could happen to a guy in prison buzzed through his mind again. It wouldn't be like the JDC. He might get beat up or raped or even shanked. He might not make forty.

As the bailiff led him back to the holding cell, Ray felt bad for his mother. He glanced back at her, sitting there in the pew, bent over, head in her hands, sobbing quietly. He hadn't meant to hurt her. And now she wouldn't even have a son to look out for her as she grew older.

Patty Higgins came in to take Ray to a conference room. He stood up when the guard opened the gate and followed his PD down the hall, but he didn't acknowledge her. What was the point? What could she do for him now? What had she accomplished so far?

"Sorry, Ray. I did the best I could. I had hoped we could get that sentence reduced, but short of striking a deal with the state, there was no way around Wolfson's election objectives. It's just one of those things."

"But what about my appeal? You said an appellate court would review it."

"And they will, but I won't be handling that for you. That appeal is based solely on the illegally obtained confession, the fact that the police interrogated you without benefit of counsel or even the presence of a parent. A new PD may visit you in prison to review your memory of the interrogation, but it's not required. The three-judge appeals panel basically looks at whether there were any irregularities in the proceedings under Judge Wolfson. And that's all in the transcript. I'm sorry. Wish I could be more hopeful."

"But what about this quick sentencing business, the judge trying to beat the election?"

"I'll look into it some more, but we might not have anything there either. I've already found precedents. A month isn't really that uncommon. We'd have to prove motive, and that's hard. Don't hold your breath on that one."

Ray watched her sullenly. She'd aged in the last year and a half. He could see it in the way she sat, shoulders beaten down a little more. She couldn't seem to look him in the eye, and she was already digging through her bulging briefcase for . . . for what? Notes on her next client? Ray could see she'd lost all hope of helping him.

"Look, Ray, you're a great kid, and I'm sorry we couldn't cut you a better deal on this, but don't get discouraged. At least it wasn't life. It could have been, you know." She gave him her card again—as though he didn't already have a half dozen of them—and then flashed a thumbs-up that kind of sagged like a melting candle. "Like I said, I won't be handling your appeal, but I'll still be in touch if anything should come up. Okay?"

"Yeah. Thanks." He reached out to shake her hand, but she was already readjusting her considerable center of gravity so she could rise from her chair. Grasping for something to say that would mask the panic erupting inside his gut and stealing his breath, he mumbled, "Don't forget to write if you find work!"

Once she finished struggling to her feet, she turned back to him. "What?"

"Nothin'. I just said, write if you find work."

"Oh . . . oh yeah. That's a good one. Keep that sense of humor, Ray. You'll make it."

He'd *make it*? What did that mean? That if he tried really hard, he could remain a living, breathing blob of protoplasm hibernating for forty years while sitting in the joint? That he would come out with no job, no skills, no friends, no family, no juice, and no connections and was supposed to *make it* in a new life? By the time he got out, all the street signs might have changed. Pagers, Popeyes, and Kmart stores might have disappeared into the history books by then. What'd she mean? How would he ever *make it*?

His public defender had reached the door and knocked. The bailiff let her out, then motioned for Ray to follow him.

Six days later, the day before Judge Wolfson's reelection bid, Ray was shackled hand and foot and loaded into a white Dodge van along with three other guys from the JDC and driven out to the Illinois Youth Center at St. Charles, some thirty-five miles west of Chicago.

In spite of the expanded steel grill over the windows, Ray's spirits rose as they cruised along the expressway and traveled through the suburbs, then crossed the Fox River. The open spaces looked peaceful, even if he was on his way to prison. But as they were passing an empty field, they suddenly turned into a drive and pulled up to a guardhouse. A high chain-link fence topped with rolls of razor wire stretched both ways. He'd never seen so much razor wire. There'd be no climbing over that. One small slip and you'd be cut to ribbons.

Though some offenders stayed in the general prison population at St. Charles, the facility primarily served as a processing center for young men who were later assigned to other youth facilities around the state. For those with less serious offenses, processing sometimes took several weeks while they underwent tests to see what kind of a facility might be most helpful. But Ray had been convicted of murder. They knew where he was ultimately headed—adult prison. In the meantime the question was, which youth facility would hold him until he was eighteen or nineteen? The only tests they gave him were designed to evaluate whether he was a high, medium, or low escape risk and how inclined he was toward violence based on his criminal history, his size, his age, and his level of aggressiveness. He had no way of knowing which youth facility was better: Harrisburg, Joliet, Kewanee, or Murphysboro, so he didn't know whether to try to appear tough or friendly and cooperative.

When Ray was assigned to Joliet within ten days, he was just as glad. Joliet wasn't that far from Chicago. Maybe his mom could come visit him—though he hadn't had any visits while he was at St. Charles, not even from his new public defender. He had no idea how long it might take for the appellate court to review his appeal. In fact, he hadn't received any communication from anyone while at St. Charles. It was like he had fallen down a hole into the underworld known as the Department of Corrections.

CHAPTER 12

Ray's *real* orientation at the Illinois Youth Center at Joliet began right after the official orientation. He and some of the other newcomers had just been issued their official DOC uniforms—loose-fitting slip-over tops and pants of heavy denim—when the orientation guard told them to put them on so he could take them to the mess hall for lunch. The sharp creases and unfaded color shouted that they were newbies.

Ray ended up separated from the other new guys when he went through the food line, so he looked for a vacant table where he could eat.

"You gonna be takin' my seat?" said a mountain of a skinhead with a wispy adolescent beard when Ray put his tray down. The guy, who looked like he had ridden in on a hog, had followed Ray through the lunch line and into the mess hall.

"Sorry." Ray moved his tray down one space.

"That's my seat too."

Ray pushed his tray across the table and started to walk around to the other side, but before he got there the skinhead bumped his tray into Ray's, pushing it off onto the floor.

"Hey, KP, got a spill over here," he called out to one of the trustees on duty.

"You clumsy elephant," Ray snarled under his breath.

"What'd you say?" He leaned across the table.

"I said you can have it." He flashed a Latin King sign and walked away.

Now it starts, Ray thought, the intimidation, the threats, the violence. *If I don't stand up for myself, I'll surely be taken down.* It wasn't his nature to live with a chip on his shoulder, but how aggressive did he need to be to avoid being taken advantage of? Trying to look casual, Ray drifted over to where the orientation guard was waiting to take the new guys to their dorms.

"You done already?"

Ray shrugged. "Wasn't hungry."

"Well, stand here until I collect the others."

All the staff at the IYC seemed to be guards of one sort or another. Not staff or supervisors or teachers or counselors like they had been at the JDC, but "hacks" or "screws" who all wore uniforms and were there primarily to manage the men and ensure prison security. And the men were no longer "residents" or "clients" as they had sometimes been called at the JDC. Here they were "prisoners" or "inmates" or "cons." Labels mattered.

The orientation guard lined up the newbies—Ray in the rear—and marched them off to their dorms. Ray had been assigned to Living Unit 4 and was the last man to be delivered. Even when they were alone, the man did not speak to Ray as they walked across the yard, and Ray didn't try to talk to him either. All the residents were in school when he arrived at Unit 4, and one of the residence guards on duty for the unit was nodding off when Ray came in. He jumped and buzzed the door open. "Take him down to 3B," he told the orientation hack. "That's the only bed we got left in here."

As they walked through the dayroom, the other guard glanced up briefly from where he sat watching TV in the dayroom. At the scarred steel door with 3B on it, Ray's escort pushed it open and said, "All right. That's your side." It was a two-person cell. "Put your stuff on the shelf. This is your new home, so sit down and acclimate. There ain't nothin' happenin' for you until supper. Good luck."

The door clicked shut when the orientation guard went out, and Ray mentally counted the number of locks between himself and civilian life: eight, if he remembered correctly, and a maze of halls, fences, guard stations, and video monitors. He was in deep!

Ray's roommate was a smaller kid than Ray with pink skin and hazel eyes but African features and kinky blond hair. Ray had seen albino African Americans before, but never up close. In this case the guy's racial features were totally overshadowed by a severe case of acne, almost as if he had taken a shotgun blast in the face. He threw a book on his chair, then flopped down on his bed and announced himself with a string of cuss words before saying, "So you my new cellie?"

"Yeah. I'm Slew."

More cussing, then, "So what's your name?"

"Told ya, Slew, Raymond Slewinski."

"What the . . . ? Well, I'm Darnell Harrison, you. . . ." And a string of profane names followed.

Ray jerked upright and glared at the kid. Was he serious cussing him out like that? Or . . . Ray thought for a moment. "Is that like stuttering or somethin'?"

This time Ray was hailed by the F-word, said three different ways—unbelievable—before Harrison asked, "What you tryin' to say? You sayin' I'm all crunked up or somethin'?"

"Just that you cuss every time you open your mouth. Sounds kinda like a stutter to me, like you can't get it out till you go through your little ritual or somethin'. Whadda they call that, Tourette's or somethin'?"

Darnell bit his lip and took a deep breath, then said—without cussing—"What you in for?"

"Shootin' a GD."

"Shee—!" Darnell caught himself. "I'm GD. What you be? King?"

Ray raised his sleeve to show his tattoo, aware he'd just admitted to shooting a member of this guy's posse. He shrugged. "Cain't help being a King," he said with a nervous laugh.

"Guess not." The kid swore a few more times, then sat up and extended his hand as a fist. "If we gotta share a cell, guess we should get along."

Ray met him fist to fist.

Harrison shook his head and cursed. "Might as well be the first to tell you. Everyone calls me Zitty, and that's somethin' I cain't help. So . . . guess we're even."

"City? Huh?" Ray chuckled. "Well, we all from the city one way or another, I s'pose."

Harrison pointed to his acne-riddled face with little pecking motions while he swore. "I said Zitty!"

"Oh . . . yeah. Got it! Somethin' you can't help."

That evening, three guys crowded around Ray when he got into the chow line. Two were obviously Latino, the other was a tall, light-skinned black guy with green eyes and cornrows. His mustache was also braided down either side of his mouth. He elbowed Ray's arm. "You sit with us, fish."

Ray looked at the guys and in a quiet voice took a chance: "¡Amor de rey!"

"Just shut up and get your food!"

Ray felt the tension drain out of him as he held out his tray for scoops of coleslaw, spaghetti, and peaches. He was hungry.

When they were seated, the tall guy with cornrows said, "You don't go flashing signs of the Almighty Latin Kings in here. In fact, no matter what you were on the outside, you ain't no King in here until we say you are!"

"Who you, el jefe?"

"*Jefe?* You don't need to know who the boss is. Until you've passed the investigation, I'm just Damion Weller to you." As Ray stared him up and down, he added, "You best not be mad-dawgin' me, boy. . . . I'll bust you up!"

"Yeah, whatever." Ray looked off in another direction, but then he turned back. "Investigation? What investigation? What you talking 'bout?"

El jefe grabbed a handful of Ray's shirt. "Never 'whatever' me, fish!" He let go and grinned. "Investigation simple. You fill out some forms, answer a few questions. We look it over, make a couple calls to your boss back on the bricks. If everything checks out and you ain't perpetratin', *then* and only then are you a King in here! *Capisce?*" he said like some godfather.

Ray couldn't imagine how inmates could conduct an investigation from within prison. "How long's all this take?"

"Couple weeks. We're thorough, don'cha know? Ain't nothin' get by us. You'll see. Course if you don't prove to be who you say you are, you just might . . . cease to exist. You feel me here?"

"You not ownin' me as a brother after I went down for crown on the outside? Man, that's cold. That's the only reason I'm in here. I smoked this GD dude, man. Everybody knows that. It's been in all the papers. What more you want?"

"*Uh-hm.* We'll see. Until then, don't be representin'.'"

Ray felt his stomach flip like a perch on the pier at Montrose Harbor. "Yeah, well, in the meantime, what am I supposed to do about those skinheads or . . . or anyone else?"

"Looks like that's your problem, now, don't it? But"—he leaned back and surveyed the mess hall—"ain't nobody's botherin' you now, are they?"

"No, but . . ." Ray caught himself. The guy was telling him that even though he couldn't announce that he was a Latin King, he could come under their shadow while he was being "investigated."

"One day at a time. That's how you do yo' time . . . *punk!*" Weller sneered. "That's right, you *my* b——h now!"

Ray recoiled. What did Weller mean by that? He'd been dreading sexual assault from the moment of his arrest. He hadn't seen any sexual abuse at the JDC, but he'd heard that anyone without the protection of a gang in the big house was likely to be forced to become someone's punk. Should he jump up and make a stand right now, call this guy out? Yet he also knew that, unlike some of the other street gangs, most Latin Kings abhorred homosexual behavior. So Weller couldn't be suggesting that! Could he? Ray shoveled spaghetti into his mouth and glanced sidewise at Weller. Weller gave him a sly smile and shook his head. Maybe . . . maybe he didn't mean anything. Maybe he was just saying Ray was a nobody, a dog, a worthless newcomer under Weller's control until he passed the investigation and would be respected like a brother.

Ray hoped.

That night Ray couldn't sleep. His mind kept going over what Weller said. If Weller wasn't *primera corona*—the top crown—here at Joliet, then Ray'd better find out who was. Homosexual behavior clearly violated the Latin King constitution and manifesto. If that's what Weller was threatening, Ray needed some protection, and the only way to get it was to bring a charge against Weller to the top crown of the gang's prison chapter. But he didn't know his way around. How would he find who the real *jefe* was?

The next morning one of the other Kings who had eaten with him the evening before slipped him a packet of folded yellow papers. He leaned close to Ray. "If a screw catches you with these, you'll be written up and thrown in segregation, probably for thirty days. But if you tell him where you got 'em, you'll never come out of segregation 'cept on a board."

Ray folded the papers once more and shoved them down the back of his pants. When he got back to his room, he opened the packet before his cellmate returned. It was a printed questionnaire on which he was supposed to fill in his name, street name, former address, detailed description of his case, list any priors, accomplices, and the names of three Latin King references. Ray couldn't believe it. How did they print such an "official" form inside the prison?

He glanced at his cell door, then read over the forms once more. It would be one thing to get caught with them when they were blank, but what if some authorities got ahold of them after he had filled them out? Would describing his case jeopardize any possibility of an appeal? Would it be the same as repeating his "confession"?

He wasn't going to fill out the dumb form. He was a King for life, and if these chumps didn't want to recognize him, that was on them. He searched for a place in his room where he might hide the papers. Even though his cell was in an older dorm, it had not been constructed with convenient hiding places. He could put the papers under his thin mattress or between a folded blanket or in a book, but if the guards called a shakedown, wouldn't those be the first places they would look for contraband—drugs or weapons . . . or, in this case, gang documents?

Then he noticed that the square sheet of stainless steel bolted to his wall that served as a mirror—scratched and foggy though it was—had a thin space between it and the concrete wall. Could he slide the papers in there? Would he ever be able to get them out again?

Well, so what if he couldn't? The only other option he had was to chew them up, spit them in the toilet, and flush them away.

CHAPTER 13

Ray's next few days at Joliet went pretty well. He got started in the school. School . . . what could he say? Classes were classes! Then he was given the after-school assignment of mopping the dorm floor each day—the most despised chore, passed on to each new guy—but he didn't mind. Someone else would come along and inherit it before long. Ray figured out how to do it fast enough to have a few minutes to play cards with Zitty and some of the guys before he went to supper.

But he had decided he wouldn't sit at the King table. If he wasn't going to expose himself by writing down all his personal information, maybe he ought to chill out as far as they were concerned. What if Weller used his information to extort sexual favors from him? Or what if the whole gang used it to blackmail him? Maybe he should become a neutron. He'd heard there were even neutrons in adult prison, though with no gang affiliation, they often had to do the dirty work for any of the heavies. Still, it might be worth it, at least until his case was totally settled.

Ray thought about Patty Higgins. Who would be his new PD? Would he—or she—get anywhere with Ray's appeal? Would he even try? Ray still had one of Patty Higgins' cards. Maybe he could call her and ask her what was happening.

When Ray went through the chow line, he tried to stick with some of the other guys from his unit, but as soon as they entered the mess hall, everyone dispersed to sit with their set.

One evening Ray took his tray to the condiment counter to squirt a mound of ketchup for his soggy fries. As Ray turned to leave, he tripped and simultaneously felt a heavy shove on his back. He went down, realizing as he fell that someone had tripped and pushed him. It was the skinhead Ray had encountered his first time in the mess hall. This skinhead, Ray had discovered, was muscle for the Aryan Brotherhood.

Ray and his tray smashed to the floor like a clattering tower of tin cans with Ray landing in the middle of the ketchup. He scrambled to his feet and whirled to face the bully. He had to put a stop to this on his own terms, no relying on the Kings this time. If he didn't show himself a man, he would be everyone's punk. "You better step off, man." But the skinhead stood there shielding an eight-inch shank from the view of the guards.

"Don't do nothin' stupid," he muttered. A sneer curled his lip. "You're a disgrace to white men everywhere, hanging with those mud races like you been doin'."

Ray wanted to protest, tell him he had stopped sitting with the Kings, but who was this scum to deserve an explanation?

"You know they're never gonna cover your back when you need it . . . like right now. Look around, sucka. Who's here to help ya? Wise up and join the AB!"

Ray glanced across the room. A prison bull had come in the far door and was watching them. Unlike the other guards, this one had a full view of what was going down. The skinhead rolled his eyes and slowly slid the shank up his sleeve, giving the guard a sour smile before walking away.

Ray couldn't believe it. The guard had seen the knife, but he hadn't done a thing. Could he be part of the Aryan Brotherhood—or at least sympathetic enough to cover for them? Maybe he was on the take! Ray's stomach tightened. If the screws couldn't be trusted to protect you in prison, there was only one other way to survive!

When Ray got back to the dorm, Darnell was busy watching TV in the dayroom. Ray hustled to his cell and tried to retrieve the "investigation" papers, but they were stuck behind the mirror. He dug at them with his fingernail. He blew from the other side. He folded up another piece of paper and slid it in. But nothing pulled them out. Finally Ray's efforts were cut off by Zitty's return and then lights-out. He never did get around to reading his history book like he was supposed to that evening.

The next morning he sat with the Kings but avoided any interaction other than to say "Hey."

On the way out of the mess hall, he picked up a few toothpicks and headed back to his cell. He got there before Darnell and went immediately after the papers. The first toothpick broke off. The second one fell behind the mirror with the papers.

His cell door opened and Zitty announced himself with a string of swear words followed by, "Whaddaya doin'?"

"Nothin', just cleaning up."

Darnell snorted, then cursed. "Why bother? You'll never get that thing clean enough to see yourself."

"What's it to ya, Zitty? Go play solitaire or learn some dirty Spanish words. You need to vary your vocabulary."

Darnell left and Ray tried again, working as carefully with his last toothpick as if he were picking a safe. Finally he got it behind the folded papers and slowly worked them toward the edge of the mirror. A fraction of an inch more, and then a piece was sticking out. He teased them a little farther until he was able to grab them with his fingernails. Success! He exhaled as if he'd been disarming a bomb and looked around. Still alone. With the yellow application tucked into his history book, he exited his room just in time to line up and march to class. He hadn't gone to the bathroom or even brushed his teeth.

Working on it bit by bit during the day, Ray managed to fill out the form while teachers talked about algebra and AIDS and the Great Depression. Great depression? Yeah, that's what he was in right now, a great depression!

Ray slipped the filled-out application to Weller that evening in the mess hall.

On Sunday when they were out in the yard, Weller sidled up to Ray. "You were asking who the *primera corona* is." With his head he gestured for Ray to follow. "He wants to talk to you."

Victor Muñoz was a solidly built Latino with a bull neck and a shaved head. He was smiling when Weller introduced Ray to him, but his eyes were so cold Ray felt he was looking into the mouth of a cave. No way of knowing what was inside.

"Slew, huh? I know who you are, and I even know Quiñones, who says everything you reported is accurate—"

"You talked to him? . . . How?"

Muñoz shrugged and raised his eyebrows. "Phone. How else?"

Ray looked from the big guy to Weller and back again. "Yeah. Sure."

"Anyway, he says you're okay. So you're a King, but don't be doin' nothin' on your own. *Comprende?* Keep a low profile. In fact, it's just as well if the prison bulls don't know about your affiliation right now. We might need someone anonymous at some point. Know what I mean?"

"But don't they already know? It's all in my case."

"Half of them can't read, and the rest don't bother."

"But what about . . . I mean, I was getting leaned on by the AB, and also, I don't want to end up somebody's . . ." He glanced at Weller.

"No one's gonna bother you. Everything's copacetic."

Ray liked it when Muñoz called him Slew. He had earned that name. It gave him status, and it began to spread. Other guys called him Slew. And even though he did not flaunt being a Latin King in front of the guards, a certain respect attended him wherever he went among the inmates. The Aryan Brotherhood left him alone, even though the big skinhead still sneered at him.

Ray had been in the Illinois Youth Center at Joliet for nearly three weeks when one day, while playing cards with Zitty, he got called out to meet Connie Mason, the mother of the guy he'd shot. Even though she had sent him the postcard, asking him to put her name on his visitation list, he never thought she'd come. He only did it so his file would have more names than just his mom and sister.

Now she'd come! Sitting across the table from her in the visitor center, Ray wondered why. Why was she here? He couldn't imagine and didn't much care, but her words caught his attention.

"I heard you went to Evanston Township High School. Did you know Greg?" Connie Mason leaned forward in her seat in the visitation room and stared hard at Ray.

"What?" Ray looked at her, his thoughts beginning to focus.

"Did you know Greg before . . . ?"

"Not really," he muttered. Her staring at him gave him the willies, like she expected more. "Couldn't afford Evanston, so we moved back to Chicago in the middle of my freshman year." He looked down—Why'd he tell her that?—and traced the lines in the tabletop with his right thumbnail.

For a long moment she said nothing, and Ray wished she would leave. Just go away and leave him alone. But she spoke again. "You know, he was a champion swimmer. He finished number one in the state. And then he started competing nationally. They were getting him ready for the Olympics. He had a really good chance.

I used to worry about him all the time when he was away at those meets. Never thought he would die so close to home. . . ."

Ray braced himself for the *you-rotten-gangbangers-are-all-going-to-burn-in-hell* part. But her voice softened. "Life wasn't a cakewalk for me when I returned to Jesus. But it was getting better. I had hope. . . ."

Ray almost stood up and walked away. Instead, he stared cold at her, rock solid, not moving a muscle.

"But it's gotten really hard lately, harder than I could ever have imagined." Her voice cracked slightly. "I really loved Greg—his murder tore up our whole family. My marriage almost collapsed under the strain." She returned his stare until he finally broke away. "But I do need to tell you this," she said, her pitch rising. *"Jesus has been with me through it all. And Jesus is the reason I had to come here today."*

Ray felt her warm hands surround one of his. Her touch drew his entire attention, but he didn't look.

It felt like an eternity before she broke the silence again. "Well, I didn't know whether you'd ever be able to ask my forgiveness for killing my son . . . so . . . so I'll go first. *I forgive you, Ray.*"

He jerked his head up. What had she said? Had he heard right?

She nodded. "That's why I came here. To forgive you."

"But . . . you can't just . . . why?" he whispered, finding himself hoarse.

She withdrew her hands as though his skin had become too hot. "You killed my son. I cannot bring him back. I could hate you forever." Her voice rose and hung there. After a moment her fingers found the little gold cross that hung around her neck. "But if I did, it would kill me as well."

Slowly she stood to her feet as if in a foggy daze. "Besides," she added, tears filling her eyes, "I, too, have been forgiven." She stepped around the table and kissed him on the cheek.

An instant later she was walking across the visitation room, weaving between the tables around which sat other inmates laughing and talking with their families or girlfriends. As she stopped at the door waiting for the guard to buzz her out, she looked back once, flashed a brief, misty smile, and then was gone.

Ray sank back into his chair. *What just happened?* Each detail was vivid, but the whole of it was encased in a fog. Then a guard called, "Hey, Slewinski! This place is for visitation, not meditation. Get on outta here!"

It must have been the cold wind that blurred his vision on the way back across the yard. He raked his wrist across first one eye and then the other.

A few moments later heads jerked up as he entered the dorm.

"Well, lookie here." Ray's card-playing partner called. "You finally back. You get the biddie, Slew? You sure took long enough."

"Shut up, Zitty. And hey, don't call me *Slew* no more. Got that? My name's Ray."

He walked over to the window and stood there a long time, staring past the paint-chipped bars into the frozen yard.

That night, with only the security lights on, Ray lay on his narrow cot trying to ignore his cellmate, Zitty, swearing in his sleep. He'd heard of people talking in their sleep, but swearing? It interfered with Ray's attempts to figure out what had happened that afternoon. The woman said she forgave him. But how could she do that?

It was strangely unsettling, to be forgiven. Yet what did that matter if he had to spend another . . . thirty-eight years, five months, and sixteen days in the joint? *Ah* . . . it was far too soon to count. Nevertheless, somehow Connie Mason's forgiving him had caused his whole world to tilt. The forgiveness itself stirred waves of remorse that grew higher, threatening to break through the wall he had built around himself this past year and a half.

Ray found himself thinking about the Mason family and the grief they had endured, and he felt new pangs of sadness, embarrassed and disappointed in himself that he'd caused it. He wondered whether Greg Mason would have ever become that champion swimmer everyone expected him to be. Probably not. But even as Ray told himself that, he knew he was saying it just to diminish the guilt he felt. Still, what difference did that make? What did it matter whether he was a champion or not? The loss his family and friends felt was just as heavy either way.

The night hours crawled. At two or three in the morning, he was still wrestling with these thoughts, sometimes sobbing silently into his pillow. The pain of what he'd done to others grew like a cancer within, and he could not choke it back.

Christmas of '98 at IYC was not like it had been at the JDC, where there had been a program with carols—redone as rap songs—paper decorations in some of the units, and a Christmas dinner, complete with turkey, stuffing, and pumpkin pie.

In Joliet there were voluntary chaplain programs—everyone from Christians to Muslims to Native Americans could worship God in their own way, or not—but as far as the institution was concerned, there were no Christmas decorations, programs, music, or special meals. It was as if Scrooge ran the place!

Someone tried to put up a green paper Christmas tree in Ray's dorm. Robert Bosco, one of the guards on duty, didn't seem to mind, but by the next morning it had been ripped down, leaving only three pieces of tape on the wall with ragged corners of green construction paper attached.

One day, however, Ray received mail from an address he didn't recognize. It had already been opened for security reasons, so he was about to toss it aside when he changed his mind at the last moment and dug his fingers in to pull out . . . a Christmas card! It was white with a silver star on the front that cast a blue light in the shape of a cross down onto a distant manger. Overall, the card had a refined look except that imprinted across the whole cover at an angle as though planted there with a ragged rubber stamp was the word "PERDONADO."

Spanish for *forgiven*.

Ray opened the card, uncertain what he might find inside. There was one image, this time looking like the inked print of a newborn baby's foot, the kind he'd seen on birth certificates. But in the center was a bright, splattered drop . . . as red as the blood that had gushed from Greg Mason's chest. And below were the words:

> *He came to pay a debt he didn't owe,*
> *Because I owed a debt I couldn't pay!*

A neat script added, *"Praying for you this Christmas season. —Connie Mason."*

Ray closed the card. *Perdonado.* How did she know that word, anyway? How did she ever find a card with it on the cover?

CHAPTER 14

Perdonado, perdonado. It clung to Ray like a new name. He plopped down on his cot and then lay back with the card on his chest. Could he ever really be pardoned, not just by Connie Mason or the state but by . . . who? Himself? Who did he really need to forgive him?

It was dark outside, and Ray was still staring at the ceiling when the albino bounced into their cell like a loose Ping-Pong ball, cussing with each step.

"Hey, Slew—"

"Don't call me that, man." Ray scowled. "I told you not to use that name no more—"

Harrison threw up his hands and swore. "What am I supposed to say? I thought *Slew* was your street name."

"So what if it was. I told you, I'm Ray now, just Ray. Okay?"

"Yeah, yeah. Okay . . . *Ray*! But guess what, I got us some squares!"

"What? Some hack drop his smokes in the yard? They're probably stale or wet from the snow."

"No, man. Look! I lifted 'em off Bosco's desk when I came in."

Robert Bosco was a large African American and the most lenient of the unit's six guards. He and Phanor Baptiste worked afternoons and evenings. Baptiste was light skinned, maybe Cajun, since he liked to slip in a little Patois when he spoke. David Talavera and Charles Barton followed them for the night shift. Barton was okay, but Talavera always threatened to write someone up or throw them into solitary. "It's 'cause he don't got no green card," said one of the inmates. "One thing goes wrong, and they'll ship *him* back to Mexico." Stephanie Beers, "Ms. Beers"—tough as any man—and Robbie Robinson came in at 4 a.m. and worked till noon. There were always two guards on duty in each unit so one could back up the other if there was trouble. And there was always one to escort the men to class or chow or anywhere else someone needed to go.

Ray saw that the pack of Camels in Zitty's hand was nearly full. "We can't smoke those now. He'll be lookin' for 'em."

Zitty swore. "No, man. Look over there in his little room. He already broke out a new pack o' squares. He's not even thinkin' 'bout these."

"You got a lighter?"

"Don't need one. Just pop a socket."

"A what?"

Darnell swore as he waved his hand at Ray. "You never popped a socket?" He scowled, then jerked his blond woolly head for Ray to follow him to the day room. "Sit there." He indicated the red plastic couch facing some infomercial on TV. He sat down on the floor just beyond the couch and leaned up against the wall. Next to him was an electrical outlet, one of the few in the whole dorm. It was used to plug in the industrial buffer for when they stripped and waxed the floors.

"Here, you hold these." He tossed Ray the pack of cigarettes. Then from his pocket Harrison pulled two paper clips, a plastic hair comb, and some toilet paper. He strained his neck to see over the back of the couch to make sure Bosco and Baptiste weren't watching. Then he twisted a couple sheets of toilet paper into a wick. He unbent both paperclips and pushed one into each side of the socket, taking care not to let them touch each other or touch them both with his fingers. Then he put the teeth of the comb over one clip and bent that clip toward the other with the twist of toilet paper between.

"Look out, man! You crazy. You're gonna electrocute yourself!"

"No way, man. My uncle showed me how to do this. He did it all the time when he was in Angola. They even started a riot this way one time, set the whole place on fire. Watch these fireworks!"

POP! The electric spark ignited the toilet paper wick . . . at the same moment the lights in the dorm went out. Harrison held up the burning wick. "See! I told you! Here's our match. Now, where those smokes?"

Ray glanced back toward the guard's cubical. The lights inside it were still on as were the lights in the individual cells, but Bosco was already standing up, pushing the alarm button and surveying the interior of the darkened dayroom.

"You idiot!" Ray snarled. "Put that thing out. Baptiste is comin'. You tripped the circuit breaker. They probably didn't even have circuit breakers down in Louisiana where your uncle was. No wonder he burned the place down." Ray rose—"You keep these"—and tossed the cigarettes into Harrison's lap as he took a step toward his cell.

"Hold it right there," shouted Baptiste as he stood on the other side of the gate. Bosco joined him, shining a bright flashlight around the darkened room. "I don't want nobody movin' 'cept when I say. If you're in your cell, come to the door. I want to see every smilin' face, and *right now*. If you ain't in your room, sit down on the floor, hands on your heads." By this time a red light was flashing above the door and an alarm just outside the unit was screeching like the steel wheels on the El tracks in Chicago's loop.

Ray sank onto the floor with his fingers laced together on top of his head. "Now you did it!" he murmured to Harrison.

Every time Bosco and Baptiste weren't looking their direction, Ray's cellmate scooted farther and farther away from the electrical outlet. But even in the dim lights coming from the various cells, one could see the scorched paperclips still protruding from the outlet and a partially melted comb on the floor below it still emitting the stench of burning plastic.

Through the outside door crashed six guards, two with riot guns at port arms and the others with three-foot-long riot batons. They wore orange helmets with plastic face shields and orange jump suits under black bulletproof vests. With the precision of a marching team, they lined up on the other side of the gate, weapons at the ready. "What's the problem here?" It was the hack Ray had noticed overlooking the skinhead's knife.

"Not sure," said Bosco, still searching the dayroom with his flashlight. "We heard this bang and the lights went out. Could be nothin', but didn't want to take a chance."

"All right," yelled the riot guard, "everyone remain in your rooms or on the floor. Anyone moving will be shot."

Shot! Ray closed his eyes. Would they actually shoot someone for moving? No one had done anything threatening. No one had been taken hostage. This wasn't a riot. Why the heavy threats? But he remained still, looking over at Zitty, who had abandoned his efforts to inch away from the incriminating outlet.

"Can we get the lights back on in there before we enter?" asked the guard.

"What's the matter? You afraid of the dark?" But Baptiste stepped back in his cubicle and made a phone call. Everyone waited—ten minutes . . . fifteen minutes . . . twenty minutes—until a man came through the door, stamped snow off his boots, stripped off a heavy parka, and stood there dressed like a washing machine repairman, not a guard. He peered past the riot bulls for a few moments as though he could diagnose the problem simply by looking into the room. Then he went to a closet behind the guard's booth. He opened the circuit breaker box and shined a penlight in it for a few moments. With his thumb he punched a circuit breaker, and the lights came on.

"Simple as that?" Bosco asked.

"Simple as that!"

"But what tripped it?"

"How should I know?" said the repair man. "But I'd check around if I were you. You don't want some electrical short starting a fire."

"No. *You* do the checking."

"Not by myself. These guys go in first and stay with me the whole time, or I'm not going in there."

There was some arguing and negotiating, but finally Bosco buzzed open the gate, and the guards filed in, taking positions next to each other like an echelon of NFL linemen. And like a scared quarterback, the maintenance man cowered behind them as they shuffled around, checking the only four outlets in the room. The cells had no individual outlets, probably to prevent the very kind of abuse Harrison had attempted in the dayroom.

"There it is," said the maintenance man from twelve feet away. "Some idiot popped a socket tryin' to get a smoke. Find the butts and you got your man."

"That cottonhead's got 'em right there," said the skinhead guard Ray had noticed in the mess hall. In one step he swung his baton down across Harrison's shoulders and back, knocking him forward. After three more wood-chopping blows from the prison bull, Harrison lay flat on his face, blood oozing from the back of his head. In another instant the screw had his stick locked around the inmate's neck and was pulling him to his feet. "Get up! Get up here! You're on your way to the SHU for thirty days, boy."

Ray stepped forward. "You're chokin' him!"

In an instant the guard swung his baton, backhand like a tennis racket, delivering Ray's raised arms a resounding whack. "You stay out of this, boy, if you know what's good for you."

Before Harrison could recover, the guard's baton was back around his throat. Harrison gasped and choked as he tried to pry it away. "Quit strugglin' or I'll pull it tighter," yelled the guard. "You seeing black yet? Dumb moron. You're lucky I'm not writing you up for arson, add a few years onto your stint."

Bosco had approached the action by then. "I'll be the one doin' the writin' up, McAfee. Just put some cuffs on him and get him over to segregation. You don't need that stick no more."

"Lookin' out for your kind, huh, old man? That'd be just like you."

That night Ray couldn't sleep. Harrison had acted the fool, and Ray had been all too close to being sucked into his foolishness. The whole incident stood as a warning of what prison could do to a guy when all his freedoms were taken away: He can go crazy. On the other hand, Ray had done a far more stupid thing on the outside when he had all the freedom in the world. So what was the point? Everyone seemed to self-destruct, whether free or constrained. The fact of it beat him down into a hopeless stupor that did not lift with morning's light.

The emotional letdown after Christmas was all the more depressing to Ray with Zitty gone. He had found the guy as irritating as a pebble in his shoe, but he missed him nevertheless. It was like he was in solitary too. Though it wasn't anything like it, really. Ray went to class every day. He worked and ate with other inmates. He played cards, gambled on ballgames and anything else they could think of, and watched TV. He got to spend time in the yard playing basketball and mixing with other men. He knew spending his nights alone was nothing like being in the hole. But he did miss Zitty.

To help pass the time, Ray got a job cleaning the infirmary three evenings a week. He would have gladly done it every night, but he shared the assignment with another inmate he never actually spoke to but left notes to telling him to rinse out the mop, which always seemed to smell sour.

Ray had counted a month and four days when Zitty came back to the unit. He looked gray, like he had been down in some literal, damp underground hole like they used to use for discipline in some old prisons. And his arm was in a cast.

"What happened? I thought they couldn't keep juveniles in segregation more than thirty days!"

Zitty sank down on his cot. "They can't, but they don't count the days you're in the infirmary."

"Yeah, your arm. What happened?"

Harrison swore as he shrugged, head down. "Don't matter." Then he looked up with a light in his eyes. "But I got an idea. It's something my uncle told me. He said the way to get out of trouble in prison—"

"Wait a minute! This the same uncle who taught you how to pop a socket?"

"Yeah, Uncle Darnell, Darnell Harrison—"

"Stop!" Ray held up his hand. "You tellin' me this world has to cope with *two* Darnell Harrisons?"

"Not exactly. He's Darnell *Edgar* Harrison, and I'm Darnell *Robert* Harrison."

"Oh, big relief! Where's he now? Still in Angola?"

"No, man. He's out. He be a regular businessman on the South-side. Runs a—"

"Don't want to hear it!"

"No, no, man. This is different. Give me an ear, dude. Makes sense."

Ray shook his head. "You're crazy, man. Now *my* uncle told me, 'Don't never drink from the same swamp twice.' Know what

I mean?" Ray's uncle had never actually said that to him. In fact, Ray hardly knew his uncle, but . . .

"Just listen, will ya? Uncle Darnell said they always respect you in prison when you get religion. So if you get in trouble, the best thing is to get religion and stick with it. Pretty soon they begin believin' you a changed man, and they lighten up on you."

"So how you gonna get religion? You gonna start praying five times a day like the Muslims? Fall down on the floor wherever you are and bow toward Mecca?"

"Nah, I don't know nothin' 'bout Islam. I'm a Christian. Least my mama was a holy woman—"

"*Holy?!* Ha! Yo mama! . . . Yo mama's so holy when she went to the Jewel, they tried to sell her for Swiss cheese."

"Yeah? Well, yo mama's so fat she sits on both sides da bus. But seriously, man. I plan to start going to all them chapel things we hear about." He paused open-mouthed, studying the scowl on Ray's face, then cut loose with a string of blue sizzlers that had no relation to one another. "I'm serious, you crow bait! Even that bull McAfee might lay off a little, 'cause you know some of those white supremacists are like, God and country and all that crap. I mean, even the Klan uses crosses."

Ray laughed. "Yeah, they use crosses, all right! They burn 'em on people's lawns. Look, Zitty, you do whatever you want, but my last time at mass was . . ." He raised his eyebrows and blew out through pursed lips. "I can't even remember the last time."

But the mention of religion did cause Ray to think about Connie Mason again and the Christmas card she sent him. Later that evening he dug it out from among his few belongings. *Perdonado,* pardoned, forgiven. She offered to forgive him for killing her son. No, she actually *had* forgiven him, whether he had asked for it or not. She had said, *"So I'll go first. I forgive you, Ray."*

He didn't feel forgiven.

But he remembered she said forgiveness was a religious thing, that it started with God. Maybe she was right. Maybe he ought to go to some of those chapel meetings and see if it made any difference.

The next morning on the way to breakfast, Ray tapped on Harrison's cast. "So, Zitty, when's this chapel meeting you're going to?"

"Saturday—" he added some blue adjectives—"morning. Want to come with me? Might help it look more real if we both got religion."

"What do they do?"

"I don't know. Pray, preach, sing? Whatever religious people do." He laughed. "Guess they don't swear. Think I can stop swearin'?"

"I dunno, Zitty. Looks like you'll have to if you're gonna get religion."

CHAPTER 15

Every Saturday morning Ray watched Zitty leave the unit, usually accompanied by the guard Ms. Beers, and go across the yard to the school building, where the chaplain's prison ministry met in one of the classrooms. Some of the guys mocked Harrison. "Hey, Zitty, the kitty kitty's waitin' to take you to Sunday school." But to Ray's amazement, his cellmate never missed attending, and his mouth was cleaning up too . . . well, a little.

"So whadda you guys do over there, anyway?"

"Why don't you come along and see?"

"Ah, nah! That's not for me." But even as he said it, Ray thought again about the Christmas card from Connie Mason that he still got out and looked at from time to time. Why did he do that? Why'd it mean anything to him?

"How do you know it ain't for you if you don't even know what we do there?"

"Just 'cause I've never been into religion."

Harrison raised his hand to hide his mouth and spoke in a stage whisper: "Me neither."

"Yeah, I know. But I see you reading that paperback Bible sometimes. It don't even look like a Bible. You might impress the guards more if you got a big black one with gold pages or something."

"*You* know why I'm readin' it and going to these meetings. But the meetings ain't half bad. I'm learning stuff about God and Jesus, stuff I never knew even though I been to church a lot."

"Like what?"

"Ah, man, I can't explain it all to you. If you want to know, why don't you come? You ain't got nothin' else to do this morning."

He made a good point. In prison there was seldom anything to do outside the daily routine. Even the smallest diversion was appreciated: a letter . . . from anyone, a trip to the commissary, a craps game, a fight, someone's stale cookies from home, or—in this case—even a Bible study.

Ray signed out with Robbie Robinson and followed Zitty and Ms. Beers out the door. Ms. Beers wore a heavy parka with a hood that wrapped around her head of short-cropped hair. Ray and Darnell wore their standard yellow uniforms.

Harrison ducked the moment the bitter March wind cut into his face and launched into his usual blue litany only to stop himself after the second curse. "Uh . . ." He glanced toward Ms. Beers and then spoke to Ray loudly enough for her to hear. "Guess the hawk's out on today!"

It was so cold Ray almost turned around and went back to the unit. Forget this; he'd stay back and catch some dumb cartoon on TV. And yet . . . "Whaddya say? You see a hawk out here?"

They were both leaning into the wind, their hands shielding their faces. "Yeah, you know, the wind!"

"What's that have to do with any hawk?"

"The wind, man. When it comes off the lake, it cuts your face like the claws of a hawk. Ain't you never heard that before? You bein' from Chicago and all?"

"Guess not." Ray still might have turned back, but by this time they were closer to the school than to the dorm, so he continued to walk beside Zitty.

Ms. Beers stopped. "All right, ladies, you want to stand out here and chat? Don't bother me none." She pulled her parka a little tighter. "You know there's no talkin' while walkin', so shut up or we'll just keep standin' here."

"Yes, ma'am," said Zitty.

Ms. Beers turned and proceeded across the yard, but more slowly now, perhaps to drive home her point.

Three civilians greeted the young men as they came into the classroom. Two were young, clean-cut, like college men. The third was older, maybe the preacher. Ray scanned the room and noticed that some of the guards had dropped off their charges and were slipping out, perhaps for coffee or a smoke. Others stood in the back with their arms crossed, keeping an eye on the men. About thirty men took seats while the civilians hustled around getting things ready to begin the meeting. One put a CD in a portable boom box and tried to encourage the men to sing along as he played some religious songs.

Either most of the men, like Ray, did not know the songs, or they simply weren't interested in auditioning for a choir. Other than the leader, who sang too loudly, those few men who did sing moaned along like the winter's wind.

Zitty leaned over to Ray and said, "Should have been here last week. There was a girls' trio, and better believe everyone sang for them."

"Women?"

"Sometimes. But they all skinny poodles. Now me, I go for a little junk in the trunk, if you know what I mean."

After the music, the older of the three civilians opened a Bible and began reading a story he said Jesus had told. Ray was only half listening until the preacher man said it was a story about a king, and for an instant Ray wondered if it was a Latin King. He realized immediately there was no way, but the mention of a king was enough to get Ray to listen.

"The kingdom of heaven is like a king who wanted to settle accounts with his servants. As he began the settlement, a man who owed him ten thousand talents [about a $100,000, explained the reader] was brought to him. Since he was not able to pay, the master ordered that he and his wife and his children and all that· he had, had to be sold to repay the debt.

"The servant fell on his knees before him. 'Be patient with me,' he begged, 'and I will pay back everything.' The servant's master took pity on him, canceled the debt and let him go.

"But when that servant went out, he found one of his fellow servants who owed him a hundred denarii [just ten bucks]. He grabbed him and began to choke him. 'Pay back what you owe me!' he demanded.

"His fellow servant fell to his knees and begged him, 'Be patient with me, and I will pay you back.'

"But he refused. Instead, he went off and had the man thrown into prison until he could pay the debt. When the other servants saw what had happened, they were greatly distressed and went and told their master everything that had happened.

"Then the master called the servant in. 'You wicked servant,' he said, 'I canceled all that debt of yours because you begged me to. Shouldn't you have had mercy on your fellow servant just as I had on you?' In anger his master turned him over to the jailers to be tortured, until he should pay back all he owed.

"This is how my heavenly Father will treat each of you unless you forgive your brother from your heart."

The logic of the story made so much sense that Ray didn't hear anything else the man said. Of course, the ungrateful servant deserved to be stomped when he tried to squeeze his homey! But that last phrase in the story—"forgive your brother"—reminded Ray of Connie Mason's Christmas card stamped *perdonado* . . . forgiven. The words on the inside of the card said, *He came to pay a debt he didn't owe, Because I owed a debt I couldn't pay!* Ray wondered whether he was kind of like that servant who owed a debt he couldn't pay? Wasn't that why he was in prison? But sitting in the joint wasn't helping him pay it off either. He had been inside coming up on two years now, but he couldn't imagine feeling any lighter after ten or twenty or even the full forty years. Greg Mason was still dead.

The card began to take on deeper meaning. God was like the king who forgave the huge debt that the servant couldn't pay, like Ray's debt to Greg Mason, to the whole Mason family. And he did it by sending Jesus. Jesus had changed Connie Mason's heart so she could pass on that forgiveness to Ray.

He remembered Mrs. Mason's visit. She had found freedom from his crime through God's forgiveness, but had he? As dramatic as it had been for Connie Mason to forgive him, Ray had never felt forgiven because he knew he needed forgiveness by someone greater, someone like God, who had the power and authority to forgive.

Was God really offering that kind of forgiveness? Is that what it meant for him to send Jesus? Ray remembered the drop of blood on the baby's footprint in the card. Now the meaning of Jesus dying on the cross—something Ray had learned about in church as a kid—began to make sense. *He came to pay a debt he didn't owe, Because I owed a debt I couldn't pay!*

The people from the visiting prison ministry were playing more music on the CD player and urging the men in the classroom to come one at a time to pray with them, but Ray just stood there. *Jesus, if you really came to pay my debt, if you really came to forgive me, all I can say is, thank you.* Somehow in that moment, in embracing the offer of forgiveness, Ray knew Jesus *had* heard him even though he hadn't spoken out loud.

So that's what prayer was. Just talking to God.

"All right, ladies, time to get back to the unit." Ms. Beers hustled them out of the classroom. Ray walked across the yard, his mind still on Connie Mason's visit, the Christmas card, and that moment when he had prayed and knew God had heard him. Had it really happened? He did not feel the hawk on his bare skin or hear Zitty's babbling. Ms. Beers didn't shut him up either. Maybe she didn't consider it "talkin' and walkin' " as long as Ray didn't respond.

For the next two Saturdays Ray went to the prison ministry meetings, learning a little more about God but not knowing how it applied to his situation in Joliet. The power struggles within the prison between gangs and with the guards threatened to boil over sometimes on a daily basis. Though Ray had the tacit protection of the Latin Kings, the fact that they hadn't owned him publicly left him feeling alone and vulnerable. Fearful of showing weakness, even for a moment, he developed a cold attitude of indifference, even though his encounter with God in the chapel meeting had stirred a hunger deep inside. He didn't want to live under that hostility and tension any longer—always watching his back, lest anyone think they could get over on him.

Harrison was behind Ray as they entered the chow hall for lunch. Robert McAfee, the racist hack who had overlooked the skinhead's shank in the mess hall weeks before, was monitoring the doorway—feet spread, hands clasped behind his back, swiveling his head to give everyone a tough-guy scowl as they came in. At the second table from the door, a black kid sat all alone, looking dejectedly at his meal tray and picking at his food. Harrison noticed him and called out, "Hey, Marco. What's happenin', man?"

"Shut up, Zitty," said McAfee. "He's in segregation and can't talk to anyone."

Then why is he in the chow hall at all if he's still in segregation? Ray wondered to himself. But it was Harrison who pushed the point. "I thought you got out of the hole yesterday. Whassup?"

"He's out, but he's not really out. He's just gettin' rebooted," murmured the kid standing behind Ray.

"Whaddaya mean?" Ray asked quietly.

"You know," offered Harrison, loud enough for McAfee to hear. "Thirty days in, one day out, and they can put him back in for another thirty days. It's a way they got of getting around the law that juveniles can only be held in segregation for thirty days. Now if you're an adult, they can put you down for a year."

By this time the chow line had moved a good fifteen feet beyond McAfee, and Harrison may have thought that gave him some protection, but McAfee came out of his stance. "That's it, you albino coon. I told you to shut your mouth. I'm writin' you up again since you seem to like our 'punkhouse' accommodations so well." He pulled out his cuffs and headed right toward Harrison.

Remembering the treatment McAfee had given Harrison the last time they had a run-in, Ray grabbed his cellmate's arm and pushed him ahead of him in the chow line. Then he said under his breath to the guys around him, "Throw up a block. Don't let the pig through." To Ray's surprise, the six or eight guys nearest him who had been watching this incident closed ranks and, with arms crossed, faced McAfee, some displaying their gang signs with their hands. Other guys shuffled Harrison on up the chow line, getting him farther and farther away from the belligerent screw. Then they, too, joined the knot of men to thoroughly block the guard's advance.

Wisely, McAfee backed down, slipped his cuffs back into his belt case, and returned to his stance by the door as though nothing had happened. A slow *thud, thud, thud* erupted among the men who had braced him as they stomped on the floor. It spread across the chow hall as other men joined in by clapping their food trays on the tables. Ray could see guys putting their heads together as they passed along the report of what happened to others who hadn't seen it. Ray and those near him pushed along in the chow line, got their food, and went to their tables. The banging continued.

In three minutes an echelon of eight guards charged through the back door of the chow hall. They were in full riot gear and all carried shotguns. Behind them came a ninth man—obviously in command—with a pistol in one hand and a bullhorn in the other.

"Everybody down on the floor, hands on your head! Everybody down on the floor, hands on your head!"

The rhythmic banging stopped instantly, but no one moved from their table to sit on the floor, and no one standing in the chow line sat down either. There was silence. This was not a planned riot. There were no further objectives, just a spontaneous flare-up over the stupid move of a racist prison bull. When the silence had continued for a full minute, the commander of the riot squad turned and spoke to one of the other guards who had been in the mess hall the whole time and was now standing with his back to the wall. They consulted for a moment, and then the commander raised his bullhorn. "Carry on."

For a moment no one moved. Then one of the guys in the chow line held out his tray for a scoop of chili, and everyone returned to eating. Slowly, hushed conversations resumed at the tables. But the riot squad remained at the ready.

Ray left the mess hall with a new roll to his walk. He had called McAfee out and "whopped" him as certain as if they had been in a physical brawl. And this was even better. Showed more finesse, leadership, and restraint. Yeah, he had demonstrated restraint. You didn't want to do things that would get a lot of people hurt. That could make them mad at you, even if they didn't admit it. But he had taken control of the situation with as little "collateral damage" as possible. And the guys had followed him—even guys from other organizations. That was impressive. Maybe it was a good thing that he wasn't too blatantly a Latin King.

Back in his cell for lockdown—a regular routine when the guards would make a count to check that everyone was present— Ray lay on his bunk and stared at the ceiling. Zitty was on his own bunk, sounding like a jackhammer as he tried to learn the words of the rap song on his Discman, but Ray paid no attention. He was thinking about the future. Maybe he could become a neutron *jefe*, a chief who could organize the men across gang lines to pressure the prison administration to get rid of scumbags like McAfee. Maybe God had forgiven him after all.

Once the lockdown was over, Ray was assigned with the other men in Unit 4 to clean their dorm. He was washing windows in their dayroom—what few there were—when McAfee showed up at the door and began speaking to Bosco and pointing through the gate toward Ray. Uh-oh. This was it. But Bosco shook his head and acted as though he was going to ignore the man. McAfee closed the door to the guard booth and started yelling at Bosco, punching his finger toward Bosco's heavy middle and then out the door in the direction of the administration building.

Phanor Baptiste came out of the shower room, where he had been inspecting the cleaning, and entered the booth. Ray pretended to continue cleaning the windows, but he was paying close attention to what was happening in the booth. In a moment Baptiste picked up the phone and made a call. He talked for a minute and then turned around to face the dayroom and looked straight at Ray. Finally he hung up, said something to Bosco, and shrugged as he turned and opened the door.

"Slewinski! Get over here! You're going to the hole."

Ray threw down his rags. Segregation! He should have known. McAfee couldn't tolerate being so publicly dissed. It would ruin his reputation and effectiveness. He had to do something! Ray was a relative newbie and held no official leadership position in any organization. He should have expected the hole at the very least, but would McAfee feel he had to do something more dramatic—such as extend Ray's time in the "punkhouse," as he called it, with a few extra days in the infirmary like he had with Harrison?

Ray felt the sweat break on his forehead as he crossed the room.

CHAPTER 16

There's prison, and then there is *prison!* The hole is *prison.* Alone with nothing to do for hours and days on end, Ray brooded. The attitude of repentance that had begun to grow with Connie's visit and Christmas card and then the chapel services shriveled. Ray thought more and more about how to bring down McAfee. Different scenarios swirled in his head: bring a legal charge against him if he hit Ray unnecessarily; set him up to get caught smuggling drugs into the prison; spread a rumor that might get him a blanket party—that shouldn't be hard. Such scheming kept Ray from going nuts with boredom in the hole.

When he wasn't devising plans to get revenge on McAfee, Ray did calisthenics or ran in place in his six-foot-by-ten-foot cell. But there were still more hours in his days and nights, hours that could not be filled with exercise and harboring hate. At those times he sat on his bunk and let his mind roam outside his cell, outside Joliet, back to the hood, at home with his mom, arguing with his freaky sister. He could make these mind trips so real it was as though he were there, and then he would startle himself when he returned to reality. What amazing—or frightening—things the mind could do. Ray had heard it said that at some point every convict breaks in prison—some after a year, some in three years, some in ten. Was this his time? Was his mind breaking?

He vowed this would not be his time. He would toughen himself. Steel his mind. Discipline his responses. Strengthen his body. He liked the way the guys had responded to him when he organized the security line to protect Zitty in the mess hall. He wanted more of that respect. He would not let himself break in the hole!

Every time the screw brought his meals, Ray tried to engage him in some conversation just to have someone to talk to, but the guy refused to respond with anything more than yes or no. Then three weeks into his detention he had a breakthrough when he said, "Hey, can I at least have something to read in here?"

"Nope!" The guard started to walk away, then turned back. "No reading material except . . . well, sometimes they let guys bring in a Bible or a Koran. You got one back in your unit?"

"No."

The guard shrugged and turned away again.

"Wait a minute. You know Zitty? Unit 4? Uh, his name's Harrison, Darnell Harrison. He's my cellmate. He's got one. He'll let me use it. Couldn't you get it for me?"

"What you think this is? Some kind of lending library, some book exchange program we got here? Look, man, that provision is only for religious purposes. If you don't have a Bible of your own, you ain't no Christian, so you'd be gettin' it for . . . for entertainment. That's not why you are in here."

"Aw, come on, man. Just say it's my Bible. Harrison'll let you have it."

The guard rolled his eyes. "Yeah, well, we'll see."

Each day Ray badgered the guard, and on the third day he finally brought Harrison's beat-up paperback Bible.

What a relief to have something to read. Ray spent all that day reading, starting in the beginning like a novel, looking for that story

Jesus told about the servant who wouldn't forgive his homeboy. He read about Noah and Joseph and Moses, but he couldn't find what he was looking for. He started skipping pages, and then he got into all these laws and genealogies. He'd nearly given up when he found that the stuff about Jesus was in the back of the book.

The next day he continued his search, uncertain why he was looking for that story in particular—maybe just to see if it was really in the Bible—but he did come across something else about forgiveness that Jesus had said, something that really disturbed him. In Matthew 6:14 and 15 he read, "If you forgive men when they sin against you, your heavenly Father will also forgive you. But if you do not forgive men their sins, your Father will not forgive your sins." Why would Jesus say that? Didn't he know that without the possibility of payback, people'd run all over you? Take McAfee. Something had to happen! Huh! This religion stuff didn't seem to make any sense.

When Ray's month in the hole was up, he was more sober and more disciplined . . . and he had not broken. But he had allowed his resentment toward the system that oppressed him to galvanize into a deeper dedication to gain power. And as far as he knew, the only way to achieve power was through the gang. Victor Muñoz would not be in Joliet forever, and neither would Damion Weller. They were both older than Ray and would soon be moved to adult prison. What he needed to do was position himself to move up. But how could he do that when the Latin Kings barely acknowledged him?

Ray's break came on the first warm Friday afternoon of spring when his unit and one other unit had open yard time. Victor Muñoz sent Ray word that he wanted to talk. Ray looked around until he spotted the Latin Kings' chief along with his bodyguards on the other side of the yard. He set off around the perimeter as though he were on an exercise walk, which soon brought him to where the Kings were.

Ray did not throw down a sign or give any other recognition as he slowed and wandered into their proximity, looking out through the fences as though something in the Illinois countryside caught his attention.

"Hey, my man. How's it goin'?" It was Damion Weller, the enforcer.

Ray glanced at the tower.

"Don't worry, Slew. It's cool, man."

"Yeah? Well, whassup?" Why hadn't he wanted to be called Slew anymore? The reasons no longer seemed important, and Ray let the matter slip.

"Victor here has a little job for you. We think you're up for something."

Ray looked at the King leader and then diverted his eyes downward. *Why'd I look down?* He looked back at Muñoz and held eye contact until the leader spoke to his bodyguards. "Hey, boys, give us some space here, huh?"

When all but Weller had drifted away, Muñoz turned to Ray. "Make out okay in the hole?"

Ray nodded and squinted his eyes. Then he deliberately looked around the yard as though he had little interest in what Muñoz was saying.

"We liked the way you handled that incident with McAfee the other day." The leader paused. "But we just got one question: Why'd you stand up for a GD?"

It wasn't a question Ray had anticipated. All he could think to say was "Once a King, always a King!"

Weller snorted to the side. "What's that got to do with it? You sound like a Burger King to me!"

Ray didn't even glance at him but fixed his gaze on the chief. "I'm down for the crown, and you know it."

Muñoz allowed that wry smile of his to wash across his face without affecting his cold eyes. "Yeah. I know. And I appreciate that you seemed able to keep your cool in a tight spot. You didn't rattle. But there's this little contradiction in my head. You're co-pacetic here on the inside, but that guy you shot? That didn't seem so cool. Seemed too impetuous, him not even being a rival or nothin'." He stopped, waiting for Ray to respond. "You know, doing the wrong thing—even though it seems bold and all—is still the wrong thing. It can get other guys hurt. Stir up trouble. You suckin' up what I'm layin' down?"

Ray shrugged and glanced down, breaking eye contact again. Muñoz was right. That shooting had not only taken the life of Greg Mason, but it had ruined Ray's life as well. It was impetuous, if not downright stupid of him to listen to Rico. He had to admit that, but not to Muñoz, not now.

He looked up at the leader. "Well, maybe there were circumstances you don't fully understand. But in any case, that's behind me, almost two years behind me."

Muñoz nodded. "Perhaps. But we'll be the judge of whether it's really behind you." He stopped and rubbed his shaved head. "That hack Robert McAfee, he was the one who sent you to the hole after you went up against him, wasn't he?"

Ray nodded.

"Well, we had some more trouble with him while you were locked away, and we need to straighten him out. It's like he's mobbed up with the AB or something. We been thinkin' one of the black organizations would take care of him, but they've been sittin' tight. So we gotta handle it ourselves. Thought you might be our man." He stopped and stared at Ray, obviously waiting for an answer.

Ray hesitated. The idea of "handling" a prison guard was a serious offense.

The Latin King leader seemed to read Ray's questions. "We're not talkin' about anything too serious. We just don't want to see him back at work for a week or so. Maybe he'll get the message and mind his own business. We gotta keep this institution running smoothly, you know. It's best for everyone that way." He waited.

Weller sighed deeply. "Like I told you, *Jefe*. I don't think he's got the brass for it. Maybe we should use someone else."

"Well?" said Muñoz. "Whaddaya say?"

"How am I supposed to do this?"

The chief crossed his arms and leaned back, almost as though there was a wall behind him to lean on. "You were going to church on Saturday, right, before you went in the hole?"

"Yeah." Ray hadn't decided whether he would return. Thirty days in the hole had made all that religion stuff seem to fade into the distant past.

"Tomorrow, during whatever you do in there, you get sick, see? The whole school is secure, so they should let you go to the rest room alone. McAfee'll be on duty at the end of the hall by the gate, but he don't sit in his little booth because he can't see the TV from there. He always pulls a chair out into the hallway. And his back'll be toward you so he can watch both the TV *and* the front door at the same time. He don't care what's happening up the hall because on Saturdays no one's in the school—except that church group, with plenty of guards inside. So if you're quiet, you should be able to come up behind him. We'll leave a sword in the trash can in the bathroom."

Ray's heart began pounding. A sword, like a shank, was a hand-made weapon, usually fashioned out of some longer strip of metal ripped from a bed frame or doorsill and used more to hack and slice than to stab. It would have been sharpened crudely against stone, leaving it uneven and jagged. And if it had become rusty, so much the better; it could spawn a good infection. Ray certainly carried a raw grudge against McAfee. He'd spent his month in the hole conceiving ways to retaliate against him. But this! Ray could end up charged with attempted murder even if he didn't hurt the guy very badly. Still . . . it might be the chance he was looking for to make his rep. Did he want it that bad?

"How am I going to keep him from seeing and identifying me?"

Damion Weller forced a laugh. "You could take his head off."

Muñoz raised a calming hand. "You could, but we're not expectin' that." He smiled with just his mouth again. "Give him the nylon, Weller."

Weller sighed as though the conversation was boring him and handed Ray the thigh section from a pair of black pantyhose. "Pull that over your head and it'll be as good as any mask, impossible for McAfee to identify you even if he sees you."

Ray hesitated. "So I whack his arm or his leg or something and then take off. Meanwhile, he's screaming 'officer down,' and we got bulls pouring out of chapel trapping me in the hall with a bloody sword in my hand and a rag over my head. That's crazy. You're setting me up."

"Ha! Like I said," laughed Weller, "samurai his head off, and he won't yell for no help."

Everyone stood there staring at each other.

Finally Ray said, "No way, man. I'm not your go-to boy on this one. It don't make no sense, and you haven't told me why this hit needs doin'. We all know he's his mama's big mistake, but that ain't enough for me to risk an attempted murder charge." He turned away and walked the rest of the way around the yard, his legs shaking so hard he feared he would fall to the ground if he so much as tripped over a shadow. What were they trying to do? Get him killed, sent to death row? He certainly wasted no love on McAfee, but hacking the guy with a rusty strip of metal? That was outrageous!

Now, however, he had refused an assignment from the Latin King leadership in the prison. It had been a directive, and he had turned it down. Where would he stand with the Kings now? He was willing to take a violation, get a beating, but what if they abandoned Ray?

Well, those were the breaks. If he had to become a neutron with the support of no organization, then he would just do that.

The next morning Ray signed up to go to chapel with Zitty. Maybe God would help him for doing the right thing. Maybe he could talk to one of the preachers, or whoever they were, and get some . . . well, he couldn't actually ask for advice. To do so would require him to describe the situation, and that would be like ratting on the Kings. Ha, some brothers they were, setting him up for a big fall!

The chapel services were led by volunteer civilians from different churches as Ray had experienced the three Saturdays he had attended before going to the hole. But this Saturday the leaders weren't from a church . . . and there were no women. The four men were from Captives Free Ministries. The little brochure they passed out said the organization worked with people who were incarcerated and helped them when they got out. Captives Free came out from Chicago once a month because so many of the young men at Joliet were from Chicago. And the chaplain's prison ministry was always glad to have them because it meant they had one less Saturday for which they had to recruit and supervise a volunteer church.

"Every other seat, please, gentlemen. No sitting next to each other." It was a stupid gesture toward security, supposedly to make it harder to pass contraband. The guys could meet in the yard or at chow. So what was the use? Still the guards nagged, "Every other seat, please!"

The leader of Captives Free was an older man, shorter than average and a little heavy, and—what was that? Ray watched him closely and concluded that the guy wore a toupee. It looked natural enough, but there was just something unusual about the way it seemed to move a little when he scratched his head. Ray was so intent on watching him that he almost missed the man's name when he introduced himself as Harvey Geevers. "But most of the guys just call me Mr. Gee."

Ray thought he might like the man. He seemed far more interested in talking to the inmates than in seeing that the chapel service ran smoothly. Ray could tell he wasn't intimidated by being in a room with a bunch of convicted criminals, not that the other preachers had appeared actually *scared*. They just didn't know what to do, what to say, how to act. After all, they might be facing a murderer . . . like Ray.

One of the other men from Captives Free stood up to lead the Bible study. Ray tried for a few minutes to listen, but he couldn't get into it. While the man talked on about some Romans and the wages of sin—whatever they were—Ray's mind drifted to the assignment Victor Muñoz had given him to attack McAfee. It teased his curiosity. Could it be done? Or had Muñoz—or Weller, most likely—been trying to mess over him, take him out of the picture? Did Weller somehow see him as a rival, not in the sense of being from another organization but as a personal rival within the Kings?

Ray turned and got Beers' attention for permission to get up and move to the back where she stood. "I need to use the rest room," he whispered when he reached her. "Stomach's real upset."

Beers gestured with her thumb over her shoulder toward the door.

Outside, Ray saw McAfee at the end of the hall, sitting outside his booth, facing the other way with all his attention on some TV game show in the outer room . . . just like Muñoz had said. Ray slipped into the empty rest room. *Maybe it could be done*, he thought. He paced nervously in the small space, then absentmindedly lifted the top of the trash bin. It was deep enough, but he had not agreed to the plan, so of course nothing was there. But before replacing the lid Ray ran his hands around the inside . . . and froze when through the plastic liner he heard something rattle in the bin. He pulled up the plastic bag, and there was a "sword," or more like a homemade machete. A thin iron strip about two feet long, wrapped on one end with tape for a handle and sharpened along one edge. With the awe of touching a golden scepter, Ray picked up the crude weapon. The tip was still square—not pointed—but it, too, had been sharpened, and there were chips of prison-green paint along one side. Obviously, the metal had been broken off of some piece of equipment around the institution. Ray felt its weight in his hand. It was flimsy, but it could deliver deadly hacks nonetheless.

Ray's heart was pounding, and somewhere inside his head he heard Rico Quiñones yelling, "Do it, man! Do it! Don't be no *cobarde!*"

CHAPTER 17

R ay dropped the weapon back into the trash can with a loud clatter and slammed down the lid. His panting kept pace with his convulsing heart as he turned, took two paces across the rest room, turned back, grabbed a paper towel, and tried to wipe off any fingerprints he might have left on the can's lid. But he wasn't going back inside the can to touch that sword. No, he hadn't actually touched the blade, had he? Only the taped handle. Prints wouldn't show on it, would they?

No, NO! This can't be!

He banged the door wide as he charged out of the rest room and back toward the classroom. From the corner of his eye he saw McAfee turn to see what had caused all the noise. The screw was still in one piece—no hacked arms, no severed neck, no missing ears.

Ray entered the classroom and stood there panting for a moment.

"Whoo!" Beers gave him a frown as she moved her head from side to side like a bobblehead doll. "You sick or something? You look as gray as old meat. You need to go to the infirmary or something?"

Ray shook his head and fled to the refuge of his seat, separated by an empty desk from anyone else. He tried to stroke his chin casually, only to realize that his hand was trembling. Was anyone noticing? Ray looked around and planted his right heel firmly on the floor to stop his leg from bouncing. What had he been thinking, just going in there to see if it could be done? Had the King leaders known he would be that curious? Or had they set up the sword earlier thinking he would agree to the plan?

It didn't matter. This was bad. They definitely planned to attack McAfee, and now Ray had become involved. Even though he hadn't done anything wrong, he had come far too close. He needed to make some changes. Maybe he *did* need some religion.

Mr. Gee had said that right after the Bible study some of the volunteers would have a little time to talk to any of the guys who had questions or wanted to pray. But Ray wanted to talk to Mr. Gee. He didn't know why, but there was something about the man that made him feel safe, like he knew what he was talking about and was on Ray's side. And right now, Ray needed someone on his side.

He stood by Mr. Gee's desk, arms crossed, then uncrossed, trying to look casual and not as anxious as he felt while Mr. Gee talked to a tall black inmate from Unit 2. Ray had never met the dude, but he had seen him shooting hoops in the yard. He seemed to get along easy with other guys and even now he had a way of using his hands to talk—like an Italian, Ray thought—telling Mr. Gee about something funny that happened somewhere in the direction he was pointing. Mr. Gee listened and commented but glanced at Ray and nodded just enough to let Ray know that he had seen him and wouldn't forget him.

"Hey, Slewinski." It was Ms. Beers standing next to Zitty. "Time to go. Sun's a-wastin'; work's awaitin'."

Ray rolled his head and glanced at Mr. Gee, hoping for a little intervention but not really expecting it. But to Ray's surprise the preacher had heard Ms. Beers and apparently saw the longing in Ray's eyes. He touched the black dude's shoulder to interrupt him and spoke across the room to Ms. Beers. "You know, if he could stay a little longer, I can see that one of the other guards escorts him back to his unit. Be okay?"

She was shaking her head even before he finished. "I don't think—"

"Which unit?"

"Unit 4, but that's not—"

"Great. I'll get him there before lunch."

Beers shrugged, then turned toward the door, ushering Zitty out of the classroom.

When Mr. Gee was free, he approached Ray, right hand out, smile broad. "So how are you doing? Don't believe I've had the privilege. I'm Harvey Geevers; Mr. Gee's good enough. And you are—?" He raised his head as he got close so he could view Ray through his bifocals.

"Ray, Raymond Slewinski."

"Glad to have you in chapel today. What can I do for you?"

Ray didn't know what to say. He couldn't help noticing Mr. Gee's hair. Was it really a toupee? Forget that. He wanted to talk, but he hadn't prepared any formal questions, so he said the first thing that came into his mind. "You know that story about the king who wiped out the big debt his servant owed, but then the servant wouldn't forgive his . . . his homie a few bucks? Is that really in the Bible? I can't find it."

"Sure it is. Hand me your Bible, and I'll show you."

"Uh. Don't have no Bible—"

"What? Oh, we can't have that. They ought to issue a Bible with every pillow when you come into this place. No one can make it in here without a Bible."

Was he kidding? Ray laughed nervously. "They don't give out pillows."

"Exactly! But they should. Don't you think? Tell you what. We have a small box of Bibles up here if you'd like one."

"Yeah. Thanks." Ray did want one. "But I'm not really the religious type."

"Oh, I wouldn't expect you to be." Mr. Gee's face grew as grave as a pallbearer's. "I would be disappointed if an obviously intelligent young man like you were caught up in a lot of religious rules and meaningless rituals."

"Really? I mean, isn't that what this is all about?"

"Oh no. Never! Here. Take this Bible. I'm turning down the page on the gospel of John. You go back to your unit and read that book. Then tell me if it sounds like a lot of rules."

Mr. Gee swept one finger in the air, like a tiny broom, dismissing Ray toward the last remaining guard, waiting at the door. Apparently, the conversation was over. But as Ray left, Mr. Gee called after him, "Oh, about that ungrateful servant. I think you'll find that story in Matthew, chapter eighteen, about verse twenty-one. Matthew is three books before John, the one I marked."

Ray was bewildered. When he had been in the hole reading Zitty's Bible, he had come across a lot of rules and laws, more than he could even comprehend. It seemed like there was a rule for every detail of life. But as he sat that evening on his bunk reading the gospel of John—instead of playing cards in the dayroom—he found a story about God's love, a story that explained even further the Christmas card Connie had given him: *He came to pay a debt he didn't owe, Because I owed a debt I couldn't pay!* Ray knew he owed a debt he could never pay, not in forty years, not even if he had been sentenced to life. He was just like that servant who owed the king so much.

Ray flipped the pages back, and after some fumbling, found and read the story in Matthew again. Yeah, that was him, in way over his head. So how could he get out? He didn't mean the physical prison around him. He meant that internal prison, that prison of guilt, that prison that almost sucked him into attacking McAfee, that prison that seemed like it was always there to mess him up. How did he get out of it?

The next day it was raining so hard that most of the guys went to the gym during yard time. But when everyone went, it became so crowded, tensions rose on the courts, and you couldn't get a turn on the weights. Ray chose to stay in his cell. He flipped through the Bible until he came to John 3, where he read about the religious leader who came to Jesus at night asking how he could be accepted by God. Maybe Mr. Gee was right. Maybe the Bible wasn't about trying to be more religious, otherwise this religious dude certainly would have known the answer to his own questions. Jesus' talk about being born again baffled Ray as much as it had the religious leader. But when Jesus said, "God did not send his Son into the world to condemn the world, but to save the world through him. Whoever believes in him is not condemned, but whoever does not believe stands condemned already because he has not believed in the name of God's one and only Son," Ray felt like he was beginning to catch on . . . a little bit. Or more accurately, he began to feel like Jesus was talking about something he wanted: to be free of the condemnation that clung to him like a monkey on his back. He had been condemned, and he knew he deserved it, but somehow he had to get out from under it. If believing on Jesus could relieve that condemnation, not just on the say-so of Connie Mason—as significant as that had been—but on the authority of God himself, that might make a difference.

And what did it mean to *believe*? Ray guessed he believed. He had heard that some people questioned whether Jesus actually lived, but as far as Ray knew, Jesus was as real as any of those old guys—Alexander the Great, Genghis Khan, Plato, or—what was her name?—Cleopatra. But what did *believe* mean? It had to mean more than assenting to a fact of history.

Another section he had just read mentioned believing. Ray flipped back a couple pages and found the passage, "To all who received him, to those who believed in his name, he gave the right to become children of God—children born not of natural descent, nor of human decision or a husband's will, but born of God." *Born of God? Born again?* Ray's head was swirling. He tossed the Bible up on his little shelf and flopped back on his bunk.

When Darnell came in sweating and smelling like a wet sneaker, Ray said, "You understand all this church stuff?"

"Whaddaya mean?"

"You know. Like Saturday mornings. . . . Do you get it?"

"What's there to get?"

Ray sat up and rolled his eyes. "The *believe* thing. What are you supposed to believe, anyway?"

"In Jesus . . . or like the Apostle's Creed. You know: *"I believe in God, the Father almighty, creator of heaven and earth. I believe in Jesus Christ, his only Son . . ."*

"Where'd you learn all that?"

"Hey, man. We went to church all the time and twice on Sundays."

"Then how come you ended up in here on a dope conviction?"

Darnell shrugged and turned away as though Ray had just made fun of his face. "I donno. Guess dealin' seemed better than flipping burgers. I supported my family, and I always tithed to the church." He looked back at Ray and grinned. "One Sunday—it had been a pretty good week—I put five thousand dollars in the offering."

"What? You gave the church five thousand dollars? Ah, man. See what I mean? Religion's just a scam, all rules and regulations to try to get your money!"

"No, man. Nobody was scamming me. I knew what I was doin'."

"But ain't you the one who told me the way to get the hacks off our backs was to 'get religion'? That sounds pretty phony to me!"

Darnell looked down at the floor. "Yeah but . . . it's more complicated than that."

"Well, I don't like complicated! You cussed and swore more than anyone in the whole unit. Then you said you were goin' to get religion, and you told me why: to get the guards off your back. Now you go to all the chapel meetings and talk like a Sunday school kid. It makes a good show, and that's not very complicated!"

Darnell sat on his bunk, staring at the floor, shaking his head slowly. "Yeah, you're right, but it's not all phony. Been trying to get back right with God for real, and he forgives. I really do believe that."

"There you go again! There's that word: *believe!* What's that mean, anyway? Doesn't almost everyone believe?"

"Not like what the Bible's talking about." Harrison sat there a moment, as though deep in thought. "Somewhere in the Bible it says even the devils believe and tremble."

"*Devils?* Whaddaya mean, they believe?"

Harrison shrugged. "I donno. Guess they believe Jesus existed, but it don't do 'em no good. Now, I don' wanna be no devil. To believe . . . well, to *really* believe in Jesus means you gotta put somethin' down on it. Look, I've heard this list a thousand times: You gotta believe that Jesus was actually God who lived here on earth. And because he never did nothin' wrong, when he died, his death paid for our sins. And finally, he proved this was for real by rising up from the dead and going back to heaven. Now, if you can believe all that, you gotta do somethin' 'bout it. You gotta ask Jesus to forgive ya, and—kinda like you Kings say—you gotta be down for the crown . . . down for *his* crown, that is! Know what I mean? *Then* you a real believer!"

Down for the crown, huh? Ray laughed.

"What's so funny? You asked me, and I tol' ya! So what's so funny?"

"What's funny is that you, a convicted drug dealer right off the bricks, sittin' here in prison, after cussin' for weeks and telling me that you are going to get the guards off your back by frontin' religion, are telling me what the Bible says."

"Hey, you asked!" Darnell flopped down on his bunk and turned toward the wall, his fuzzy blond hair looking like a cotton ball at the head of his bed. "But there's one more thing that you don't get," he muttered over his shoulder, "and that's that a guy can change his mind. Maybe I started out planning to scam the screws, but that don't mean I can't decide to change for real!"

The lights went out, and Darnell was silent for a few minutes. Then he added, "You ever hear the story of the Prodigal Son?"

"No."

"Well, read it some time. A guy *can* turn around if he wants to. And God does forgive! It's in the Bible."

CHAPTER 18

Forgiven . . . *Perdonado* . . . Ray lay there in the dim light that came through the door of his cell and thought again about the card Connie Mason had sent him: *He came to pay a debt he didn't owe, Because I owed a debt I couldn't pay!* It was basically what Zitty had been telling him. Maybe the albino was right, but it all seemed too . . . too unbelievable. Did that mean Ray wasn't a believer? He guessed so. But then he recalled the verse he read where Jesus said, "Whoever does not believe stands condemned already because he has not believed in the name of God's one and only Son." Whew, that was heavy! But it was exactly the way he felt: *condemned already.*

Ray bolted out of bed the next morning to the blaring of the alarm outside their unit. Had he been in a submarine, he would have known they were preparing to dive, the thing was so loud, so grating, yanking everyone from their sleep while it was still dark outside.

Both Ray and Darnell came to the door of their cell wearing nothing but their underwear. Stephanie Beers was on the phone while Robbie Robinson switched on all the lights in the unit, but neither of the guards pushed the buttons that opened any of the cell doors. Apparently, it was not a fire or a fire drill.

Pretty soon Robinson picked up the mic. "Everyone just chill out. We're on lockdown until further notice!"

Someone in another cell yelled, "Just our unit? How come?"

"No. The whole prison's on lockdown."

Ray looked at the clock in the dayroom: 5:22 a.m.—quite a while before breakfast. He returned to his bunk and curled up under his blanket with his fingers in his ears, but there was no blocking out the wail and no falling back to sleep.

Two hours later, when the alarm had finally been silenced, Zitty was banging on the door of their cell and yelling. "Hey, Mr. Robinson, when we gettin' some breakfast? We're gonna miss chow if you don't let us out of here."

"We're on lockdown," Robinson said into the mic that broadcast to the whole unit. "Nobody's going anywhere right now. So just chill out"—apparently his favorite term this morning—"and listen to your stomach growl. They say they'll bring breakfast around when they can get to it."

Zitty turned back toward Ray. "Wow! Must be a riot or somethin'. Last time there was a lockdown, we at least got to go to the mess hall by units."

When breakfast finally came, it was delivered as individual boxed meals filled with plastic containers: a petrified biscuit, a fruit cup, a cup of gelatinous goo labeled "ham and eggs," and a juice box.

"How long these been in the warehouse?" Ray asked.

"Probably since they invented plastic."

They had been allowed to come out of their "cages," four at a time, to get their boxed meals, but they had to return to their cells to eat. "Mr. Robinson, what's goin' on? How come we can't eat in the mess hall?"

Robinson raised both hands over his head as though shooing away a swarm of pestering flies. "Don't ask me. I just work here!"

But Ms. Beers spoke up. "A guard's dead. They're trying to figure out whether he had an accident or was attacked."

All the guys in the unit began clamoring for more information: "Who was it?" "Where'd it happen?" "How come they have *us* locked down? They don't think we did it, do they?"

"Look! You'll hear about it soon enough anyway, so I'm gonna tell you what I've heard so far," said the female guard. "It was Robert McAfee. They found him at the bottom of the stairs in the north end of the administration building. What they're trying to figure out is whether he slipped and hit his head on one of those concrete steps or whether someone hit him over the head with a pipe or something. And as far as who they suspect, until they know for sure what happened, they suspect every swinging one of you cons in this whole prison. That's why you get the recycled breakfasts-in-a-box. Understand? There ain't nothin' you or we can do about it . . . unless one of *yous guys* is ready to confess."

Confess? Everyone slipped back into his cell without saying a word.

McAfee dead? Ray's mind swirled. *He* had no question whether it had been an accident or not. But what if he'd been part of it? What if he got accused even though he had nothing to do with it? What if they found the sword in the bathroom and his fingerprints were on it? He should have wiped it off! He never should have gone in there!

After a few minutes Darnell spoke up in a cautious voice since the door still stood open. "I guess I ain't too sad. It ain't too much to say that he was my enemy!"

"Thought you were supposed to love your enemies!" The comment popped out even before Ray was sure where the idea had come from.

"Yeah, but you know I ain't a very good Christian . . . least not yet."

"I know what you mean." It was tempting to tell his cellmate how close he had come to attacking McAfee himself. It was almost as if he had to tell *somebody*; after all, if he *had* been involved, it would have been partially as payback for how the racist hack had treated Zitty. But Ray kept his mouth shut. He'd grown to like Harrison, but there was no telling what might loosen his lips if Ray told him too much.

They were allowed to go to the chow hall one unit at a time that afternoon for a late midday meal. It took three hours to feed the whole population, and it was the last meal of the day. The food was dried out or cold when Unit 4 got its turn. With nothing to do back in their unit except watch TV or play cards, the guys became restless, and two fights broke out.

Two days later the lockdown was lifted, and the public word was that McAfee had had an accident. He probably slipped and fell, hitting his head on either the railing or the step.

Ray knew from the moment he heard the report that it was a coverup. If McAfee had hit his head in a fall, there would have been skin and hair samples at the point of impact and there wouldn't have been any question as to whether his head had hit the step or the railing. The administration knew McAfee had been taken out, so why put out this false story? Were they playing politics with the public, not wanting the prison to look like a dangerous place to work? Or were they biding their time until they could pin the murder on someone specific? Ray would need to be extra careful. The whole situation was a sleeper.

"Hey, Slew," called Victor Muñoz as Ray made his way through the mess hall. "Here, sit with us."

What could Ray say? He put his tray down and took the seat across from the Latin Kings chief. But something was different about the little huddle of Kings around the table, and then he realized: "Where's Weller?"

"Didn't you hear? Damion got sent to Pontiac yesterday."

"Pontiac?" Pontiac was the toughest maximum security facility in the state, not where anyone wanted to be placed when transferred from a juvenile facility to an adult prison. "How come?"

"He was nineteen." Victor smiled his cold-eyed grin. "And that's why I want to talk to you. I'm impressed with you, Slew, and was wondering if you'd be willing to take his place." When Ray did not respond immediately, Muñoz continued. "Hey, man, I can arrange for you to move into Unit 2 with me. We got a good arrangement over there. You can have a room of your own, TV, coffee maker, almost anything you want . . . 'cept women. Haven't worked that one out yet." He grinned again. "Whaddaya say?"

Ray stared at his tray, avoiding eye contact with Muñoz while he heaped his mashed potatoes into a peak. Finally he said, "I don't know. I need some time to think about it."

"*Think about it?* Of course, sure. That's copacetic. You're a thoughtful guy. That's why I like you. But I can't hold that room for long. They'll stick someone else in there without consulting me. I have some pull, but not that much."

Ray thought he had an awful lot of pull if he could arrange a private "room" with special concessions for his henchmen. And what did he mean, "*room,*" as though this were a hotel? This was prison, and everyone lived in cells, not rooms!

Ray got up with his uneaten tray of food. "I'll get back to you . . . tomorrow." He made the sign of a crown with his free hand and muttered, "*¡Amor de rey!*" Then left.

Now what was he going to do? Why was Muñoz interested in him? Ray had kept a low profile in terms of the Kings for the last few months. It didn't make sense. Yeah, he was down for the Crown, but there were a lot of other guys far more outspoken and more experienced in leadership. Why not promote one of them? On the other hand, it was a fantastic opportunity. To be number two—or maybe even *numero uno*, once Muñoz was gone. Muñoz had

to be older than Ray, so he would be transferred first, leaving . . .
perhaps Ray in charge. Even if it were only for a short time, being
number one in Joliet would position him well when he went to
adult prison. And he might need that kind of juice. He was facing
a lot of years in the slammer. It only made sense to position himself
as strongly as possible.

Could he do it? Gang leadership in prison meant tough decisions, like laying the smack down on errant members to keep the
discipline clear. Ray was sweating on his bunk as he dreamed about
it. Maybe he was the guy who could reform the Kings at Joliet, keep
'em strong but just and fair. Muñoz was right in noticing that he was
a thoughtful guy, someone they could trust, someone who would
keep his head and not do rash things like Weller. Weller probably
whacked McAfee on his own. Isn't that what he was threatening,
egging Ray to do it with the sword the way Quiñones had talked
him into smokin' Greg Mason? But Ray was more mature now.
And like Muñoz had said, rash actions were a threat to everyone.
That must be why Muñoz was interested in raising up Ray into
leadership.

This was his opportunity.

"Hey, Ray . . . Ray! RAY! What's the matter with you? It's like
you're off in la-la land."

Ray turned toward his cellmate. "Sorry, just thinkin' about
some heavy decisions I gotta make. What you want?"

"You goin' to chapel tomorrow?"

Tomorrow? Saturday? It hardly seemed like a whole week had
passed. Ray had completely forgotten about chapel, about the questions concerning Jesus Christ he had been considering just a few
days before. At this point they seemed so remote . . . not trivial,
but irrelevant.

"Hey, you know what? I really can't deal with the church thing
right now. I caught myself a forty-year bid. So the first thing I
gotta do is look out for myself. Know what I mean? Maybe later

I'll check out God. I got plenty of time. In fact, that's about all I got—time."

"Yeah," Harrison sat up. "You got time. You been inside—what?—almost two years? Your time gettin' better?"

"What you talkin' 'bout, man? I'm makin' it."

"You been reading that gospel of John like Mr. Gee said, right?"

"I read . . . some . . . but not for the last couple days. Why?"

"Well, if you read far enough, you'da come across where Jesus said, 'I am the way and the truth and the life.' That's all I'm talkin' about. Jesus can give you life, man. I've decided that's the only way to survive in here."

"Whaddaya talkin' 'bout? I'm still alive."

"Yeah, well, you breathin', but there's more."

"In here? Not much. But if the religious thing's your choice, that's cool. Just don't be preachin' it at me. Okay? I liked it better when you were swearing and callin' me names."

"Oh, I can still do that too, you . . . you pile a . . . what ya clean up after your dog."

Ray smiled and shook his head at Harrison's attempt to sanitize his speech.

"Though there's one difference," Harrison added. "I don't use the Lord's name in vain no more. That's my choice. But there's a choice *you* gotta make. Know what I mean? . . . So you goin' to chapel tomorrow or not?"

"Nah. Maybe later. I got some other business to take care of. You tell me what happens, though. Okay?"

"I'll be glad to, but you know you can't get life secondhand. You gotta get it for yourself."

"Ah, man. Just quit preachin' at me. Okay?"

CHAPTER 19

H ey! Whassup pawtna?"

Ray looked at Zitty and frowned. *Partner?* Darnell considered him his partner just because they were cellmates? That was a new one. "Hey, man. So how was chapel?"

"Oh, it was good, but there's somethin' else you ought to know."

"Yeah, like what? You gonna preach at me again?"

"Maybe, but that's not what I'm talking 'bout." He sat down on his bunk and leaned back against the wall so his whole body was like a ski jump. "Word's out you goin' down for a fall."

"Whaddaya mean?"

"Well, I wouldn't usually mess in some other set's business, but you stuck up for me when you didn't have to, so . . ."

"So? So whassup?"

"You bein' set up, dude, by your own crew."

"Whaddaya mean?"

Harrison sat up and leaned forward with his elbows on his knees. "Victor Muñoz, he's the head of the Latin Kings in here, ain't he?"

Ray nodded.

"And he's offering you some sweet deal, right?"

"How do you know that?"

"Don't worry 'bout how I know something! It's either true or it ain't true."

"I don't listen to no hearsay. Rumors can get a guy in trouble." Ray got up and went over to the little metal washbasin and splashed some water on his face.

"All right. All right. I heard it from Tyrone Taylor. He's that tall black dude from Unit 2 who comes to chapel all the time. He knows I'm your cellmate, so he pulled me aside and talked to me on today."

Tall black dude from Unit 2? Yeah, Ray remembered him. Talked with his hands a lot. And Unit 2 was where Muñoz was, where Muñoz had promised to transfer Ray to a private cell. Perhaps Tyrone Taylor did know something. Ray dried his face and turned back to Harrison. "So . . . wha'd he say?"

"He said Muñoz waggin' the dog with you."

Ray stared at his cellmate until Harrison continued.

"He said the administration thinks the Kings were behind McAfee's death. Maybe Weller did it on his own. Maybe not. Maybe Victor Muñoz ordered the hit and Weller dropped a dime on him when he was leavin'. Taylor didn't know. But he said the Kings are worried that the administration still considers it an open case—probably murder—even though they put out that accident story. He said Muñoz is moving you into position to catch any heat."

"How can that be? I wasn't in any leadership when McAfee got hit. I didn't order nothin'. How can they pin that on me?"

"Don't know, but Taylor said you gettin' promoted so quickly could look like you was bein' rewarded."

"That's crazy." But Ray had no sooner said it than a chill skittered up his back. It might be crazy, but it had the ring of truth. And there was also the sword in the trash bin . . . that might have his prints on it. Even if the guards hadn't found the sword or his prints, perhaps there were other Latin Kings who knew Ray had been recruited to put a hit on McAfee. They might be enticed to testify against him if the heat got turned up high enough.

Still, Ray wasn't quick to abandon the advantages of King leadership. He could see the dangers, so maybe that was enough to help him avoid them. To be forewarned is to be forearmed, right? He could stay out of trouble and benefit from the position all at the same time. And besides, who was Tyrone Taylor to be warning him? That seemed suspicious too, didn't it?

"How come you bring all this to me, Zitty? And who's this Tyrone Taylor? What's he? Who's he mobbed up with?"

"He's GD."

"And the GDs aren't going to be all over him—and you—if they find out you're helping me? No. Something doesn't make sense here."

"Taylor's a Christian, and maybe he thought after seeing you attend chapel a few times that you were too, or . . . at least almost. But that doesn't matter. We don't like to see anyone get hurt. There might not be any way to get unhitched from our set, but we're no one's enemies, not anymore, anyway. Jesus made us all brothers. Besides, you stuck your neck out for me. Did that make any sense?"

"Guess not."

The call for chow came, and as they left their cell, Ray knew he had to make a decision. Muñoz would be expecting an answer.

"So how's my man?"

"Hangin'. Whassup?" Ray touched fists with Muñoz and the other Kings at the table.

"We gotta talk." The King chief smiled his dead grin and jerked his head to the side, indicating that Ray should follow him to an empty table where they could talk alone.

"So you gonna be my number two, make everything copacetic?"

"Uh . . ." Ray looked around the mess hall as though the answer were posted on the wall somewhere. "Uh . . . could I have another day to consider it? I mean, it's a great opportunity and all, but I don't want to go into it blind."

"What's the problem? What's there to think about? You crappin' out on us again? When your brothers call, you not ready to step forward for the Crown?"

"You know I'm down for the Crown. It's just—"

"No, Slew. I *ain't* sure you're down for the Crown. You keep *sayin'* you are, but every time we ask you to do something, you hesitate. I mean, we wanted to teach that McAfee a little something, but you wouldn't handle it for us—"

"So you had Weller do it? Is that what happened?"

Muñoz scowled and looked back at the table with the other Kings. "Who said that? Don't go spreadin' that around!"

"Yeah, but you gotta tell me *why* you want me to take his place, 'cause I'm no farmer walking through the barnyard. Know what I mean? I don't want to step in anything."

"Ah, Weller's gone." Muñoz waved his hand as though shooing a fly away. "Besides, they ruled that an accident. So there's nothin' to step in."

"Yeah. Weller might be gone, but I don't think the administration thinks it was an accident, and you can be sure they haven't forgotten McAfee either." Ray paused and stared at Muñoz, who was still grilling him. His dead eyes looked away, unable to hold Ray's gaze. Harrison had been right. Muñoz wanted some insulation, and he was looking to Ray to provide it. Finally Ray sighed. "No. My answer's no! Find someone else to take Weller's place."

That night after lights-out Ray said, "Hey, Harrison, you still awake?"

"Yeah."

"I sure hope you were right. 'Cause I put everything on the line. And now some pretty heavy guys are not too happy with me."

"Think of it this way, Ray. You didn't suspect they were settin' you up. That came to you. Taylor overheard it, and I tipped you off. But who was really lookin' out for you?"

"Whaddaya mean?"

"I mean, maybe God was looking out for you. Ever think of that?"

"God? What did he have to do with it? Why would he do that?"

"I don't know. Why does anything happen? Why'd I catch my case? Maybe God was trying to get my attention, and now I'm tryin' to listen. Same with you. Maybe he's lookin' out for you too, trying to get your attention."

"Yeah? Think so?"

"Could be."

Neither spoke for a couple minutes. Finally Ray said, "Hey, Harrison, you pray?"

"Pray? Yeah, sometimes. Least, I'm tryin' to more than I used to. Why?"

"Well, I was wondering if you would pray for me. I think I'm gonna need it."

"Pray? Yeah, sure, but only if you pray for yourself."

"Aw, I don't know how to do that." But then Ray recalled that time in chapel when he had simply said, *"Jesus, if you really came to pay my debt, if you really came to forgive me, all I can say is, thank you."* He knew that he had somehow connected. Maybe that was praying, just talking to God.

"Okay. Uh, God, if you can hear me, I need your help."

"Yeah, God. Ray needs your help. Keep him strong and don't let nothin' bad happen to him."

They were both silent for a moment.

"Thanks, man—"

"Hey, I ain't done," injected Darnell. "And, God, help him believe. Amen."

Ray heard Darnell flop over on his bunk and then a muffled, "G'night."

"Yeah, tomorrow."

Ray lay staring up toward the dimly lit ceiling. Did he believe? He tried to recall the things he had read in the Bible about believing. It had been a couple weeks. What had Harrison said *believe* meant? *Not only that Jesus lived and died and rose again, but that his death paid the penalty for your sin. . . . If you believe that and ask him to forgive you and are 'down for the crown,' then you are a believer.*

Yeah, he was there. He *did* believe like that. "I mean, what else can I do, God? You kind of brought me to this point. Where else can I go? It's worth a try!" Ray whispered. "If you can hear me, God, please forgive me for shooting Greg Mason . . . and for all the other bad things I've done. I want to give my life to you and change up so I can live like you want—" He stopped for a few moments as he thought. "I guess that's all. G'bye."

Did that make Ray a Christian? He didn't know, but in a few moments he drifted off to sleep.

The next morning when Ray got up, he tried to tell if he felt different. He didn't . . . but then again he did. He didn't feel more holy or more religious. He didn't feel less like a convicted criminal or less like a murderer. All those things were still true. But the monkey wasn't on his back anymore.

He took a deep breath like a pearl diver upon bringing up a rare find. "Hey, Darnell, I did it!"

"Did what?"

"You know. Prayed."

"Yeah, I remember. That was good."

"No, I mean I prayed to be a Christian."

There was a long silence. "Last night?"

"Yeah, after you went to sleep. I told God I believed and asked him to forgive me."

"Hey, that's good. That's real good!"

"So now what?"

"I don't know."

CHAPTER 20

C opacetic was how Victor Muñoz liked his world. But when SORT, the Special Operations Team, brought in CSI detectives the following day and began putting the screws to everyone about McAfee's death, Ray knew Muñoz would be sweating bullets. The SORT guys had all kinds of leverage: "Talk, and that drug charge you're still facing will go away." "Talk, and we can get you into a minimum security facility when you go adult." "Talk, and we can get your time reduced."

Sooner or later, someone would rat out Muñoz if they knew anything about McAfee's death. But did anyone else know about it? Did anyone know that Weller and Muñoz had tried to recruit Ray to put the hit on McAfee? Maybe, maybe not. Ray recalled that Muñoz had been careful to make sure no one overheard their conversations and had warned Ray at the lunch table not to *"go spreadin' that around"* when Ray speculated that Weller had been the hit man. So maybe no one else knew.

If that was the case, obviously Weller hadn't flipped or the DOC would have nailed Muñoz without ramping up a new investigation. That left Ray as the only other person at Joliet who knew of the conspiracy. Now with SORT snooping around, Ray could see that Muñoz might consider him a threat, the kind of threat Muñoz might want to eliminate. Knowledge can be dangerous.

Ray sat on his bunk, alone in his cell, head in his hands, worrying. This gang life was crazy! It had never done him any good. It had incited him to kill an innocent person, had stolen forty years of his life, had nearly gotten him set up for a second murder, and now might get him killed! Ray had to drop the flag. Forget all that commitment trash—"¡Amor de rey!" "Down for the Crown!" "Once a King always a King!" It was gonna get him killed. He knew too much!

He sat there for a long time. Yes, information could be dangerous, but—a plan began to slowly take shape in Ray's mind—information could also be powerful!

"Muñoz," Ray said that evening at chow, "I gotta talk to you, alone, right away."

El jefe gave Ray his dead grin. "No problem, man. Meet me in the yard tomorrow."

"No. Tonight. I need to talk now. Listen, I'm on duty in the infirmary. Get sick. I can arrange for us to be alone." Ray got up and left the table.

A couple hours later Muñoz came into the infirmary moaning and groaning, saying his stomach was cramping something awful. The nurse gave him some Pepto-Bismol and told him to lie on the cot with a heating pad on his stomach. She then went back to her office while Ray came in to mop the floor.

Ray closed the door. "Hey!"

"Hey, yourself. What's all this drama about?"

"It's about the SORT guys. They're lookin' pretty close, and I was thinkin' you might be concerned 'bout what I know."

"You don't know nothin'!"

Ray worked the mop along the edge of the floor. "Yes and no. I been thinkin' 'bout that. No, I don't *know* how McAfee died, so

I don't have to say anything. On the other hand, you and Weller did try to recruit me to put a hit on him—"

"I never said kill him!"

"True. That was Weller talkin'. But you did say enough to go down as a conspirator. And if that led to indicting Weller, he might flip in order to get the charges reduced, and that might implicate you further. You're in it up to here." Ray stopped mopping and saluted with his hand just below his nose.

Muñoz sat up. He wasn't grinning anymore. "You say anything, and you're dead, *muerto*, nothin' but *una memoria para su madre!* You hear me?"

Ray stood there, leaning hard on the mop. Could he stand up to Muñoz? Or would he let *el jefe* rule him? "When do you get out? Two more years, isn't it? Just a drug charge? But McAfee counts as a cop. If I talk, you go down for life. And maybe, or maybe not, you'll get the chance to waste me. It's a gamble. But I have a suggestion that could improve your odds. . . ."

"Yeah. Can't imagine it's worth anything. But go ahead."

"I swear to not say anything if you discharge me from the Kings."

"What? You *loco*? You want out?"

"Yeah. And I'll keep my mouth shut. If I ever say anything, you have just as much chance at a 'remedy' as you got now."

"And if I don't discharge you?"

"Well, you never know, do you? This way you got a little more peace of mind."

"Ha! No more than your word!"

"Have you ever known me to lie? It's more than you got now."

"Ah, I dunno. Nobody gets released from the Almighty Latin King Nation. I mean, I guess some old guys kinda go inactive. But you know, it's 'Once a King, always a King.' "

"That ain't necessarily so. I've heard of guys gettin' out for religious reasons. You know, they get religion and want to follow

God rather than the Inca." Ray waited until he saw Muñoz shrug a tacit acknowledgment. "And that's why I want out. I've become a . . . a, you know, a Christian, the real kind, and I don't have time for the organization anymore."

"No time? That's bogus!" Muñoz flopped back on the cot. "In here everybody's got time. Besides, if I was to let you go because you got religion, you'd have to get V'd out at the very least."

A violation. Accept a voluntary beating? Ray hadn't thought about that.

Muñoz continued. "If I let you go without a violation, somebody would get suspicious. They might think you were holdin' something over my head. Then they might sweat it out of you."

Ray was already sweating, breathing hard. Could he go all the way?

"All right. I'll take a violation. Just no permanent injury!"

Muñoz sat up. The grin returned to the bottom of his face while his eyes remained as hollow as caves. "You know there ain't no guarantee what might happen in a blanket party. But I will make you this promise: If you break this deal and rat me out, I'll make sure someone tracks you down and wipes you out, even if I have to buy the hit from death row."

Ray couldn't sleep that night. In the morning he said to Harrison, "You ever hear of anyone getting beat down because they became a Christian?"

"Where you think *martyr* come from? People gettin' stoned, cut up, burned, all that crap."

"Yeah, in the Bible. But what 'bout now?"

"Still happenin', man."

"What?" Ray dropped his yellow Bic razor in the sink.

"In China and some of those radical Islam countries. I heard about it."

"How 'bout in the good ole U.S. of A? Like right here in Joliet, Illinois, man?"

"Whaddaya mean?"

"I'm . . . gonna get V'd out of the Kings."

"What? You crazy? How come? Ya don't have to, ya know. I'm still a GD."

"Ah!" Ray waved his hand. "It's more complicated. I just can't take this crap anymore. It gets crazier and crazier. I figured since I prayed, this is my time to step down."

Harrison frowned. "Maybe you can arrange it to happen someplace where the guards'll step in 'fore it gets too bad."

Ray snorted. "Not likely. It's gonna be a blanket party. I won't know when or where till they throw a blanket over my head and start hittin' me."

"Oh, man, that's cold."

It didn't come the next day or the next week or the next month. But during that time the SORT investigators squeezed everyone who might have had a beef with McAfee, and that included Ray, of course, since McAfee had written him up and sent him to the hole.

Ever since Ray had made his deal with Muñoz, he worried about whether he was doing right. He had information that could be relevant in solving a murder, but he didn't actually *know* whether it had been a murder. So was withholding it from the authorities a crime in itself? He feared it might be, but what could he do? In prison the very worst thing to be was a snitch. Even the guards and the administrators despised a snitch. Prison operated on a different set of rules than outside, where law and order was maintained by vigilant civilians who reported crime, or even the possibility of a crime. But it didn't work that way on the inside! Justice seldom followed an informant.

Ray sat in the chair in the small office being used by the detectives. There was no bright light, no good cop/bad cop routine, no sleep deprivation, and—to Ray's surprise—no offers of special rewards if he would serve up some incriminating evidence. They just calmly asked factual questions concerning Ray's whereabouts during the night McAfee died, how long he had been in the hole and why, and whether he had ever threatened McAfee. Then they asked him about his involvement in the Kings and whether he held any kind of rank in the organization. Ray answered the questions in a straightforward manner, knowing the investigators could check out every detail.

"All right, Mr. Slewinski," said the lead questioner, "is there anything else about this event that you want to tell us?"

There it was! No, he did not *want* to tell them anything more. Ray did not have any firsthand knowledge concerning the cause of McAfee's death. But there were things he could tell, things they would like to know. Only, keeping silent was his ticket out of the Kings. What should he do? What did God want him to do? Certainly God didn't want to keep him in the gang. It was a godless, violent organization that destroyed lives.

Ray looked down and shook his head, not so much in answer to the detective's question but at the dilemma he faced.

"Okay then, Mr. Slewinski. Thanks for your cooperation. You know how to reach us if anything comes to mind."

Ray walked out and followed the guard back to his unit. Maybe they really didn't want to hear any more about McAfee's demise. Maybe they knew he had been a bad guard who got what he deserved. No, that's not really the way things were supposed to work.

"Oh, Father God. Nothin's clear and easy. You gotta help me!"

The investigation wound down with no change concerning the "official cause" of McAfee's death. Day by day, Ray began to breathe easier and put it all behind him. He even hoped he would never have to take his violation out of the Kings. Maybe they would just let him drift away, nothing said . . . nothing done. He cut his hair—not so short that he might be mistaken for a skinhead, but so it no longer fell over his eyes. He quit eating at the Latin Kings' table, hanging with them in the yard, or walking like a gangbanger and slinging fake hand signs when he talked. If he could, he would have removed the LK crown tattooed on his shoulder.

To keep himself busy, Ray concentrated on studying and received his GED on October 15, 1999, after which he celebrated by splitting a liter of Pepsi with Harrison. He also volunteered for every prison chapel program, even helping in the services put on by other churches. By Thanksgiving Mr. Gee arranged for Ray to receive Bible correspondence courses that increased in depth until he was working on a college level.

If it hadn't been for Harrison, Ray might have felt lonely, since most of the other neutrons were loners by nature or misfits who sabotaged any friendship, but Darnell proved loyal. In fact, it was one day when a heavy rainstorm kept everyone in the gym during yard time that Ray heard Darnell yelling at the top of his lungs from across the gym: "Look out! LOOK OUT! Ray, look behind you!"

Ray turned just as the blanket dropped over his head, and he was knocked to the floor. Blows began landing from every side, and he was barely able to pull himself into a fetal position, hoping to protect his face and vital organs. His attackers were yelling, cussing him out, and kicking him. He heard Muñoz scream, "A King is for life! You are no longer a royal member of the sacred and Almighty Latin King Nation. Go to hell!"

At least two of the goons had some kind of clubs that landed vicious blows. One clipped him across the lower back so hard Ray felt it in his kidneys, but his movements were so restricted by the blanket and the fact that he couldn't see from which direction the blows were coming that he could do nothing to defend himself. Like Muñoz had said: There was no guarantee he wouldn't receive permanent injury . . . or even death! Ray knew it now. How stupid he'd been to agree to be V'd out. There had to have been some other way.

At least six men were beating him, and none of them held back. Typically, a violation restricts a beating to a specified number of minutes as a measured punishment, but to Ray the time went on and on. When would they stop? Where were the guards? He heard Harrison's voice cursing and yelling and obviously struggling to intervene, but it did no good. And Ray knew he couldn't hope for help from the other inmates. This was obviously an internal matter, and no other set would jump in without starting a riot.

Ray feared he was losing consciousness when he got hit again in the kidneys. The pain was so intense that he involuntarily straightened from his fetal position. That's when some guy's foot connected with his face like he was kicking a forty-yard field goal.

All Ray heard after that was the fading whistle of the wind past his ears as he sailed through the uprights . . . or was it the whistles of the late-arriving guards? He couldn't tell as everything faded into merciful silence.

CHAPTER 21

W hen Ray regained consciousness in the infirmary, he pissed blood for three days. After it finally stopped, he was allowed to return to his unit with a plastic guard on his face to protect his broken nose. Both eyes were black, and he had bruises all over his body. Other than that . . . he grinned at Darnell. "I'm officially out of the Kings!"

"Man, you paid one high price. But what difference does it make?"

"Nobody's tellin' me what to do. Nobody's settin' me up to get me in trouble. But most of all, I feel free!"

"Free? You forget where you are?"

"No way. But there's different ways to be free."

A year and a half later, shortly before Ray turned nineteen—or rather, shortly before the State of Illinois *thought* he would turn nineteen—he was transferred to the Stateville Correctional Center for adults, not far from Joliet. Ray had survived two prison riots, thirteen shakedowns, and six lockdowns. He thought he could handle Stateville. Of course, he would have preferred a lower-security prison, but if he had to go to maximum because of his murder conviction, he could survive Stateville. Reportedly, it was not as rough as Pontiac and no worse than Menard. Besides, Stateville would keep him close enough to Chicago for his mother to continue visiting him, though the frequency of her visits had dropped off because of her health and her heavy work schedule. In addition, the Captives Free Ministries had weekly—not just monthly—meetings at Stateville. And Mr. Gee had taken a special interest in Ray as he finished his GED and began taking Bible correspondence courses. It had been great to have such a concerned mentor.

His eagerness to go to Stateville—if anyone could ever be eager for a prison assignment—fizzled, however, as soon as the gray prison bus turned in the gate at three in the afternoon on May 15, 2001. If Ray hadn't been shackled to the ring below his seat on the bus's floor, he might have jumped right through the expanded steel covering the window when he saw Stateville's thirty-three-foot-high concrete wall with ten guard towers. This was no progressive reformatory; it was a prison like in the movies—horror movies!

Once inside, fourteen-foot chain-link fences topped with coils of razor wire dissected the yard into mazes to control prisoner movement. There were other buildings around, but the structure that seized Ray's attention was a round building, perhaps fifty feet high with a slightly domed roof and a central turret on top. If it had been in any other setting, Ray might have taken it for a colossal water tank, a reservoir large enough for the city of Chicago. But on closer inspection, the checkered pattern on the wall was created by scores of barred windows.

"What's that?" Ray asked the guard who helped him out of the bus so he wouldn't trip. Four-piece shackles hobbled Ray's legs.

"Oh that? That's F-House. We used to have four of them round-houses. But now all we got is the one—special accommodations, if you know what I mean—and the only one left in the whole country." He gave Ray a shove. "Come on. You'll get a tour later."

Ray entered a small building and descended some stairs into what had to be a basement, where he was searched and unshackled.

Then he waited for an hour while a clerk filled out paper work. Finally she called down the hall, "Hey, Coleman, your fish is ready. Take him on over."

The same guard who had taken Ray off the bus came out of a doorway, tossed an empty coffee cup in the trash, and jerked his head for Ray to come with him. They went through a series of locked doors and down a long corridor that ended with more gates. On the other side Ray could see a ramp that ascended into what had to be F-House.

He balked. "Hey, wait a minute! I ain't supposed to be in there. How come you brought me here? I had a good record at Joliet. I'm s'posed to go in one of them new units in the gen-pop."

"Sorry, pal. I didn't write this order. I'm just doin' what's on the sheet."

Locks buzzed, and doors clanged open. Ray shuffled up the ramp, through air thick with disinfectant, and onto the highly waxed concrete floor of a huge arena as though he were a gladiator brought in to face the lions. The walls of the cavern, all the way up to the roof, were lined with hundreds of cells, four tiers high. From the center of the bare floor rose a pillar that resembled an air traffic control tower, but the glare of the sodium lights at the top prevented Ray from seeing into the booth on top.

"Don't be watchin' the gods, now. They're there to watch you. From that tower they see every move you make, day or night. Whether you're sittin' on the stainless steel throne or cryin' for your mama, they know if you're naughty or nice. They control the lights. They control the heat. They control the cell doors. Anything you need, you bow down to them. Got it?"

Banging started like steam pounding up through radiator pipes in an old tenement building. Hooting and yelling followed as the inmates noted Ray's arrival. "Here comes fresh meat, boys." "Hey, punk, want some of this? I'll take *real* good care of you." A soggy sandwich hit Ray in the back of the head. "Come on, fish. Come to papa. You *know* what I like!" Coming from all sides and all the way up to the rafters, the screaming and banging grew louder than an NFL game in Houston's House of Pain.

A riot stick jabbed Ray in the back. "Suck it up, son, and get moving. This is your new home away from home! Right across to those stairs on the far side. You're up on tier three, all the way around to the right."

"But how come? How come I'm getting put in here with these. . . ?"

"Probably 'cause of overcrowding. This is supposed to be for segregation. But I can't help that. You'll be okay. According to this"—he slapped the sheet of paper with the back of his hand—"you got a cell of your own. So no one'll bother you . . . 'cept maybe in the shower." The guard choked on a guttural laugh. "That's where you're going to have to be careful."

Two weeks later, Ray hadn't yet taken a shower when the loudspeaker barked, "Number K17868 . . . K17868! Hey, Slewinski, you awake?" Ray rolled off his bunk and came to the bars of his five-by-ten-foot cell just as the door rolled open. "Gather up all your—" The PA squealed with feedback. (Ray thought the guards enjoyed making the inmates grab their ears.) "—and come on down here. You're goin' in gen-pop."

When Ray stepped onto the arena floor with his plastic bag of dirty underwear, a second uniform, and his Bible, Coleman, the same hack who had escorted him into F-House in the first place, stood waiting, feet apart and riot stick horizontal, gripped at both ends like he was ready to use it. But he was grinning . . . at least until Ray got close. Then his face screwed up as he turned away. "Oh man, you're too ripe for G-House. They'll never let you in. Might as well go back upstairs to your tier."

"G-House? I'm going to G-House?" G-House was an open-cell "honor" house with the rooms laid out along a central common area, not all that different from what Ray had experienced at the Juvenile Detention Center. "I'll take a shower as soon as I get there. I promise."

"Yeah? You better believe you will. In the meantime, stay downwind of me. I'm a sensitive guy, you know."

Sensitive, ha! Sensitive was a color no guard came in, but Ray had to admit that Coleman was better than most. Ray followed him across the yard to G-House and stood as far away as possible while Coleman waited for the guard on duty to sign off on Ray's transfer sheet.

The gate rolled open with a clank and a grumble. "You're down there in room 5. Coleman says you need a shower . . . bad, so you can take one as soon as you stow your stuff."

Ray paused in the doorway when he got to room 5. A heavy black man sat at the desk with his back to the door. The gray in his hair and sag to his massive shoulders suggested he was older—maybe forty. But the nightmare that slowly turned to stare at Ray could have seen fifty or even sixty hard years. It was crisscrossed by several scars, some still pink against his dark skin. Similar scars were on his arms, crosshatched in a way that caused Ray to wonder what possibly could have caused them.

"Oh mama!" the man growled. "What have we here? A snot-blowin' cracka?"

"Uh . . . yeah. I'm Ray, Raymond Slewinski. . . . Been assigned to this cell."

The heavy face turned back to his desk. "Get outta here, fish. You smell like worm food."

"Yeah . . . sure. I was just gonna take a shower."

After showering, Ray walked slowly back to his room, reluctant to face his new cellmate. As he passed room 3, he glanced in and stopped. The body on the cot with a Marvel Comic book over its face looked familiar. Wooly, blond hair showed above the image of Iron Man leaping off the cover. "Harrison! Hey, Darnell! That you?"

The figure sat up. It *was* Harrison, all right, rubbing his eyes and mumbling, "Hey, man, what you doin' here? I thought you went to Menard."

"Not me. I been holed up in F-House. Reception's all screwed up."

"Tell me about it. They sent me straight here. I didn't even go through Reception." He stepped forward and met fists with Ray. "Where's your cell?"

"Five. I'm in cell 5."

"You in there with Moon?" Darnell cursed then pursed his lips and sucked in. "Man, he be one mean pit bull."

"Moon? Moon who? I ain't never heard of no Moon."

"Johnny 'Moon' Riviera. You know, like Moon River? Or maybe it's Moon 'cause his face is round like one. I dunno. Anyway, he's El Rukn, but old school back from the Black P Stone days. Don't nobody mess wit' him."

"Well, apparently *somebody* did. He might have a moon face, but with all those scars on his face and arms, looks to me like he got ran over by a lawnmower."

"Ha, but there were three of 'em, and they all dead. One was an undercover cop. That's why he's been in here for so long."

"Hey, maybe I can get transferred into your cell."

"Don't hold your breath. With all this confusion they got goin' on—the crowdin' and all—they ain't cuttin' nobody any slack. They be cracking on all the little things just to show they's in control."

Moving to G-House and finding Darnell there were gifts from God, but rooming with Moon Riviera seemed more like a gift from hell. Other than ordering Ray out of the cell before he went to take a shower, the only thing the man said to him when he returned was, "Touch any of my stuff, fish, and you're chips. Any of your fish stuff ends up on my side of the room, and *poof!* Am I transmittin' on a frequency you're capable of pickin' up?"

Ray got the message. To reduce the chances of Moon finding some other excuse to "deep fry" him, Ray spent as much time as possible outside of his cell, reading, continuing his correspondence courses, playing cards, or watching TV in the common room. He took any classes that were offered and volunteered for extra du-ties—anything that would insulate him from Moon. With time his friendliness and good deeds became their own reward. Most of the guys ignored the fact that he wasn't mobbed up and didn't hassle him. Ray noticed, however, that anytime tensions broke out in the unit along gang lines, he was numbered with the Latin Kings, especially by their rivals. It was as though they assumed that in spite of his independence, he would support them in a fight.

During the next several months, Ray and Darnell hung out together whenever possible. The albino's face cleared up until it showed only a few pock marks from his former severe acne. Maybe it was better food and regular sleep or maybe he just outgrew it. Ray had no idea, but he stopped calling him Zitty, and that helped the name fade into extinction among the other inmates.

"Hey, dawg," Darnell said one day as he sat down next to Ray in the mess hall. "Where you when I need ya?"

"Whaddaya mean?"

"Ah, some guard tried to kick me outta the chow line. Said I already ate. You 'member back at IYC how you guys threw up a block for me when we were in line that day? Man, that was somethin' else."

Ray laughed. "McAfee didn't know what to do. I'd take another stint in the hole just to see that look on his face again."

"Yeah." Darnell shoveled some beans into his mouth. "Hey—" He chewed. "You hear about Victor Muñoz?"

"Muñoz? No, what?"

"Now they're saying McAfee was murdered, and they've indicted Muñoz for it. Guess somebody must have fingered him."

"Really?"

"Yep. That's what I heard."

Harrison turned to talk to the guy on the other side of him while Ray's mind tumbled with the news. He hadn't thought about the King leader for months. Who could have ratted on him? Ray and Muñoz and Damion Weller were the only three who knew about the threats against McAfee, and Ray had always thought it had been Weller who actually pulled the hit. But what if Muñoz thought Ray was the one who dropped a dime on him? He remembered the threat Muñoz had made to him: *"You say anything, and you're dead, muerto, nothin' but una memoria para su madre!"*

From time to time Ray and Darnell applied to be transferred to the Stateville Farm unit.

"But what if they take only one of us?" Ray said.

Darnell shrugged. "If you get moved, you've earned it. I'm gonna be paroled pretty soon anyway, so whether I stay or go, you're gonna be on your own."

"Yeah."

Mr. Gee had often mentioned the value of believers praying and studying the Bible together, but somehow in the context of prison, it seemed too intimate or something. But they talked. They often talked about their faith and the things God seemed to be showing them. Even having another brother in the same unit often helped Ray consider God's perspective on what he was facing, more powerful than merely asking the theoretical question: WWJD? But soon Darnell would be gone.

"I'm gonna pray that you *will* get moved over to the Farm as soon as I go," Darnell said the week before he got paroled. "You deserve it."

"Maybe. But it'll just mean more work: mowing grass around here, collecting litter along roads, providing work crews during lockdowns. I don't know. . . ."

"Hey, they can't work you more than you're doin' on your own now. Least then you wouldn't have to room with Moon. And it would look good on your record."

"Gettin' some space from Moon wouldn't be bad. But who cares about my record? You're going home, but me . . . Long as I don't commit no more crimes, they can't extend my time, but nothin's gonna shorten it either."

"Well, one day at a time. I'm still gonna pray you get moved. Every bit of freedom counts."

"Yeah, guess you right 'bout that."

CHAPTER 22

I t was warmer than usual near the end of March 2003, and Mr. Gee hoped to get permission to hold Friday's chapel outside in a fenced-olf section of the yard, visible to other men, which might attract some of them to a future service. But it ended up raining that day, so the Captives Free Ministries used one of the classrooms as usual. But after an abbreviated Bible study, they served cake and soft drinks to celebrate Darnell's going home.

"So you be gettin' paroled on Tuesday?" one of the guys said during the little party.

"Yeah. Can't wait!"

"Can't wait, huh? Ever cross your mind what day that is?"

"No, why?"

"It's the first of April, man, April Fool's Day. I wouldn't be surprised to see you back here next Friday feedin' us cake!"

Everyone laughed and slapped Darnell on the back to wish him well. But Ray decided to save his good-bye until Tuesday. He couldn't deal with the prospect of losing his best friend right then. Later, yeah, later he'd say good-bye.

After the party Ray stayed behind to help clean up—sliding desks back in place, picking up napkins and paper cups. When all the other inmates had left, Mr. Gee said, "Ray, you got a little extra time? The guy I'm riding with has to go up to Administration to fill out some papers."

"Sure." Mr. Gee often tried to grab a few minutes to talk with the guys who came regularly to chapel to see how they were doing and pray with them. But today was different. Mr. Gee asked Ray about his case. In all the years Ray had known the chaplain, he had never heard him talk to a man about his individual case, and for good reason. He explained to the trainee prisoners who helped in the ministry, "None of you are ordained ministers, so you don't have the legal privilege of confidentiality. If a man told you something important, you could be subpoenaed and required to testify, perhaps against him. You wouldn't want that."

Though Mr. Gee was a minister and could claim confidentiality for himself, he had also explained, "Our purpose is not to give men a false hope that we can influence their case by any means other than prayer. We're not lawyers. We're representatives of Jesus Christ. We can pray, but we don't need to know any details. God knows!"

So Ray was surprised when Mr. Gee said, "So, Ray, I've never heard about your case. Nothing is pending in terms of an appeal at this point, is it?"

"Nah. My PD filed the routine appeals long ago, back when I was at Joliet, but they came to zip." Ray shook his head. "'Cept for Jesus' return, I ain't waitin' on nothin' or hopin' for nothin', I got five down on my bid and thirty-five to go." He bit his lip and smiled. "I'll be as old as you 'fore I get out of here, Mr. Gee."

"I doubt that." Mr. Gee absentmindedly scratched his head, causing his toupee to shift back and forth a little even though it was a new one and otherwise looked pretty good. "Anyway, have a seat. Let's talk. Tell me how you caught your case."

Ray told him everything, beginning with how Rico had egged him on to prove his street name. "I don't go by Slew no more. It took me a couple years after I shot that kid before I could even admit I was a killer. Doin' so was part of my coming to Jesus. That's what I mean when I give my testimony and say, 'Jesus paid a debt I couldn't pay.' But I ain't proud of what I did, so I don't use that name no more." Ray looked down at the desk with a flop-eared rabbit carved in its top, evidence that a member of the Two-Six gang had an object sharp enough to leave his mark while he sat in class. Ray looked back up at Mr. Gee and took a deep breath. "I'm just grateful that Jesus did pay my debt."

"Amen." Except for an occasional question of clarification, Mr. Gee had listened quietly to Ray's whole story. But then he frowned. "How old did you say you were when you did this?"

"Fourteen."

"But they recorded you as fifteen?"

"Yeah. That was because of the school thing. My mom had to get me in school, so she said I was born a year earlier. So when they checked my school documents, they said I was fifteen, and that's what went on my police report."

"And you didn't object?"

"Well, I told 'em, but I was almost fifteen, so it didn't seem to matter. Besides, I'd always been taken for a year older, so—"

"And your PD didn't make an issue of this in court?"

"No. She focused on trying to get me off 'cause the cops had acquired my confession without my mom bein' there. 'Course, that didn't work." Ray frowned as he looked hard at Mr. Gee. "Why are you askin' 'bout my age?"

"Ah, I'm not sure. I'll have to talk to Alan Sondano. He's a defense attorney who sometimes helps us in the ministry. Excellent man, excellent. He'll know if there's anything to it. You said you were *automatically* transferred to adult court? That it wasn't a judge's ruling? Are you sure no judge made a ruling?"

"I don't think so."

"Well, we'll need to check that out. It could be important. I'll talk to Sondano, see what he says."

Ray went back to his unit with his head swirling in a fog. What was Mr. Gee suggesting? For five years Ray had disciplined himself to accept his forty-year sentence. Acceptance had finally brought him emotional peace. He couldn't upset that now with this little tease. No, he didn't dare think about it. He was number K17868, a man convicted of murder, a man doing his time for having committed the crime. He didn't deserve anything else. . . . Yet the flicker of a reprieve pestered the edge of Ray's mind like a dream of an impossible woman. What if . . . ?

The possibility that Ray's case might change floated between him and Darnell the next couple of days. Ray wanted to tell him, but it seemed so farfetched that he felt embarrassed to mention it. On Tuesday morning, when Darnell was about ready to leave, Ray realized he'd never gotten around to really saying good-bye. He reached out to shake hands, but Darnell pulled him close and spoke in a hushed tone. "Ray, if you can get transferred to the Farm, you better take it. There's smoke on the horizon, man, and you don't want to be here for the fire."

"Whaddaya mean?"

"Look around, bro. Everyone's tense, standing off in their sets like they fixin' to . . . to—"

"Have a little riot, maybe? Hey, I been through riots before. Besides, I'm not mixed up in all this gang drama anymore."

"No, man. This is different. I dunno what it is, but I heard somethin' big's goin' down. You just keep outta the way. Okay? I'll be prayin' for you. And take that Farm if you can."

He slapped Ray on the back and was then buzzed through the gate to be paroled to house arrest with a monitor around his ankle for three months, but after that, life could start over for Darnell.

Ray sat down across from his mother at the small table in the visitor center. She had put on a lot of weight in the last few years, unhealthy weight, in Ray's opinion, but today she had a big grin on her face. "So whassup, Mom? You look like you won the lottery or somethin'."

"I know. I know. It's because I got some good news." Her eyes widened as though she expected Ray to guess for himself. Finally she reached out and laid her hand on his arm. "It's that we just moved from Rogers Park to Elmhurst. A really nice little apartment, sunny kitchen. And it's only the second floor; even though the number's 3B, they're countin' the garden apartments as one." She fluttered her hand at her face. "I don't think I could make it if I had to climb to the third floor all the time. Oh, Ray, you'll just love it. . . . Oh . . ." Her hand clapped over her mouth. "I'm sorry, baby. But you still need the address. Here, let me write it down for you so you don't forget."

Ray handed a crayon from the paper cup on the table to his mom and she wrote the address on a paper towel. Crayons were the only writing instruments the prison allowed in the visitor center. They didn't want an angry inmate taking someone hostage and threatening to drive a pencil or pen through the visitor's temple if they didn't get their demands.

She started to hand the paper to him, then pulled it back. "Oh yeah. Almost forgot our new phone number." She scribbled for a moment. "Here. Now, you call me anytime. I'll always accept the charges."

Ray folded the paper towel and stuffed it in his pocket. Should he tell her *his* good news, the questions Mr. Gee had raised about his case? No, no! It was too remote . . . and yet . . . No, he wouldn't raise false hopes. "Uh . . . so, Mom, how come you moved?"

"You know . . . don't you? Puts me nearly an hour closer to you. Besides, I had to get Lena away from those friends of hers in Rogers Park or wherever she goes. But she's eighteen now and does whatever she wants. She takes off two or three days at a time, and I have no idea where she is or what she's doing."

"She go back home?"

"I try calling her old friends, but . . ." Ray's mom shrugged. "She's going to end up in as much trouble as you. Think you can talk to her, Ray? You learned the hard way, but maybe you can convince her to turn her life around before she ends up in the same fix. I couldn't take it if both my children . . ." She put her hand over her mouth again.

Ray grimaced. Yeah, he'd speak to his sister, tell her how he'd learned the hard way. But on most days it didn't feel like he had turned his life around. At most he'd stopped making it worse.

It was months before Ray's mother came to visit again—so much for moving closer—but she did manage to drag Lena along with her. Ray stared at his sullen sister. How was he supposed to talk to her? He watched her out of the corner of his eye—looking for some ideal opportunity to speak to her—while the three of them played cards in the visitor center. Finally, when no good opening came and his mother had for the third time frowned at him, nodding her head toward Lena, Ray dove in. "So what's with the look? Why you dress like that?"

Lena scowled at him. "Who, me?"

"Yeah, you. You look like a ho!"

Lena just rolled her eyes and slapped down her hand of cards to stare off in another direction. That was the end of their game of hearts. Ray watched as his mother and sister finally left the room.

Ray felt awful. He'd blown it. His sister probably wouldn't ever come back. But she also made him mad.

Two weeks later Ray got a letter from his mom. She said she wasn't feeling too well. Thought it was nerves; she'd been worrying so much about Lena.

She left right after we got home from visiting you, and she's been back only once that I know of. She came by one day when I was at work and picked up some of her stuff. I've tried calling all her friends again—the numbers she put in the speed dial of the phone—but they say they have no idea where she is. I don't believe them. I think they know, and they're just lying for her. Well, write when you can. Love, Mom.

That evening was chapel, and Mr. Gee gave a teaching on prayer, using the text from Jeremiah that says, "Call to me and I will answer you and tell you great and unsearchable things that you do not know." Ray felt bad that he had not been praying for his sister and his mom, and he promised himself—and God—that he would begin praying more. But the next morning, right after breakfast when he had planned to pray, a guard came to escort Ray to the administration building. Deputy Warden Parker wanted to see him.

Prayer was forgotten. Ray had never talked personally to the deputy warden. The man often gave speeches to the prisoners, like the time he came to the mess hall and explained that there would be no coffee until further notice because someone had tried to smuggle packets of cocaine into the prison in the bags of coffee. *"You'll have to wait until we can find a new source for our coffee, one that puts it in sealed cans so no one can hide contraband in them!"* Ray thought all but the fancy coffee, like Starbucks, came in cans.

"Sit down, Slewinski," the little man said when Ray entered his office. He stabbed a sausage finger at the wooden chair on the far side of his desk. "I just gotta finish this report. Be with you in a minute."

Ray watched the man as he pecked at the keyboard of his computer with one finger from each hand. Finally he tipped his head back so he could look through his bifocals as he moved the mouse and hit the button on it hard enough so his hand sprang into the air.

He leaned back and turned to Ray. "So how's it going?"

"Pretty good, sir."

"You like it in G-House?"

"Yes, sir. It's pretty good."

"And yet you keep turning in these applications for transfer to the Farm." He waved some papers from a folder on his desk.

"Well, yes, sir. I think anyone would prefer the Farm."

The deputy warden frowned, making his mouth form an inverted moon. "I s'pose. Well, we're going to give you your wish, young man, and see how it goes. But you mess up, and we'll yank you right out of there, and with the crowding, there's no telling where we might have to put you." He flipped through some more papers in a thick file. "I see you spent a few days in F-House when you first arrived, so you know the range of accommodations we offer here at Stateville-U." He looked up and grinned at Ray as though he hoped to get a laugh for his lame humor. "Anyway, you'll move on Monday."

"Uh . . . there's a possibility that I might—" What was he doing telling Warden Parker about a remote chance that his case might get reviewed? That was really stupid.

"What was that, son?"

"Never mind, sir. Thank you. I'm lookin' forward to the Farm." Ray sat there blinking his eyes at his near disaster.

"You know, Slewinski, there are psychologists and psychiatrists and palm readers, but no one can judge character better than those of us who work in corrections. So don't try to pull anything on me. Got that?"

Ray nodded.

"Get outta here!" The warden pointed toward the door with his fat finger.

Ray was halfway back to his unit, trying to keep his mind on the present as he walked beside the silent guard. Moving to the Farm, that was great! But he already had one of the best jobs in the prison, working in the infirmary, cleaning up and doing odd jobs. What he really wanted was to get out, and Mr. Gee had raised that possibility. . . .

Reality, Ray! Reality . . . focus on reality, one day at a time. That's the only way to do your time! Moving to the Farm sounded like it was going to happen; that was reality, and Ray ought to be ecstatic! But . . . well, reality sometimes had two sides when you looked it in the eye. He'd been in G-House for over two years. He knew all the men. They came and went, but some had become friends, and others at least left him alone in that tenuous truce rivals reached in prison just to survive. Even his cellmate, Moon Riviera, didn't hassle him, terrifying though he still seemed with the scars all over his face and arms and, as Ray had discovered, his chest and stomach, as well—how could all that be from a street fight? But Ray was not sure what he'd find at the Farm.

Darnell Harrison had promised to pray for this move, and now it seemed like it was going to happen, but did Ray really want it? Maybe if God actually answered prayer, Ray ought to be praying to get released. Besides, the dream of getting out had fewer downsides even though it was just a fantasy.

CHAPTER 23

Arif Nazim, the hack on duty in G-House, hung up the phone and craned his neck to search the common room. "Hey, Slewinski, over here!"

Ray sighed deeply and got up from the green leatherette couch where he had been watching news about the frustrating search for Saddam Hussein and his weapons of mass destruction. He staggered with exaggerated slowness toward the guard booth. "How come, man? I just got back from workin' in the infirmary. I need a break."

Nazim glared at him and held out a slip of paper. "You're supposed to call this number and ask for Amanda Clifford. Then give them this code." He pointed to a four-digit number across the bottom of the slip.

Ray walked over and took the paper. "Hey, I can't read this. What's this number?"

"It's a seven, stupid. Can't you see the little mark across the middle?"

"I see it, but I've never seen a seven written like that. Is that the way you write sevens in Iraq?" Ray turned away. He knew Nazim was Iranian, but so what?

"Slewinski."

Ray looked back over his shoulder. "They said it was an emergency."

"Emergency?"

Nazim shrugged.

The two phones at the end of the unit were both in use, with several men waiting their turn. One was a "People phone." The other for Folks. Most of the seventy Chicago street gangs belonged to one or the other of these two alliances, and though there were significant tensions within the alliances, gangs in the opposing alliance were prime enemies. In spite of formal prison policy to the contrary, the dominant People gang in any housing unit ended up controlling the "People phone," while the dominant Folk gang controlled the "Folk phone." Supposedly, it was a way for everyone to get a chance, though independent gangs like the Aryan Brotherhood as well as neutrons had to negotiate for their turns. In G-House there were more Conservative Vice Lords than any other People set, so they controlled the "People phone," supposedly on behalf of the Latin Kings, El Rukns, and other People gangs. But there was very little tolerance for one another. Nevertheless, out of habit, Ray always went to that phone.

"Hey, man," Ray said in a stage whisper to the man on the phone. "I gotta make an emergency call. Any chance you could call back later?"

"Don't be yankin' my chain, Anglo." The caller was a Conservative Vice Lord, as were the other two men waiting.

"Come on, man. You had plenty of clicks on that phone already. I got some kind of emergency. Need to make a call."

"Emergency? Hey, chump, I thought you were supposed to be a neutron. Neutrons ain't supposed to have emergencies."

The guys in line laughed.

An hour passed while Ray waited for his turn.

Finally Moon Riviera emerged from room 5. "Hey, give the man his turn. He got a 'mergency!"

Everyone stared. All the men in the dayroom stared. No one moved.

"You deaf as well as dumb?"

The Vice Lords looked at one another. "Sure," the guy on the phone said. "No problem, *mon*! 'Specially seein' you his new war daddy." Then the caller turned to the phone. "Sorry, babe. Gotta go. Get back to you later." He hung up, and the Vice Lords drifted away from the phone as though they had never intended to be there in the first place.

Ray looked at Moon and nodded ever so slightly before the big man returned to their cell.

Within a few moments Ray had dialed the number. He could hear a woman's voice on the other end agreeing to accept a collect call from an inmate. It was a voice he did not recognize. When the line finally opened, he asked for Amanda Clifford.

"I'm sorry, she's off duty now. Uh . . . are you really in prison like the recording thing said?" She asked it like she was talking to a celebrity.

"Yes, ma'am. I'm Raymond Slewinski. I got a message that there was some kind of an emergency, and I was supposed to phone this number. This is as soon as I could get through on the phone."

"Raymond Slewinski . . . Raymond Slewinski." Ray could hear papers shuffling on the other end of the phone line. "Ah, here it is. Is your mother Maria Slewinski?"

"Yeah, that's my mom. What's the matter?"

"Could you please verify her birth date?"

"Yeah . . . uh," Ray had to think a minute. "Yeah, August 14 . . . uh, I think it was '59. But why? Is something wrong?"

"Well, this is Elmhurst Memorial Hospital." Her breathy voice made the information sound like a secret. "Your mother was admitted to the hospital this afternoon. . . ." She stopped like she was expecting Ray to finish the sentence.

"How come? Is she okay? What happened?"

"I'm sorry, sir. We cannot give out any details without a patient number. Privacy issues, you know."

"*Patient number?* How come? Listen, just tell me what's happening."

"Like I said, sir, our privacy policy is very strict. It's for the protection of the patients . . . especially since you are in prison—"

"But I'm her son. Can't you just . . . Wait a minute." Ray looked again at the slip of paper Nazim had given him. "Four, three, one, one."

"Almost, sir, but—"

"One, seven. Seven. The last number is a seven."

"That's right, sir. And we thank you." There was silence.

"So . . . tell me about my mom!"

"Of course, sir. She was admitted with what appears to be a hemorrhagic stroke. She's in ICU, but she's conscious for the moment. However, that may change if we can't stop the bleeding in her brain. You should probably come right away. But, of course, you being in prison—"

"Right. Is my sister there? What about her?"

"No. Your mother was brought in alone. We called her brother in Indiana, but so far no one has showed up. We got your number from a card in her wallet. But isn't there some way you could get out of jail for a little while, you know, just to visit?"

"Uh . . . I'll do my best."

Ray dropped the receiver and staggered away from the phone. How could this be? It was true that he hadn't seen his mother for . . . Wow! How long had it been? Time got strange on the inside, sometimes racing past without a person realizing it, sometimes coming to a near standstill. This was August 2003. Ray hadn't heard from his mom for four months, not since she had brought Lena for that disastrous confrontation. His mom had looked okay then, hadn't she? Maybe a little haggard, but . . . but who wouldn't when trying to raise someone like Lena? Now Mom was in the hospital, in intensive care. The woman said some kind of a stroke. She needed Ray. He had to go to her.

"Hey, Nazim, I mean Mr. Nazim, that emergency phone call? Well, it was a real emergency. My mom's in the hospital, and I have to go see her. I need a pass to visit her. Can I go to the warden's office?"

Nazim kept reading his *Playboy*. It would bring him ten bucks when he was finished with it, maybe more.

"Uh . . . Mr. Nazim? I gotta go to the warden's office."

Without glancing up, he said, "Warden doesn't want to see you, you little . . ." He looked up, frowning with squinted eyes. "How do you say it *in this country*? You little . . ." He motioned as though pushing a lever down and said, "*ker-swoosh?*"

Ray stood there a moment. "Hey, I'm sorry 'bout what I said about the seven."

"Good, because that's not the way we write a seven in Arab countries. Our sevens look more like your letter V."

"Yeah, whatever. But I really need to see the warden."

Nazim looked at his watch. "I doubt it would do you any good to go over there now. By the time we got someone to escort you, Parker'd be gone for the day."

"Couldn't you phone ahead and ask him to wait till I get there? Tell him my mom's dying!" Ray hadn't said it in those words before, not even to himself. But was it true? Was she dying?

Nazim stared at him for a few moments. "All right. See what I can do."

"Thanks." Ray paced back through the common room, going from one end to the other. The worst thing about prison was that you were no longer in charge of your life, not even the most crucial aspects of it, like being able to go to your mother when she needed you.

The next time Ray got to the end of the room where the booth was, Nazim said, "Warden's gone for the day. Guess you'll have to wait till tomorrow."

Ray was waiting outside the office when the deputy warden arrived the next morning. The man's eyes looked as puffy behind his glasses as did his fat fingers. "What you doin' here? It's not Monday yet, or have you changed your mind about the Farm?"

Ray followed him into his office without being invited and began explaining his emergency.

Warden Parker sat down in his squeaky chair, laced his fat fingers behind his head, and leaned back. "We don't give leaves just 'cause someone's family member is sick. Otherwise we'd be having half the population out every day. Somebody's always sick."

"But this is a stroke. The hospital said she was in ICU. She might die."

Parker sat there rocking back and forth. "You appear kind of desperate, Slewinski. Desperate men aren't a good security risk. No tellin' what they might do. I'm not sure the Farm is the right place for you unless you can get hold of yourself." He sat there waiting for Ray to respond.

"I'm not a desperate man, sir. I just need to go see my mother."

"But you are desperate, right? Desperate enough to give up the Farm for a trip to the city?"

Ray thought a moment. "I don't think I should have to make that choice, sir. But right now, the most important thing to me is my mom."

The warden rocked forward in his chair. "What you think doesn't matter. If that's your choice, I'll see what I can arrange, but don't count on anything."

"Thank you, boss. Thank you. You'll see. I'm not any kind of a security risk."

"Yes, I'll see. Go back to your unit, but like I said, don't count on anything. First thing I gotta do is confirm with the hospital that you're tellin' the truth. Even then, it usually takes several days to arrange a leave. Gotta find a deputy who's free and a car. Today being Sunday, who knows. . . . So get back to your unit and cool your jets."

Ray tried to "cool his jets," but his mom was in ICU. She needed him. He'd assured the warden that he wasn't any kind of a security risk, but that afternoon when he still hadn't heard from the warden and was at his job in the infirmary, he gritted his teeth and mumbled under his breath, "Prison officials operate mind over matter: They don't mind, and you don't matter!" Nothing made sense. He began fantasizing about ways to escape. *Of course, I'd return, and I wouldn't hurt anyone,* he told himself, *but there's gotta be a way!*

Two weeks before, an older inmate had died while still in prison—died in his sleep, was the word that went around. And his body had laid there on a gurney in the infirmary storage room covered by nothing but a green sheet. It was the first time Ray had been around a dead person. He had nearly freaked out and could hardly force himself to clean the floor in the little side room. But now he began imagining: What if someone died and was brought to the infirmary? What if the body lay there waiting for the morgue or funeral parlor or whoever came to collect it? Wouldn't that be a perfect way to escape? A guy could stuff the body into the utility closet and tie the coroner's tag onto his own big toe, climb up onto the gurney, cover himself with a sheet, and wait to be transported right out of the prison. Who would know? People didn't go around pulling sheets off dead people just to have a look.

Could he do it? Could he touch a dead body, pick it up and stuff it in the closet?

Ah, how stupid! It would never work. The administration wasn't that dumb. As far as Ray knew, no one had escaped from

Stateville since 1942, when mobster Roger "The Terrible" Toughy made it over the wall only to be recaptured three months later during a bloody shootout with the FBI, led by J. Edgar Hoover.

When Ray got back to his unit from work that afternoon, Nazim was on duty again. "Got another call," Nazim said as he buzzed Ray in through the gate.

"Warden's office?"

"No. I think it's the same number you called yesterday. Here." Nazim held out another slip of paper. "Can you read the seven this time?"

Ray took it and didn't even try to respond but headed for the phone. This time the phone was free. His hand trembled as he punched in the numbers. Perhaps his mom was better and was on her way home. He should still go see her. He wouldn't tell the warden she was better. It was legitimate to still consider this an emergency. His mother needed him. He'd just have to convince the deputy sheriff to take him to her house. Or maybe she needed a ride home from the hospital, and the deputy could play taxi driver.

Again, Ray's collect call was accepted. Ray thought it was strange that a hospital would do so, but maybe it was just the same breathless airhead as the day before . . . who probably wouldn't last for too long on the switchboard if she kept it up.

"Hello? This is Raymond Slewinski. I received a message to call you."

"Oh yes, Mr. Slewinski." Her voice dropped like she didn't want anyone to hear her. "One moment. I'll transfer you."

Ray waited and waited until a deep male voice said, "Mr. Slewinski? This is Father Rockford. I'm the chaplain on duty, and I'm very sorry for your loss."

"Loss? What loss?"

"Uh . . . you don't know? I had assumed . . . You mean no one's told you about your mother?"

"I knew she was in the hospital. I was coming to see her, but . . . what do you mean, *loss?*"

"I'm sorry to have to tell you, but your mother has passed. She died about twelve-thirty this afternoon."

"She what? . . . She died? Alone?"

"Oh no. Her brother—your uncle, I guess, an Alex Kovacsik, or something like that, from Indiana was here."

Ray dropped the receiver and turned. He looked around at the four walls, at the bars, at the guys playing cards, at the guard. He had learned how to survive in here. But now the same prison that had become like a womb to him had turned and destroyed his outside world, the memories and images that kept him sane.

Ray's mother had needed him, but he could not go. She had died, and he could not even imagine it.

CHAPTER 24

Ray hung up even while the chaplain was trying to say something more about offering his condolences or something.

The slight smell of the dead man in the prison infirmary came back to Ray, not rotten like an old carcass, but different, like something he had never encountered before. Did his mother smell like that now? He hoped not. He remembered her smelling faintly of the Jovan Island Gardenia she sometimes wore. He didn't really like it, but now it was the scent of freedom to him.

Ray shook himself and drifted away from the phone. Why was he even thinking of how she smelled? How morbid! She couldn't be dead.

It must have been a cruel hoax. His mother had to be fine. Maybe that airhead was playing with his mind, having a big laugh with her friends. She could have picked his name at random off the Illinois Department of Corrections Web site and called claiming to be from the hospital. Yeah, that had to be it. No hospital would have accepted a collect phone call from a prison inmate. If it had been a real emergency, the news would have come through the warden. Right? By now Warden Parker would have checked his story about a sick mother. He must be furious at Ray for trying to stage a phony trip.

But who was that "chaplain" who came on the line offering his condolences? And how did that airhead know his mother's name? It didn't make sense.

Ray's heart was pounding, skipping beats, causing him to gasp for breath.

"I gotta go see the warden," he yelled. "I gotta go see the warden right now."

Prison policy allows for inmates to attend funerals of immediate family members—at the discretion of the warden—provided the round trip can be made within one day, if a prison officer or deputy sheriff is available to escort the inmate, and if the inmate's escape risk ranks medium or lower.

"I think you qualify on the distance to Elmhurst and your escape risk is low," explained Deputy Warden Parker as Ray sat dazed in his office. "But I can't say about the other variables. We'll have to work on 'em.

"Uh . . . hey, Slewinski?" The warden moved his head from side to side across Ray's line of sight. "You trackin' with me here, son? Look, I'm sorry you lost your mother, but don't let this get you off course. I've been in corrections a long time, and a death in the family can often throw a man, cause him to lose his focus, do things he wouldn't ordinarily do. So I'm going to keep you in G-House until you've stabilized. Know what I mean? No Farm for now, okay?"

That was all the warden had to say before he ushered Ray out to be escorted back to his unit. Ray felt like a fly ball that had been hit into left field, floating through the air, on its way down. Now there was no question about his mother having died. But would Ray even be able to attend the funeral? He was unaware of walking down the hall, hearing the gates buzz open and closed behind him, following the guard back to his unit. Even the fact that some of the Conservative Vice Lords were standing outside his cell, yelling at Moon and daring him to come out and "get what's comin' to ya!" didn't phase Ray as he walked past them and went in to flop on his bunk.

An hour later the CVs had given up, but Ray hadn't been able to remain on his bunk more than twenty seconds. Moon said, "Chillax, man. How come you can't sit still? You like some four-year-old."

Ray sat down again . . . for the tenth time, feeling electricity buzzing through him. "I just wish he'd told me whether I can go or not. It'd be easier to deal with being told no than with this uncertainty."

"Ya think so, huh? Don't be so sure. Right now there's at least a little part of you that has hope, and that hope keeps your rage in check. Without hope you could let your rage fly and even have someone to focus it on. You could feel sorry for yourself while you hated the deputy warden. You may think that would feel good, but it's all negative and won't get you nowhere. You're better off learning how to suck up the tension, 'cause hope—even a trace of it—is a rare thing, especially in here."

Ray sat down on his bunk. Moon was right.

Whether he was to go to the funeral remained uncertain for the whole week, until at the last minute, on Sunday morning, Ray was summoned to the front gate, where a Cook County Deputy Sheriff was waiting with a car just inside the gate. A prison social worker provided Ray with a poorly fitting used suit and some street shoes. Ray felt almost human, but the deputy insisted on putting four-piece shackles on him. Wasn't it enough that he would arrive at the funeral home in a marked Cook County Sheriff's car accompanied by a deputy in full uniform?

"Hey, man, do I gotta wear these when we go in?"

"We'll see when we get there. I need to reconnoiter the premises first. Last funeral I was at was for a kid younger than you who got shot on the streets. His whole posse attended, and guess what? Some rivals drove by in a war wagon and sprayed the place with a MAC-10! Can you believe it? So I gotta know what I'm walkin' into before I relax any security. Who knows, you might have a bunch of—what's your set, anyway?—doesn't matter, you might have a bunch of your boys from your crew there wantin' to spring you. I take no chances!"

The deputy was a chatterbox, talking all the way to the city. Ray feigned interest in hopes of getting on his good side, but he couldn't care less what the man had to say, whether it was about the White Sox or the weather or the war in Iraq. From the backseat, behind the wire divider, Ray mumbled "Yeah," "Uh-huh," "You might be right," "Uh-huh," just often enough so the guy didn't think he was asleep.

But Ray's mind was years away in a place that seemed like another universe, one that vacillated between vivid memories of his mom and sister and himself living in their apartment, sometimes fighting, sometimes ignoring one another, but together, nonetheless. Then his mind would flip to far more foggy, unreal images of the day of the shooting: blood spurting, pedaling away like a maniac on the bike, throwing it in the back of the Dumpster, and then the cops coming to question him until he confessed in that stark eight-by-ten-foot cell at the 24th District station. Ah, that scene was vivid—the two rings embedded in the concrete floor, the steel bench mounted to the wall. What was that cop's name? He couldn't remember, but he did remember Officer Percell, the stout African-American woman with half-moon glasses and short, cropped hair tinged red at the tips, red like blood! In that scene Ray flamed out, confessed the shooting, and watched his life go up in smoke. Is that what Mr. Gee meant when he said that the devil "comes only to steal and kill and destroy"? If so, he certainly had succeeded in Ray's case, killing Greg Mason and stealing Ray's freedom. Steal, kill, and destroy! It sure felt like it as Ray rode shackled in the back of a cop car to his own mother's funeral.

Ray watched the strip malls and monotonous warehouses of Chicago's suburbs slide by the car window. What had the devil left him but thirty-four more years of misery? And yet Mr. Gee had read the rest of that verse where Jesus said, "I have come that they may have life, and have it to the full." How could that be? Was that just true for the "good" people of this world? Ray couldn't believe it included him. He believed God had forgiven him in a spiritual sense and would grant him eternal life, but what about this life? He couldn't even forgive himself. He belonged in prison. He had a debt to pay society. And yet . . .

He came to pay a debt he didn't owe,
Because I owed a debt I couldn't pay!
What did it mean? How far could forgiveness go?

The deputy left Ray locked in the back of his car while he went into Gibbon's Funeral Home to "peruse the scene," as he called it. Ten minutes later—why did it take so long?—he returned.

"Okay, this is the situation. We got here just in time. They're about ready to start. So I'm going to release you from the four-piece, and we'll walk in together. It's the little chapel to the left as soon as we enter the front door. I'll remain standing in the back of the room. You can go down front and view the remains, then take a seat on the front row reserved for the family. I'll be watching you the whole time during the service. When it's over, come back and check in with me before talking to anyone. Understood?"

"Yeah, but I gotta take a piss."

"Sure, but I'll be going with you, and I can't guarantee they won't close the casket before we get in there. You might not get to see the remains."

The remains, what a gross way to speak of Ray's mother!

"Well, I still gotta take a piss."

The deputy opened the back door and unlocked Ray's shackles. "Uh, on second thought, it don't seem natural to me that someone who was so eager to attend his mother's funeral would pass up an opportunity to see her. You wouldn't be thinkin' 'bout boltin' or nothin', would you?"

"No way, but I just cain't hold it no more. So can we go in now?"

"Okay. But if you give me any trouble, I'll throw you back in here so fast your eyeballs will be left behind, and we'll be outta here. In fact, you need to know this: I wouldn't hesitate a cat's breath to shoot you if you tried to flee. You got that?"

"Yeah."

There were only about a dozen people in the small chapel. Taped organ music crackled through tinny speakers. Ray avoided looking at the casket as he walked slowly toward the front. Some of the guests looked up at him. He recognized a couple from the old Rogers Park neighborhood, but they looked away quickly, probably not knowing how to respond to a murderer.

Finally Ray was close enough that he could not avoid looking at the casket, and his attention became riveted on what was within. The lid was up on one end, and Ray didn't know if he dared to look. Would it be his mother? He glided forward slowly until he could see a forehead and a bit of hair—it was her color—and a nose—it was the shape of his mom's nose. And then he could see her face! It was, but it wasn't Mom. Maybe it was her sister. Did he have an aunt? He had an uncle—his Uncle Alex—but . . . By this time Ray was at the edge of the casket.

The more he stared, the more he realized that it had to be his mother's body. There was the familiar small mole to the left of her eye, and the clothes were hers. He recognized the earrings and glasses and dress. But the skin looked so . . . so dead, and her cheeks had sagged down to make her neck look fat. It was her, but she was gone, really gone!

Ray reached out to touch the hands crossed on her chest. They were cold, stiff, and leathery, not at all like the soft warm hands of his mother. She was gone! Tears spilled over the brim of his eyes, and he sniffed hard.

Ray had no idea how long he stood there. A stranger wearing white gloves and dressed in a black suit touched Ray on the arm. "I'm sorry, sir, we need to close the lid and begin."

Ray looked around. "Where's the priest?"

"Her brother didn't arrange for a Catholic funeral. He said she didn't need one."

Ray turned and stared at the front row. There sat Uncle Alex and his wife, Catherine, and Ray's sister, Lena.

"Excuse me, sir. Are you family?"

Ray glanced to the back of the room where the deputy stood, arms crossed, scowling at him. "Yeah. My mom."

"Then why don't you have a seat over here with the other family members." He guided Ray by the elbow to sit by Lena in the front row.

When Ray looked back, the lid of the casket was closed and the funeral director was reading some generic, nonsectarian service that meant nothing to Ray. How had it come to this? No reference to God. No promise of eternal life. No real comfort for the family.

Ray should have been there. He should have been there for his mom. Instead, he had been stuck in prison, unable to be with her in her last hours, not even able to help arrange for her funeral.

Before he knew it the service was over. Ray looked at his sister, tears in his own eyes blurring her image. He swiped his wrists across his eyes. Her clothes were appropriate enough for a funeral, but she looked as hard and rough as concrete—her once shiny ebony hair died dead black, heavy makeup, and an eyebrow ring. "So are you going to stay in the apartment?"

"Why would I want to? Besides, there's no way I could afford the rent."

"What are you going to do, then?"

Lena shrugged. "I got friends."

"I bet." Ray looked her up and down. "What's the matter with you, anyway?"

"Whaddaya mean?" She rolled her eyes. "What do you expect? Mama just died."

"Yeah but . . . you look so goth, like death warmed over." He pointed to his own eyebrow but nodded toward her.

With an empty stare, she opened her mouth, letting her tongue loll out to reveal a silver stud through the middle. "Plus I got three more rings where the sun don't shine . . . at least not usually!" She turned and walked away.

Ray turned to his Uncle Alex and shrugged. Then he glanced at the deputy standing at the back. The deputy gestured for him to come . . . NOW!

"Uncle Alex, Aunt Catherine, thanks for helping out."

"Well, if you'd been here—"

"Sorry. Gotta go." The deputy's inflexible insistence that he leave immediately after the service didn't seem so ruthless after all.

To Ray's relief, the deputy sheriff didn't try to carry on a conversation while driving back out to Stateville. He just listened to the White Sox beat the Oakland Athletics, 5 to 1. "How 'bout that?" the deputy said as he guided the cruiser off I-80 and north into Joliet. "Loaiza retired seventeen out of eighteen batters between the second and seventh innings. I guess he's provin' the critics wrong. I can see the White Sox goin' all the way."

Ray didn't respond. His mind was still back with his mother. Where was she now? Ray had found faith in Jesus, but that had never seemed important to his mother. Maybe he should have told her. Why hadn't he told her? What if she was—?

"Hey, want a Big Mac or something?" The deputy was looking at Ray through the rearview mirror. "We can use the drive-through. I'm not supposed to make any stops, but if neither of us gets out, they can't really call it a stop, can they?"

"Huh . . . Big Mac?" Ray hadn't had one in eight years. "Yeah, but I didn't bring no money."

"It's on me. Besides, we might not get you back in time for chow. What time they serve out there, anyway?"

"Usually from five to seven. They cycle different units through."

"So you want one or not?"

"Sure."

The deputy made a right turn and looked up at Ray in the mirror again. "I know how you feel, kid. Lost my mom year before last . . . Alzheimer's, so I didn't really have her with me, if you know what I mean, for five years before that."

Ray stared at the back of the deputy's head, short hair flecked with gray. It had been over six years since he had been able to enjoy being with his mom, even though she visited him as often as possible. Visits in prison only reminded you of home; they weren't like home. Maybe Alzheimer's was like that. Ray had heard it said that sometimes a person with Alzheimer's has good days when they can remember things and act nearly normal but then bad days. And they "visit" the real world less and less often.

"Sorry 'bout your mother," Ray said to the deputy. He remained quiet for a few moments, thinking about the analogy. "My mom used to visit regular, but lately it was longer and longer between when she came. I hardly noticed the change and had no idea this was gonna happen." Why had he never talked to her about God?

The deputy swung in at the sign of the Golden Arches and stopped at the two-way speaker. "Okay. Whaddaya want? Big Mac, fries, Coke? The whole meal?"

CHAPTER 25

Deputy Warden Parker had been right. Ray had to admit it: "A *death in the family can often throw a man, cause him to lose his focus, do things he wouldn't ordinarily do.*" But Ray didn't care. He wasn't going to start a riot or attack some guard or try to escape. Nothing like that. He just sat. Whenever he wasn't required to be somewhere doing something mandatory, he sat. He sat on his bunk in his cell.

"So what you lookin' at, chump?" Moon challenged.

"Nothin'."

"Then go look at nothin' someplace else. You creep me out!"

Ray got up, went out to the common room, and flopped on the couch . . . and stared.

"Hey, you watchin' TV or not?" challenged one of the Conservative Vice Lords.

Ray shook his head.

"Then get off the couch so we can watch the game!"

Ray moved to the chair by the magazine stand, but he didn't pick one up to read it. He just sat.

It kept on like that, day after day, for weeks. He went to work. He went to chow—though he didn't eat much—but he did very little else. He seldom shaved and let his hair go wild, and he dropped out of attending chapel or reading his Bible. After all, where was God in all this? Several times Mr. Gee sent word that he would like to see Ray, but Ray didn't respond, didn't list him as an approved visitor. Why should he?

One day Ray tried to phone his sister. All he got was a recorded message: "We're sorry, but this number is temporarily out of service." Well, she'd said she wouldn't be staying in Mom's apartment, but Ray had hoped she might change her mind. Where else could she go? And how was he supposed to get in touch with her? He retreated to his cell and flopped on his bunk, burying his face in his crooked arm so if Moon came in he wouldn't see the tears streaming from Ray's eyes. He'd lost his family. How had that happened? Family was one thing that had kept him going while he did his time, or at least that's what he told himself. *Mama's still there. And she's working hard and taking care of my sister. Someday my dad'll show up. Maybe when I get out, we can all get it back together.*

None of that was true anymore . . . if it ever had been. Now his mother was dead, he couldn't reach his sister, and he had no idea where his father was. Maybe his uncle . . . no, his uncle had never liked him, and Ray didn't have an address or phone number for him anyway. Just somewhere in Indiana . . . Michigan City, last time Ray had heard.

Ray had made such a mess of his life, and even prayer didn't seem to help—not that he'd been praying much since his mother died. Maybe this was all a bad dream, a nightmare. What if he hadn't pulled the trigger that day?

What if something snapped inside my head that day and I just thought I'd shot Greg? What if I was holding the gun but couldn't pull the trigger? Rico was mocking me, egging me on, but maybe I didn't actually pull the trigger. But then the memory of the gushing blood flooded his mind. No, it was too real. Greg had been shot, right in the chest!

But maybe, maybe not by me. What if I just froze until Rico grabbed the gun from my hand, pulled the trigger, and then said, "There, that's the way it's done," as he slapped the gun back into my hand and rode off yelling, "Come on, man. Let's get outta here. Five-Os be comin'!"

Ray recalled the police coming to his house and taking him to the station. But they also picked up Rico. He knew that now. *Maybe Rico rolled on me from the first, and that's why the cops drilled me so hard, until . . . until I panicked and confessed. Panic can screw up a guy's mind, cause me to think that I actually did it when I hadn't. Maybe all these years I've been imagining something that I didn't really do. Yeah, I think Rico shot him!*

Then he fled. The other guys in the car saw that I had the gun in my hand, but they didn't see Rico slap it there. And there was one guy in the car who wasn't sure that it was me—that's because Rico did the shooting. Rico said, "Come on, man. Let's get outta here." But I shouldn't have run. That's what made me look guilty. Of course that's what the onlookers saw. What could I do with a gun in my hand? I dropped it in my pants and rode off on my bike.

Ray recalled the crazy ride down the street, seeing the garbage truck, and tossing the gun in—and the bike—before he went home. *Yeah, that's what happened. What else could I do? But from the time I got home until the cops made me confess, I maintained that I didn't shoot anyone. That's gotta be because I didn't do it!*

"Ray . . . hey, Ray! What da matter wit' you, man?"

Ray sat up to look into Moon's scarred face. "Uh?"

"You layin' there shakin' like you havin' some kind of a fit or somethin'. You okay?"

"Yeah. I guess so."

"Man, you gotta get holda yo'self. You trippin' out. You cain't let 'em mess wit yo' mind, 'cause that's all you got! Know what I mean?"

Ray nodded, but the possibility that he had not done the shooting swirled in his head. "You know, Moon, I don't think I killed that kid. I think Rico did it, and I think the cops scared me so bad that I confessed. You know, I was just a kid."

Moon stared at him for several moments, then shook his head. "Huh. I can't tell you whether you wasted that guy or not. Here on the mainline, everybody claims to be innocent . . . 'less they frontin' a rep. But there's something else that happens on the inside: Everyone breaks. Sometimes after a couple years, sometimes not until ten years, but sooner or later, everyone breaks!"

"Yeah, I heard about that. But that ain't me." Ray recalled the time he was in the hole at Joliet. He had kept his mind active so he wouldn't break. But what was happening to him now? "So whaddaya gettin' at, Moon?"

Moon stripped off his shirt and wrapped a towel around his waist, getting ready to go to the shower. "It just gets too much and you crack. You cain't help it. I seen some guys freak out and start fightin' everyone around 'em. I seen others go catatonic—or whatever that word is—and not be able to speak or do nothin'. It happens. Maybe that happenin' to you."

Ray stared at Moon, distracted by the ragged pink scars that crossed the front of his body. "What happened . . . ?"

"Hey, I ain't tryin' to get all up in yo' biznezz or nothin', but it's somethin' to think about."

Ray wiped a thin film of sweat from his forehead. Moon probably didn't want to talk about that fight. And as for himself, nah, he wasn't cracking up. He was just trying to figure out the truth. And the more he thought about it, the more he began to wonder whether the whole system had sold him a wolf ticket. What was the truth?

Mail? Someone had sent Ray a card? No one sent him mail anymore. There was no one out there to send him mail . . . unless it was Connie Mason sending him another Christmas card. He brushed aside that fantasy. Even though Christmas was coming, he hadn't heard from her in five years. Ray ripped open the card and read: *"We've been missing you in chapel. Is everything okay? Drop in and see me this Friday; I have some news for you.–Harvey Geevers."*

Mr. Gee had written to him? Memories of chapel, of God and Jesus swirled in Ray's mind. It all seemed so remote, like something from another life, like life on the outside. And that wasn't such an unrealistic comparison. Ray had experienced something different after becoming a Christian, a strange freedom in being connected to God through prayer and the Bible, like some kind of pipeline that freed his spirit even though his body remained incarcerated. But all that had faded away since his mom had died. Could he get it back? Harrison had said something. What was it? *"A guy can turn around if he wants to. And God does forgive! It's in the Bible."* Yeah, Darnell had mentioned the story of the Prodigal Son. After two years of chapels and some Bible correspondence courses, Ray knew the story almost by heart. Nevertheless, he pulled his Bible off the shelf—where he had left it for the past month—and turned to Luke, chapter fifteen, and began reading from verse eleven.

Tears came to Ray's eyes when he got to the part where the father had joyfully welcomed his wayward son home. "For this son of mine was dead and is alive again; he was lost and is found." Ray hadn't intended to turn his back on God. It was just that with the pressure and grief of his mother's death, he had neglected his relationship instead of going to God for comfort and strength.

But God had not forgotten him. Ray picked up Mr. Gee's card and realized that God was reaching out to him, inviting him home. Then Ray looked at Mr. Gee's message more carefully: *"I have some news for you."* What could that be about? Ray would go to chapel tomorrow and find out, and, if he could get some time alone with Mr. Gee, Ray would tell him about this possibility that he had not really pulled the trigger. Maybe Mr. Gee could help him sort it all out.

"Hey, Mr. Gee, you got some time?"

"For you, I've always got time. What's been happening? I've been worried about you. Haven't seen you for months. You don't come to chapel. You don't put me on your visitor list. Did I do something to make you mad at me?"

"Nah, nothin' like that." Ray told him about his mother's death and how he couldn't seem to shake the cloud that hung over him afterward. "But maybe it's all for the best."

Mr. Gee frowned in disbelief.

Even though they sat in chairs at the side of the classroom where the Captives Free Ministries volunteers couldn't overhear them, Ray looked around nervously. "You see, I been thinkin' 'bout my case. And maybe I didn't pull the trigger. So maybe I didn't kill that kid after all." Ray stopped to see how Mr. Gee would respond.

Mr. Gee looked down and scratched his head, making his toupee move slightly. When he looked up into Ray's eyes, Mr. Gee's lower lip protruded and he frowned. "Well, somebody killed him."

"Yeah, but that's the thing. I think it might have been Rico, the gangbanger who was egging me on. Maybe I couldn't pull the trigger, so he grabbed the gun from my hand, shot the kid, and then slammed the gun back into my hand." Ray leaned forward and held his breath.

"Is that what happened, Ray?"

Ray's shoulders sagged and he exhaled like a leaky tire. After several moments his voice rumbled barely above a whisper, "I don't know." Then with more enthusiasm: "But it might have happened that way. Rico was really the one who wanted me to shoot him. I didn't have nothin' against the kid. In fact, I don't even have anything against GDs. It was just that they are a rival set."

"Then where'd all this come from? This idea that Rico might have done it?"

"I dunno, Mr. Gee. It just came on me after Mom died. I couldn't help her, and now I don't know where my sister is. Our whole family's fallen apart. We don't even exist anymore."

"Yeah, that's tough. That's one of the toughest things about being inside. You can't help. You can't be there." The chaplain stopped, leaned forward with his elbows on his knees, and folded his hands in front of himself. "I gotta ask you this, Ray—" This time he was the one who looked around the room to see if anyone was listening. "Did you shoot that kid or not? Don't play with me, and don't play with yourself."

Ray exhaled again and was quiet a long time. But when he answered, his voice was clear. "Yeah. Guess I did it."

"You sure?"

"Yeah, but I ain't proud of it. I wish I hadn't done it."

"I know. I know, Ray. I've never doubted the sincerity of your repentance. But listen to me. It's important—important to you—that you hang on to reality. We're talking about more than the truth for its own sake here. We're talking about your sanity. If you lose hold of the truth, as painful as it is, only God can bring you back. Do you understand what I'm saying?"

"Yes, sir."

"Okay." Mr. Gee leaned back. "There's something else I wanted to mention to you. You remember last spring when I asked you about your case and wanted to know exactly how old you were?"

"Yeah."

"Well, our attorney friend, Mr. Sondano, has been looking into it, and he wants to come out and interview you. You up for that?"

"You kiddin'? I mean, yes, sir. I'll put him on my visitor list right away."

"Now, don't let your hopes carry you away. Like I was saying, keep a grip on reality, and right now, your reality is that you are working off a forty-year sentence."

Ray grinned. "Yeah, but I got life."

CHAPTER 26

Alan Sondano was a balding Swede who over the years had allowed his large, soft body to sag into the shape of a pear. But according to Mr. Gee, his mind was a virtual law library and his courtroom savvy was seldom outflanked. If a case could be made, Alan Sondano was the man to do it.

He sat across the table from Ray in one of the small attorney-client conference rooms in Stateville's administration building.

"So Harvey Geevers says you were fourteen when this shooting took place. Is that correct?"

"Yes, sir."

"Then why were you booked as a fifteen-year-old?"

Ray frowned as he tried to remember. "I guess I always passed as fifteen—"

"Wait a minute. You couldn't have always passed as fifteen. You were a baby, a little boy; you weren't always fifteen. So go back and start from the beginning. I need to know everything, every little detail."

Ray closed his eyes and held his forehead, elbow on the table. Then he took a deep breath and looked up at the attorney. "I was born on July 10, 1982, but my father left the family shortly after we moved to Chicago from Michigan City, Indiana. I think that's where my uncle still lives. It's less than fifty miles around the bottom of the lake."

"Yeah, I know where Michigan City is." Sondano waved his hand for Ray to get on with it.

"Anyway, I was only four at the time, and Mom couldn't afford to pay for two kids in day care, so she put Lena in the nursery school and enrolled me in kindergarten—"

"At the age of only four years?"

"Yeah. But she convinced them that I was five years old and just a little small for my age. I guess I was kinda verbal and acted a lot older. So she told them I was born on July 10, 1981, and apparently they believed her, 'cause from then on, all my school records showed my birth date as July 10, 1981."

"R-i-ight." Sondano dragged out the word as he flipped through the thick document in front of him and frowned. "And I see from your trial transcript that they confirmed your age by your school records. Is that right?"

Ray nodded.

"But why did the police think you were fifteen in the first place?"

"I told 'em. Like I said, I'd been passing for fifteen. I didn't think it mattered. It just came natural, so when I first got picked up, that's what I said."

"Didn't you ever correct them, tell them you were only fourteen?"

Ray punched a finger in the air as though ringing a doorbell. "Yeah. Yeah, I did, when they actually booked me, but the cop saw '81 on the other form, my initial intake form. He asked what my school records said, and that's what he went by."

"Yes." Sondano ran his hand over his shiny head fenced by a band of thin blond hair. "And those are the very records the DA used in court to prove you were fifteen, which is what got you automatically tried as an adult. Did you know that?"

Ray shrugged.

Sondano opened an envelope and pulled out an official-looking certificate, which he unfolded and showed to Ray, displaying an embossed seal and fancy writing. "This is a certified copy of your birth certificate from the La Porte County Health Department in Michigan City, Indiana. It shows your true birth date as being July 10, 1982. So you were right, you were only fourteen when the incident for which you were convicted took place."

Ray reached out and took his birth certificate. It was a record of himself, written the day he came into the world. There was his father's name and occupation: *Antoni Otto Slewinski, steel mill worker*. And his mother's: *Maria Ewa Kovacsik, housewife*. And the date and time of his own birth: *Raymond Peter Slewinski, July 10, 1982, 4:36 a.m., 8 pounds, 11 ounces.*

Looking at it gave Ray a sense of connection to the day when a kicking, pink boy had come into the world giving his parents joy and hope for the future. He imagined how proud they must have been. He had seen a copy of this certificate before, in the baby book his mother kept on the top shelf of her closet. It was followed by happy pictures of him—held up by his smiling father, in his mother's arms, naked in the kitchen sink bath, with a double chin as he sat propped up on pillows by a Christmas tree. What had happened to all that hope? What—even—had happened to that baby book and all of his mother's keepsakes? Perhaps lost forever.

"Ray . . . Ray, I asked you if you understand why your birth date matters."

"Uh, not really."

"Let me explain. Illinois law dictates that any minor over fifteen charged with an offense as serious as first-degree murder, armed robbery with a firearm, aggravated criminal sexual assault, etc., is to be transferred automatically to adult criminal court. That is what happened to you because they thought you were fifteen. Minors who have not yet reached the age of fifteen can *also* be transferred, but not automatically. They are entitled to a hearing on the question, a hearing where a judge must decide whether to order the transfer. The judge would consider the accused's history of delinquency, school records, psychological evaluations, level of participation in the offense, testimony of teachers, clergy, even family members. Now, you might not have scored very high on some of those, but you did not get such a hearing or the benefit of a judicial decision."

For a moment, Ray's hopes swelled, and then he thought of the judge he had first appeared before, Judge Gregory Romano, as he recalled. "My PD said the judge was a fair man, but I doubt he would have cut me any slack. He'd have sent me to adult court anyway."

"Perhaps. But nonetheless, you were deprived of due process, and I think we may be able to get your case reviewed on that basis. How old are you now?"

"Twenty-one."

"You turned twenty-one last June?"

"Yeah."

"And how long have you been incarcerated?"

"I been locked up for . . ." Ray closed his eyes and frowned for a moment. " . . . for 2,408 days."

"Ri-i-ght!" Sondano smiled and shook his head. "I'm surprised you didn't give it to me in hours. Now, break it down so a civilian can understand."

"A little over six and a half years." Ray extended both hands, palms up. "But what I don't understand is what good it would do me to get a review on whether I should have been tried in adult or juvenile court. Given my confession, which my PD did everything she could to get it thrown out, I'd still have been convicted even in juvenile court."

"I hate to say it, but your PD was focusing on the wrong issue at the wrong time. Even before it was clear that you were going to be convicted, she should have made sure you were positioned to spend the least amount of time possible *should* you get convicted. In order to do that, she first should have concentrated on making sure you didn't get tried as an adult. Then she could have worked on getting your confession thrown out."

"But you said a judge still might have sent me to adult court. And I think that's exactly what Judge Romano would have done."

"No one knows that for certain, and that's where we can ask for redress. Because if he had sent you to juvenile court and even if you were convicted—which you probably would have been—the state could have held you only until your twenty-first birthday. Then they would have had to let you go."

Ray's eyes widened. "You mean . . . I would be out now?" Ray felt like he was riding on a Tilt-A-Whirl.

"Yes, as long as you didn't get convicted of any other crime while you were in prison, crimes that might have tacked on additional time as an adult offense."

"Well, I haven't." Ray recalled the time he got thrown in the hole. But that was a disciplinary event, not a crime. "No, no other convictions."

"I know. I've checked on everything about you." Sondano smiled, and Ray couldn't tell whether it was a smile of kindness or the grin of someone who had all his ducks in a row. But maybe it didn't matter; either way, it was in Ray's interest. But—he felt the ground crumble beneath him—what if he had committed another crime after he turned fifteen? Ray's mind raced through how many times he came close to getting in trouble since being locked up — the time he cracked Doug Davenport with a soap-sock, trying to grab leadership of the Kings, nearly seeking vengeance on McAfee, almost getting framed for the same, even that stupid idea of trying to escape by taking the place of a corpse. It was like somebody had protected him from all those things.

Maybe Somebody had!

Ray came out of his reverie. "If you can get me a review, will they have to let me out?"

"Not hardly. This is just the first step on a very long and precarious path. But I need to know: Do you want to start down that path . . . with all its uncertainties?"

"Do I? Of course I do!"

Ray walked back to his unit behind the escort guard. The northwest wind dropped in over Stateville's thirty-foot gray wall and peppered Ray's exposed skin with freezing rain and snow, but he hardly noticed. *Out at twenty-one.* He'd have been out for more than six months by now. *Let's see, how many freedom days would that be? No, I wouldn't have to count days anymore. How many days isn't the right question. The question is, what would I be doin' now? Would I have a girl? A car? A crib? Yeah, a really cool loft somewhere. And I could paint the walls whatever color I wanted, eat whenever I wanted . . . whatever I wanted!*

The glee of it all brought tears to Ray's eyes until he didn't see the crack in the walk and stumbled, causing the hack to wheel around and whip out his riot stick until Ray righted himself and held up both hands, palms out. "Just tripped, man. Stay cool."

"Don't be telling me to stay cool. Just watch where you're going. And hurry it up. I don't like being out here suckin' up this arctic sweat!"

Ray didn't either, but he'd walk a mile—even an extra mile—if the guard asked him to, he was so happy. Of course, the hack hadn't done anything for him except threaten to crack his head open, but Ray was feeling grateful, grateful to be alive, grateful for the possibility of a review, grateful that he might get out. It was amazing how your perspective can change everything. He had his hope back, the hope Moon had warned him never to lose.

When Ray got back to his cell, Moon was out, so he closed the door and sat down on his cot. He was feeling so grateful! To whom did he owe thanks? It was God. It had to be God. Ray leaned forward with his head in his hands. "Oh, God, how could I have drifted away from you like I did? How could I think you didn't care? You were protecting me from committing all those crimes while I've been in here. Now I know you're making a way for me out of no way, God. I can feel it in my bones, and I'm sorry for ever doubting you."

Two weeks later—two weeks filled with anticipation and hope that bubbled up in Ray like a broken water main in the street that no one could cap—Ray noticed an announcement on the bulletin board for a House of Healing program. Over the years theories about criminal justice had changed from trying to rehabilitate offenders to merely separating them from the community as punishment. And so there was very little left of the old rehab efforts. But since most offenders return to the community at some point, the House of Healing Programs hung on, designed to help inmates prepare for civilian life before they got out. Darnell Harrison had taken one before he was paroled and had said it was pretty much a joke in terms of getting a guy ready for life on the streets: "Mostly all they do is warn you of all the things that can go wrong. Very depressing." Nevertheless, attendance was open, and Ray knew that some inmates took the class even though they weren't scheduled for release. It was something to do. Ray had never gone because he had so many years left on his sentence and hadn't wanted to fill his mind with dreams of the street. He had even done his best to quit thinking about women, because they weren't going to happen for him.

But now, now things were different! He might have been out by now. He'd better get himself ready. So on Wednesday evening, Ray, along with three other short-timers from Unit 4, followed Philip Coleman over to the classroom where the House of Healing program was to be held.

"Whaddaya think you're doin', Slewinski?" the guard said as they walked across the yard, weaving in and out of the high chain-link barriers. "You ain't gettin' out any time soon."

"Maybe not, but there's a chance—I mean . . . just thought I'd check it out. Anything wrong with that?"

"Nothing that I'm aware of. Just seems a little out of your universe, that's all." Coleman turned away and picked up his pace.

The session was organized and moderated by some of the prison chaplaincy staff, though not anybody from Captives Free Ministries. It began with a volunteer from McDonald's University talking about how to get and keep a job. Apparently, the famous fast-food franchise had made a recent commitment to helping ex-offenders integrate back into the community. This presentation was followed by a boring and seemingly bored parole officer who explained what happens if a man doesn't report at his scheduled check-ins and what happens if he fails to pass his drug screening tests.

Finally the chaplain said he was pleased to introduce their special guest of the evening. "Let's give it up for none other than State's Attorney Peter Musselman." A lame *pat, pat, pat*—mostly from the chaplain—was the only applause the DA received, but Ray recognized the name and a moment later knew why: The tall, thin man with a short-cropped dark beard outlining his jaw was the DA who had prosecuted Ray almost seven years earlier. In that time Musselman had graduated from an assistant DA to full-fledged, elected state's attorney.

"Gentlemen," he began, surveying the room and letting his gaze rest a moment too long on Ray, "I'm pleased to be here this evening because some of you are going to make it and fit back into your community as useful members of society." He looked around again with a narrow-eyed smile on his face. "However, I'm sorry to say that the majority of you—86 percent, according to the most recent figures—will fail. And I will be the one to throw your sorry butts right back in the slammer when you do!"

Ray didn't hear any more of what the DA had to say as he realized that his threats came from the same glee with which Musselman had prosecuted him in the first place.

After the session Ray tried to make his way out without acknowledging Musselman, but the inmates were dismissed by rows, and it was Musselman who zeroed in on Ray and came right toward him.

"You," he said, pointing. "I want to talk to you."

Ray took a deep breath, peeled off from his row of men, and went over to the smartly dressed DA. "Yes, sir."

"I heard some fancy do-good lawyer is trying to pull a trick out of the bag to get you released. You don't deserve to be out of here. You still owe society a big debt. So don't try it! I'll snatch you off the streets in twenty-four hours, and you know I can do it!"

CHAPTER 27

The close, warm air of the unit stung Ray's cold cheeks as he stood in the vestibule cage waiting for the house screw to buzz him in. Arif Nazim was on duty again and acted like punching one button was far beyond his call of duty. So Ray stood there. He was in no mood to smile or make nice. His earlier hopefulness had taken a heavy hit, and the only thing he could think to be grateful for was that he hadn't told any of the other inmates or guards that he might get released, so now he didn't have to come up with some way to save face. But even for himself, Ray never should have imagined he could get out early. It was worse, he decided, than dreaming about women.

He went to his cell, mind tumbling like a rock down a landslide, picking up momentum with each bounce. The DA was right. Ray didn't deserve to be let out. He had committed that murder, and there was no question about his guilt in spite of his recent flights of fantasy. He had finished six and a half years of his sentence—the 2,408 days he had told Alan Sondano had now grown to 2,422 days. Big deal! Not even one grain of sand through the hourglass of his remaining time. He may have made a start on paying his debt, but now he needed to finish it. Long ago he had given up all hope of release until he became a middle-aged man. And with all the crimes he had *almost* committed in prison, chances were, sooner or later Ray would end up doing something that would extend his time, perhaps for the rest of his life. Yeah, maybe he would end up a lifer. The chances were high. Just to survive, Ray had made prison his life, his home, his mother, his father, his girl. He had done all he could to forget the streets. His mother was dead; his sister was . . . She might be dead too. He had no idea.

Connie Mason may have forgiven him, and maybe God had too. Ray actually believed that and was glad for it. But society hadn't forgiven him. If he got out of prison on a technicality, he would be cheating society. Besides, what would he do? Where would he go? Who would hire him? He would still be a murderer. No, he belonged in prison: *If you do the crime, you serve the time.*

Ray would go to chapel on Friday and ask Mr. Gee to call off Alan Sondano, forget his case. Sondano himself had said it was a *very long and precarious path.* Why get all revved up about something so unlikely? Release was as much a fantasy as imagining he hadn't pulled the trigger.

But when Friday came, Ray was sick with the flu, so sick he was having diarrhea every fifteen minutes and was transferred to the infirmary.

When Ray returned to his cell three days later, Moon was sitting on the can, reading a paperback novel, and making pained faces. The stench that slugged Ray in the nose like a baseball bat the moment he walked through the door was so rank it could peel the last of the paint off the concrete block walls.

"What died?"

"Nothin'. O-o-oh! I just caught that flu you had last week. O-o-oh!"

"Then why don't you go to the infirmary? I can't breathe in here!"

"Cain't go to no infirmary 'cause that doc's a ford. He don't like me."

"Why not?"

Moon held out both arms, exposing the scars, especially on the undersides of his arms. "O-o-oh!"

"So what's this mean?" Ray stuck out his arms mirroring Moon's gesture.

"It means he the one who sewed me up, and he done lost all patience with me."

"I don't understand. Thought you got those in a street fight when you killed that cop."

"These?" Moon repeated his arm-out gesture. "Nah! Got this"—he pointed to a roped scar that went through his left eyebrow and up to his hairline—"from the cop. But these . . ." He rolled his arms. "These were from the time I broke."

He crossed his arms across his stomach and leaned forward, another wave of pain washing across his face. "O-o-oh!"

When Moon relaxed and looked up again, Ray said, "You mean you broke, like you were talking to me about the other day?"

"Sure did, kid. Couldn't take it no more. Thought I could make it over the wall, but it would have been easier to fly outta here, 'cause that razor wire can tangle with you somethin' fierce, don't ya know."

"But how . . . how did you—?" Ray stopped. It didn't matter how Moon got up as high as the razor wire. What was more amazing was that someone as tough as Moon had broken. Ray shook his head. "Listen, I really can't breathe in here. We gotta get some ventilation, or you gotta go to the infirmary. How can you stand the smell?"

"Can't smell that well. Ever since I had trouble with my thyroid, I lost most of my sense of smell."

"Yeah, well, I haven't."

"Then why don't you just move on out into the dayroom for a while? 'Cause I cain't do nothin' 'bout the air up in here, and I fo' sure ain't goin' to that infirmary."

Ray went out into the common room and flopped onto the green couch, slouching down so far that his back was parallel to the seat while only his neck and head curled up onto the back. *Moon broke?* Ray could hardly believe it. He tried to imagine what could have driven the man that far, but he knew without asking. Ray had seen a couple other guys break; he just hadn't known what to call it until Moon had explained it. It had started out with their eyes as wide as if they had just seen a semi highballing it right down the centerline toward them. One had burst into uncontrollable bawling, taking no care who might see him. The other started kicking the wall with first one foot and then the other. He ended up with four broken toes before the guards got there to restrain him.

Guess I was pretty lucky, Ray thought. *I mostly broke on the inside instead of outside.* But the more he thought about it, the less certain he was. Losing his hold on reality and thinking that Rico had shot Greg—when he was right there and knew that he had done it himself—that was pretty serious. What if Mr. Gee hadn't helped Ray get a grip? How much further might it have gone? He might have ended up a raving lunatic. "Thank you, Jesus, that I'm clothed in my right mind!" He repeated the words again. He had heard some of the black brothers pray them in chapel. At the time Ray had dismissed them as a quaint colloquialism they dropped in when they couldn't think of anything else to say. Now he was beginning to learn otherwise. Being in your right mind was something to be thankful for and never taken for granted.

But to stay in his right mind, Ray felt he had to concentrate on reality—just like Mr. Gee said—and the reality was he was in prison, and he would be staying in prison for a long, long time. Keeping that in focus was the way he had to do his time. He had been sick the last Friday, but at his next chance he would tell Mr. Gee to call Sondano off his case.

Ray had an urge to run this all by Moon. As hardcore as Moon was, he had never made fun of Ray, and he had never known Moon to break a confidence from anyone. Moon had never told Ray anyone else's business, and that gave him hope that Moon wouldn't tell anyone his secrets. By that evening Moon's stomach had calmed down enough for Ray to return to his cell, but Moon remained in a sour mood, so Ray went to bed and read his Bible. It was something he had been neglecting.

Ray went to chapel on Friday, determined to have Mr. Gee tell Alan Sondano to forget trying to get his case reviewed.

"It's just not gonna work, Mr. Gee. I 'preciate everything you've done for me, and I enjoy helping out in the Bible studies and chapel, but what Mr. Sondano's trying to do for me . . ." Ray shrugged, tipped his head to the side, and grimaced like a salesman who doesn't like the offer you've made him on a used car.

"What do you mean, 'It's just not gonna work'? Does that mean you don't think Sondano can get a hearing or you don't want him to try?"

"I dunno. It's just that I *did* kill that kid—like we talked about— and that makes me a murderer. So I owe this debt to society. It's taken a long time for me to adjust to institutional life, but I think I'm comin' around. And I can help even more in the ministry, be a witness here on the inside. I also been thinkin', what would I do if I got out? Where would I live?"

Mr. Gee coughed in a way that made Ray suspect it was covering a laugh. He scratched the back of his head. "You know, you might have to do what most law-abiding citizens do: Get a job and find an apartment. It's not all that bad a gig."

"Yeah, but . . ." Ray didn't want to say anything about the DA's threat to find a way to put him back in prison within twenty-four hours.

"Let me ask you a question, Ray: Do you believe God has really forgiven you? I'm not talking about whether you think he might let you sneak into heaven in spite of the fact that you'll always be known as the murderer of Greg Mason. I want to know whether you have been *completely* forgiven."

"Well . . . I'm not sure." Ray paused and thought about all the times and ways that he thought of himself as the murderer of Greg Mason. It had become his identity, the reason he was in this prison to begin with, the reason he didn't believe he deserved to get out or ever would get out. "I guess I'd have to say that I'd leave that up to God and see what he says."

"Very diplomatic, Ray, very diplomatic. Maybe you could get a job in the U.S. State Department. But if you want to know what God thinks, you need to read the Bible, because he's already spoken on the issue. He's made it clear how he sees you now and when you're in heaven. Did you know that in Hebrews, chapter ten, the Lord said, 'Their sins and lawless acts I will remember no more'? That's you, Ray, and I could show you several other verses that say the same thing. In Christ, God has completely forgiven you. 'Though your sins are like scarlet, they shall be as white as snow; though they are red as crimson, they shall be like wool.' God said that in Isaiah, chapter one."

"Yeah, guess you're right."

"No guessing about it."

"Yeah, but—"

"Boy, you got a lotta 'yeah-buts' today!" Mr. Gee paused and held up a hand. "I'm sorry. What were you going to say?"

"I was just gonna say you once gave a teaching at chapel that we needed to understand that just because God forgave us doesn't mean we can escape the earthly consequences of our behavior. I guess that's all I'm thinking about."

"Yeah, I did say that, didn't I? And it's true." Mr. Gee nodded. "That's usually the way it works. God isn't a Coke machine who produces a can when we insert a dollar. We gotta live in the real world. If we walk in the rain without a jacket, we're liable to catch a cold, just like other people. But you've got to let God be God. You've got to let him do what he wants even when it doesn't make sense."

Ray frowned. "Whaddaya mean?"

"Usually people whine and complain when God doesn't protect them from their own foolishness, doesn't heal them when they ask or get them a better job, or—like a lot of guys in here—when he doesn't spring them from jail the first time they pray. I'm always having to explain that God has a better plan, that he sees a bigger picture and loves us so much that he does what's best even when we don't understand it."

"Yeah. I've heard you say that."

"Are there any times in your life when you had to trust God and accept that he is just and loves you even if he didn't do something you prayed for?"

Ray thought about his mother, who died in spite of his prayers. And about his sister, for whom Ray still prayed—though not enough. Both were tough situations, but though it had been hard, he'd finally come to accept—most of the time—that God was in control. Sometimes Ray's faith wavered, and he felt angry that God had not done what he asked. Finally Ray nodded in agreement with Mr. Gee's question: God was just and loving even when he didn't understand it.

"Okay, then." Mr. Gee scooted forward to the edge of his seat. "You know you need to trust that God is doing what's best for you even when he doesn't answer your prayers the way you want. In the same way, you now need to trust that if he *does* do a miracle for you, it's also because he's doing what's best for you." Mr. Gee turned his head to the side and held up a finger. "Now, I'm not saying he will get you out of here, but be humble enough to accept it if he does. In other words, let God be God!"

CHAPTER 28

L *et God be God!"* Ray turned the nugget of wisdom over and over like it was gold from an ancient treasure box as the guard escorted him across the yard in the freezing temperatures of early February, their feet crunching on the trampled and dirty snow that still covered some of the walkways.

"Your unit's in the gym. I'm takin' you there. It's shorter, and I've got five more cons to escort before chow."

"Yeah, well, I had to wait for nearly an hour."

"Shut up, chumpion! We're short-handed here. You're lucky you're not still waitin'!"

The air in the gym smelled like the inside of a rotten shoe. Ray winced and looked around. He didn't really feel like working out right now. He was cool with letting God be God, but he was still human and needed to think how to manage his expectations if Sondano opened his case. How do you "pray without ceasing"? How do you pray that earnestly for something without presuming God's there to serve you rather than you serve him? Ray realized that for him it had been easier to ignore the question and reject the possibility that God might have other plans for him. In reality, the possibility of getting out was as frightening as a stint in F-House. He'd rather stay where he was, maintain the status quo!

He'd never been an adult outside. He'd only been a kid back then, making a fool of himself on the streets. He was a completely different person now and didn't know how to act, how to be a man, how to be among women.

He spotted Moon pumping iron and walked over to where he was doing squats with 220 pounds on the bar across his shoulders. No one was spotting for him as he blew sweat off his lip with each dip.

"Ahhh," he groaned as Ray helped him put the bar back on the rack. Then he sat down on the bench and began rubbing his knees. "You know, they hot. They actually hot like a motor with bad bearings." He looked up at Ray, water streaming down his round face like he was defying an Illinois rainstorm. "I may be gettin' older, but I ain't quittin'." Then he grinned. "Don't look at me like you cain't figger dat out, kid. Old's still better'n de alternative."

"Yeah." Ray looked abstractly across the gym, trying to see a mile into the future. "You ever dream about gettin' out, Moon? I mean, like you had a real chance?"

"You don't mean like tryin' to go over the wall?"

"No, no! Like somethin' legal might break your way."

"The way I figure it, somethin' did break my way when Governor Ryan moratoriumed the death penalty last year. Otherwise, I'd be walkin' the green mile fo' dat cop."

Ray stifled a smirk at the word *moratoriumed*. "Yeah, that's what I'm talking about, somethin' legal. You ever think about anything else maybe happenin', somethin' that might even get you reprieved?"

Moon looked at him, his eyes squinting almost imperceptibly. "What you talkin' 'bout, boy? You got somethin' cookin'?"

"Not sure. But even if I did, I don't think I'd know how to handle it."

"When you up in here for smokin' a dude, you gotta remember somethin' like a get-outta-jail-free card is as rare as crackers on the Southside. It happens, but no person of color with any sense would ever count on it!"

Six weeks later it was still cold and partly cloudy when Ray climbed aboard a van and rode into Chicago for his initial hearing before the Illinois Appellate Court, First District. It was going on seven years. Even though he had admitted to Moon that he didn't know if he could handle an early release, he didn't know if he could tolerate being locked up for thirty-three more years either. He watched cars whiz by, models he had never seen except on TV. New buildings going up. The world would no longer be recognizable if Ray had to serve his full sentence. He felt like kicking himself: *Can't stand to stay in, too afraid to get out!*

All that morning Ray's hearing was dominated by motions and legal details that didn't seem to address the substance of his appeal. Afterward, Alan Sondano was noncommittal. "I think it went as well as could be expected, but there's no way of foreseeing the outcome. The assistant state's attorney is sharp, but I hope the judges will be fair. I've stood before Judge Miriam P. Kaplan before, and she's good. But I know the other two judges only by reputation."

"And . . . ?"

Sondano sighed. "And what I've heard is not too good. They're inclined to leave rulings stand when the challenge is solely procedural, so I may have to expand things, demonstrate that you have genuinely reformed. Frankly, I wish we had a different panel. You've got to remember, Ray, our chances are slim that you'll get a new trial." He watched Ray. "But in the meantime, it's your job to keep praying."

"Oh yes, sir. I've been prayin' twenty-four/seven." But it wasn't really true. Ray had seldom prayed about the matter, not because he didn't want to, but because he didn't know how to pray about something like this. He was afraid, afraid that God might *not* answer—and what would that mean?—and afraid that God *might* answer and Ray wouldn't be able to handle it. But after the hearing, Ray began trying, praying the only honest prayer he could come up with: "God, help me become the kind of person who can let you be God and not be blown away by whatever you do!"

Three continuances—all requested by the state—delayed Ray's case for weeks, until finally on May 24, Alan Sondano was scheduled to present his arguments. Sondano had arranged for Ray to appear in court without restraints and dressed in civilian clothes. "It's always better to look as normal and upstanding as possible," Sondano had said. "Be sure you shave and have a fresh haircut. Look sharp."

And Ray felt good—almost normal—sitting behind the defense desk beside his legal team, Alan Sondano and two assistants. But as the court assembled and was called to order, Ray watched in shock as Peter Musselman, the newly elected state's attorney, slid quietly into a seat behind the DA who had been handling the case.

Mussleman leaned forward to speak to his colleague and glanced Ray's way. He shook his head ever so slightly as they made eye contact. *He's here to deep-six me!* thought Ray. Was Alan Sondano up to that kind of firepower, the state's attorney himself? Ray's hopes melted.

Sondano spent an hour providing background, then concluded by saying, "There are two components of our claim, Your Honors. First, the court did not adequately research my client's age in determining—falsely, I must emphasize—that he was fifteen. Second, he did not receive adequate counsel to challenge that ruling. My client was just a youth. He had no way of knowing the momentous implications of that error. But his public defender should have known it and challenged it!"

Ray watched as Peter Musselman whispered into the DA's ear, coaching him, Ray thought. As soon as Sondano stopped, the DA was on his feet. "This is a waste of your time, Your Honors. The plaintiff is pinning this entire appeal on a technicality that makes no difference. The shooting was so violent in nature that the judge would have unquestionably transferred the case to Criminal Court anyway. He was going to be tried as an adult one way or the other. There's no question about that."

"Objection." Sondano stood up. "Doesn't this issue turn on the very charter for the court of appeals in Illinois: to determine whether the procedures and rights guaranteed by Illinois law are granted to every citizen? In this case a deleterious error was made. Because my client was under fifteen, he deserved a judge's opinion as to whether he was to be tried in juvenile or adult court. He was not granted that right, and therefore the judgment against him was in error."

"Oh, come on." The DA was back on his feet. "The defense is not challenging the guilty verdict. In fact, he has not offered any testimony to suggest that a judge might have granted a trial in Juvenile Court. The murder was too heinous. A Criminal Court trial was a given."

"Not necessarily, Your Honors. Mr. Slewinski's behavior since being incarcerated suggests a far more benign character influenced temporarily for evil by an older and manipulative youth, who—by the way—was never prosecuted or even thoroughly investigated for his role in this crime—"

"Objection, relevance. We're not here to discuss whether someone else should have been indicted."

"Sustained."

One of the members of Ray's team handed Sondano a note. "If it pleases the court, may I draw its attention to Mr. Slewinski's record: one minor disciplinary event in nearly seven years, and that was for intervening on behalf of a prisoner being threatened by a guard who had previously beaten the inmate severely. Otherwise, Mr. Slewinski has been a model prisoner. Our justice system used to focus on rehabilitation, reforming offenders so they could reenter society as productive citizens. We spoke of 'reformatories' and 'correctional institutions' precisely because we believed some people could be changed for the better. Mr. Slewinski's good behavior for seven years demonstrates that he has changed. But more important, it demonstrates how out of character—and therefore the result of youthful foolishness and negative peer pressure—his actions of June 10, 1997, were. He was not 'an adult' at age fourteen as the state tried to portray him. If he had been an adult, there is reason to believe that he might have acted more wisely—"

"Objection, speculation."

"Not speculation, Your Honors," Sondano quickly offered, "but a judgment call, one that a judge should have had the opportunity to make nearly seven years ago. But because of an error—an error on which the prosecution hastily capitalized—that never happened, and my client was consequently denied due process."

Sondano stopped, looked down at Ray on one side and then his assistants on the other, and took a deep breath as though he were preparing for the final sprint. "We are calling on this court of appeals to rectify that error."

Judge Kaplan leaned back in her chair and raised her hands off the bench, turning them palms up as she looked from side to side at the other two justices. "Toward what end, Mr. Sondano? Suppose we agree that this young man should have received that judicial consideration, what redress remains? He was convicted of a cold-blooded murder, and there's no evidence that a juvenile court would have found otherwise."

"Perhaps not, Your Honor, but had he been convicted as a juvenile, his sentence would have been completed on his twenty-first birthday, over ten months ago. Should you find for the plaintiff, you would have to release him, not only because he has served his sentence but because he is a changed man, ready to take a productive place in his community."

"Objection." This time it was the state's attorney, Peter Mussel-man, who jumped to his feet, taking over the DA's role. "You can't turn a convicted murderer out onto the streets of Chicago."

"Please be seated, Mr. Musselman. We release convicted crimi-nals all the time, as you very well know." She took a moment to confer behind her hand with the justices on either side. Then she pointed toward Ray while speaking to Sondano. "Even if we were to concede that a judge should have actively determined jurisdiction based on the defendant's age, we don't live in a perfect world, and this seems like an honest mistake exacerbated by the youth's own equivocation concerning his birth date. But looking beyond that procedural matter, my colleagues and I must consider whether or not this young man presents a threat to the community today. Do you have anything to say about that, Mr. Sondano?"

"Your Honor," Musselman interrupted, "the statistics show that the vast majority of felons return to a life of crime. The recidivism rate is 86 percent at this point. Given the gruesome nature of his crime, I don't think there is any way you can free him."

"I'm familiar with the statistics, Mr. Musselman. You may also be aware that murder is rarely a repeated crime except in the case of a hit man or someone like that. So what we're concerned with today is whether this young man is one of the 14 percent. Do you mind?" She extended her hand to Alan Sondano.

Sondano then called on Rev. Harvey Geevers from Captives Free Ministries. Mr. Geevers made a strong statement concern-ing the responsible character Ray had demonstrated through his leadership in the prison chapel program. Ray expected Mr. Gee would give a positive report, but what he didn't expect was the next testimony. Deputy Warden Parker took the stand, and with his fat sausage finger pointing at Ray, he said Ray had been a model prisoner whose only influence on others had been positive.

The state countered with testimony from two staff persons from the Illinois Youth Center at Joliet who said Ray had been surly and difficult while there. "I would say," said one of the guards, "that if you are trying to determine what kind of a person this prisoner was when he came to us—which was closer to the time any judge would have had to evaluate—then his character fit the profile of most of the other gangbangers we see all the time."

Musselman then added, "He may have just turned fifteen by then, but you'll notice that he was already behaving like a hardcore criminal adult. There was no miscarriage of justice. How he has changed since then—if indeed he has—should have no bearing on that judgment."

Sondano had been flipping through some papers shortly after Musselman had started to speak. He handed them back to his assistant and stood up. "Objection. Mr. Slewinski was nearly sixteen and a half by the time he arrived at the Illinois Youth Center at Joliet. His behavior then—which could hardly be described as hardcore—provides no basis for determining his character a year and a half earlier."

"Wait a minute," said Musselman. "It was you who proposed that we look back through the lens of time and extrapolate from his present behavior to conclude that he was basically benign nearly *seven* years ago. If you can do that, it is certainly legitimate—maybe even more valid—to do the same from the closer vantage point of only a year and a half after the shooting."

"Gentlemen, gentlemen. That's not getting us anywhere. You will please address the court and not one another. We cannot speculate on how a judge might have ruled when he was fourteen, even if we agree a judgment should have been made then. What we are looking at now is what he has become. Do you have anything more to add in that regard, Mr. Musselman?"

"No, Your Honor."

"Mr. Sondano?"

"If the court will allow, we have one more person we'd like to hear from, Mrs. Connie Mason, the mother of the victim."

An audible gasp spread through the courtroom as everyone turned to see Connie rise and come to the bench.

"Your Honor," said Musselman, "this is highly irregular. Her testimony is irrelevant. She did not know the offender at the time of the shooting. How can she give witness to anything you are presently considering?"

Judge Kaplan turned to her associates, who each whispered behind their hands. Then Judge Kaplan addressed the state's attorney. "Nevertheless, we would like to hear what she has to say. Please be seated, Mrs. Mason. By the way, we are all very sorry about the death of your son. We hope you and your family are beginning to . . ." Her voice trailed off, as though she feared it would be offensive to suggest that one could truly recover from the murder of a family member.

After being sworn in, Connie told how she came to the point of forgiving Ray and even went to see him in prison to communicate that forgiveness directly. "When a crime is committed, the fabric of our society is rent," she said, "but no one is more offended than the victim. But in this case, love has covered a very terrible sin. He is forgiven. I know him to be a new person, and if Raymond Peter Slewinski—yes, I know his full name—is released, I would welcome him as my neighbor and brother in Christ."

The courtroom was absolutely silent.

Finally Judge Kaplan said, "Do you have anything else, Mr. Musselman?"

The state's attorney shook his head and looked down to the floor, his thin beard pulsating where it outlined the edge of his jaw.

"Then we will recess and consider our decision," said Judge Kaplan.

CHAPTER 29

Ray sat there, elbows on the table, head in his hands, waiting for the bailiff to escort him back to the holding cell. What would the judges decide? Had Sondano made his case? As far as Ray was concerned, Sondano's argument sounded convincing: The judges would have to agree that because he had been only fourteen at the time of his arrest, a judge—and only a judge—should have determined whether he got tried in juvenile or adult court. But Ray had been in the system too long to take any comfort in what made sense.

Ray wished the judges would hurry up; his bladder was uncomfortably full. He had been sitting in court for over two hours. He looked around. Most of the observers had stepped out, including Connie Mason and Mr. Gee. The clerk and the court recorder had also left the courtroom, perhaps availing themselves of the rest room, Ray thought, and shifted awkwardly in his seat. Musselman and his team stood by their table talking among themselves. Every few moments the state's attorney looked over at Ray, and Ray imagined they were plotting some legal trick to prevent his release even if the judges decided in his favor.

Alan Sondano sat beside Ray, scribbling furiously in a yellow legal pad while one of his assistants scanned an inch-thick sheaf of papers Ray knew was the transcript of his original trial. The other assistant had left the courtroom.

Minutes passed.

Ray squirmed. "Uh, Mr. Sondano, excuse me, but I gotta use the rest room. You think—"

"Of course." He raised his arm and beckoned with his fingers. "Bailiff."

One of the two guards standing to the left of the judges' bench broke away from talking to the other and came over.

"Thank you, bailiff. My client needs to use the rest room. You think you could . . ." He gestured with his hand toward the door through which prisoners entered the courtroom.

"Sorry." He turned to Ray. "We can't take you back there because the plumbing in the holding cells is all backed up. It's a mess, and the plumber's got the whole place torn up. Some fool stuffed a whole roll of toilet paper down one of the johns. Guess we'll have to start issuing it square by square." He turned away to return to his partner.

"Wait a minute. The man's still got to use the facilities. You can't deny him that right."

The bailiff came back. "Look, counselor, I didn't cause the problem. Far as I know, your man here is responsible. In fact, maybe it wasn't toilet paper after all. Maybe somebody . . ." He glared hard at Ray. " . . . tried to dump a stash of drugs down the hole."

"That's uncalled for, sir. Escort my client to a rest room immediately, or I'll file a complaint that could threaten your job."

"Wow!" The bailiff held both hands up in front of him. "Take it easy! Uh . . ." He rolled his eyes. "Come on, then."

Ray got up and followed as the bailiff headed down the aisle between the benches. What was happening? He hadn't even cuffed Ray and was leading him to the back of the courtroom, past the few remaining observers. The bailiff stopped, turned, and took Ray by the elbow, guiding him through the heavy oak door and out into the hallway. "Just down here," he muttered.

Ray looked both ways down the wide hall. Only a few people could be seen: A couple of men who looked like lawyers with expensive suits and heavy briefcases were just topping the stairs at one end. A small huddle of civilians stood talking at the other end. A black woman with frazzled hair and a child in tow was reading the docket on the door of the adjacent courtroom.

Across the hallway and down thirty feet was the doorway designated MEN. On the floor by the door was a yellow A-frame sign reading CAUTION, Wet Floor. Beside it was a janitor's bucket on wheels with a heavy metal-handled mop sticking up. The bailiff pulled the door open and gave Ray a light shove into the rest room, releasing his elbow. "All right, now. Don't take all day."

Ray stopped at the first urinal, and the bailiff passed him to use the fourth one, following "man law" of not standing too close to another if there were options.

Ray realized his situation: No one else was in the rest room, and he was at least three steps closer to the door than the preoccupied guard. Furthermore, outside the door was a metal mop handle that could be rammed through the D-shaped door handle and wedged into the heavy oak frame surrounding the door.

Could he do it? Instead of trying to run after Ray and catch him, would the guard simply pull his gun and shoot? Ray didn't think so. But who knew? What if he couldn't wedge the mop handle into the doorjamb in a way that would delay the guard from following him? What if someone were right outside and saw what Ray was doing before he could walk casually down the hall unnoticed in his inconspicuous civilian clothes? What if someone who had been in his courtroom recognized him, someone like Mr. Gee or Connie Mason? No, he couldn't do that to them. Besides, even if he could get out of the building, where would he go?

On the other hand, if the judges refused to grant his appeal, Ray still had thirty-three years to serve, and this might be his only chance to cut that short.

The pros and cons flipped through Ray's mind like calculations on a computer screen as he stepped to the washbasin and turned on the water—two steps closer to the door, and the older, heavier guard was still "busy." Ray ran his hands under the water, turned it off, and moved to the paper towel dispenser. Now he was just a couple steps from the door, and there was no question that he could get out before the guard could respond . . . but should he?

"So, Slewinski, what's it like out there at Stateville? You guys got cable and DVD players in every room now? Steaks for dinner?"

"Nah. One TV in the dayroom for thirty men." While he answered, Ray's mind continued to race. "And last night we had moosh for dinner." He was remembering a Bible story about David before he became King of Judah.

"What's moosh?" The guard was backing away from the urinal and zipping up.

"Uh . . . mush. You know: rice, soybeans, and potatoes . . . all mixed together. No flavor." Ray had read the story as part of his Bible correspondence course: Twice David had easy opportunities to kill King Saul and take over the throne, which God had actually promised to David. "Oh yeah, they also fed us some wilted lettuce they called salad and gave us our choice of either milk or Kool-Aid." But even though David had the chance, he didn't take the shortcut to the throne because it would have been doing the wrong thing. It would have meant killing God's anointed.

Ray made his decision and stepped back away from the door, waiting for his guard. *If I'm going to be free, it's gotta be the right way. Gotta do the right thing!*

Without washing his hands, the bailiff waddled toward Ray like a Weeble doll, took Ray's elbow again, and nudged him toward the door.

Just as Ray reached for it, the door swung open, and there was the other bailiff from his courtroom coming into the rest room along with two Chicago cops. They were moaning and groaning about such a dull day as Ray slipped past them.

"Oh, God, thank you . . ." Ray almost collapsed from shock. "Thank you, Jesus," he whispered. What if he'd run? He'd be a dead man.

"Hey, Murphy," said the incoming bailiff, "better get him in there. Clerk said the judges were ready to return."

"All rise."

Everyone did as instructed as the three judges filed in.

"You may be seated," said Judge Kaplan. "Let the record show that we are still in session." She and her associates took their seats, and then she continued. "In the case of Slewinski versus the State of Illinois, we find in favor of the plaintiff."

Ray gasped. *"In favor?"* Alan Sondano grabbed his arm and gave him a look to be quiet. The judge had more to say.

"Since Mr. Slewinski was only fourteen at the time he committed the crime, a judge should have determined whether he was tried as a juvenile or as an adult. That did not happen, and we agree that was in error. Normally, when the appellate court affirms an appeal, the case is referred back to the trial court for review. However, in this case the question was jurisdiction, not anything that happened during his trial. Furthermore, Judge Gregory Romano, who made the error, has since deceased and cannot revisit the question of jurisdiction with the knowledge that Mr. Slewinski was only fourteen.

"Therefore, this court has assumed that responsibility and unanimously agrees that he should have been tried as a juvenile based on his age and lack of priors and his achievements in school. That being the case, as Mr. Sondano pointed out, he would have served his time by now even if he had been convicted. Given his good conduct while incarcerated, we find no legal or practical objection to releasing him immediately."

Ray nearly leaped from his seat and was again restrained by Sondano's firm grip.

The judge turned to the clerk. "Since this court considers Mr. Slewinski to have served his full sentence, he will not be supervised by the Community Services Division of Illinois Department of Corrections." Judge Kaplan turned back to Ray. "That means you will not have to report to a parole officer. So listen to me: Instead of having to serve forty years, which your crime richly deserved, you are getting a second lease on life. Life, Mr. Slewinski. We are resentencing you to *life*! Do not squander it. Several people have testified on your behalf, convinced that you are a new man, capable of serving your fellow human beings in a responsible manner. Live up to that confidence, stay out of trouble, stay away from negative influences, and don't ever come back to stand before this court or any other court as a defendant for as long as you live.

"You are free to go!" She slammed down her gavel with a mighty smack. "Court adjourned!"

This time Alan Sondano did not prevent Ray from leaping to his feet, cheering, and shaking his arms in joy and celebration.

Ray had hoped and prayed for this for so long—but now that he'd been freed, he could hardly believe it. Was it a trick? Maybe he'd wake up—like he did from that wild notion that he hadn't pulled the trigger—and find out he'd been dreaming.

Ray wasn't shackled as he rode in the van back out to Stateville to collect his belongings, but he had had to force himself to get into the van. What if . . . ? Maybe he should have had someone at the prison send his stuff to him so he'd never have to look at the prison again. But he knew prison bureaucracy and the high probability that his few meager belongings would get lost or damaged if he left it to some guard to collect, pack, and ship. And of course, such a "complex task" could take weeks, and Ray had no permanent address yet anyway. Where would they send the stuff? Mr. Gee said Ray could stay at his apartment a short time while he got settled, but how long would that last? Maybe he could stay with his sister . . . if he could find her. And where could he find a job? Ray knew very few employers were willing to risk hiring a con. His mind was buzzing with the future, but he could not forget his past. He also hoped to say good-bye to Moon and a few other guys.

Ray arrived at Stateville in the late afternoon. The deputy sheriff who had driven him escorted him into the administration building. Ray started to protest, to say he was a free man now and did not need an armed guard. But why make the guy mad? It would only be a few more hours, and he wouldn't have to say "Yes, boss" to anyone . . . except maybe an employer.

"Prison's on lockdown. You'll have to see Deputy Warden Parker about your stuff," the guard at the front desk said.

"Lockdown? 'Bout what?"

The guard opened his mouth like a fish, then stopped. "Better ask the warden."

Ray knocked on the warden's door with a crisp rap.

"Enter."

"Evening, Warden." Ray couldn't help but grin. "Thank you for testifying for me. Did you hear how it came out?"

"Yeah, I got a call shortly after I got back here."

"Again, I want to thank you, sir. Your testimony might have been the very thing that tipped the scale in my favor. So I had to come back here and say good-bye to you and pick up my stuff. I was gonna say good-bye to Moon and the guys, but what's this I hear about a lockdown? What's going on, sir?"

"You haven't heard?"

"No. The guy at the front desk told me to ask you."

"Hmm." The deputy warden tipped back in his chair and removed his glasses, putting one stem in his mouth and examining

Ray with squinted eyes. "You're lucky I know where you've been all day long."

Ray felt a chill. "Why's that?"

"You really don't know?"

"No, sir. I haven't been around since six o'clock this morning."

The warden leaned forward with one elbow on the table and put his glasses on again. "Your cell was blown up this afternoon, son. With Moon in it."

"What?" At first the words didn't make sense. "Blown up? But . . . Wait! Is Moon okay?"

"Moon's been taken to the hospital with burns all over him. They don't know if he'll make it or not."

Moon! Ray could hardly believe what the warden had said. "Where? What hospital? Can I go see him?"

"They got him at Silver Cross in Joliet. But they might move him to the burn unit at Cook County Hospital. I don't know if you can see him or not."

Ray ran his fingers through his hair and sank into one of the warden's chairs, unbidden. "But how? How could anything explode? There's nothin' in those cells that would even burn, let alone explode."

"Yeah, unless someone sneaks in a little calcium carbide. You know what that is?"

"No, sir."

"Looks like crushed gravel." The warden squinted as though cigarette smoke were drifting into his eyes. He leaned forward, one elbow on his desk, his hand supporting his chin. "Dangerous stuff, unless it's in an air-tight container, like maybe a ziplock plastic bag." He paused, studying Ray closely. "Know why the stuff needs to be sealed?"

Ray shook his head. He had the feeling the warden was testing him . . . as though trying to evaluate how much Ray might know.

The warden continued slowly. "Calcium carbide reacts violently when it comes in contact with water. You know what it releases?"

Again, Ray shook his head.

"It gives off acetylene gas, you know, like for welding. All that needs is one small spark—like a burning cigarette butt, maybe—and it explodes. Big time! You smoke, Slewinski?"

Ray shook his head. He hadn't smoked in years. "But wouldn't it smell?"

"The gas? Some. Kinda like garlic, but enough of it might collect in a cell to create a serious explosion before anyone outside noticed the smell."

"Yeah . . ." Ray turned and stared at the warden's bookshelf, filled with more cheap travel souvenirs than books. "Yeah, and Moon wouldn't smell it 'cause he can't smell." Ray looked back at the warden. "So you think someone filled our cell with gas and then blew it up?

The warden shrugged. "Too soon to be sure, but we found a bunch of carbide lime in the bottom of the toilet bowl." He paused and studied Ray as though still deciding how much Ray knew. "Carbide lime's what's left over when calcium carbide is put in water. It was definitely enough to have generated the gas for a lethal explosion."

"But . . . but how would anyone in here get this calcium carbide or whatever?"

"Ha!" The deputy warden threw up both hands. "Like you guys aren't able to smuggle *anything* in here that you want. . . . Who knows where that stuff came from? But it sure did a job on Moon. . . . And I don't think there's many of your personals left in that room either."

Suddenly retrieving his old Bible, his correspondence courses, and his other personal items—including that old Christmas card from Connie Mason—seemed very important to Ray, but he was embarrassed to say anything about them at the moment.

"Did you guys have a coffee percolator in your cell?"

"Yes, sir. A little one, but it was an approved appliance."

"Well, you don't have one anymore. It's probably what created the ignition spark when Moon plugged it in."

Ray sat there, looking down at the floor and shaking his head.

"Son, you got any idea who might have wanted to take out Moon?"

"Not really, sir. I mean . . ." Ray stopped himself. There was that beef with the Conservative Vice Lords. Ray wouldn't have been surprised if it had led to a fight or something, but blowing Moon up? That seemed a little extreme . . . unless it was to settle some old score. Moon did have quite a past.

"How about you?" the warden said.

"Me?" The idea shocked Ray. "No, no, sir. I been cool with just 'bout everyone."

Muñoz's threat came to Ray's mind: *"I will make you this promise: If you break this deal and rat me out, I'll make sure someone tracks you down and wipes you out, even if I have to buy the hit from death row."* Now Muñoz was on trial for murdering McAfee. Could this be payback if he thought Ray had broken their deal?

"Slewinski? What's going on, man? You look a little pale. Come on, you're not an inmate anymore. You can tell me. It might even save someone's life."

But the old taboo against being a snitch was too strong. Ray couldn't say anything. Telling the warden about Muñoz even now would break his promise. And besides, he'd have to talk to Moon before he would know who had been the target. If Moon was in danger, he could ask for isolation. He'd better just keep quiet.

The warden shook his head. "Yeah, yeah. Once a con, always a con," he mumbled, then spun around in his chair and punched the Start button on his computer with his fat finger. "But listen to me. If you ever want to get something off your chest, you give me a call." He looked back at Ray as though surprised he was still sitting there. "Have one of the guards take you over to G-House. Tell the state police detective workin' the case that I said to release your belongings unless he thinks there's specific evidence involved . . . probably like with that coffeepot. Good luck on the outside. And Slewinski, don't you ever come back in here! You hear me? 'Cause if you conned me into testifying for you," he chuckled at his own pun, "I won't be a nice guy next time."

When Ray still didn't leave, the warden took a deep, loud breath and nodded. "So where you going?"

"Maywood. Gonna stop over with Mr. Gee, the reverend who leads the Captives Free Ministry."

"Know how to get there?"

"I think so, sir. My mom used to take public transportation when she came out to visit me."

"You got any money in your account?"

"Yes, sir, 'bout thirty-two dollars. I already withdrew it."

"Okay then. I'll give you fifty bucks gate money. That's all I can do. You'll need some of it for bus and train fare, but since you've got somewhere to stay . . ." He broke off as he counted out five tens from a petty cash box in his desk and handed them to Ray. "Wait! You gotta sign right here."

CHAPTER
30

With a large paper bag under his arm and eighty-two dollars in his pocket to start a new life, Ray exited the gates of Stateville Prison on his own steam for the first time at 5:13 p.m. on May 24. He walked the third of a mile down the entrance drive to Route 53 and the Pace bus stop, where a uniformed prison guard was already standing. Ray had seen him before but didn't know his name.

"Hey!" the guard said. "Just released?"

Ray nodded and maintained enough distance to discourage conversation, but the guard still volunteered, "Me too. Actually, I ain't feelin' so good. The wife told me to stay home and take a sick day, but you know how it is. Now I'm leavin' early and gotta catch the bus instead of ridin' with Coleman. Where you headed?"

Ray's shrug finally encouraged silence except for the occasional passing car and the light breeze through the trees and brush that spotted the surrounding wasteland. He needed to think. Seeing his blown-out cell had shaken him. What if that hit had been meant for him? He'd be in the hospital instead of Moon . . . or perhaps dead. But this was the second time in one day that he had avoided disaster: He could have been shot had he tried to escape from the rest room at the courthouse, and he could have died in the cell explosion. Someone was looking out for Ray; there was no other way to understand it.

Mr. Gee always said God had a special plan for his life, and it was Ray's job to discover it and submit to God by following it. But what if he missed the plan? He had come so close in that rest room, too anxious to take things into his own hands. But the explosion, he'd had no idea that was coming—like a stealth bomber sneaking up on him. How many other times had God protected him? The guys in Greg Mason's car could have been GDs after all, and they could have pulled a gun and shot him before he shot one of them! How many other times should a car have hit him when he ran carelessly across the street? Should he have fallen from that light pole he climbed to throw a rival's hundred-dollar Nikes over the high power line? And then there was that time when he was a little boy and so terribly sick. He couldn't even remember what he'd had, but his mother had told him he almost died.

Someone was looking out for him!

Pace bus number 831 rolled up to the stop, and Ray climbed aboard after the guard, the door hissing closed behind them.

As the bus lumbered away, Ray watched the prison fade into the distance. He was free. Really free! Back out in the world. Could he figure out why God helped him get out early? Could he find God's plan? Could he follow it? Would God's protection follow him wherever he went? What was it that Psalm 23 promised? "Surely goodness and love will follow me all the days of my life, and I will dwell in the house of the Lord forever." What did that mean if he didn't even know where he was going?

Still, Ray did sense God's mercy and protection that evening as he caught the Metra Rock Island train, transferred to the CTA's Blue Line El, and caught two more buses before he finally ended up ringing the doorbell for Mr. Gee's Maywood apartment at ten o'clock that night.

The door opened on a small living room with half a dozen guys sitting around. "Well, look who we have here," said Mr. Gee, swinging the door wide, "one of our fine young gentlemen from the far western suburbs." Ray winced. Did everyone in the room know that meant Stateville prison? But Mr. Gee shook his hand as though he were a foreign diplomat and urged, "Come in, come in. I have some of the boys over here to help plan our next United Nations meeting. And I want you to meet them."

Ray felt awkward. The day had been long and momentous. He had escaped death twice—or rather, twice *God* had protected Ray from death. Thirty-three years had been cut off his bid. He had navigated Chicago's public transportation system—all over the city, it seemed— for the first time in over seven years. He was starving, and he had no idea where he was going to sleep that night. He just wanted to be alone, get some food, and go to bed. But he made nice and went around shaking hands with a Latino from the Two-Six Nation in South Lawndale, an Insane Spanish Cobra from Bucktown on the north side, a tall blond guy who was an Almighty Gaylord, and a Black Gangster/New Breed from the near west side. They all seemed about seventeen or eighteen.

Ray looked around. This was amazing: Guys from various "nations," as gangs were often called, coming together, not as rivals ready to kill each other but "united" to plan some larger gathering in the name of Christ. "If Jesus is our brother," Mr. Gee had once explained, "then we're brothers to each other, and we ought to act like it."

Then Mr. Gee introduced Ray to the only guy who looked to be Ray's age, an African American "who is one of Chicago's finest: Carl Franklin. But he's off duty tonight, so you don't need to worry." Mr. Gee chuckled at his own joke and scratched the back of his head, causing his toupee to shift.

A cop? Ray was spinning. He couldn't imagine being in the same room with so many rivals, and certainly not with a police officer. What was going on?

"Now you can see," said Mr. Gee, "why we need to plan our United Nations meetings. We wouldn't want an 'international incident,' now, would we? But here, pull up a chair for yourself. How 'bout some pizza or Colonel Sanders? I'm afraid they're kinda cold. But there's Pepsi on the table. Anything you want, feel free."

Ray grabbed a paper plate and piled it high, then sat down to feed his face and listen to the end of the planning meeting—talking about where they would meet, who should be invited, and what the risks were. Ray had no idea what that meant.

After the meeting Carl Franklin reached out and shook Ray's hand. "Just out, huh?"

"Yeah . . ." Ray tightened inside. He remembered how State's Attorney Peter Musselman had vowed to put him back in prison if he ever managed to get out. Was this already the first move? A cop sidling up to him, putting the squeeze on? "Just got in this afternoon."

"Where'll you be staying?"

Ray shrugged. "Haven't figured that out yet."

"Mr. Gee has lots of connections. He can fix you up if anyone can. But if that don't work out, here's my card. Why don't you give me a call? Might be able to find something through our church. And that's also an invitation to come to church with me. We got some really fine older folks—" he grinned a warm, disarming smile—"and a lot of young people too. You might like it."

Somehow, Ray's tension subsided. "Thanks. I'll keep that in mind." He put the card in his pocket.

It was nearly midnight before Ray stretched out on Mr. Gee's couch. How could a nearly seventy-year-old man keep up such a pace, going all the time with energy into the night? Ray lay there listening to the sounds of the city—cars going by, the thud of someone's stereo in a neighboring apartment, and even a siren in the distance. Altogether they created a symphony he hadn't heard in nearly seven years. He sighed. He was out! And long before he expected to be. Darnell was out too. And even Moon . . . sorta. Ray should go see Moon, see how he was doing, find out what had really gone down that day of the explosion. What if Moon had taken a hit meant for Ray? The weight of it was too heavy to dwell on for long.

The next morning Mr. Gee came in brushing his teeth and mumbling about going to IHOP for breakfast. "Then, young man, you need to find a job. You got enough money to pay for transportation?"

"I think so. After the buses and trains last night I've still got a little over seventy bucks." Ray hesitated. "But I was thinkin' I oughta find my sister. I'm gonna need a place to live, and she could probably put me up for a while till I get on my feet."

"Well," Mr. Gee waved his hand. "I'm sure finding your sister is important. But you might want to think long term. You know, getting a job's not like selling drugs on the street. You don't usually get paid the same day. You have to wait for payday. If you only have seventy dollars . . ." He shook his head and frowned so that his unruly eyebrows almost met. "That might not last until your first paycheck. Once you get set up, you'll have the means to keep looking for your sister for as long as it takes."

Ray sat up and pulled on his sneakers. "Yeah, but she's my only family, and I haven't heard from her in over a year. Seems like I oughta track her down first."

"Oh, there's no doubt family's important, but maybe you could work on both—look for a job *and* try to find your sister. I'll tell you what: Captives Free has a halfway house less than a mile from here. It's called Timothy House and is primarily for younger guys coming out of the Sheriff's Boot Camp or even the JDC if their home's not a viable option. But we just lost one of our live-in support staff members, so there's an empty bed. You think you could help some younger guys go straight?" His eyebrows went up. "At least it would give you a base to work from, and you might make some connections. Whaddaya say? We're always trying to help guys get jobs."

"Yeah! Yeah, that'd be great, Mr. Gee." Wow, two offers in as many days. Well, Carl Franklin hadn't actually made a specific offer, but . . .

The food at Timothy House—all cooked by the residents—was even worse than it had been at Stateville, but Ray did his part and hoped he wouldn't get sick. He tried to juggle looking for his sister *and* looking for a job, but jobs for an ex-con without any "outside" experience were hard to find. Having a place to live took the pressure off getting a job, so he focused on finding his sister.

He went to the apartment where his mother last lived, on Poplar Avenue in Elmhurst. But someone else was living in Unit 3B, an Asian woman with three screaming children. She wouldn't take the chain off the door and kept saying through the three-inch crack, "No English! No English!" Ray tried some of the other doors. People either weren't home or had only recently moved in and didn't remember his mother. No one knew anything about a young girl named Lena Slewinski.

Ray came back the next day in the late afternoon and found an older couple living in 1A who said they had lived there for eight years. "Yeah, I remember a Mrs. Slewinski," said the woman. "Ambulance came and took her away one afternoon, and we haven't seen her since. Sorry, can't help you."

"She was my mother, and she died. But I'm looking for my sister. Did you ever see her? She's a little younger than me, black hair, and kinda . . . kinda freaky-looking, actually."

"How 'bout it, Bob?" She turned to the man who was still sitting across the room on the couch watching the news. "Didn't we see someone like that around sometimes?"

He glanced up. "Oh yeah. Real strange lookin'. I 'member seeing her. She really your sister? She didn't look much like you."

"Yeah, she's my sister. I'm just trying to find her."

"Well, I ain't seen her since way before the older woman left. Got no idea."

The next day Ray went to the post office, but the clerk there said no forwarding address had been registered, so they began returning all mail to the sender. Ray called Nicor Gas and ComEd, but they both said they had finally written off Mrs. Slewinski's unpaid utility bills. "However, if you are her son, why don't you give us your address and we can—"

Yeah, Ray knew what would follow: a bill. "Thanks anyway." He hung up quickly.

He checked the phone book and AT&T. Then he asked one of the guys at Timothy House if he knew how to use the computer in the office to search for someone: "Lena Slewinski" or "Magdalena Slewinski." Still no luck.

Ray began to panic. He'd been out of prison a week and had attempted every means he knew to find a "missing person" without turning up a trace of his sister. Half his money was gone. Maybe Mr. Gee had been right: He should have concentrated more on finding a job. Actually, Ray had filled out fourteen applications, going from one fast-food place to another, one convenience store to another. But he had heard that it sometimes took ex-offenders several times that number of applications before they landed a job. He knew the line that always killed him was the one where they asked for his most recent address. Yeah, "Stateville Correctional Center, Joliet, Illinois." Should he lie?

No. The day he had considered taking a shortcut and fleeing out of that rest room at the courthouse was still fresh in Ray's mind.

If this was God's path for him, if God would never leave him or forsake him, then he had to "do the right thing," and that didn't include lying.

The next day, however, Ray couldn't stick with job hunting. He had to find his sister. He went to the Elmhurst Hospital, but they said all medical records were confidential. The police, at least, checked their records for him. But no one matching the description of his sister had been booked.

He wondered if there had been an unclaimed body that matched her, but he couldn't bring himself to ask. *This is crazy*, Ray thought as he left the station. *My sister can't be dead! Why am I even thinking about bodies?* But then again, the hard facts were pointing more and more in the direction of disappearance by some means. She was simply gone! "Oh, God, please help me! Nothing's working out, and I'm running out of time. I gotta find my sister, and I need a job."

Money was getting tighter, and so the next day Ray went back to job hunting. He came back to Timothy House in the middle of the afternoon with nothing more encouraging than what he'd left with in the morning. "Have you talked to Carl Franklin?" Mr. Gee said.

"The cop?" Ray laughed. "I don't think my background would make me a very good candidate for the police academy."

Mr. Gee frowned in his get-serious manner. "Oh, that would be out of the question, my man. You simply don't have the taste for all those donuts and coffee. However . . . I wasn't talking about becoming a cop. Carl meets a lot of people in a lot of places, and he's helped several guys find jobs. Why don't you give him a call?"

CHAPTER 31

Ray called Carl Franklin and, to his amazement, the police officer *had* heard of a job opening, one with the TechClean Corporation. They provided janitorial service to businesses all over the Chicago area, and they had an opening on the crew that cleaned the Air Route Traffic Control Center at O'Hare International Airport.

"I'll give them a call right away," Ray said. "Thanks a lot. I really appreciate it."

"Do you really?"

The question startled Ray. People never questioned someone else's thanks. It was just what you said when someone did something for you. "Well, yeah. Of course. I been lookin' under every brick and behind every trash can for over a week. This is the first possibility I've turned up. Yeah, I really appreciate it."

"Then do me a favor. Did you go to church with Mr. Gee last Sunday?"

"No." What was this about?

"Then come to church with me Sunday. I'll pick you up. Whaddaya say?"

"Uh . . . yeah! Sure." If that was all he wanted. "But I don't got no church-goin' clothes."

"No problem. Wear whatever. Some folks come in jeans, some in suits. It doesn't really make much difference."

"Okay, if you say so."

Maybe Carl Franklin wasn't such a bad guy after all. As soon as Ray got off the phone with him, he wasted no time taking the El into the city, where he found the TechClean offices and filled out an application.

"Thank you, Mr. Slewinski. We'll call you if anything turns up," said the secretary as she threw his application in a bin.

"But I thought there was an opening to clean those offices out at the airport."

"You mean ARTCC?" She pronounced it *artic*. But when Ray frowned, she spelled it out. "The Air Route Traffic Control Center?"

"Oh, yeah! Carl Franklin, a Chicago police officer, told me you needed someone."

The secretary pulled out Ray's application and scanned over it again. "Well, we do need someone, but you marked on here that you were only available in daytime hours. It's only twenty-five hours a week, but that crew works at night. Actually, most of our crews work at night when people aren't in the offices."

Ray didn't know what to say. His responsibilities at Timothy House involved making sure the guys weren't sneaking out at night. Some had ankle monitors on, but others could get in a lot of trouble, and their sponsors wouldn't know about it until their PO sent a sheriff by to pick them up.

Seeing Ray hesitate, the secretary smiled.

"Air traffic slows way down after 10 p.m., and most of the staff goes home. Our crew doesn't even come in until midnight and works till 5 a.m. Would that be possible for you?"

If he didn't have to be out there until a little before midnight, perhaps he could do what was needed in getting the guys at Timothy House "tucked in," and he'd be back before most of them got up in the morning. Ray would try to work it out with Mr. Gee. Besides, he had to have a job, even if it meant losing his position at Timothy House. "Yeah, I can do that. When do I start?"

The secretary laughed. "First you have to have an interview with Mr. Gilmore. Then we need to check out your references. But if everything works out, could you begin next Monday night?"

"Sure!"

Sitting on the leatherette sofa on the other side from the secretary's desk while she went in to speak to her boss, Ray felt like he was waiting to see the dentist. In a few moments she came out. "Could you come back after lunch, say at 1:15? Mr. Gilmore's busy at the moment."

"No problem. See ya then."

Ray left and walked up the block. He didn't want to be loitering outside TechClean's offices if Mr. Gilmore or the secretary came out. He found a McDonald's and had a hamburger, then ordered a pie and a cup of coffee . . . and burned his tongue on it. Maybe he could sue and never have to work! Ha! Finally it was one o'clock, and he headed back to TechClean.

Mr. Gilmore must have spent part of his time going over Ray's application, because when he went in for his interview, it was obvious the man had not only looked it over but had called the Illinois Department of Corrections to check on his case. Nevertheless, Mr. Gilmore spent most of the interview asking about Ray's criminal background, which caused Ray to lose hope.

"So you actually shot somebody? That's pretty serious. Did you ever get arrested for any other crimes?"

"No." This wasn't going well, but Ray decided total frankness would be best. "To tell you the truth, Mr. Gilmore, I probably didn't get arrested for anything else because I got pulled off the streets with my murder case. I was in a gang, and . . ." He shrugged. "That would have led to more trouble sooner or later."

Gilmore leaned back in his chair and stroked his chin. "'To tell the truth,' huh? Well, I hope you're doing that, because we check out everything." He pursed his lips like he'd been sucking lemons. "How 'bout gang affiliation? You in a gang?"

"Not anymore." Ray turned away and rolled his head. "In prison, it's almost impossible to survive without the protection gang members provide each other. But there are things you can do. I was in the Latin Kings, but I got V'd out." He saw Gilmore frown. "That means I took a beating in order to get out. For the last couple years, I spent all my free time studyin' and helping in our prison ministry—the chapel program. Out in the yard and in the gym, I worked out or played hoops. I didn't hang with the Latin Kings, but sometimes—like when there was trouble—other sets counted me as a King. But that life's behind me."

"I see." Mr. Gilmore leaned forward. "Well, I appreciate your frankness, Mr. Slewinski." He waved Ray's job application. "And we'll consider this and give you a call one way or the other. Okay?"

Ray nodded. "Thank you, Mr. Gilmore." But as he left the office, he didn't expect a call of any kind. The promise of a call had just been a subtle way of telling him the interview was over and it was time for Ray to leave.

The urgency to find his sister consumed Ray's thoughts so much the following day that he put job hunting out of his mind. Or maybe it was the depressing experience of being turned down again and again that drove him to switch priorities. After all, he could only take so much rejection at a time.

The haunting possibility that his sister might be dead kept rising like a flood, swirling currents eroding the last remnants of family life. Why had he been so harsh when Lena came to visit him in prison? If he'd been more understanding, perhaps she would have stayed in contact.

Later that morning, when the Timothy House guys were off to school or occupied studying for their GEDs with the volunteer coach, Ray got on the El and headed into the Loop and up to Rogers Park. It made sense to search their old neighborhood, but Ray had hesitated to go there because of the memories of the shooting. He told himself that his mother had called all of Lena's old friends without any luck, but he knew that was inconclusive. As he rode along, Ray was so preoccupied with thoughts of his sister, trying to imagine where she might be, reviewing what he had done so far to try to find her, that he was oblivious of the El ride as though he were being teleported, not only across Chicago but back in time.

Ray got off at the Jarvis stop, determined not to face Howard Street—the next stop—and the scene of the shooting, and headed west a few blocks, then south to Jordan. The apartments, the stores, the corners. This had been his old stomping grounds, his hood. Everything was familiar . . . but different. Could Ray have made something more of it than a gateway to crime? Probably. He stiffly pushed the thoughts of the old days out of his mind—he was here for one purpose—and spent the afternoon knocking on doors. Many people were not home or wouldn't answer, most were strangers, but the half-dozen neighbors who remembered him and his family had not seen or heard of Lena since his mother moved.

It was a bust!

Ray went home discouraged—but glad, actually, to get away from the old neighborhood and all the memories that threatened to overwhelm him. There had to be another way to find his sister. Without her, he had no family at all . . . none, that is, except the uncle who lived in Indiana. Ray had barely spoken to him at his mother's funeral, and even then there had been blame and disdain in his uncle's few words. But maybe he was still the key to finding Lena.

The next day Ray walked to the Elmhurst library and found the phonebook for Michigan City, Indiana. It was his only chance. If his uncle didn't still live there, he might never find him. *Kovacsik, Alex and Catherine Kovacsik.* Ray ran his finger down the page. There were only two Kovacsiks listed for Michigan City: Justyna Kovacsik and A. Kovacsik. The second name had to be it. The A could stand for Alex or Alexander. . . . Ray wrote down the number and headed for a pay phone in the foyer. He would have to get a cell phone as soon as he had a job. They were so much more convenient, and every one of the guys at Timothy House had one.

Ray dialed. It rang and rang, and finally a woman's tired voice said, "Hello."

"Is this Catherine Kovacsik?"

"Who's this, please?"

"Ray Slewinski."

"Raymond? No, no! Alex said we should never accept a collect call from prison. Good-bye."

"Wait! I'm out of prison. This is not a collect call."

"It's not?"

"No."

"But you're not coming here, are you?" Her voice quavered in fear.

"No, Aunt Catherine. I'm in Chicago. I'm just trying to find my sister. Have you heard anything of Lena?"

There was a long silence as though she were searching through her last year's memories. "What did you say your name was? I know you are Maria's son, the murderer, but I've forgotten your name. Oh never mind. We don't want you to come here!"

"I'm not coming there, Aunt Catherine. I'm just trying to find my sister. Is Uncle Alex there?"

"He's working on the car."

"Well, could you get him for me?"

"He doesn't like for me to disturb him—"

"Just go tell him it's important, and it'll only take a minute. Please."

Ray heard the phone being put down, and in a few moments his aunt's distant words: "It's that boy from prison, Maria's son. He say's he's not coming here, but he wants to speak to you."

In a few moments Ray's uncle picked up the phone and said, "Yeah, Raymond. What do you want?"

"I'm trying to find Lena. I've been released from prison, and I'm trying to find her."

"We haven't heard a thing from her since the funeral. Look, I'm glad you're out, but there's nothing we can do for you. So please don't call again. You upset Catherine—"

"But—"

"No. Good-bye, Raymond."

The phone went dead. Ray stared at it, then hung up. That was that!

Ray spent the rest of the day hanging out at fast-food places, especially the McDonald's and the Steak 'n Shake nearest York Community High School in Elmhurst. Anytime teenagers came in looking goth, he asked them if they knew his sister. It was fruitless. Most of them treated him like he was a cop, and the few who responded said they didn't know anyone named Lena.

The next day Ray took the plunge and rode the El back into the Loop to the Cook County Medical Examiner's office on West Harrison. It took him nearly two hours before he filled out all the forms and got his answer. To his relief, there had been no unclaimed bodies during the last year that resembled his description of his sister. That, however, did not help him find her.

He was back on the Blue Line, headed west toward Timothy House, studying the city map Mr. Gee had given him and trying to figure out what to do next when he realized that he had been only three blocks from Cook County Hospital. That was where Moon was! He should have gone to see him. Ray looked out the window. Should he get off at the next El stop and go back? It was getting late. He might have to wait twenty minutes for the next train. He could come some other day, but he wondered how Moon was. Was he recovering from his burns? Would he be cuffed to his bed? Would there be a guard outside his door? Could he even receive visitors?

Ray stared out the window as the train clattered and rocked along the tracks down the center of the Eisenhower Expressway, screeching to a stop at each El platform while the traffic on the highway cruised past unhindered. If only he had a car, Ray could easily turn around and go back right now. If he had a car, it would be easier to find a job too, or more important, conduct an unhindered search for his sister. But there he was sitting in the El, almost twenty-two years of age, and he didn't even have a license.

When Ray arrived at Timothy House, there was a note on the door of his room telling him to call TechClean. He punched in the number with a cynical obligation. Most places didn't even bother to let you know when they didn't hire you. But to his surprise, TechClean wanted to know if he could come to work Monday night. Ray slapped his head with the heel of his hand. Unbelievable! He had been so doubtful that they would hire him that he hadn't even talked to Mr. Gee about getting off at night. "Yeah, I'd love to take the job, and I think it will work out, but can I call you right back? I need to check something first."

Mr. Gee was reluctant to lose Ray as a house parent during the night, but the guys in the house at that time were pretty stable. "The job is a good opportunity for you, Ray, so go for it. We'll work things out."

Ray called TechClean right back and landed his first paying job with the glee of a Chicago fisherman cranking in a record-setting salmon at Montrose Harbor.

CHAPTER 32

When Carl Franklin picked Ray up Sunday morning for church, he was driving a black 1998 Ford Mustang convertible that rumbled like a volcano when it idled and roared like a tiger when it took off. Ray had never experienced anything like it and had never imagined that a black cop might be into cars, but Carl was—big time.

"I got that job," he said when he caught his breath as soon as they were underway.

"At TechClean?"

"Yeah, I'm going to be working out at O'Hare, cleaning some offices at night, the air traffic center or something."

"Hey, that's great. Oh, forgot to tell you. I'm gonna have to kick you into the back, bro, soon as we get to Alicia's house."

"Oh yeah? Who's Alicia?"

"My fiancée." He glanced over to Ray with a grin that caused his eyes to squint. "We're getting married October 15, and you're invited . . . at least you are if you're willing to ride in the backseat. Gotta give my queen shotgun."

Wow! Everything about Carl Franklin was blowing Ray's mind and all his presumptions about cops, black men, and Christians.

Alicia Turner's petite form made Carl look like a defensive line-man for the Bears when they came bouncing out of her apartment building. A pink scarf contrasted with her mahogany skin in a way that set off her electric smile with beautiful teeth. "Sorry to chase you out of your seat," she said. "My name's Alicia. Carl tells me he bribed you to come to church by helping you find a job."

Ray laughed nervously as the doors closed and they drove off.

"You know Carl. He takes the Scripture seriously where Jesus said, 'Go out into the highways and hedges, and compel *them* to come in.'"

"All I care about," laughed Ray, "is that he don't put those cuffs on me to get me there."

"Not a chance," said Carl.

The Westside Christian Fellowship was as different from any church that Ray had ever attended as Chicago summers were from winter. Some three hundred people met in a converted warehouse as bright and busy as an airport concourse. Worship was irresistible with the pounding praise band and occasional dancing in the aisles—which Ray didn't try. But the freedom of it all made him feel welcome in the congregation that was two-thirds black with the remainder white and Hispanic. The preaching was as rich and practical as the Bible studies he had experienced with the prison ministry.

After the service Carl invited Ray to go with him and Alicia and several other young people out to the Olive Garden for din-ner. Ray hesitated, knowing how thin his wallet was, but he finally had a job and, after all, this was the way to make friends and find his place in the world again. Besides, "Sister-in-Christ Cynthia" was going with the group. Ray didn't even know her last name, but already Ray couldn't keep his eyes off her toffee-colored skin, green eyes, and long, beautiful hair.

In the days that followed, Ray found the work with Tech Clean hard, swinging a mop, running the industrial vacuum cleaner, and buffing the floors every night. Ray got home with just enough time before the residents of Timothy House had to start their day that he was able to eat breakfast with them—such as it was—and then he fell into bed and slept until early afternoon. When he got up, he helped with maintenance around the halfway house and thought about Cynthia until he came down to earth, worrying about his sister. Was there anything else he could do to find her? The quest was seeming more and more hopeless, and Ray was out of money—maybe he shouldn't have gone to the Olive Garden—and wouldn't get paid until the first of July. He had tried everything he knew to find Lena but with no results.

Slowly, worry about her was replaced with pursuing his own life. He really ought to go visit Moon at Cook County Hospital or look up Harrison on the south side. And there were girls everywhere with their bare bellies and their push-up bras. Wow, he'd been in prison too long, but he'd better not go there! But there were women at Carl Franklin's church who were different, women like Cynthia. Perhaps . . .

But first Ray ought to find his sister, Lena. He felt guilty for kind of giving up and letting her go, but what else could he do? Life moved on.

Then one day Carl Franklin dropped by. He was in uniform, and most of the Timothy House guys scattered to their rooms.

"Hey, Carl, you're scaring them off with those blues," Ray said.

Carl waved his hand. "Don't worry 'bout it. They can smell cop no matter what I wear. I just show up in uniform sometimes to demonstrate that I'm not trying to work undercover. But I hope their duckin' out like that doesn't mean they're holdin'."

"I don't think so. But it takes time to get over the old fears that somethin' bad's bound to happen when blue shows up."

"All the more reason to wear a uniform occasionally. So how ya doin'? How's that new job?"

"It's goin' great. Thanks for giving me the referral, but . . ."

"But what?"

"It's not about the job. I've come up dry tryin' to find my sister."

Carl had Ray go over what he had already done and then nodded. "Missing persons is the kind of thing where family and friends usually hold the key, they just don't know it."

"Whaddaya mean? You sayin' I know where she is but I don't know that I know?"

"Not exactly. Actually, in spite of the shows on TV, police don't get involved in missing persons very often unless there's indication of some kind of crime. A lot of people just disappear for their own reasons. And frankly, the only way to track them down is to hire a private investigator. Even then it's kind of a crapshoot."

"How much do PIs cost?"

"Well, like I said, you've already done the easy stuff, so you'd have to hire a good one at, say, eighty-five dollars an hour plus expenses. They'd probably require five hundred bucks as an advance. And of course, don't let any of them fool you. They cannot guarantee success, not even the best agencies."

Five hundred dollars! There went all hopes for a car. But Ray had to find his sister. He owed it to her!

A week later, on July 3, Mr. Gee dropped by. "Hey, Ray, could you come to the United Nations meeting today? We might be a little short on numbers if some of the guys are absent, getting an early start celebrating the Fourth."

Ray had wanted to talk to Mr. Gee anyway, so he jumped into the gray Buick. Once they turned north on Harlem Avenue, he said, "Got paid Thursday. Been thinkin': Maybe I should get my license and a car someday. Whaddaya say?"

Mr. Gee tipped his head from side to side, his lower lip protruding, as he navigated the traffic. "Sounds like a good idea if you can get somebody to teach you. They got these driving schools now, but they usually rip off Latinos or Asians or anyone from another country who needs a license. It's like, become a cab driver in fourteen hours or less, but I wouldn't pay them a penny."

"Well, who can I get to teach me?"

Mr. Gee glanced at Ray, then looked straight ahead as he stopped at a red light. When he turned again to Ray, his right eyebrow was raised. "I could teach you, but before you respond, let me tell you why I'm offering—other than just as a friend, of course."

The light turned green, and Mr. Gee pulled ahead. "The doctor's been telling me that I've got to slow down. But we can't afford to put a new person on staff for Captives Free, and I need more help than the once-a-week volunteers. Now, you've got a job that's a little better than half time, and you could continue staying at Timothy House without the house parenting responsibilities—I've got someone else who can take over—if you could help me in the ministry. You'd need transportation, though, 'cause one of the most time-consuming things I do is run all over the city, meetings here, meetings there, Bible studies at the jail and prison, and checking in with the guys on the streets or in the hospital. Some of that you could learn to do . . . if you could drive. Would that interest you?"

Ray gaped at Mr. Gee. "Sure would!" Almost like a spring shower, Ray felt meaning and purpose raining down on him. Up to this point he'd been consumed with simply getting out of prison and surviving. But this would give his life direction and purpose. It couldn't be described as anything but a gift from God. And if he could drive . . . well, he knew mobility alone wouldn't find his sister, but it might help. This was a gift from God, and Ray was thankful. But if he was going to find his sister, he needed a miracle.

They set a time the next afternoon—"after church," Mr. Gee said—when he would take Ray to the large parking lot of a factory that he knew would be empty on Sunday. "We can see how it goes, and if you have any aptitude—and I'm certain a man with your impressive skills won't have any trouble—then you can apply for a learner's permit on Monday, and we can go from there."

Nearly twenty guys were at the United Nations meeting that afternoon, young men Mr. Gee said had made a serious commitment to Jesus and had demonstrated enough self-restraint that they weren't likely to go off on a rival. "Letting these guys meet their brothers in the Lord, even if they are from a rival organization, has been a way to avert a lot of killings on the streets," Mr. Gee said. "But mixing members of rival gangs can be deadly, so I'm very careful who I invite."

They met in Mr. Gee's church, a large Gothic structure of gray stone. Ray joined the guys in playing hoops in the dual court gym until everyone was winded. Then Mr. Gee broke out the pizza, and the guys gathered in a circle for Bible study, much like those Ray had attended in the chapel at Stateville. After that one of the guys—a tall handsome Latin King—gave his testimony, but Mr. Gee had to interrupt him. "Okay, Mr. Perón. We got the picture. You don't have to tell us about all your exploits. Why don't you move on to when you heard about the Lord and tell us how he changed you?"

After José Perón finally told how God had given him a new direction, Mr. Gee introduced Ray. "Right now, Mr. Slewinski is helping us out at our Timothy House, but one of these days, he'll give us his testimony too. He's got a magnificent story of how God helped him get out of prison thirty-three years early. I mean completely out. He's not even on parole. Let's give God a hand." Everyone clapped as they looked at Ray and nodded. Seeing and hearing other people praise God like that over something that had happened in his life made him realize at a whole new level just how much of a miracle it was, and that was more than just his private opinion too! Wow, how good God is! Ray couldn't stop the tears that flooded his eyes and threatened to spill out the corners.

Then Mr. Gee introduced a Christian businessman who was the regional corporate manager for the White Hen Pantry convenience stores. The man talked about getting and keeping jobs.

"At our next meeting," Mr. Gee said when the job discussion concluded, "we hope to have Alan Sondano, a very fine attorney who has helped many of us. He'll come and talk about how to behave so you won't get a crime pinned on you that you didn't do. So be sure and show up. And remember, if there are any new guys who want to come, you need to check it out with me first. Okay?"

Afterward, as they were cleaning up, José Perón moved up beside Ray as they were carrying chairs. "So you're at Timothy House, huh? Saw the crown on your shoulder when we were playin' ball. You a King?"

Ray shook his head as he placed his chair on the stack. "Not anymore. Why?"

Perón spoke more softly. "Ah, man, I can dig that, 'cause you know, once a King, always a King. And these United Nations meetings, you know, they da bomb, and I'm cool with the God thing too. Praise the Lord! I picked up some information at the last meeting that helped out my boys."

"Oh yeah? Whaddaya mean?"

"Gave 'em a little heads up, you know. Kept 'em from walking into a trap. It was the inside dope, man. Real useful. Praise the Lord." He said it loudly enough that others might have heard, then he turned his body so his back was to the rest of the guys and he faced only Ray and returned to a quiet voice. "There's something you could help me with . . . know what I mean, man? As a brother."

Ray stared at him, trying not to show any emotion.

"Yeah." Perón glanced behind him. "I gotta ice some assets . . . just for a few days. Wouldn't be no risk holdin' it 'cause no one would look to you, you bein' inactive, so to speak. Know what I mean?" He watched Ray closely. "I'll make it worth your while: Ice my stash for cash, say, five benjamins until next Thursday, whaddaya say?"

CHAPTER 33

Five hundred bucks in five days—enough to engage a PI to search for Ray's sister! Wow! Ray's head was spinning. This must be God's miracle! And all he'd have to do is hold this guy's bag. He wouldn't have to deal or transport or collect from delinquent street vendors. Just take a little package home, put it in his drawer—no, it better be a more secure place than that—and give it back to Perón on Thursday. It wasn't like he was trafficking. This pharmacy was already in the hood. Somebody was going to get it and use it. He wouldn't be the one creating or adding to the drug problem.

On the other hand, some of that *ooowee* was nasty stuff. "So what is it?" he asked Perón, as though that made the difference. "What you got?"

"You don't need to know." Perón stared dead-eyed. "All right, all right. Just some ice, you know, crank. Nothin' big."

"Not big, huh? I seen a guy trying to come off crystal meth at Joliet. Turned him inside out. Sucker nearly died."

"That ain't my problem. Besides, this stuff goes to rich white kids. They're smart enough to know what they doin'. You gonna hold it for me or not?"

Ray hesitated. Who was this guy, anyway? Like Moon had once said, "*Somethin' too good to be true probably ain't true!*" The image of

Peter Musselman sneering at Ray and promising to put him away if he ever got out of prison passed through Ray's mind. What if this was a setup? What if this guy was a narc? And yet, how could he be, coming to a United Nations meeting? And five C-notes! It would take Ray a long time to save that much, a long time of not knowing where his sister was. He needed that money.

"So, why you like . . . frozen? Look man, this ain't about no heat from the popo. It's just a little territorial issue at the street level. I gotta establish some boundaries, and I can't do that if I'm holdin', know what I mean?"

Ray didn't know, but five hundred dollars—five days? Just until Thursday? Ray ran his fingers through his hair. "Okay. Where do I pick it up, and how do I return it?"

"Easy, man. That little red and black bag I brought my sneakers in—sitting right over there next to the wall." He jerked his head toward the other side of the gym. "You just pick it up and take it home like it was yours. Then on Thursday, I come by your place and swap you for the bones. Piece of pizza, man. You don't have to do nothin'. Deal?"

Ray nodded. Perón smiled and walked away, and Ray began to sweat.

The next day when Carl Franklin picked Ray up to go to church, he was still sweating every time he thought about the little red and black bag under his bunk. Carl was a cop. Cops smell drugs as well as a beagle, even meth, which was relatively odorless. And Ray hadn't thought of a better place to hide it in Timothy House. People might wonder if they saw him climbing up into the attic or digging through all the stored items out in the broken-down garage. But he ought to find a better place.

This was the third time Ray had gone to church with Carl. He'd also tried Mr. Gee's church, a local Catholic church, and "Bedside Baptist." But Carl's church brought Ray closest to God . . . only today he didn't feel like getting anywhere near God. Still, Cynthia was there, Cynthia *Braithwaite*, Ray had learned. She was in her first year of teaching third grade and felt overwhelmed, eager to talk about her experience, even to Ray. As Ray listened, he was even more impressed with her care for the children and her ingenious ways of managing thirty-two kids in an ill-equipped classroom—like looking up the meaning of each child's name and making a poster of it. Or the "Darn Lucky Box" where she put all the gloves and scarves and things the kids left laying around, and they were "darn lucky" to get them back . . . after they did some classroom chore. She was something else.

But now Ray was risking it all—any relationship that might develop with Cynthia, his job, his place at Timothy House, and the kindness of Mr. Gee in trying to get him set up so he could succeed as a free man.

The worship was as vibrant as usual, but Ray couldn't engage. In fact, his mind was back at Timothy House, thinking where he might hide the drugs, until halfway through the sermon when the preacher's words snagged his attention. "The Bible says, 'No temptation has seized you except what is common to man. And God is faithful; he will not let you be tempted beyond what you can bear. But when you are tempted, he will also provide a way out so that you can stand up under it.' "

Was he talking to Ray? How did he know about the temptation Ray had just faced . . . and had given in to, in the gym of a church, no less?

"But if you have been tempted," continued the preacher, "and have given in"—it was like the preacher was reading Ray's mind, one thought after another!—"you don't have to stay on that train. You can always get off. There's always a way out. It might not be easy, but it is always possible. And the sooner you take God's escape route, the better."

Ray didn't hear anything more. This was unbelievable, but if that preacher was actually speaking to him—he knew what Mr. Gee would have said: "It's not him, it's the Holy Spirit speaking through him, and it is to you. So listen up!" But if that were true, what *was* "God's escape route"? Ray had told himself the five hundred bucks was God's miracle to help him find his sister. But that was a stupid presumption, and he had known it all along.

Oh, God, what am I supposed to do now? he said to himself as he leaned forward, elbows on his knees, head in his hands. *What escape is there?* His mind searched for options: He could dump the drugs down the toilet, but then he'd have to face Perón empty-handed, and if the guy was willing to pay him five hundred just for Ray to hold them, then they had to be worth . . . what? five thousand, maybe more? He'd be in debt . . . forever, perhaps forced to do worse things. Maybe he should follow through with his commitment and just count this a hard lesson learned and never do it again. Yeah, that sounded pretty good, and he'd get his five hundred too.

Ray was still thinking about it that afternoon when Mr. Gee picked him up from Timothy House and was driving toward the empty parking lot. "You okay, Ray? You know, we don't have to do this driving thing right now if you're not ready for it."

"Ah, no, Mr. Gee. I'm okay. Let's go do it." But Ray couldn't get the question out of his mind: What was the way out God provided for *this* situation? Ray knew God's way would have been to say no in the beginning. "Just say no!" So easy to parrot but always so hard to do in the situation. Still, he should have done it. But he hadn't, and now it was too late. He was already on the train! But if the preacher was right, that you can always get off the train—all you gotta do is quit—then what did that mean? Quit! Quit means *quit!* Quit now! Find the guy, give back his drugs, and tell him you're not holdin' them for him anymore, not now, not ever. Just quit doing the wrong thing.

A sense of relief melted over Ray as they turned into the parking lot where his first driving lesson was to take place.

There was one problem, however. Ray did not know how to get hold of the guy whose drugs he held. But having made his decision, the drugs sitting under his bed seemed as explosive as the acetylene that had blown up Moon. And this explosion would most definitely take Ray out! He had to get rid of them . . . and soon!

That evening Ray called Mr. Gee and got Perón's cell phone number.

The thought crossed his mind: If he really wanted to do the right thing, he ought to destroy the drugs so no one else's brains would be fried by them and take the heat himself from the dealer. Or maybe he could tell Carl Franklin and secretly arrange to have Timothy House raided. Then he wouldn't be responsible for the loss of the drugs, but no one would be harmed by them either. But if the cops found drugs in Timothy House, either Ray or one of the other residents could end up being blamed. Once a raid was in motion, Carl might not be able to control the final outcome. Somebody could end up back in prison . . . *someone like me!* thought Ray. Even if he engineered a way so the drugs couldn't be pinned on anyone specific, it would reflect poorly on the halfway house and damage the ministry.

No, there was no other way to do it. If he was going to get off the train, he'd just have to return the drugs. Taking them off the street was too risky. Yet a little voice in the back of his head sounding somewhat like Rico Quiñones whispered: *Cobarde! Cobarde!*

The voice niggled at Ray all Sunday night while he swung the heavy Merit 2000 buffer down the hall floors of the ARTCC offices. But he wasn't a wuss! He was doing the right thing, getting off the train, quitting now! Only . . .

The next morning when Ray got back to Timothy House, he made his call. "Hey, Perón. This is Ray Slewinski. We met last Saturday in the basketball gym. I need to talk, today."

"Can't do that. In fact, don't be callin' this number again. See you Thursday."

"Not if you want your gym bag back . . ."

The phone was quiet for a few moments. "What's that mean?"

"It means if you want your gym bag back, you meet me today, at noon, at the Burger King, the one on Roosevelt Road."

"Nah, man. I don't know what you're tryin' to pull, but if we're gonna meet, I'll tell you where: How 'bout the North Gate of the Brookfield Zoo in thirty minutes. Very public."

"I can't get down there that soon. Give me an hour."

There was silence. "Okay. One hour, but no more." The phone went dead.

Ray got there in forty minutes and sat on a bench with the red and black bag between his feet, waiting for Perón. Every cop, zoo attendant, or anyone in uniform who came anywhere near Ray caused him to quake inside like the San Andreas Fault. He couldn't help feeling like the bag sitting between his feet was broadcasting like a boom box: "Drugs, got drugs, anyone for some ice, crank, meth, crystal. Whatever you call it, I got it!"

Finally Perón came strolling up, pants halfway to his knees, left leg rolled up, cap turned to the left—looking every bit the Latin King, surveying the crowd like he expected some kind of a hit at any moment. "Whaddaya doin' with my bag. You *loco*? If you lost that, you'd be dead, man. What's happenin', anyway?"

"I'm just returnin' your merchandise, man. You ever heard of downsizin'? Well, this is a major downsize. The lock-up's closed." Ray got up and started to walk away.

"Wait a minute." Perón grabbed the bag and came after him. "You can't do this, man. You short, man. I ain't payin' you nothin'!"

Ray held out both hands, shrugged, and began to walk away again.

"Hold on." Perón grabbed Ray's arm and whirled him around, opening his jacket just enough with the hand that held the bag to display the gun stuck in his belt. "How do I know this bag still holds what it's supposed to?"

"You don't. But you'll find out soon enough. You make a scene here, and you'll attract attention, get yourself collared. Then you'll know what's inside . . . when the cops open it in the evidence room. Frankly, that wouldn't bother me at all. Or you can take it back to your ride or your crib and check it for yourself. If anything's missin', you know where to find me. But I don't want no more to do with it."

"What? What's the matter? You want more money? Man, I paid you plenty—"

"It's not the money. I just made a mistake in takin' it in the first place. Walk away, all right? And I'll do the same."

Perón released his grip on Ray's arm and dropped his shoulders, staring ahead like he had been hit with a stun gun. He stood there, his red and black gym bag hanging at his side as Ray walked over and got on the 331 PACE bus and headed home.

Whew! That was tight. Ray smiled at his own reflection in the bus window as it rumbled along. He was no *cobarde*. He hadn't caved, not even when Perón flashed his piece. He'd done the right thing. God helped him. "But now, God, what am I gonna do to find my sister? I'm broke. I don't get paid again till next Friday, and then it'll barely be enough to pay back the people I've borrowed a five-spot from and see me through to my next check. What am I supposed to do to find her? Go to Pay-Day Loan?" He knew that was a poor-man's trap, but what else was he to do?

Was God going to help him? Had he not prayed enough? Should he have trashed Perón's stash? "Oh, God, I did as much as I could do! What more do you want?"

"*Cobarde,*" Quiñones seemed to whisper. "*You'll never get your sister back!*"

CHAPTER 34

Most evenings, after Ray had slept through the afternoon and had gotten himself something to eat, he used his learner's permit to drive Mr. Gee to the hospital to pray with a kid who had been shot or to a Bible study at the Cook County Sherriff's Boot Camp or to visit some guys on the street. Ray went into neighborhoods he never would have gone into alone, neighborhoods he didn't even know existed in Chicago. Even to the suburbs where gangs and gangsta styles flourished. On Ray's own time, Mr. Gee expected Ray to study the "Illinois Rules of the Road" booklet. Ray thought his getting a license would be so Mr. Gee could slow down . . . like the doctor had suggested. But Mr. Gee seemed to have forgotten that objective. "As soon as you get your license there'll be two of us, and we'll be able to do twice as much ministry. Don't you think?"

Ha!

Sometimes Mr. Gee picked up Ray earlier, and they ended up on one of Chicago's expressways during rush hour, where Ray sat in traffic, looking out the window, watching the El zip past as he had once longingly watched cars pass the El. Six of one, half dozen of the other.

Mr. Gee was a good driving teacher. In no time Ray had passed his driving test and received a license to drive by himself.

"The ministry actually has an extra car someone donated, an old Chevy Capri," Mr. Gee said when Ray waved his license in triumph. "It mostly sits in the garage of one of our board members out in Wheaton. Last time I used it was when someone sideswiped my car in a hit and run." His eyebrows went up and his eyes got big. "If you ever get in an accident, don't you ever drive off, or you could be back out at Stateville. Anyway, I used that Capri for a week while mine was in the shop. Like I told you earlier, the ministry can't afford to pay you for your help at this point, but that Capri runs and it's licensed and insured, if you'd like to use it."

"You bet, man! That'd be great!"

With his head tipped slightly to the right and a skeptical look on his face, Mr. Gee eyed Ray. "'Course, you're going to have some personal errands you need to run with that car. I think we understand that. I go shopping and do whatever I need to do in mine, but the car is for the ministry and to support you so you can minister effectively. There's no way to lay down rules saying you can go here but not there because 'there' might be on the way to someplace I've sent you. However, you need to use wisdom and practice moderation. Let's try it out for a month, but I want you to keep a log of where you drive, the purpose, and the distance. And then we'll go over it and see if there needs to be any adjustments. Sound fair?"

Ray didn't know what to say except yes. *Fair* hardly seemed the word. He was glad to help out in the ministry. Doing so was like answering a call from God, but to get the use of a car in return was another gift. "Thank you, Jesus!" All kinds of benefits and options flitted through Ray's mind. He'd go see Darnell and Moon. He definitely would go see Moon. Maybe he'd go down to Indiana and see his uncle. His uncle had claimed not to know anything about Lena's whereabouts, but perhaps . . . perhaps if he could get his uncle to talk to him face-to-face, they might come up with some clues Lena had dropped at the funeral, or even something his mother had said before she died that could lead to finding his sister.

Would a trip to Indiana qualify as *wise and moderate* personal use of the car?

Mr. Gee was talking again. " . . . and I'd suggest you get a cell phone and a credit card, but use that card only to pay for gas and in case of emergencies—and by emergencies I don't mean snack attacks or new sneakers! Too many people get in trouble with credit cards. But they can be helpful."

A credit card! Ray felt like a kid on Christmas morning. And instead of trying to hire a private eye with the little money he saved from his first paychecks—or getting a loan to hire one—he got a cell phone . . . "for the sake of the ministry," as Mr. Gee had suggested, of course.

A week later Ray received his new Visa card through the mail. "That was quick," he said to Mr. Gee. "I didn't even have to mention my last permanent address on the form, like I did on all those job applications."

"You mean Stateville! Ha," laughed Mr. Gee. "Figures. They only require enough to know how to come after you if you fall behind on your payments. And believe me, they'll get the money out of you, and a lot more if you have to pay interest. So don't let it get out of hand."

Ray filled the Capri with gas on the way to work and felt a new sense of freedom. A crib, a gig, a ride, a cell, and now plastic: He was finally set up to function like a tagged-up civilian. But what a sweat popper; when you come out of the joint, it takes a lot of effort—and a lot of help—to get in the groove.

A couple weeks later as Ray was coming home from work in the morning, Mr. Gee called him. "Ray, I know you're just getting off work, but I need a favor. You remember David Hickman, the young man in our Bible study at the Sheriff's Boot Camp? I believe he's a Latin King."

"Uh . . . sorry, can't place him. But whaddaya need?"

"That platoon graduated last week, and he's home on house arrest with an ankle monitor. But I promised I'd get a Bible to him, so I was wondering if you could take him one."

Ray had been looking forward to catchin' a few Z's, but . . . "Sure."

"Great. I've got to be in court all day. Alan Sondano wants me to testify on behalf of one of our boys. So if you could go up to Rogers Park and see David for me, that'd be great."

Rogers Park? His old hood? Ray stiffened. He felt so uncomfortable that day he went up there to look for his sister.

"'Course, if you need to get some sleep, I could probably see David some other time. It's just that—"

"No, no. It's okay. I'll go. You want me to drop by and pick up the Bible?"

"Yeah, I'd appreciate it, unless you've got one of those paperback NIV Bibles we've been passing out. I don't want David to think we've forgotten him now that he's out. For a lot of guys, this is the most critical time, you know."

Ray did know. Mr. Gee had done everything he could to help Ray get on his feet after coming out of prison. How could he even hesitate helping another guy? But Rogers Park—Ray didn't know whether he was ready to visit his old neighborhood again. He still had occasional nightmares about shooting Greg Mason. Would his blood never stop spurting?

Nevertheless, Ray agreed to go straight there as soon as he got a little breakfast.

He drove to the address on Ashland that Mr. Gee had given him, but no one would answer the apartment buzzer. Ray was about to walk away when he remembered his cell phone. If David was on house arrest, he would have to answer his phone, and Mr. Gee had given him the number. He called.

"Yeah." It sounded like the voice of someone not too happy at being awakened.

"David Hickman?"

"Yeah."

"David, this is Ray Slewinski. I work with Mr. Gee. We met at the Bible study when you were in the boot camp."

"Oh yeah." The voice had changed, and the door buzzed open. "I remember. Come on up."

Off the third-floor landing, the door to one of the apartments was open. "David," Ray called.

"Come on in. I was just trying to pick up a little."

Once his eyes adjusted to the dark, Ray saw that the job would have taken all day. A small, overworked air-conditioner in one of the shaded windows made noise but did little to cool the close room. A TV with rabbit ears lit the space with a snowy picture and the laugh track of a *Frasier* rerun. "Here," said a muscular, young African American in sweat pants and a ribbed, sleeveless undershirt, "let me move that clothes basket so's you can sit on up in that chair. Want somethin' to drink? Pepsi, or . . ."

"Pepsi'd be great." Ray frowned at himself as David went into the other room. Why was he surprised to find that David was African American just because Mr. Gee thought he was a Latin King? Ray was white and had sported the crown.

David returned and tossed Ray a warm can. "Sorry." He shrugged. "Ice tray's empty." Then he flopped down on the beat-up sofa and stared at the TV, but Ray did not think he was really watching.

Ray held the Pepsi, fearing the flight it had just taken would result in an eruption if he popped the top. "So how you doin'? How's it feel to be out?"

"Hard to tell, with this thing." David kicked his leg up to display the strap around his ankle. "Pretty tired havin' to lay up in here all the time, but guess it's better than the joint." He paused for a moment. "Though I didn't mind the boot camp all that much. Least there was something to do that didn't end up getting you shot."

"Yeah. Know what you mean." Ray gingerly opened the Pepsi with a *psst* that he sucked up before it foamed over. "Mr. Gee seemed to think you were a Latin King."

"Oh yeah? *¡Amor de rey!*" And he gave a King hand sign.

David took his eyes off the TV and looked at Ray. "You were in the big house, weren't you?"

"Just got out in May."

"What was your organization on the streets?"

"Kings. This my old hood too. I just lived up on Jordan."

"Get out! Hey, man, when I get unbuckled, we'll have to go kick it, and maybe you could put in a good word for me with the boys."

Ray shook his head. "That ain't me no more, man." Ray told him about the forty years he'd been workin' on when God worked a miracle. "But let me tell you somethin' I been learnin' lately. When we're facin' certain disaster, especially of our own making, God always offers a change-up if we'll take it. This could be your change-up, man, a chance to make a clean break. Know what I'm sayin'?" What was he saying? He was talking like he knew all about it, when he had taken the easy way out of returning Perón's stash to him rather than destroying it. *Cobarde, cobarde!*

But easy way or not, God had helped Ray quit holdin' the ice, and that was a way for him to escape. And it had worked. He had to quit listening to those little accusations that bounced around in his head like pinballs.

"Here's the Bible Mr. Gee promised you. Look here." Ray flipped to 1 Corinthians 10:13, the verse the preacher had been talking about last Sunday. "It says it right here that God will make a way to escape."

"You mean you were a King and you got out? I thought once a King, always a King, you know, for life?"

Ray told him about getting V'd out of the Kings. "It can happen, especially for religious reasons. But you need to have something to go to, like the Lord, and the support of people like Mr. Gee. 'Cause if they find out you're hypocritin', you're dead. Literally! I'd suggest you get involved in a real good church. You can get permission to go even though you're still on a monitor." Yeah, and now who was "hypocritin'"? Ray liked Carl's church, but he hadn't been going regular. But he knew it was the right thing to say, so he continued. "Then when you get off house arrest, go to your posse and tell them you want out because you're a Christian."

"Oh, man. I don't know if I could take a violation. That's cold, man!"

"Yeah, well I'm not the one to tell you to crack the hard nut. But sometimes there are ways, steps you can take in the right direction, even if you can't go all the way. I'm not telling you what to do, but you might check it out with your *jefe*, see what he says, see what's likely to happen, and then ask God for the courage." Ray stared at David, thinking about what he had just said. Was that what he'd done? Taken a step in the right direction even though he hadn't been strong enough to go all the way? He rubbed the back of his hand across his mouth like he was wiping away a bad taste.

"Yeah." David looked back at the laughing TV screen. "I'll think about that. Could you ask Mr. Gee to pray for me?"

"I'll be sure to do so. But you want me to pray for you right now?" It was the thing he knew Mr. Gee would have offered, but Ray had never prayed for anyone like this before. Oh, he'd prayed for other guys when they all sat together in a Bible study, but to be the one to suggest it in such a personal way . . . what would he do if the guy said yes?

David pulled his eyes away from the TV. "Sure. I could use some prayer!"

Ray leaned forward, elbows on his knees, head in his hand. "Father God, David needs your help right now. Please be with him like you were with me. Give him the strength to do the right thing. Amen." There! He'd prayed for someone. He let out a sigh and stood up. "Guess I'd better go."

Three minutes later, Ray was down on the street walking toward his car. He was afraid he didn't make a very good street chaplain—didn't even attend church every Sunday himself—but he was learning. Maybe next time he would be able to pray a little longer than ten seconds. On the other hand, did God listen more closely to long prayers than short ones? Didn't Jesus say something about not babbling on and on like the pagans, thinking that we'll be heard for our many words? Yeah, something like that. He'd have to look it up when he got home.

His mind was so on ministering to David—God had really used him, hadn't he?—that when he pulled out of his parking spot, without thinking, he turned left on Lunt. *I gotta tell Mr. Gee about prayin' with David!* Then, almost automatically, he turned north on Clark and headed into his old neighborhood.

CHAPTER 35

Popeyes still anchored the corner of Clark Street and Jordan Avenue with the small parking lot where he'd first seen Greg Mason riding in that Taurus. *Ah, man.* Ray wished he had never seen him that day. One little incident changed his whole life . . . and *ended* Greg Mason's life! Ray turned west on Jordan again and drove slowly down the block. Somehow the neighborhood didn't stir the same haunted feelings as it had the day he came looking for his sister. Ray let the old memories seep in from the day he frantically pedaled the bike this way, hoping to ditch the cops.

He pulled over to the curb opposite his old apartment building and sat staring at it, thinking of all the good times before he'd gotten caught up with the Latin Kings. Funny, back then, he hadn't thought of them as "good times," but they were. Very good times compared to what came after that. Life had been simple—a Christmas tree in the window in the winter, hoops in the park in the summer, and the smell of home-cooked food every night when he walked in the door.

Ray remembered the day he'd been playing basketball with some other kids on the court in the park when three cute girls stopped to watch. Oh, had he played that day, sinking two jump shots and a lay-up. Then along came a couple older guys Ray knew were Latin Kings. In five minutes the girls had gone away with them. That was the day Ray became a wannabe. It wasn't long until he was a shorty and then a full-fledged gangbanger.

Oh, if things had only taken a different course . . . No, if Ray had only chosen a different course!

Ray pulled away and went around the block, back to Clark Street, where he headed north again toward Howard Street. But what was this on his right? The old stores a block before he got to Howard Street were gone. In their place stood a huge Dominick's food store and a strip mall with all kinds of new stores. The place was getting gentrified. He pulled into the parking lot and got out of his car, taking his first steps gingerly as though he were walking in a dream. It was so different, but so much the same. Slowly he made his way toward the corner of Clark and Howard, the scene of the crime. Over seven years ago, right there in the street was where the green Taurus had stopped, blocked by traffic. Ray had raced up on the bike with Rico right behind.

No! He didn't want to recall what happened next. He'd been over that all too often in his nightmares and his daydreams. He walked quickly past to the intersection of Clark and Howard, where he turned east on Howard.

Howard Street hadn't changed that much. Could anything change Howard Street, the ugly seam where Chicago and Evanston met? It was as though Evanston had bulldozed everything and everyone they didn't want down to the border while the Chicago riffraff had been stopped there from going north—drugs, prostitutes, pawnshops, homeless people, violence of every kind lurked in the grungy doorways and narrow alleys.

Obviously some business people were attempting to salvage the neighborhood with the new shopping center less than half a block away, but it hadn't yet been enough to upgrade Howard Street. Even the El stop was too scary for most people to use at night. Then Ray noticed a smartly dressed businessman coming along the sidewalk toward him. Maybe money and success were making their inroads.

Wait a minute! Ray knew that face. No, it couldn't be. Rico Quiñones? No, no, not Rico looking like he had just come out of a downtown office building, stepping smartly as though on his way to a power lunch.

Ray didn't want to meet Rico. There was too much baggage between them. He wanted to turn away and flee, but it was so unbelievable to find Rico looking so sharp that he couldn't resist staring at the man as he approached. Was it really him?

"Rico . . . hey, Rico?"

"Hey, my man!" Rico's eyes opened wide. "My man, Slew!" He threw his hands into the air like a televangelist and stood there, waiting for Ray to come to him. "I never expected to see you—not now, not here!"

"Guess you didn't, 'cause as you know, I went down for forty."

"Ah, yeah. That was too bad. But it's so good to see you now! How'd you get out, bro?"

"Actually, it was somethin' of a miracle." Ray was ready to tell him the story. Maybe God would convict Rico right there on Howard. Certainly there were few people in this world who needed to repent more than Rico Quiñones, and Ray was the street chaplain to do it!

But before he could say more, Rico jumped in: "You're right, must've been some kind of miracle for 'em to let *you* out. But hey, you know, it's good to see you. I'm glad you're out. Let's get together sometime. Okay?" Rico started to slip past Ray.

"Hey, hold on a minute, *compadre*. What's the rush?" Why was Rico so eager to get away? Was he afraid Ray might extract revenge for having egged him on to do the shooting, an act that had robbed Ray of seven years of his life and might have cost him forty? He wasn't about to let this guy bolt after what he'd done. Ray might have been ready to let bygones be bygones—after some sincere groveling—but he wasn't about to let Rico act as though nothing had happened years before.

Ray hadn't seen the homeless guy coming up behind him until the guy spoke over his shoulder. "Hey, Mr. Rico, Mr. Rico, can you help me out?"

"Get lost, Henry. I'm busy."

The guy stumbled into an alcove, where he continued mumbling as though he were talking on a cell phone.

"Sorry, Slew. Didn't mean to be rude or nothin'. Tell me, how's it going? You got a place to stay? Gettin' set up?"

"Yeah, I'm doing all right. I'm out in Maywood. How 'bout yourself? Looks like you're doin' mighty fine. What are you up to these days?" Ray was thinking how being sent away set you behind. If he hadn't been sent to the pen, he, too, might have had a career and some fine threads like Quiñones.

Just then the homeless guy staggered out of the alcove like a drunken cuckoo bird. "Mr. Rico, Mr. Rico . . . a dollar'll do. Just a dollar, any ol' dollar."

"Now I warned you, Henry. Not now. Go away." Rico gave the man a push, which only served to push him back into the alcove. Then he turned to Ray. "I'm doing okay." He looked down at his clothes, arms slightly spread as though demonstrating his success. "As usual, I been takin' care of business."

"Yeah," said Henry, stepping back up to the two of them. "You the *businessman* of Howard Street, Mr. Rico. But, Mr. Rico, could you just lend me—"

"I'm warning you, Henry, get on outta here 'fore I smack you upside the head!"

Henry turned to Ray. "Yeah, he's the *el primo* pimp of Howard Street. He's good. Ain't no other like him." Then he turned back to Rico. "Come on, Mr. Rico, can you help me out, just this once?"

Sensing that Rico was about to detonate on the poor guy, Ray tried to deflect him. "You a *pimp*, Rico? And what's with this?" Ray reached out and flipped the lapel of Rico's suit. "You don't look like no pimp. Where's the gold chains and flashy clothes?"

Rico gave Henry a threatening stare while speaking to Ray. "Times are changin', Slew. Times are a-changin'. Don't need no gold and flash. Just quality. Hey—" He turned to Ray; maybe the deflection had worked. "I got me a regular ride, now, just a plain-lookin' Lexus. Nowdays we invest in personnel, not the trappings."

But Ray hadn't taken into account how touching Rico's suit might embolden the homeless man. The guy reached out and tapped Rico's shoulder, trying again for a handout. This time Rico back-handed him so hard it knocked the man to the sidewalk. "I told you to leave me alone, Henry. You want that I hurt ya?"

"Rico, Rico, Rico." Ray put a hand on his shoulder and stepped between him and the man on the ground. "Chillax, man. He don't know no better. Leave him be." Ray dug into his pocket and pulled out a dollar. "Here, man. Here's a buck."

"Thank you. Thank you!" The man staggered to his feet, using the side of the building as a prop to help him up. "Thank you. I really want to thank you."

The man's nagging was getting to be too much for Rico. Ray could see him boiling. He needed to change the subject. "Hey, Rico, you remember my sister, Lena? She used to live with us down there on Jordan, but I lost track of her while I was in the joint. You seen her round here? She used to have some other friends up this way."

Rico stepped back and brushed at the front of his suit with his finger tips. "Nah. She was probably too young for me back then. Sorry."

"Oh yes, you have, Mr. Rico. You know Lena. She works for you."

"Works?" Sharp slivers of ice churned in Ray's stomach. "Whaddaya mean, *works*?"

"Ain't nothin'. He don't know what he's talkin' about. That's why I didn't want to give him any money. He's just an old burned-out wino. His mind's . . ." Rico twisted a finger beside his ear. "Shouldn't encourage 'em."

"I do too know what I'm talkin' 'bout. Lena's his best ho! Everybody round here knows that." Henry threw up both hands to protect himself. "No, don't hit me, Mr. Rico!"

Ray grabbed Rico's arm with a grip like a Chicago winter. "What's he mean? You pimpin' my *sister*?"

Rico jerked back but couldn't break free. "Don't mind him, Slew. He's just a homeless bum. He don't know nothin'.'"

"But you, *you're* workin' my sister, aren't ya?"

"Look, look." Rico finally pulled free, and Ray shoved him once, then a second time until Rico planted his feet and shoved back. "So what if I am? You ought to be thankin' *me*, man. I been taking care of your family. You owe me!"

"Owe you? This is all I owe you!" Ray slugged him hard on the jaw and then drove a solid left to his middle. "Where's my sister? Give her up before I turn you into a grease smear up the side of this building."

Rico doubled over choking.

"Uh-oh, popo! Uh-oh, popo!" warned Henry, rocking from side to side with his hands clasped in front of him. "Evanston's finest comin' round the corner! Uh-oh, popo!"

Ray backed off before the cruising cops noticed what was happening.

"Okay, okay." Rico stepped back, took a couple deep breaths, and tried to stand tall, straightening his suit. "You want to know where your sister is? I'll give you her address. Go see her for yourself!"

Rico recited an apartment number on Juneway Terrace. "Like I said, go see for yourself."

Seething, Ray turned and headed back to where he'd left his car.

"Hey, Slewinski, won't do you no good. She's all mine anyway."

CHAPTER 36

Something Ray had never felt began to bubble up inside him, like sulfur smoke that caused him to gasp and cough even as he resisted doing so. It was worse than the CS gas the guards had used at Stateville to quell the riot, but it was coming from within him. Ray got into his car but found he was shaking so badly that he tried five times before he managed to get the key into the ignition.

Juneway Terrace! The infamous little street that had given the whole neighborhood the tag "Juneway Jungle" was just a couple blocks north and east. Ray had found his sister . . . almost. But if Rico was pimping her . . . "Oh, God, don't let that be true!" He bent over, clutching his stomach and coughing. In spite of being too inexperienced to handle a car safely without thinking about it, Ray headed out of the parking lot and almost ran the first signal he came to. He managed to stop with the Capri halfway into the intersection. The honking from the traffic that had to swerve around him didn't even penetrate his consciousness, which was focused exclusively on going after his sister.

In five minutes Ray pulled to a stop outside the apartment address Rico had given him, blocking a fire hydrant. But in this neighborhood the cops were unlikely to notice. They had more important things to worry about . . . like staying alive. Ray ran to the door and stepped inside the vestibule, looking for the doorbell for 4A. It was not to be found. In fact, the whole mailbox/doorbell unit for the eight apartments in this stairwell had been torn from the wall. All that was left were a few dangling wires and some trod-on advertising circulars and bills on the floor.

"Lena! Lena!" Ray filled his lungs. "LENA!" He yanked on the handle of the inside door. It swung open, almost hitting him in the face . . . having not been locked in the first place. Ray dashed up the steps, lit only by a single bulb on the second-floor landing, past the gang graffiti on the walls, and through the overwhelming smell of urine, until he came to the fourth floor. A . . . B. A would have to be the left door. He pounded on it with his fist. "Lena! Lena Slewinski!" No response, but from somewhere within he could hear the sound of a TV. Sounded like a soap opera.

"Lena? It's me, Ray. Let me in. Lena!"

He heard movement, someone approaching the door, and then the sound of locks being opened. "She don't work this early. 'Sides, you ain't supposed to come here anyway. You know better 'n that."

"Let me in." Ray pushed past the frowzy redhead who wore an oversized Cubs T-shirt stretched halfway down her thighs. "Where's Lena? I want my sister! LENA!" He stopped his charge, not knowing where to head.

"Man, you her brother?"

"Yeah. Where is she?"

"I can tell you, she don't want to see you or nobody else right now. Why don't you get on out of here and come back later . . . after she's up."

"Up? Which room's she in?" The clue gave Ray enough direction, and he headed down the hall, opening the first door and flipping the light switch. No light. All he could see by the dim gray coming through the shaded window were a couple mattresses on the floor with piles of clothes on them. Or was that a person?

He stepped across the room, tripping over shoes and other items on the floor. "Lena?" He shook the lump. It *was* a person. "Lena, wake up. It's me, Ray. I came for you." The figure groaned and pulled away from him. "Come on, sis. Gotta get up." Ray took another couple steps to the window, where he tried to raise the paper blind. Instead, it tore loose and came crashing down in a cloud of dust. Behind it, glass so dirty it looked frosted revealed a brick wall no more than three feet away. "Come on, Lena. We gotta go." He turned back.

A half-dressed woman sat up on the mattress, head flopping down as though her neck were broken, her skin as dark as Moon's.

"You ain't Lena! Where's Lena? Where's my sister?"

As Ray stumbled out of the room, he heard commotion down the hall. He followed the sound and found the redhead in the kitchen, helping a girl—who sat half on, half off a broken kitchen chair—pull on some too-tight jeans.

This time Ray could see it was his sister. "Whatcha doin'?"

The redhead glared over her shoulder at Ray. "What's it look like? Helpin' her get dressed. Do you mind?"

"Oh, sorry!" He glanced briefly around the trashed kitchen. "This must be the place for modesty, all right. Why can't she pull on her own pants?"

"Can't you see?"

Ray had been looking, and now it was registering. Lena was so stoned she couldn't even sit straight in the chair. He moved toward her, his hands out to help, but Lena threw up her own hands and ducked her head down behind them. "Stay away."

"What?" He backed off.

"Just leave me alone."

"I ain't gonna hurt you."

"Still . . ." She lowered her hands and stared at Ray, her eyes losing focus and her lids dropping like jerkbait that had to be yanked up every few moments with a twitch of her head. "Thought you were in prison."

"Got out in May, over six weeks ago. Been lookin' for you the whole time. Where have you been?"

"Well . . . I . . . I don't think you'd understand." She looked like she was falling asleep.

Ray went to the sink and grabbed a rag. It was wet and sour. He threw it down and ran the cold water into his hands, then stepped behind his sister and put his cold, wet hands on her face.

She pulled away. "What are you doing?"

"Come on, Lena. Wake up! We gotta get out of here!"

"Where we goin'? I ain't goin' nowhere with you."

"I'm gettin' you away from Rico, away from this crunked-up hellhole."

She staggered to her feet and turned to face him. "Yeah? And to where? What better do ya have for me?"

"Anything's better than workin' the streets and being strung out on . . . what're you on, anyway?"

"What difference does it make? I ain't goin' nowhere."

"Yes we are!" Ray reached out and grabbed her arm, checking the inside for needle tracks. "Oh, dear God. What are you shooting?"

"I ain't shooting anything. That's just . . . we got fleas here. Look at her legs."

The redhead's legs had bites all over them. Some looked infected. "These on your arms aren't bites. Whaddaya been shooting?"

She yanked her arm out of his grip. "Just a little white. So what? Sometimes I need a little somethin', you know?"

"Look, I don't care what you say. We're leavin' here, *now*. You got anything you want to take with you? Clothes or anything?"

"I can't, Raymond. I can't. Rico would kill me if I left."

"Not before I kill him!" Yeah, that's what he would do. He'd kill that shank-eatin' pimp! And that's the way he'd do it too. Make him eat a shank! Feel every inch of it going in.

Lena started to cry. "But I can't. He'd kill me."

"Look, Lena. He's already killing you. You could have HIV or even AIDS. He's destroying your life just like he destroyed mine."

She sniffed in a great gulp, trying to hold back the tears. "Whaddaya mean?"

Bile rose in Ray's throat. "He's the one who . . . oh, forget it. We're gettin' outta here!"

The black girl came into the kitchen, and the redhead advanced toward Lena. Ray couldn't wait any longer. If Lena left something important behind, he'd come back and get it later. He grabbed her arm again and pulled her toward the back door. At first she came easily, like she didn't realize what he was doing, but once he turned the lock and got the door open, she began yelling. "No! No! You can't do that!" But she still wasn't resisting as he pulled her out onto the porch and started down the stairs.

The thought ricocheted through Ray's mind that Rico had demeaned Lena so much that she was incapable of resisting anything physical. Or maybe deep down she was glad he was rescuing her. Whatever the explanation, they made it down the four flights of stairs with nothing worse than a lot of yelling and screaming from Lena and the two other whores who followed her. "You let that girl go! You can't do that to her. Help! Help! Somebody call da po-lice!"

Yeah, like they wanted the police up there in their apartment. Ray saw a couple people stick their heads out their back doors and watch for a moment, but once they saw it was just a man dragging a "ho" down the steps, they went back inside. . . . Only in the Juneway Jungle!

But when Ray got to the ground and Lena realized that all her wailing hadn't fazed him, she began to fight and resist for real.

Finally he just picked her up and threw her over his shoulder like a bag of cement mix and carried her across the courtyard, through the gangway, and out to his car while she kicked and screamed and pounded him on the back.

It must have taken all the fight out of her, though, because once Ray opened the door of his car and threw her into the seat, she just sat there when he yelled, "Don't you dare move a muscle." Before she had a chance to catch her breath, he ran around to the other side, jumped in, and took off.

Lena whimpered softly, bent forward with her head in her hands.

Ten minutes later, they were cruising down the Outer Drive with the city on their right and the lake on their left. He had made it. Once he got down to the Loop, he'd head out the Eisenhower and . . . yeah, where would he take her? He couldn't take her to Timothy House. It was only for men. Maybe he could take her to Cynthia's apartment. No. That was crazy. Cynthia might be a compassionate person, but dumping a strung-out hooker on her was over the top. He might as well kiss her good-bye for good if he brought that kind of trouble to her. He wasn't even sure he wanted her to know what had become of his sister. It would look like the whole family was bad: One committing murder and snagging a forty-year sentence, the other turning into a prostitute and a junkie. Besides, she was gone all day, and Ray knew that Lena would need some baby-sitting for a while. Maybe Mr. Gee would have an idea. Ray pulled out his cell phone and flipped it open, then he checked his rearview mirror to make sure a cop wasn't close enough to notice him breaking Chicago's local law.

What he saw, however, caused him to put down his phone as fast as if a cop were on his tail. The first car—not fifty feet back—was a slate-gray Lexus, and Ray could clearly see Rico Quiñones behind the wheel.

CHAPTER 37

Rico Quiñones following them? It certainly wasn't because he graciously wanted to return a sweater Lena accidentally left behind! He was after them . . . or at least after Lena. Rico probably didn't care a whip about Ray as long as Ray didn't disrupt his "bizniz." But Ray was messing with his merchandise, something Rico wouldn't tolerate.

Ray gripped the wheel, pulling himself forward to get a better view in his mirror. It was Quiñones, no question about that! There was that crooked grin across his face just as if he were saying, *"Cobarde! Cobarde!"* And a red and black garter hung from his rearview mirror. In spite of the hot summer air that blew through the window, a chill shook Ray. Unconsciously his foot pressed harder and harder on the accelerator. Most cars traveled five, ten, or even twenty miles per hour above the speed limit on the Outer Drive, but Ray was passing them all. Still Quiñones kept pace, hanging back no more than a couple car lengths as the Capri began to shudder and strain.

"Raymond! Whatcha doin'?" Lena had raised her head out of her hands to protest through the streaks of last night's mascara. "Slow down! Ya gonna kill us both!"

Ray glanced down to see the speedometer vibrating close to eighty and turned what had been involuntary into a deliberate attempt to outrun his pursuer by slamming the gas pedal all the way to the floorboard. The gasping engine pulled harder but barely increased the speed of the car. Ray looked again in the mirror and admitted the obvious: There was no way his old car was going to outrun a new Lexus. Without realizing it, Ray began to shake as much as his car. What if he had an accident? What if a cop saw him?

Lena was crying again. "Please, Ray. Slow down!"

Movement in the mirror caught his attention, and he saw that Quiñones was pulling up on his left side. The side windows of the Lexus were tinted too dark for Ray to see within until Rico lowered his right-front power window. And there sat the pimp laughing as he paced him, cruising smoothly and easily at eighty-five miles an hour while Ray could only watch for a second or two at a time. He saw Rico pick up something from the seat beside him but had to wrestle the Capri's steering wheel in order to keep the car under control as it shimmied over a few bumps. He glanced back at Quiñones. His arm was extended toward Ray holding a large chrome-plated handgun. Rico gestured for Ray to take the next exit.

No way! Ray was not going to let himself get trapped in some side street by a thug like Rico. He drove on, pressing ever harder on the gas—though he gained no further speed—as he fought to keep the Capri in his lane. On the other hand, if he could get into the neighborhood of some rivals . . . maybe Rico, who was obviously Latino, would hesitate to show muscle when alone. They were coming up to the Lincoln Park Zoo on their right. Beyond it was the Gold Coast. Not much chance to find rivals hanging out in front of those million-dollar condos, but beyond the Gold Coast, some blocks were Gangster Disciple territory. Could he find them?

Ray glanced over to see the Lexus slow down and drift back. Ray let up on the gas as he extended his lead, watching in his rearview mirror as Rico fell so far behind that he disappeared in the traffic. Whew! Maybe the pimp was letting them go. But what

Ray had not seen until he whizzed past it was the Chicago police car parked on the side of the highway running a radar speed trap.

"Oh no!" Ray said as the cop's blue lights began flashing and the cruiser lunged onto the highway. "Quiñones must have a radar detector. Now we're fried!" But at least no one was pointing a .357 Magnum at him any longer.

He slowed down quickly as the cop car came up behind him and signaled that Ray should take the next exit, which was La Salle Drive, curving around the bottom of the zoo. As he got off, there was no safe place to stop, so Ray kept going until he turned north onto Stockton Drive.

Whoop. Whoop. "Pull it over right now."

Ray stopped the car and sat there waiting while the cop ran his plates. Then he watched in his side mirror as the cop came up to the left corner of Ray's car and said, "Driver's license, please?"

Ray held his open wallet out the window with his license showing through the plastic window.

"Take it out and hand it to me."

Ray complied, dropping his wallet back on the console between his and Lena's seat.

"Please step out of the car slowly, and put your hands on the roof."

What was happening? The cop had stepped back and had his hand on the butt of his sidearm. Which would be better: to be shot by the chrome-plated gun of a fancy pimp or by the blue-metal special of a Chicago cop? But Ray hadn't spent seven years in prison without learning how *not* to spook a cop. He got out very slowly, keeping his arms away from his sides until he could put them on the roof of the Capri.

The cop studied his driver's license with a frown. "Hmm, new driver, huh? What's your hurry, anyway?"

"You're not gonna believe me, but a guy in a Lexus was pointing a .357 Magnum out of his window at me."

The cop coughed a laugh. "And you could tell that it was a .357 while driving at eighty miles an hour? What'd you think you were gonna do? Outrun a bullet?" The cop looked toward the other side of the car. "Ma'am, ma'am! Please stay in the vehicle. Close the door and stay in the car!"

"I can't. I'm gonna be sick." Lena finished opening the car door, fell out onto the lawn on her knees, and proceeded to throw up.

"Ma'am, you gotta get back into the vehicle. Right now!"

Lena just rocked back and forth on her hands and knees. After a moment the cop gave up and began writing a citation, copying information from Ray's driver's license onto the ticket. In a few moments Lena stood up and stared back across the park toward La Salle Drive. Ray followed her gaze . . . and saw parked no more than a block away the familiar slate-gray Lexus. Lena started walking toward it.

"Lena, no. No! Lena, come back. Don't go." Ray started to follow.

"Stay where you are, and keep your hands on the roof of the car."

"But that's my sister. She's getting away." Then he yelled. "Lena. NO! Don't go to him. Come back. Officer, you gotta stop her. She's getting away."

"Getting away from what? You? A guy who threatens her life by driving eighty miles an hour on the Outer Drive? Get serious."

"You don't understand. He's her pimp, and she's going back to him. He was the one who was following us, pointing a gun out his window. You should go search his car. You'll find it."

"Look, Mr—" he held Ray's license a little further from his eyes—"Mr. Slewinski, I don't work vice. I can't do nothin' about it if she wants to go back to her Mack Daddy. That's your problem. And I don't have a warrant to search the guy's car."

"But he has her shootin' up cocaine, all strung out so he can keep her in his stable. That's why she's going back to him."

He kept writing his ticket. "You might be right, or you might be pullin' a fast one on me, trying to distract me so you can drive away. But don't forget—" he held up Ray's license, waving it at him—"I still got this."

"Exactly! So what could I do?" Ray threw up his hands and started to turn toward the cop.

The cop stepped back and reached for his gun. "Put your hands back on the roof."

Ray's shoulders slumped as he complied. He again looked across the lawn. Lena was getting into Rico's car. He'd lost her again.

"Here, sign this," the cop said. "It's not an admission of guilt, just confirmation that you received the citation." Ray signed the slip. "You were doing better'n eighty, but I gave you a break, Mr. Slewinski, and put you down for fifty-nine. That's only fourteen over the posted limit. It'll save you some money. But I hope you've learned your lesson."

"Thanks." Ray got back in his car, not feeling at all thankful, and waited until the cop drove around him and on up the street. Then he hammered the steering wheel with his fists. So close! *So close!* But she had gotten away! He wanted to scream, he wanted to rage. Rico had his claws deep into Lena. Ray had to get her away from him, or he'd kill her with the cocaine or an STD. At the very least he'd leave her a human wreck. Ray had to get her back!

His jaw clinched. He pulled out and headed north, back to the Juneway Jungle.

He took the city streets rather than going back by way of the Outer Drive. He needed time to think. The pumping adrenaline that had for the last couple hours found an outlet in *doing something* to get his sister back began to sour into a rage that seethed and searched for a focus. It was Quiñones, Rico Quiñones who had ruined his life, literally stealing seven years of freedom from him, and now he was ruining his sister's life. Ray had thought all he needed to do was get her away from the devil, but the devil came with her. He wanted to . . . he wanted to hurt Quiñones the way Quiñones had hurt him. No, more than that, he wanted to kill the lousy pimp!

The realization settled on him like snow in summer. Leaving no trace, but having fallen just the same, it changed the weather. But he couldn't kill Quiñones. That would be murder, and he was no . . . Yes, he was. Nah! Nah! Ray shook it off and drove on through the Rogers Park neighborhood until he crossed Howard Street and found the apartment in which Lena had been living.

This time, however, no one answered his desperate pounding on the door of 4A, no one, that is, except a woman in 4B who cussed him out for making so much noise. Ray went around to the back and climbed the porch steps down which he had so recently dragged his sister. Even before he reached the top, he knew no one was there. The back door was locked, but the window to the side that was above a sink was open a couple inches, and there was no screen. Ray looked around, then tried to lift it—just checking—but ancient layers of paint bound it in the frame.

"Lena . . . you in there?" Ray put his head down near the gap but heard no movement from within. On the other hand, when he'd come by earlier, everyone had been so stoned, he'd been lucky to get any response at all. "Lena! Open the door! Let me in. I want to talk to you." He tried the window again, lifting harder. It moved a few inches, enough for him to get his arms under it for some leverage. He looked around—no one watching—and lifted with all his might. The window went up. One more check for nosy neighbors, and then he climbed inside.

Was this breaking and entering? No, no. Couldn't be. His sister lived here, and he had reason to fear for her welfare. Besides, there was no neighborhood watch in this hood.

"Lena . . . ?" Ray walked through the dim apartment. There was stuff scattered all over the place, worse than he remembered from before: a tattered couch, a tipped-over chair, clothes on the hall floor, shoes, newspapers, mattresses on the floors of the bedrooms. In the bathroom the medicine cabinet was open and empty, but there was a toothbrush and an empty Excedrin bottle in the sink. It looked like some stuff had been taken, but how could he tell? He didn't even know what belonged to Lena and what didn't.

Ray sat down on one of the chairs in the kitchen and considered waiting for the whores to return—Ha, there he was, calling his own sister a whore! But that's what she was, and Ray could end up waiting all night. What would he do when they came in? He was staring at nothing but seeing the scene in his mind: The redhead, the black girl, and Lena coming in, staggering down the hall, probably so drunk or high that they were holding up both walls, maybe torn up too, and exhausted. And Rico was right there behind them, herding them like horses. Wasn't that why they called this a stable?

Ray raised the 9 mm, holding it with both hands straight out in front of him. He pulled the trigger. The blast was deafening. He could see blood pumping, spurting, gushing red and frothy from the hole in Rico's chest. Ray had never seen so much blood.

Oh . . . yes he had. He'd seen that much blood when he shot Greg through the window of the Taurus. He'd never meant to do that. He had nothing against the poor kid, no animosity, no hatred, no score to settle. He'd only seen him a few times in high school, and the guy wasn't even a rival. He'd tried to tell Rico that, but Rico wouldn't listen. Ray hadn't wanted to kill Greg.

But now he *did* want to kill Rico! Wanted to see that red blood spurt right out of Rico's chest! Rico was behind all the bad things in Ray's life, and now he was destroying Ray's sister too! His only sister, his only family. Rico had to be stopped. That was the only way he'd ever be able to get his sister free—eliminate the source of the problem, the source of her drugs, and the death-hold he had over her.

Yeah! He was gonna shoot Rico!

CHAPTER
38

R ay jumped up from the kitchen table. "Oh, dear God. What am I saying? What am I thinking?" In two strides he crossed the kitchen, flipped open the deadbolt, went out without bothering to lock up, and fled down the apartment's back stairs.

In his car he sat trembling. It was almost like he had really shot the pimp. The imagined scene flooded back over him until he shook it off like a swimmer flinging water from his face with one quick snap of the head. Then with deliberation Ray put the key in the ignition, started the car, and drove away from the apartment.

Where might Lena be? Probably working! Ray knew Rico always made sure his people worked, whether it was shorties selling eight balls or . . . or his sister doing tricks, something too dreadful to envision. But since housing in Juneway was relatively cheap, and that was where Rico kept his "ladies of the night," it was probably because they worked nearby, like on Howard Street.

Ray drove around, checking out everyone he passed on the street, but he didn't see Rico or Lena or anyone who looked like the other two girls. He turned into the parking lot for the new Dominick's and its adjoining strip mall and walked back to personally buttonhole people along the strip.

"Hey, you know Rico Quiñones, drives a dark gray Lexus, runs some girls around here?"

"Nah. Never heard of him."

"You gotta know him, man. How 'bout Henry? You know a homeless guy named Henry?"

"Oh yeah. He's probably round somewhere."

"Where?"

The guy shrugged and walked off.

Ray tried another and another. Some said the same, as though that was what they had been told to say. Others wouldn't even respond to him at all, giving him a threatening stare if they were big enough or scurrying off like kicked dogs if they were the used and abused of Howard Street.

Ray tried to remember the other two hookers in the apartment. One was a redhead with bites on her legs; the other girl was African American, kind of dark skinned, as best as he could recall. But such vague descriptions were unlikely to bring recognition from people on the street, especially if they didn't want to get involved or had been warned to keep their mouth shut. For some reason Ray couldn't bring himself to ask people if they had seen a prostitute who looked like his sister, even though he could describe her more thoroughly. She wasn't goth anymore with the black lipstick, and he hadn't seen a stud in her tongue. Her hair had been frosted but it was just as dull, her skin just as dead-looking, and there'd been needle marks on her arms. He just couldn't say it.

At midnight Ray gave up and headed home. Remembering that a McDonald's just north of the Loop on Clark Street stayed open twenty-four hours a day, he headed that way to get something to eat. It began to rain, with lightning silhouetting Chicago's dramatic skyline. While he drove, Ray flipped open his cell phone and called work to say he had a "situation" and couldn't make it, but he'd be in tomorrow night.

"You sure?" said his supervisor. "You know, we don't like hearing about 'situations,' especially from someone with your background, Ray. You've been a good worker so far. Don't blow it."

"I won't." He closed his cell phone. He had every intention of being at work the next night, unless . . . what if he was still chasing his sister? What if he was dealing with Rico? "Oh, God, will this ever end? Please help me find her!" Ray knew he ought to pray. But that *was* a prayer . . . short and wimpy though it seemed. "God, I don't know how to pray to you, not really, not like people in church who go on and on. What do I say after 'help me'? I just don't know." He flipped open his cell again and imagined being able to punch in God's number and talk to him through something he could hold in his hand, something by which he could know they were connected, something that would allow God to talk back to him.

Instead, he punched in Carl Franklin's number. Carl hadn't been able to help when there was nothing much to go on, but that might be different now that Ray knew for sure his sister was alive and caught up in the wrong kind of lifestyle. But all he got when the phone rang was, "This is Carl Franklin. I'm not available right now, but you know what to do."

Ha, he couldn't connect with Carl either. Had God also been "not available right now"? Or had God heard Ray's wimpy call for help? Ray knew what the answer was supposed to be, but . . . it hadn't *felt* like he even got through to God's voice mail.

Ray closed his phone without leaving a message for Carl. He pulled into the McDonald's and ordered a Big Mac, fries, and a Coke. Maybe it was better he hadn't gotten through to Carl. While finding Lena was Ray's most urgent goal, one where Carl might be able to help, getting her away from Rico had already proved an even bigger challenge. And the only solution Ray could think of . . . well, Carl was a cop, and you didn't tell cops that you felt like shooting someone.

Ray eased the Capri forward to pay for and pick up his order, but when he opened his wallet, he had only two dollars in it. *What's this? I know I also had a five in here!* But there was no five. Today everything seemed to be going wrong. He dug in his pocket for some additional change.

"Forget the burger. Just give me the fries and Coke."

"Here." The attendant nearly threw the items through his car window. "And you don't need to come back here again. Got that?"

Ray roared out of the McDonald's. No, he wouldn't come back either. He drove on to Timothy House, not getting in bed until 2 a.m.

Ray spent a sleepless night trying to figure out how he would find his sister, presuming Rico had moved her. Knowing that she was a prostitute working for a pimp should narrow the search, but other than Howard Street, where were the hot spots around the city? Ray had heard that girls worked Broadway, but he had been away for seven years, and before that he'd been just a kid, barely aware of such things. Again, Carl came to mind. He ought to know someone in vice who could provide a clue.

The next morning Ray gave Carl a call. Perhaps the issue of what he'd *like* to do to Rico needn't come up.

"I found my sister," he said into his small flip phone. "But then I lost her." Ray went through the whole saga, including the speeding ticket he had gotten.

Carl laughed at him trying to do eighty down the Outer Drive in his old Capri. "Now if you'd had my Mustang, he'd have never caught you!"

"Oh yeah? Maybe we should swap cars for a while."

Carl laughed again. "Sure, just as soon as the Cubs win the World Series." Then Carl got serious. "I'm real sorry to hear about your sister. But, Ray, don't do anything stupid about that Quiñones perp. Know what I'm saying?"

"What? Rico? Nah! Don't worry." How had Carl picked up on that? Was he psychic? Or had Ray let something slip? He thought he'd been careful not to make any threats. Besides, just because he *wanted* to smoke the hog didn't mean he was going to.

"Good. But just remember, it's the rock that's got a hold on your sister. Even without her pimp, she'd find it again."

"Yeah, I hear ya. But you think you could talk to someone in vice? See where streetwalkers are most common? I couldn't find anyone to help me on Howard Street."

Carl laughed without humor. "Just read this report the other day that said there are sixteen thousand prostitutes in the Chicago area. 'Course, most don't work the streets anymore like your sister apparently does, but that's still gonna be like finding a nickel on the beach."

Ray's insides sank. "Yeah, but right now, I don't even know which beach to walk."

Carl was quiet for a few minutes. "Okay. I'll see what I can do."

"Thanks, dawg. That'd be a big help."

"Hey, what you doin' callin' me dawg . . . dawg?"

"Oh, sorry, Officer Franklin, *sir*! Didn't mean to dis ya none."

They both laughed, and Carl said, "I'll get back atcha."

It was two anxious days before Carl dropped by Timothy House with a page torn from his notebook listing the top ten locations for street-level prostitutes in the greater Chicago area.

"Now, I wouldn't worry about these Southside locations. It's not that there aren't any white hookers down there, but a Latino pimp would be shut down cold in those neighborhoods unless he had a whole lot of juice. And unless he has a lot more fillies in his stable, he's not that big." Carl ran his finger down the list. "You might try these areas in Bucktown or Humboldt Park or Garfield Park. Or possibly along Mannheim Road in Melrose Park. They pick up a lot of out-of-town business traffic from O'Hare airport. But I wouldn't waste my time on these other locations. He's not likely to have gone there. Prostitution is very territorial. It's not easy to break into a new location."

"Thanks, Carl. I'll see what I can turn up."

"Be cool, now. You know, on the job they say the most dangerous thing about workin' vice is gettin' caught in the vice. Happens to a lot of guys. Know what I mean?"

Ray nodded, but Carl pressed on. "A guy thinks he's fightin' drugs or prostitution or some other vice, but the closer you get, the easier it is to get sucked into the very thing you're against. Happens to a lot of preachers too. But as the Bible says, though sin may appear pleasurable for a season, Satan 'comes only to steal and kill and destroy.' "

"Yeah, I know. Sounds like you'd make a pretty good preacher yourself, Officer Franklin."

Carl opened both hands, palms up, and grinned. "Never can tell. Sometimes there's not that much difference between a good preacher and good cop." He studied the quizzical look that pinched Ray's face. "You know, we're both supposed to be about public safety?"

"Yeah. Yeah. *Public safety*, as in not going to jail or hell, right?"

"You got it!"

Ray showed up for work every night, but he spent every un-scheduled hour for the next few days cruising the streets Carl had suggested. He didn't expect to see Lena walking them during the day, but there was also Rico's Lexus to look for. Every time Ray found one the right color, adrenaline shot through his veins like hot water. But rarely did one have smoke-tinted windows, and none had a red and black garter hanging from the mirror. Sometimes, out of frustration, Ray parked and staked out one of the Lexuses for a while anyway, thinking that if Rico went to all the trouble to hide his girls, he might also have altered the unique features that identified his car. But no luck.

Once, Ray went up to the Juneway Jungle again to check out the old apartment. A young Puerto Rican woman with three children had already moved in and couldn't speak enough English to answer any of his questions about the former tenants or who managed the building. But that was a lead he hadn't pursued. He began knocking on the doors of the other apartments until he found someone who told him they sent their rent to Maxwell Management Partners at a Chicago post office box but had no idea who owned the building. They'd seen people get evicted, but it had always been by a professional server.

Ray went back to searching the streets, but the frustration served only to heighten his rage at Rico. The man was evil incarnate and deserved to get smoked. Ray would film little movies in his mind featuring how he might do it, what he would say before he pulled the trigger. He had shot Greg without malice, but now he wanted to kill someone, and he wanted to tell him exactly why it was coming. The words were so bitter in his mouth that he knew he was being poisoned, but he couldn't help it.

Maybe that was what Jesus meant when he said evil thoughts are as serious as the act, that indulging anger or lust was as serious as murder or adultery. *Maybe so*, Ray thought. *Maybe that's why God won't help me find Lena.* But the scolding only served to suppress his rage temporarily. The very next disappointment or dead end in his search for his sister triggered all those mental execution scenes again.

What Rico had done—was still doing—to his sister . . . No! Ray could never forgive that! And no reasonable person, no one who truly loved a family member, would ever expect him to suck it up either. He was justified!

It was a Friday when Ray received his first Visa card bill: $418.64, and it wasn't even for a full month.

What? That couldn't be! He'd only used the card once to fill up the Capri at the Citgo station near Timothy House. Not wanting to rack up too high a bill, he'd paid cash the second time, right after cashing his August 1 paycheck. And then he read the itemized list of charges: The first was for $17.16 at the Citgo, just as he had expected. But then came $235.41 at Wal-Mart on North Avenue, $14.76 at the IHOP on Winston Plaza, $86.09 at Walgreens on North Avenue, and finally $65.22 at the Kinky Tease on Mannheim Road.

Kinky Tease? He hadn't been to any of those places and certainly hadn't spent that kind of money. It would take him months to pay it off! Something was wrong. Very wrong! Mr. Gee had warned him about the dangers of credit cards—interest, identity theft—even if he kept his own spending under control.

He couldn't deal with this. He'd cut up the plastic and throw it away. He pulled out his wallet and found . . . that his card was missing!

CHAPTER 39

Ray dropped down onto his bed, crumpled over, hands hanging between his legs as he let the bill fall to the floor. Someone had stolen his Visa card and ran up over four hundred dollars. What was he going to do? Maybe he should call Carl. Surely this was a crime. But did local police investigate identity theft?

No. Not Carl. The first thing he ought to do was call Visa and cancel the card and try to convince them that these weren't his charges. Yeah, like an ex-con orders a credit card and protests paying over 95 percent of his first bill —not likely! But he did have to put a stop on the card. Whoever had it could keep racking up charges.

He made the call and spent forty minutes arguing with the customer service agent. Finally the woman agreed to list those charges as "in dispute." "But I can tell you, sir, unless you have additional proof of foul play, they most likely will come back to you for collection!"

"Whatever. Just put a stop on my card, and no, I don't want a replacement!"

He hung up the phone and looked at the bill again. Where were these places? Where had he lost his card? This was raw. If you lost a twenty-dollar bill, you were out twenty bucks. But if you lost a credit card, the finder could max out your card before you knew you'd even lost it.

When had he lost it? The first bogus charge was on August 9. What had he been doing that day? Where had he gone? He'd been looking for Lena . . . all over the place. He could have lost it anywhere. And then he remembered the five-dollar bill he *didn't* have when he went through the McDonald's after losing Lena the night before.

Five dollars.

Missing credit card.

Lena getting out of his car and walking across the park to Rico.

Ray snapped his fingers. That was it! After the cop asked for his license and told him to get out of the car, Ray had left his wallet on the console. When he got back in the car, he'd returned his license to his wallet and put it into his pants pocket without checking anything. Why check?

Stupid! He slammed the heel of his hand against his forehead. Lena had taken the money and his card. "That cheap little whore!" Ray said out loud. "Tryin' to help her, and she rips me off!"

He looked again at the bill. Wal-Mart on North Avenue, IHOP on Winston Plaza, Walgreens on North Avenue, and the Kinky Tease on Mannheim Road. The *Kinky Tease?* What was that? Sounded like a strip club.

Mannheim Road, that was one of the places Carl said sported prostitutes. How had he put it? Something about them hooking a lot of business travelers flying into O'Hare. And where were these other businesses Lena had used his card? Ray got out the Chicago area street map he used when Mr. Gee sent him to unfamiliar neighborhoods and checked. They were all in the Melrose Park area, near Mannheim Road.

That's where his sister was! And not so far away, at that!

Ray ran out and jumped into his car and headed west.

Two hours of driving up and down Mannheim Road turned up a lot of restaurants and motels that looked greasy and cheap in the daylight and probably flashed lots of jumpy neon at night. A couple said "Live XXX Show" and "Girls, Girls, Girls," but no Kinky Tease. Finally Ray stopped in a gas station, an older one that offered a mechanics garage on the side rather than nine pump islands and a party store.

"Kinky Tease? Yeah, I know it. It's a topless bar, right? 'Bout a half mile south on your right there's a big used-car lot, Joe's Deals on Wheels, I think it's called. Turn in just past it, and go around behind. But it don't open till six."

"Thanks. Thanks a lot."

Ray drove there anyway and found the front door of the windowless, white clapboard building locked. He went around and tried the back door. It was open, and a large Latino was inside mopping the floor with a strong disinfectant.

"How ya doin'? Got a minute? I'm lookin' for someone and need your help."

"*No sé. No hablo ingles.*"

"But I'm looking for a girl." He gestured an hour glass, then realized his sister wasn't that shapely. "She's my . . . *mi hermana. Si. Mi hermana.*" Struggling, he made another try. "*¿Dónde está mi hermana?*"

"*No sé.*" The man lifted his shoulders. "*¿Quien es su hermana?*"

"Lena. *Su nombre es* Lena."

"*No sé. No sé.*"

"Rico. Rico Quiñones." Ray thought he noticed a flicker of recognition cross the man's face. "You know him? *¿Le conoce?*" Ray wasn't sure he had the Spanish right, but as the man returned to his mopping with nothing but a shake of his head, Ray realized he wasn't getting anywhere.

Maybe he should just wait in the club and see if Lena showed up. Maybe she worked out of here and had spent all that money buying drinks and something to eat. Or maybe she'd run up a tab that Rico wouldn't cover and had to pay it off. Ray slipped into a booth while the Latino continued cleaning. But after a few minutes the dingy place began to get to him, and he kept wondering what was happening outside along Mannheim Road. He was close, so close! Lena . . . and Rico . . . had to be around here somewhere, in one of the cheap motels, perhaps. He should go cruise the strip again.

Ray left and drove north. No luck. He turned around at Grand Avenue and drove south, watching both sides of the street. It was just as he was approaching Joe's Deals on Wheels that he saw a dark Lexus come out of the drive beyond and turn south. Ray stepped on the gas, then realized that if it was Rico, he didn't want to be recognized. The guy would just leave him in the dust and perhaps move his girls again, so Ray hung back, letting several cars separate him from the Lexus.

But the Lexus continued south, beyond the cheap motels, car lots, and nightclubs, and took the overpass above the train yard. Ray followed because there was no way to turn around on the overpass, but he had given up hope. This guy wasn't Rico. He needed to get back to his prime target area. But when the Lexus came down off the overpass, it turned into the parking lot for a wholesale plumbing supply center. Ray almost drove past before he noticed there appeared to be an apartment above the plumbing supply.

Ray took the next right and stopped. He should check it out. It probably wasn't Rico, but . . . He got out and started to walk back toward the plumbing store when he got a better view of the Lexus. It had tinted windows. He made his way between the buildings and approached the car. There was a back stairway that went up to the second floor. Perhaps it was just business offices for the plumbing company, but he had to know. And then, as he stepped through a broken-down hedge that separated the two buildings, Ray saw the red and black garter hanging from the rearview mirror.

Rico's Lexus. No question!

That was his car, and he was upstairs, probably with Lena. Should he wait for Rico to leave and then go up and get her? But what if he took her with him? He could hear arguing coming from the apartment, Rico and one of the girls, but he couldn't be sure it was Lena. The arguing escalated into shouting, and then he knew it was Lena. And then she screamed.

Ray hurtled up the steps two, three at a time, leaping to the landing and yanking open the door to see Lena sprawled on the floor, Rico above her.

Rico's upraised hand froze in midair, poised for a backhand to Lena's face. Already her nose was bleeding and tears staggered down her cheeks. "What're *you* doin' here?" shouted Rico, his voice continuing at its previous level. With his other hand he held Lena's wrist.

"You hit her again and you're dead."

"Haven't you learned yet, you fool? She's *mine*. She don't want you! Look, I brought her out here to Melrose Park so she could work with my tourist ladies, class up a little. So get outta my face and mind your own business."

Rico's sharply pressed dress shirt had dark stains under the arms, and his suit coat had been thrown on the table behind him. On top of it lay Rico's chrome-plated pistol. And, yes, it was a .357 Magnum. With one quick step Ray lunged toward the table and grabbed up the weapon. With both hands extended in front of him, he aimed it at Rico. His angle was perfect. With Lena on the floor and Rico standing between her and Ray, there was no way Rico could get behind her and use her for a shield before Ray could pull the trigger.

It was just like Ray had imagined it!

Rico held out his free hand, palm down. "Now, let's calm down, homie. We go back a long way. There ain't no need for us to complicate things here. Your sister and I are in a business arrangement that requires a little negotiating sometimes. But she's not hurt. I wouldn't be the successful entrepreneur that I am if I damaged my merchandise. Know what I mean?" Rico was moving around behind Lena.

"Take another step, and I'll blow your head off." No, it wouldn't be his head. Ray would shoot him right through the chest just like he had Greg Mason, and the blood would come pumping.

Rico stopped his shuffle to gain position. "Look, Ray, if she wants to leave, I ain't holdin' her. This is a free country. Take her with you right now if you want. No hard feelings. Okay?"

"No hard feelings, huh?"

"No, man. You saw what happened before; she came back to me on her own. But if she wants to go now, I'm not stopping her. Why don't you ask her?"

"Let go of her arm."

Rico dropped Lena's arm and straightened up, raising his hands to shoulder level.

"Lena, get away from him. Move over there. I wouldn't want his blood to get all over you."

"Hey now. Come on, Ray. Don't you think we can work this out? Ain't no harm been done. If she wants to go, how 'bout I give her some severance pay. You know, like those golden parachutes big execs get?"

Ray stepped to his right to get closer to his sister. "Golden parachute, huh? You mean something she can retire on?"

"Well, retire from this profession, at least. How 'bout it?"

"Man, you have no idea. That wouldn't even begin to repay what you owe our family!" Ray cocked the hammer on the heavy revolver.

Lena screamed. "No, Ray! Don't do it!" She clapped her hands over her ears and clinched her eyes shut. "Ray, you can't. You'd go back to prison. Just forgive this guy. Please!"

Forgive? Did she say *forgive?* No. Couldn't have been forgive! How could he forgive Rico? Even Lena's appeal showed just how totally this lowlife controlled her. She was still trying to protect her Mack Daddy. All the more reason to smoke the dude. Why should he forgive?

Because I forgave you!

"What?" Ray spoke aloud without even realizing it.

Forgive . . . you can forgive him because I forgave you!

A swirling dizziness came over Ray. What was this, *Pay It Forward?* Rico hadn't even asked for forgiveness. A guy's gotta at least ask for forgiveness, get down on his knees, beg a little, do something to show he's really sorry!

Had you asked for forgiveness before Connie Mason forgave you?

No. But . . . but that was different. . . . Or was it?

Ray's hands slowly lowered the heavy handgun as though he were putting down a too-full cup of coffee. His right thumb found the hammer and gently uncocked it while his eyes focused on Rico's face, where a crooked grin spread over the pimp's features.

Rico lowered his own hands from "surrender" and leaned forward to stab the air with his right index finger. "*Cobarde!*" A deep laugh shook him. "*Cobarde!* You've always been the Clark Street *cobarde!* Ha, sucka!"

CHAPTER 40

C *obarde?* That was too much! You don't call the guy who just spared your life a coward for having done so! Acrid vapors rose through Ray's sinuses as he raised the .357 again and sighted along its barrel, covering the whole of Rico's chest. But would he be a coward if he did *not* shoot Rico? Or had he been the coward seven years before when he yielded to this . . . this nose-thumbing agitator's taunts? Yeah, that's what Ray had been afraid of. He knew he could pull the trigger again if he wanted to, and he knew Quiñones deserved it. But what had driven him and haunted him ever since he'd killed Greg Mason was the mocking. Until now he hadn't been able to stand up to it, not from someone else, not even in his own mind. *Cobarde! Cobarde!* the little voice had jeered, but no longer.

"No cobarde. ¡Estoy perdonado! I have been forgiven! . . . And as much as it galls me to say it, so have you." Ray tipped up the muzzle of the weapon, flipped open the cylinder, and shook the five cartridges onto the floor, then threw the Magnum through the window with a crash of glass followed by a thud and a clatter as it dropped on the top of Rico's Lexus. "Come on, Lena. Let's get out of here!"

"But—"

"Just come! There's nothin' here you need more than to get out of this hellhole right now. Come on!" He took her arm and headed out the back door, down the steps, and through the broken-down hedge.

For the second time Ray had found his sister. This time he would not drive eighty miles an hour and get stopped by a cop or create any other excuse for her to run away. He may not have the resources to help her get the crack monkey off her back, but he would find someone who did. Then, as Carl had said, it would be up to her. He looked over at her as they headed north on Mannheim Road.

"Open the glove box. There're some Kleenexes inside. Your face still has blood on it, and your eyes . . . Well, use those tissues."

"Ray, how come you came after me again?"

"Me? 'Cause you owe me over four hundred dollars!"

"Four hundred dollars? What for?"

"On my Visa!"

"Oh, that."

"Yeah, that! And you're gonna get a job and pay for every penny of it too."

"But, Ray, how can I . . ." She sniffed as she wiped her nose and tried to clean off her face. "How'd you find me, anyway?"

"Listen, you can't imagine how hard I looked or the places I went. But when my Visa bill came with all these strange charges on it, I realized you'd stolen it that day when the cop stopped us. Every place you used it was in this neighborhood, so I knew you had to be around here. And when I saw Rico driving his Lexus, I just followed him back to that . . . whatever it was where you lived."

Ray reran the scene in the apartment, imagining what it would have been like if he'd pulled the trigger. The rush from tension shut out everything around him until the .357's blast knocked Rico across the room. Yeah . . . he could have shot him, but he was glad he hadn't. Did that mean he'd really forgiven the man? Perhaps, perhaps as much as was possible at this point. Ray took a deep breath and felt the tension in his gut unwind.

"Hey, Ray, did you really come just to get your money?"

Ray shook his head and stiffened his arms with his hands gripping the top of the steering wheel. Tears flooded his eyes so he could hardly see the traffic. "I came for you, sis. Someone had to, and I'm the only one left."

Lena was silent, as though trying to take in the ramifications of Ray's words. Finally she said, "Where you takin' me?"

He glanced over at her while he drove and shrugged. "Dunno. My place is just for guys. But maybe we can stop there and get something to eat while I call around and see if I can get you into rehab somewhere."

"Rehab? Ray, I can't do rehab. I tried to stop several times, and I just can't do it." She turned to look out the window so Ray couldn't see her face. "You know, I still got some old friends up in Rogers Park. I can go stay with them."

"And end up dying a crackhead? You think I'm gonna let that happen? You're my sister!"

She snapped back to glare at him. "Like you can stop me? It's my life, you know." She buried her face in her hands and tried unsuccessfully to stifle three huge sobs. Finally she raised up, wiping her eyes on the back of her hands, smearing further what remained of her dark eye makeup. "Look, Ray, what can happen to me that hasn't already happened?"

Ray stopped for a red light and stared straight ahead. He knew she thought she'd already experienced the worst that life could dish out, and maybe she had. In spite of his seven years in prison, who was he to argue over someone else's pain? But there was another answer to her question. "What can happen to you? For one thing, you might get straight, get your health back, make some new friends who won't use you and throw you away. You might find God's purpose for your life. There are a lot of things that haven't happened to you yet! Good things!"

As he stepped on the gas, she shook her head. "Not for me there ain't. It's too late for me."

"It's never too late, Lena. Look how God rescued me! I was workin' on forty years, and he turned it around."

"Yeah, but—"

"Hold on. There's a lot you don't know. It wasn't just gettin' out of prison. God turned it around long before I ever had a chance at an early release. It began with a woman who forgave me for murdering her son and told me she did it because God had forgiven her. Then there was this cellie who swore like a rapper, but he got me to go to chapel. That was God turning it around, 'cause I met him there and gave my life to him. And then . . ." Ray thought of God helping him to not pull the hit on McAfee, keeping him out of his cell when they blew it up, holding him back from not making a run for it in the courthouse. There were so many. Someday he'd have to tell Lena about them all.

"But it wasn't just what happened before I got out or even the gettin' out. God keeps makin' a way, giving me a chance to turn it around." Ray was almost too embarrassed to go on. But she might as well know. "Even after I got out, this guy, José Perón, offered me five-hundred bucks to hold some drugs for a few days. I agreed so I could get enough money to hire a private investigator to find you. But I knew I was messin' up, big time. Then God gave me a way out, offered me a change-up—"

"Did you still get the money?"

"No. That wasn't the right way. . . ." Ray paused while he made a right turn. "Even today, God used you to give me a chance to turn it around."

"Me?" She looked at Ray, her face contorted with disbelief.

"Yeah, you." It was so new, Ray barely realized what had gone down. "I was really gonna shoot Quiñones. I've been wantin' to kill him ever since I discovered he was pimping you. First he destroyed my life, and then he was destroying yours. I came so close to pullin' that trigger . . . but then you said, 'Don't do it, Ray! Just forgive this guy!' and I began to think—"

"Wait a minute! I never said to *forgive* him. I didn't want you to shoot him, but I never said forgive. I said *forget* him!"

"Really?" Ray thought back over the confrontation above the plumbing store. He was sure he had heard *forgive*. Or could that have been what God let him hear? "Lena, don't you see? That makes it all the more a God thing. I'm not sure what you said— forget or forgive—but the word *forgive* is what I heard. And I began remembering how I'd been forgiven, and I knew that was my way to escape, if I'd only take it."

"Yeah, but a moment later you almost shot him again."

Ray sighed deeply, as though tired from a long fight. "You're right. I don't always get it the first time. Know what I mean?"

"Who does?"

"It was when he called me *cobarde* that I almost lost it again. But then it struck me—no, I believe it was God who spoke to me and showed me I was a coward seven years ago when I didn't stand up to Rico's taunting. But I'm no coward anymore. I didn't need to buckle. I'd been forgiven. God offered me a little window where I could choose to escape. And when I did, he turned the whole scene around." Ray looked over at his sister. "See, here you are . . . and I didn't shoot him."

Lena was quiet until they pulled up in front of Timothy House. She stared at Ray through squinted eyes. "So you think this is God's window for me to get out?"

"I sure do. But the longer you wait, the harder it might get."

"Maybe. But I think it's already too late for me. Like I said, I done tried to crack the crack . . . several times. Just don't work for me."

"It's never too late, Lena. Again and again, it's never too late as long as we have breath! There's even a promise in the Bible where God says he will always make a way to escape . . . if we'll just take it."

"That really in the Bible?"

"Yep." Ray opened his car door. "Let's go in and get something to eat."

Epilogue

Getting Lena into rehab was not as easy as Ray had imagined. It certainly wasn't the kind of thing he was able to arrange in one evening before he had to leave for work. The best he was able to do was ask Cynthia Braithwaite to let Lena stay at her apartment for the night. The next day Cynthia couldn't figure out how Lena managed to go out on the streets of a strange neighborhood and score enough cocaine to leave her like a zombie by the time Cynthia got home from work. But she had.

Ray shook his head. "It's like, if you're lookin', it'll find you!"

Cynthia wanted Lena out of her house immediately, but Ray negotiated Lena's remaining a little longer by promising to pick up his sister in the morning and keeping her with him all day until Cynthia could watch her at night. "But only if you can get her into rehab soon. Because I can't take this happening under my roof, in my home. No way! I've got to deal with too much chaos in my classroom every day at school."

It took Ray two days before he found a program for his sister.

But after two months Lena left rehab to move in with a new boyfriend. Fortunately, he was not a pimp; in fact, he held a good job as a collections agent for a company that contracted its services to the IRS. Lena got a job also, working at a dry-cleaners. One day when Ray was in her neighborhood, he stopped by to say hi.

She looked better. She still had a ring in her eyebrow, but her hair was soft and even had a shine to it. "So how's it goin'?" he asked when she finished with a customer.

"Pretty good. How 'bout yourself?"

When she talked, Ray could even tell that the stud was out of her mouth, but she pulled down the sleeves of her blouse so quickly that he became suspicious. "Lena, what's that about?"

"What's what?" she trilled in a carefree voice as she turned and took down several garment bags and laid them over her left arm while she moved away to hang them on a new rack . . . slowly.

"You know what I'm talking about, Lena. Why are you covering up your arms so fast?"

"Oh, habit, I s'pose. You know I feel self-conscious about those old tracks."

"Lena! Let me see your arms."

Her face got red. "Go drown yourself, Ray."

"Lemme see!"

"For what? So you can put cuffs on me and take me back to rehab? You think you run my life? Just get outta here!"

Ray left without saying more. Was she using again? He feared so, but she was right. It was her life, and he couldn't run it. He had tried to help her, and from now on, he'd do his best to stay in touch, but he couldn't save her. Only God could save her . . . if she would turn to him, and that turning might take a lifetime.

Ray's work with Mr. Gee continued to expand. In addition to ministering to kids in gangs, in jails, in hospitals, and at Timothy House, the board of Captives Free funded a new outreach Mr. Gee had proposed: a center offering young people job training, coaching in life skills, and GED tutoring. Ray ended up spending several afternoons a week helping convert the old storefront location into the "Equip-U Center," or "the U," as Mr. Gee liked to call it. There were rooms to paint, carpeting to put down, chairs and tables to bring in, and a dozen donated used computers to install and set up, not that Ray had any experience with them. He just did what he was told.

In the flurry of all this ministry, and in his efforts to find and help his sister, Ray had not contacted his old friends from Stateville Correctional Center. On one hand, he missed them, but in his mind there was something about their association with his time in prison that haunted him. Until his final showdown with Rico, when Ray had found the courage *not* to pull the trigger, he had always feared that someday he would do something to put himself back in the joint. But that fear had been broken. He knew he was not perfect or beyond mistakes, but as the Bible said, "Through Christ Jesus the law of the Spirit of life set me free from the law of sin and death."

As a new sense of freedom settled on Ray, he began wanting to see his old friends. Darnell Harrison was somewhere on the Southside, but Ray had no idea where. Moon, on the other hand, had been sent to Cook County Hospital—now called the John H. Stroger, Jr. Hospital of Cook County. Knowing that burn victims took a long time to heal, Ray thought his old friend might still be there. He called, but Jonathan Riviera was no longer a patient in the burn unit. He had died two weeks before from the third-degree burns that had covered 85 percent of his body!

Ray folded his cell phone and went outside Timothy House. There was a bus stop at the corner, and he sat on the bench, letting his shoulders sag and his hands fall between his legs. His head bowed forward until his chin rested on his chest, then began to bob as great, silent sobs shook his body. He had let Moon down—his cellie, the guy who stood up for him in the joint when he had no cover from a gang, the guy who took a hit that may have been intended for him. Had he suffered for months in pain and agony in the hospital, perhaps without a single visitor? As far as Ray knew, no one had come to see Moon when he was in prison.

Ray wiped his eyes on his sleeve. How could he have been so selfish! Getting his own life together, finding a job, searching for his sister, getting a car, meeting a girl, even going to church . . .

But all along he had put off visiting Moon. Didn't the Bible say something about visiting people who were sick and in prison, that Jesus counted it as a service to himself? But Ray had failed! Why? Yeah, he was busy, but he had also been afraid, afraid of any contact with his old life . . . afraid that in talking to Moon he might discover the truth about the explosion. As long as they didn't talk, Ray could imagine someone was settling an old score with Moon. But if Moon was in the clear, then the hit had probably been meant for Ray.

Now he would never know the truth.

A bus pulled to a stop in front of him, and the doors opened. Ray sniffed deeply and waved the driver on.

What should he do? The least he could do was find Harrison, face his past life, and try to bring it together with his present. He had found Lena; maybe he could find Darnell.

Finding him wasn't easy, however. The Southside of Chicago was a huge part of a city of 2.8 million, and none of the methods Ray had used to find Lena seemed to apply to Darnell. But the volunteers at the Equip-U Center who came in to teach computer said Google could find anything. Ray was just learning how to use a computer, and out of curiosity, he typed in the name "Darnell Harrison" along with the word "Chicago." To Ray's utter amazement, he got six hits. Two had to do with family trees and people who lived a century ago or more. Three more names were completely unrelated to the fact that the word "Chicago" also appeared on the same Web site. But one entry read "Wings 'n' Things, The Best Hot Wings and Ribs on 63rd Street. Darnell Harrison, proprietor. Phone for carry-out. . . ." Ray clicked on the entry and went to a restaurant directory page with the only additional information about Wings 'n' Things being an address and phone number.

Ray's heart beat faster. Sixty-third Street was on Chicago's Southside, and Darnell had lived on the Southside. Could he have started a business in the few months he'd been out? No way! Ray recalled how hard it had been to merely get a job. Starting a restaurant that quickly would be nearly impossible even for a man with money and connections. Then Ray recalled Darnell's uncle—the one who'd taught him how to pop a socket and encouraged him to "get religion" if he needed to get prison hacks off his back. *Uncle* Darnell Harrison, Ray recalled, had been released from Angola Prison much earlier and was now a "successful businessman" on Chicago's Southside.

Ray punched in the number. The phone rang and rang. Finally . . .

"Yeah. Whatcha want?"

Ray hesitated a moment. "Uh, is this . . . Wings 'n' Things?"

"None other, you sorry . . ." The string of curses that followed made Ray smile before the man ended by saying, "Gimme your order."

"No order. I'm just lookin' for Darnell Harrison."

"Tha'd be me. Whassup?"

Ray knew he wasn't speaking to his cellie, and he couldn't remember Darnell's middle name, so what was he supposed to say: "I'm looking for an African-American albino who was recently released from prison; guys on the street call him Zitty, and he used to swear just like you"? No, that would never work! He settled for, "Do you have a nephew named Darnell?"

"Oh yeah." The man's voice went flat. "What's he done now?"

"Nothin', far's I know—"

"Humph! You right 'bout dat! He's s'posed to be workin' up in here all this afternoon, but he's off over to that church again, hootin' and hollarin'."

A tickle of excitement came on Ray like an impending cough. "And what church would that be, sir?"

"*What church?* What do you mean, *what church?* If you his friend, you oughta know. He spends more time over there than anywhere else. Now they workin' on some Christmas program or somethin'."

"But where?"

"Buelahland . . . that New Buelahland Baptist, I think they call it. Up there on King Drive, almost to the park. Can't miss it. Big ol' barn on your left."

"Okay. Well, thank you, Mr. Harrison. And you have a great day, now. Sorry to have bothered you."

It *had* to be Darnell! And in spite of all his old cellie's shuckin' and jivin', it sounded like his spiritual renewal had stuck.

Grinning inside, Ray got in his car and headed for South Martin Luther King Drive. He'd waited too long to see Moon. He wasn't going to wait one minute longer to see "Zitty."

Acknowledgments

Neta Jackson, my wife, best friend, encourager, and toughest editor, who took time away from writing her amazing YADA YADA novels to help me with this project.

Bethany House Publishers, especially **Carol and Gary Johnson,** and my fine editors, **Natasha Sperling** and **Kyle Duncan,** who fought hard for this project.

Gordon McLean, the head of the Juvenile Justice Ministry of Metro Chicago YFC, who knows the streets and the criminal justice system, and with whom I was privileged to serve for two years leading Bible studies for young men in the Cook County Juvenile Detention Center.

Xavier McElrath-Bey, who now works as a Gang Intervention Specialist with Catholic Charities, but was kind enough to share about his former gang life and thirteen years as a "guest" of the Illinois Department of Corrections.

Mario Ramos, who remains in prison serving a sentence for the incident that inspired this novel, but whose life was transformed by forgiveness, first from his victim's mother, but more profoundly from God through Christ Jesus.

Karen Evans, friend and mental health therapist with juveniles on parole, whose practical insights and literary suggestions were invaluable.

Julia Pferdehirt, author, friend, and former teacher at a residential school for boys connected with the Illinois Department of Corrections.

The guys in my Tuesday night Bible study who are my best friends, prayer warriors, accountability partners, truth seekers, and real MEN!

About the Author

Dave Jackson is coauthor, with his wife, Neta, of the award-winning TRAILBLAZER BOOKS and the HERO TALES series, as well as *No Random Act*, the story behind the 1999 murder of Coach Ricky Byrdsong. Dave holds a degree in journalism from Judson College and has a prolific writing career, including books on racial reconciliation and ministry to kids in gangs. Dave and Neta are members of Chicago Tabernacle, a multiracial congregation and daughter church of the Brooklyn Tabernacle. They live in Evanston, Illinois.

Learn more about Dave and his writing at *www.daveneta.com*.